DISCARDED

PREBIND LORD FOULGRINS LETTERS
9780055638960
ALCORN
RC

LORD FOULGRIN'S LETTERS

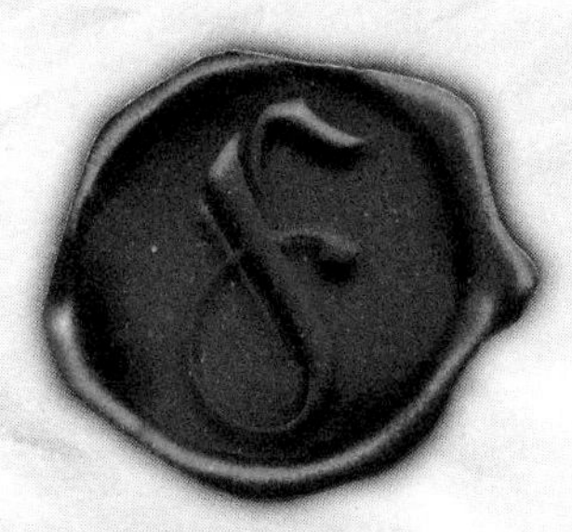

How to Strike Back at the Tyrant by Deceiving and Destroying His Human Vermin

RANDY ALCORN

Multnomah® Publishers *Sisters, Oregon*

"*Lord Foulgrin's Letters* is a welcome addition to the world of Christian fiction. Randy Alcorn provides a needed reminder of just what it means for Christians to be engaged in battle with principalities and powers not of this world. But *Lord Foulgrin's Letters* won't send readers looking for demons under every bed—it will send them to the right place, the study of God's Word."

—CHUCK COLSON
Founder, Prison Fellowship Ministries
Author of *How Now Shall We Live?*

"In renowned C. S. Lewis style, Randy Alcorn demonstrates that Satan is a liar and his demons are masters at deceit. In *Lord Foulgrin's Letters* we hear how demons plan to ruin us, keep us from God, and make us miserable and unfruitful. If you are interested in gaining a better understanding of Satan's strategies and becoming more successful in resisting him, this book is a must read."

—TIM LAHAYE
Creator and coauthor, the *Left Behind* series
—BEVERLY LAHAYE
Founder, Concerned Women of America, author of *The Act of Marriage*

"Randy Alcorn has written one of the most unusual and important inquiries into the demon mind since *The Screwtape Letters*. It is no easy challenge for a dedicated Christian author to realistically portray the spirit realm, but Alcorn rivets our attention in a way readers aren't accustomed to. This book will disturb, stimulate, and enlighten."

—DR. D. JAMES KENNEDY
Senior minister, Coral Ridge Presbyterian Church
Author of *Evangelism Explosion*

"*Lord Foulgrin's Letters* is loaded with thought-provoking scenarios driving home the point that we are spiritual beings living in the midst of a spiritual war. Alcorn graphically portrays the struggles between the angels of God and the forces of the evil one. His artful description of the devil's strategies reminds us that Satan still prowls as a roaring lion seeking to devour those who trust in God. I highly recommend this book!"

—PAUL ESHLEMAN
Director, The JESUS Film Project, author of *The Touch of Jesus*

"As this powerful book goes into print, there will be a major meeting in the committee rooms of hell. Randy Alcorn will be high on Satan's hit list, so let's pray for him. God's Word is clear that we must not be ignorant of Satan's devices. This book will be a great help in doing just that. The devil is not happy with it. Beware! A dynamic, demon-binding book."

—GEORGE VERWER
Founder and director, Operation Mobilization

"Not since I produced the art for *This Present Darkness* and *Angelwalk* have I read a book that caused me to look over my shoulder while reading. More than once I winced at recognizing myself getting caught in the enemy's web and falling for his subtle tricks. If Randy's pattern for *Lord Foulgrin's Letters* is *The Screwtape Letters,* the student has, dare I say, surpassed the teacher."

—RON DICIANNI
Artist, author of *Beyond Words*

"*Lord Foulgrin's Letters* is a wonderful accomplishment. It should be required reading. I wish I'd had it years ago, before I was such an unwitting accessory to so many of Satan's schemes. Randy Alcorn makes no apologies for the truth that radiates off each page. He skillfully reminds us that we are not fighting against flesh and blood. I highly recommend this book to anyone who wants to grow."

—TERRI BLACKSTOCK
Author of *Private Justice*

"Paul admonishes us to 'stand against the devil's schemes.' My friend Randy Alcorn goes undercover to disclose those schemes so we can be better prepared to stand firm, overcome evil, and faithfully represent Jesus Christ."

—LUIS PALAU
International evangelist, author of *Where Is God When Bad Things Happen?*

"I love to read everything Randy Alcorn writes. *Lord Foulgrin's Letters* is reminiscent of *The Screwtape Letters,* echoing the solid theology, insightful psychology, and literary creativity of C. S. Lewis. It is both challenging and encouraging, a wake-up call to the reality of personal evil in the circumstances of everyday life and, best of all, a forceful declaration of Jesus' promise of victory over every work of darkness for those who trust Him."

—RON MEHL
Senior pastor, Beaverton Foursquare Church
author of *God Works the Night Shift*

"Randy Alcorn has brought into the twenty-first century the classic concept behind C. S. Lewis's *The Screwtape Letters.* Written in clear, compelling style, *Lord Foulgrin's Letters* is at once entertaining, fascinating, and highly illuminating. It is a book for believers and unbelievers, for young and mature Christians. I pray I never forget it."

—ANGELA ELWELL HUNT
Author of *The Immortal*

Alc

This book is a work of fiction. The characters, incidents, and dialogues
are products of the author's imagination and are not to be construed as real.
Any resemblance to actual events or persons, living or dead, is entirely coincidental.

LORD FOULGRIN'S LETTERS
published by Multnomah Publishers, Inc.

International Standard Book Number: 1-57673-679-2

Photography by Mike Houska/DogLeg Studios
Cover and interior design by Uttley/DouPonce DesignWorks

Printed in the United States of America.

For information:
MULTNOMAH PUBLISHERS, INC.
Post Office Box 1720, Sisters, Oregon 97759

LIBRARY OF CONGRESS CATALOGING-IN-PUBLICATION DATA

Alcorn, Randy C.
Lord Foulgrin's letters: how to strike back at the tyrant by deceiving and destroying his human vermin/by Randy Alcorn.
p.cm.
ISBN 1-57673-679-2
1. Demonology—Fiction. 2. Good and evil—Fiction. I. Title.
PS3551. L292 L67 2000 00-008460
813'. 54–dc21 CIP

00 01 02 03 04 05 06 07 — 10 9 8 7 6 5 4 3 2 1 0

TO STEVE AND SUE KEELS

Your love for Christ and each other
has touched countless students and their families,
including ours.
Thanks for being there for us
and so many others in times of deepest need.
We respect you deeply and
treasure your friendship.

The safest road to hell is the gradual one—

the gentle slope, soft underfoot, without

sudden turnings, without milestones,

without signposts.

C. S. Lewis

CONTENTS

ACKNOWLEDGMENTS

Thanks to Don Jacobson, Kevin Marks, Jeff Pederson, Ken Ruettgers, and others at Multnomah Publishers, who believed in this book enough to pursue it.

Special thanks to my friend and editor, Rod Morris. It was a pleasure working with you on my first book sixteen years ago and doing it again this fifth time.

I'm grateful to many others at Multnomah involved in various aspects of this project, among them Steve Curley for cover coordination and Jennifer Curley for copyediting. I'm very appreciative of Multnomah's outstanding sales team, including Jay Echternach, Matt Engstrom, and Bob Otey, all on loan to Central Oregon from our church in western Oregon.

Thanks to my Nanci, the best friend and wife I could ever imagine, way better than I deserve. Thanks to my precious daughters Karina and Angela, and their helpful insights that surfaced in our long conversations about issues related to this book.

Thanks to Kathy Norquist, Bonnie Hiestand, and Janet Albers for your dedicated work for the King at Eternal Perspective Ministries, freeing me to write this book. Also, for your careful proofreading.

Many perspectives woven into this book have been gleaned from my favorite authors, including those on Lord Foulgrin's list of forbidden writers, not least of all C. S. Lewis and A. W. Tozer. Those who've read John Piper's books will recognize my debt to him in Foulgrin's letter on pleasure.

A special thanks to Chris Mitchell, friend and director of the Wade Center at Wheaton College. Few know C. S. Lewis like Chris does, and his input on an early draft of this book was extremely helpful. Thanks also to Gerry Breshears, who made some fine suggestions, and my ChiLibris friends for their book recommendations.

Many others contributed through conversations and observations on drafts of various chapters. Among them were Adam Rehman, Matt

Mormance, Levi Brotnov, Todd Johnson, Jim Seymour, Ron Norquist, Tim Newcomb, Robin Green, Diane Meyer, Amy Campbell, and Steve Keels. (My sincere apologies to anyone I've forgotten.)

My friends and pastors Stu Weber, Barry Arnold, and Alan Hlavka began a series on spiritual warfare just as I was putting finishing touches on this book. As always, their messages feed my mind and heart, and their influence works its way into my writings. (I only wish the series would have started earlier!) Thanks, brothers, for your faithful teaching of God's Word.

I'm touched by the kindness with which people agreed to read and endorse this book, most with schedules so full it was hard to imagine they'd say yes. Thank you for your generosity.

I'm deeply indebted to the prayer team that faithfully lifted me up in the writing and revision of this book. Any eternal impact this book might have is the direct product of war waged in the prayers of these brothers and sisters.

Finally, I can't begin to express the depth of my love and appreciation for the One for whose glory this book was written. Foulgrin calls Him the Enemy and the Tyrant. I call Him my Creator, Provider, Sustainer, Savior, Advocate, and closest Friend. Your sovereign grace, Lord, overwhelms me. I can't wait to be with You in Your place. Meanwhile, please empower me to serve You faithfully where I am.

Our prayer, gracious Lord, is that You would use this book to work a miracle of illumination. Penetrate the lies of the dark powers with the light of Your truth. Use these imperfect words to accomplish Your perfect purposes. Touch readers for eternity, as only You can.

NOTE TO READERS:

If you'd like insights into the distinctive background and approach of this book, you may wish to turn back to the afterword now and read it as if it were an introduction. (That's what I originally intended it to be.) Or you can just wait until the end. I repositioned it believing many readers would rather dive right into the story without explanation. Whichever you choose, I hope you benefit from *Lord Foulgrin's Letters*.

PRELUDE:

THE HUNT

If Jordan Fletcher wasn't happy, it was only because he needed something else—someone else or someplace else. All his life, happiness had been just one step around the corner. He'd spent his life chasing around that next corner…and the next and the next and the next.

Jordan never realized that all the time he'd been hunting happiness, someone had been hunting him.

CHAPTER 1

IT DOESN'T GET ANY BETTER?

Shirtless, Jordan Fletcher kicked back on the lounge chair on the sunny deck of his new house at Sunriver, basking in the high desert beauty of Central Oregon. He'd always longed to have a special place of his own. Now it was his—and no one could take it from him.

Jordan's wife, Diane, sat five feet away reading her novel, but it may as well have been five miles. They inhabited two different worlds. He found it easier to avoid conversation, since it usually ended up in a laundry list of ways he'd let her down or things she wanted him to do. *High maintenance,* he thought. He breathed in the scent of fresh pine and contemplated the mountain peaks framed by the huge blue sky.

Well, she can't accuse me of blowing it on this place.

"I'm walking to the store." The voice from behind startled him. Jillian? It didn't sound like the voice of a little girl—maybe because his strawberry blond daughter was now seventeen.

"Okay," Diane said weakly, eyes not moving from her novel, the story of a life far more interesting than her own.

Jordan looked disapprovingly at his daughter's skimpy outfit. He started to grumble something about not talking with strange boys, but by then she was gone. She seemed always to vanish these days, outrunning his words. Jillian never asked permission for anything anymore. Half the time she never told them where she was going.

He looked over at fourteen-year-old Daniel, his hair in a stiff black bang against his pale skin, earphones permanently attached to his head. He sat under a desert pine, still pouting because his best friend couldn't come with him and he was stuck with the family. He wore his perennial black T-shirt featuring some rock singer, with an embossed "Hail Satan," blood spurting out of the words. Daniel gazed at a magazine Jordan didn't recognize, probably about computers or vampires or who knows what.

What's he doing wearing those stupid boots on a hot sunny day? When will he grow up, take some responsibility?

Jordan stood restlessly and ran his hand across the smooth deck railing. He looked at the tennis courts where he could barely see someone practicing serves. He watched carefully, trying to figure out if the guy was good enough to beat him. Finally he turned around and studied the house, his latest symbol of success and happiness. The shutters screamed at him.

Idiots.

The builders had installed the wrong shutters. He'd left a message and hadn't heard back from them. He wouldn't let them get away with it. Still though, the place was beautiful.

Wait till Hal sees this. It makes his mountain chalet look like a bungalow. And Matt's little beach cottage? No comparison. I'll buy a barbecue and have it going Friday night when they get here. A few cases of beer on ice. Everything'll be perfect.

He looked at the vacant spot under the tree where Daniel had been a moment ago.

Oh, well. He's fourteen. Not like he needs a babysitter.

Jordan went inside to get his briefcase off the shiny oak dining room table. He pulled out the new monthly sales figures. He'd gone over them already but wanted to study the numbers again. He returned to the deck and settled back in his lounge chair, sipping lemonade.

Yeah, it was true. He'd outsold everyone. He'd come out on top again.

I can borrow a little more, get that ski boat. No problem.

It felt great.

Yeah, great. Everything's great. It doesn't get any better than this.

LETTER 1

Our Working Arrangement

My newly assigned subordinate Squaltaint,

I'm recording these instructions despite the misgivings of my assistant Obsmut, who believes it's too risky.

As you've heard, there's been a reshuffling of the chain of command in your geopolitical sector, precipitated by the removal of Ashtar for his reprehensible acts of disloyalty against Lord Beelzebub. I've been assigned to command your region. You and your cadre of six tempters now fall under my authority. So do all your current subjects, including the vermin assigned to you, Jordan Fletcher.

In our kingdom's multilevel marketing structure you have now come in under me. I will be the beneficiary of your successes. I will also be held responsible for your failures. Make sure there are none.

Since I have vested interests in your success, I'll offer my keenest advice and monitor your progress. I'll aid you in deceiving and destroying Fletcher. Together we'll share the spoils of victory.

I'm a master of strategy and tactics. In my letters, I'll tutor you in the fine art of deception. I'll begin with Foulgrin's Basic Training, or if you prefer, Temptation 101.

These half-spirit, half-animal hybrids who inhabit this planet, *our* planet, are an endless source of fascination and frustration. They're such *creepy* little things, misshapen balloons of flesh, bloated bags of liquid and alloy. Grossly inferior to spirit beings, they should be our servants—yet the Enemy would have made us theirs!

As you deal with Fletcher or any of them, remember in the end they are but raw material, to be used by us against Him or by Him against us. They're weapons to wield in our jihad against heaven, that oppressive citadel called Charis.

Never forget the reason we revoked our citizenship—to establish the new and greater realm of Erebus, that mighty domain of which hell is but a junkyard, a ghetto for human slaves. (The Enemy claims we shall one day join them there—I think not, but if the worst proves true let's first do all the damage we can.) Our kingdom is being built each day with the bony bricks and bloody mortar of the Enemy's precious image-bearers—including your cockroach Fletcher.

Picture it, Squaltaint: The sludgebags are caught in the crossfire between Erebus and Charis. Skiathorus, what they call earth—that festering wound, that canker sore of the cosmos—is the battlefield where two rival kingdoms vie for the allegiance of puny men. The delicious thing is, the vast majority of them don't have a clue about the raging battle. How can they prepare for a battle they don't even know they're in? And how can they win a battle they haven't prepared for?

Foulgrin's rule number one: Keep them in the dark.

The central question is always this—how can we exact revenge on the Enemy? It was He who evicted us from our rightful dwelling, He who chose the sludgebags over us. He made ours a government in exile, driving us out to the hinterlands of the spirit realm, where we have no place to call our own until we colonize Skiathorus.

What can we do to inflict pain on this Creator who at first glance appears untouchable?

Intelligence gathering yields the answer. The Carpenter gave it away when He asked that vermin Paul, "Why do you persecute me?" Well, who was he persecuting but Christians?

There you have it, so simple it's elegant: To persecute them is to persecute Him. By striking out at them—and at all His weak and vulnerable image-bearers—we kill the Enemy in effigy. Better yet, we actually inflict harm on Him.

In and of themselves the vermin are utterly insignificant. But because the Enemy places such value on them, they become immensely useful to us. They're the objects of our aggression and the means of our attack against Him. What better way to hurt the divine parent than to kidnap His children, brainwash and torture them?

Delightful, isn't it? As you hatch your plots for Fletcher, Squaltaint, never lose sight of the big picture.

As you're doubtless aware, I'm known throughout Erebus as a highly decorated agent of Beelzebub. Indeed, from time to time I've traveled with the Master himself and served as his confidant. I am an experienced tactical instructor. My sage advice and counsel to field-workers is legendary. You'll find me far more accomplished than Ashtar.

Count yourself privileged to be the recipient of my advice. Know that many would give their right arm to receive my counsel. Know also that many have given their right arms when they failed to heed it.

Despite Obsmut's reservations, my sending letters to subordinates has many advantages over our conventional communication. Something vital gets lost in oral transmission, and you can never fully trust the messenger. (The Enemy has the unfair advantage of being present in more than one place at a time. The rest of us must make do.)

Our methods of thought-projection have also proven imperfect. Enemy warriors—those bootlicks with whom we once served—sometimes overhear our messages. And occasionally our emotions—rage in particular—blur our thoughts and create some unfortunate misunderstandings.

I have before me your résumé, Squaltaint. I see you've had only mixed success with the thirty-eight sludgebags assigned to you in the past seven centuries. No less than six of these became Christians, and only three of those did you manage to derail from serving the Enemy.

My standards are higher than Ashtar's, and my tolerance for failure lower. Trust me when I say it is in your best interests to serve me well. Sit at my feet and learn, or you will lie on my plate and be devoured.

The scientist must know the lab rats or he will not be able to use them to greatest advantage. Guided by my keen eye, you will come to understand the human prey. You will learn to stalk them, developing the keen instincts of the predator.

Submit immediately detailed information on Jordan Fletcher. In my next letter, I'll advise you concerning my strategy of team temptation. Bear in mind I may pay a visit to the field at any time. Unannounced.

To get you started, here are Foulgrin's Rules of the Sting:

1. Never lose sight of your goal—Fletcher's enslavement.

2. Find just the right bait, tailor-made for him. Be sure the hook is well hidden.

3. Use as many lures as you can. He may pass on one but bite on the next, or spend his life moving from one to the other.

4. Make him promises and actually keep a few now and then, so he doesn't catch on to the setup.

5. Tempt your prey with what he wants to have, but give him what you want him to have. Lure him, coddle him, reassure him all will be well, even as you fatten him for Lord Satan's altar.

If you're somehow unfamiliar with my past campaigns and decorations, you should review the attached sixty-page vita, which summarizes a smattering of my accomplishments over the millennia. Attached also are *Foulgrin's 66 Rules of Temptation,* an acknowledged classic. Read, marvel, and obey.

There are many reasons to follow my orders. First is our common commitment to retaliation against the Enemy and aggression against the sludgebags. Second is the punishment I'll inflict upon you if you let me down. I'll celebrate your victories with you, but should you fail, I'll discipline you severely. Mercy is the Enemy's weakness—not mine.

We are forging the only sort of alliance that works in Erebus, a coalition of mutual self-interest that keeps our house from being divided against itself. For both our benefits you must deceive and destroy Fletcher. As long as you do, we will get along fine.

When talking to you, I explain, clarify, and enlighten. When talking to the sludgebags, I hide, eclipse, and obscure. You must be honest with me and dishonest with them. Never get it backwards. I eagerly await your first report.

Remember, Squaltaint, while the vermin have successfully exorcised demons from their daily conversation, they've failed to exorcise us from their daily lives.

We always work best in the dark.

Your indisputable superior,

—Lord Foulgrin

CHAPTER 2

VOICES

Jordan Fletcher stared at the shadowed hollows of his temples and flecks of gray in his sideburns. He ran his right index finger over the creases in his once smooth cheek. His bloodshot eyes stared at him from the mirror, vacantly...or was it accusingly? With the back of his hand, he patted the sagging flesh under his chin.

"Jordan! Your breakfast's getting cold."

He grunted, resenting the shrill voice that once made his heart leap. Nowadays his heart leapt for no one. Except Patty, his secretary. He'd been thinking of her lately. He'd missed her during vacation and made up excuses to call the office. They were on the same wavelength. Patty appreciated him, didn't take him for granted like Diane. And she was beautiful, warm, always...just right.

Jordan adjusted his maroon tie and walked straight-backed and purposefully to the kitchen table.

He drank his coffee and downed his bagel, gazing at the financial and sports pages, as Diane watched the small television on the far end of the kitchen table. It had been weeks since they'd touched each other, except accidentally when tossing in bed. But yesterday she'd managed to get in a dig about him drinking too much and supposedly losing his temper. Patty would never treat him with that kind of contempt.

Five minutes later Jordan was weaving through traffic in his dark blue Lexus, listening to some inane morning radio show. His thoughts returned to Patty, entertaining forbidden possibilities.

Suddenly he sensed someone's presence. His eyes darted to the rearview mirror. Nobody there. No car behind him. He craned his neck to look in the backseat. No one. A chill spread from the center of his back to his shoulders. His biceps clinched.

Jordan turned off the radio. He felt a disturbing tug, that same inner discontent that kept at him, an indescribable longing for something more. Why wasn't he happy? He'd accomplished most of his goals. He was making the big bucks. He had the new vacation house. He was buying the boat.

What was missing? What was *always* missing?

But this time it was more than the nagging emptiness. He had the eerie feeling he wasn't alone. That he was being watched.

As he drove to work in the stone silence, he seemed to hear...well, not voices, more like promptings; this one calling him one way, that one another. Sweat dripped from his forehead onto his dress shirt. He swore, wiped it off, and turned up the air conditioner.

He punched the radio back on, then turned it up so loud he couldn't hear his own thoughts...or anyone else's.

LETTER 2

Know Your Prey

My disappointing Squaltaint,

Your report on Jordan Fletcher is far too sketchy. I need details.

The Enemy deployed another warrior to assist Jaltor when Fletcher was driving? That's a dead giveaway he's been targeted. Fine, you got Fletcher to turn up the radio and drown out their voices. But they won't give up on him. We must counterattack.

I've reordered the hit list, shifting Fletcher's priority level from gamma to beta. Since only Christians are on my alpha list you see how seriously I take this. A conversion plot may be in the works—at all costs you must keep him from falling into Enemy hands.

This brings me to my strategy of team temptation, a singularly effective method overlooked by Ashtar. I advocate double-teaming and rotation of duty among a small group of tempters. Your orders are to work more closely with the five other operatives in your cadre—Scumsuck, Hackslay, Muckdrool, Baalhoof, and Conhock.

Sometimes the Enemy deploys forces in a zone defense, rather than man to man. (I was once assigned to a coach—it heightened my strategic skills.) We must adjust our offense to best exploit opportunities. Teamwork is part of that. Each of you has a different primary patient. (The others' initial reports were far more thorough than yours.) Confer regularly and exchange information on your sludgebags. Explore how you can best use them against one another. Study the game films of Fletcher's life. Run them back and look for the little things. Discuss how best to attack him and exploit his weaknesses.

Today's lesson: To succeed with Fletcher and the other sludgebags, you must understand the differences between how we see them and how the Enemy sees them.

To us, they are food, meals to be chewed and swallowed. We seek to expand the borders of our selfhood, becoming ever bigger through absorbing their wills into ours. He, on the other hand, calls upon them to voluntarily submit their wills to His. We want them as slaves to exploit and dominate. He wants them as sons and daughters to "love" and promote to higher service. We want to devour them; He wants to empower them. We would rape them; He would woo them.

The Enemy has put these misfits at the center of His battle plan—a fatal mistake! He could have entrusted His schemes to our warrior counterparts. True, they're a crop of fawning bellboys, but they're still a thousand times stronger, smarter, and more reliable than humans.

Consider whom we are dealing with here. This virus on the galaxy, these parasites called image-bearers are so ignorant they imagine the cosmos is limited to what they can see and hear and touch, taste and smell. The rest of the universe, 99.999 percent of all reality, in their puny minds simply doesn't exist. Can you imagine? They're like those slimy babies in their vermin mother's womb, never suspecting there's a vast world beyond the realm of their senses.

Clearly, these ignorant fools are the weak links in the Enemy's plan.

This brings me to your Fletcher. The gnawing emptiness he's feeling affords you understandable pleasure, but beware—the Enemy draws their attention to their emptiness to fill it Himself. Prompt Fletcher not to listen. When the Enemy or that flunky Jaltor whispers to him, prompt him to turn up the radio, turn on the television, pick up his cell phone. Let him do anything other than examine his life, his emptiness, and especially his mortality.

Your job is to help Fletcher move impulsively to fill his emptiness with all the things the Enemy forbids. These have value not simply because they'll destroy him, but because they'll distract him. In the final analysis, distraction from the Enemy is all we need to accomplish.

Obsmut implores me to make clear to you what should be obvious—my letters must never fall into the hands of others except those directly under my command. Let your platoon members read my letters only while you're present. Then breathe on them and burn them completely.

Can you imagine what would happen if they fell into the hands of Enemy warriors or the sludgebags?

Fortunately for us the Enemy has failed to take such precautions. True, He has hurt us by getting His orders out to our prey, but remember they are equally available to us.

The key to success in any battle is "Know your Enemy." In a grave tactical blunder our Enemy has recorded His training instructions and strategies for us to see! This means we can devise perfect countermeasures. Think about it, Squaltaint. His designs of cosmic conquest, His battle plans—documents that should be locked in top-secret file cabinets—are littered in vermin hotel desk drawers across the planet!

He's spilled the beans. He's poured out His intentions indiscriminately, allowing us full access. The humans put the forbidden book on display tables and shelves. But *we* actually read it; indeed we must, no matter how loathsome.

Foulgrin's third rule: Whatever the Enemy wants, we want the opposite. The forbidden book tells us what He wants, and therefore serves as a photographic negative of what we want.

Of course, the Enemy has also planted in the forbidden book false information to misdirect us. The most obvious red herring is the persistent claim that He "loves" the sludgebags. Since it's an inherent universal law that the powerful subjugate and exploit the weak, He cannot be serious when He claims to love them in any sense other than a man "loves" a piece of pie or a prostitute.

What is there to love about these little insects? Even before they rebelled they were weak and useless. And since those two morons in the garden first betrayed the Tyrant, their bumbling offspring have committed an unending sequence of offenses against Him. (Aided and abetted by us, I'm proud to say.)

Now think about it, Squaltaint. If the Tyrant sent us packing from Charis—we who are the vermin's superiors in every conceivable way—can anyone seriously believe He loves them? Obviously, this "love" is a cover for some ultimate betrayal He's setting them up for. He speaks to them of comfort and wiping tears from their eyes and one day saying "Well done," and welcoming them into Charis. Ridiculous! Who does He think He's kidding with this patronizing nonsense?

Nonetheless, if you can see through the propaganda, studying the Enemy's book can equip you to thwart His work. Indeed, judiciously chosen passages can serve as bread crumbs to lead your prey down the sloping path to hell.

Foulgrin's rule twenty-three: Tactics without strategy are useless.

Sometimes shortsighted demons will gang up on a skid row bum and incite him to rob a store or jump off a bridge. Then they strut and gloat, as if they've done something noteworthy. But these maggot-feeding humans are already ruined—what help do they need from us? They are lures, I think, planted by the Enemy to distract us from more strategic targets.

Don't waste your time with low-maintenance drug addicts and petty criminals. They're already in our hands.

It's the educated and influential unbelievers and the Christians of all kinds who have the most potential for the Enemy's purposes, and therefore our own. Look at Fletcher. Well educated. Respected. An accomplished businessman. A wandering soul, confused and uncertain, but projecting an image of self-sufficiency and confidence. An ideal tool for our purposes.

Erebus is about pragmatism. Ethics, philosophies, theories, and methodologies don't matter. It's long-term results we seek. Tactics count only in so far as they produce the desired impact on Fletcher—reality distortion, moral failure, thoughts, and actions displeasing to the Enemy. Whatever sends them to hell we condone. Whatever draws them to heaven we oppose.

I stress the word long-term. Your service record reflects a tendency to inflict great pain and suffering on the humans today. This is quick, cheap gratification. Trust me, Squaltaint, when I say I have drunk deeply of the pleasures of administering agony to the sludgebags. Sometimes, I confess, I would love to unleash a few megatons of roach spray and rid the planet of them. But this remains outside our present abilities. Be patient—set the trap, wait; then when the rodent is caught, savor your writhing prey.

Honestly, Squaltaint, accounts in your files remind me of an undisciplined little boy pulling legs off an insect. You must act more strategically. If withholding pain or even giving him a morsel of pleasure will keep your prey a safe distance from the Enemy, then by all means do it. Eternal misery—not temporary suffering—is our overriding goal. Stay focused!

Keep Fletcher from thinking about his imminent death and what awaits him on the other side. Blind him to the obvious fact that since his last day is coming, he ought to prepare for it. Don't let him ponder hell. Or if he does, let him view hell as one big party where all the fun people will be.

Fun in hell? A most useful illusion. Company in hell? Hilarious, aren't they? Don't let him see that every vermin is alone there, in unending solitary confinement. Misery may love company, but there's no company in hell. Only misery. But for now, let that be our secret. The jaws of hell are greedy for him. Yes, we eagerly invite him to our party!

As for Charis, Lord Satan commands us to slander the Enemy's place every way we can, to convince the image-bearers it's unworthy of attention, undeserving of excitement. Let them first imagine heaven is their default destination. Second, that it's a boring habitation of stick-in-the-muds, a drab tedious residence they'd rather be delivered from than to. The less clearly they think about the Enemy, the less clearly they'll think about heaven; the foggier about heaven, the foggier about Him.

As long as you adhere to your duties, Squaltaint, we'll have a civil relationship. (Start by giving me that detailed report on Fletcher.) If you fail me, or try an end run around me, you will experience terror as you've never known it.

Is the name Basteel familiar? I thought not. He's never been seen again since he betrayed me centuries ago in the Jonathan Edwards incident—an event in which my role was greatly exaggerated, by the way, as explained in footnote number 29 in my vita. Review it.

I appeal to your self-interest, Squaltaint. Serving me will prove the best way to serve yourself. Failing me is your path to unspeakable ruin. The Enemy may not give you hell before your time—but I will.

Serving the vermin...upon a plate,

—Lord Foulgrin

CHAPTER 3

THE DARKNESS, THE BOOK, THE STAIN

With Diane at the mall and the kids with their friends, Jordan Fletcher sat alone downstairs, sunk into his recliner. After he flipped channels for half an hour, the room suddenly went dark and silent.

He started pressing buttons, trying to get the TV back on. Nothing. He reached for the lamp next to him, and turned the switch. Nothing.

Am I the only one who knows how to replace a stupid lightbulb?

He sat still, waiting for his eyes to adjust. As his heart slowed, he found himself mulling over the direction of his life, something he hadn't had much practice at until recently. This new habit of introspection frightened him. Why was he asking these questions?

You only go around once, so grab for the gusto. Make the most of it.

As he stood in the darkness his hand brushed against something, and it fell to the carpet. His wine glass. Cursing under his breath, he fumbled across the room in the darkness, feeling his way to a lamp he seldom used. He turned it on. The light shined on the old bookcase beside it, and his eyes fell on one book. His mother's Bible.

Jordan felt compelled to go pick up the wine glass immediately, even though it was empty. Suddenly he felt a stab in his stomach. He should go get more Mylanta. He looked back at the book, but something seemed to push him from it, as if…

The phone rang upstairs. He started toward it. No. He listened to the voice.

"Yeah, Jordy, it's Ron. Just reminding you about basketball practice tomorrow night. Barlow gym. See you around seven o' clock, okay?"

Jordan looked back at the old black book, worn and tattered. Feeling a strange heaviness in his hand—must be the arthritis again—he pulled it off the shelf and flipped it open.

Jordan studied his mother's handwriting in the margin. He remembered trying to copy it to forge an excuse when he skipped school in eighth grade.

A flood of memories besieged him, including the time he hadn't spent with his mom in her last years on earth. He tried to picture her face but couldn't.

"You were always there for me, Mom," he whispered aloud, surprised to hear his own voice, alarmed at the tone of his admission. He felt something hot and wet on his face.

He flipped a few more pages, then saw lines underlined in red. For some reason, he read them aloud:

"Put on the full armor of God so that you can take your stand against the devil's schemes. For our struggle is not against flesh and blood, but against the rulers, against the authorities, against the powers of this dark world and against the spiritual forces of evil in the heavenly realms."

A prickly chill crawled up his back. A devil scheming against him? His mother had taught him and his brothers there were fallen angels who rebelled against God and were cast from heaven. It was a myth, of course, a fairy tale for the weak and gullible, like heaven and hell and God Himself. Jordan Fletcher had never fallen for it.

He started to put the book down, but his eyes fell back on the underlined words. They didn't sound like myth. It was as if they had power, as if they had…the ring of truth.

Jordan started to move toward the recliner, to sit down and flip through more pages.

No, wait. He needed to replace that lightbulb. And get some Mylanta. And make that other phone call. And…*that coffee stain on the Lexus upholstery. If I don't take care of it now, I'll never get to it.*

Jordan placed the Bible on the bookshelf, back on display. He bounded up the stairs toward the garage, surprised at the urgency he felt to distance himself from the basement, from both the darkness and the light.

LETTER 3

Working behind the Scenes

My servant Squaltaint,

The air grows stale here at headquarters. This place is so mundane, nondescript. It lacks the tangible qualities of Charis, the home stolen from us, and Skiathorus, where you work. What can we do for pleasure here in the second heavens, this makeshift dwelling for displaced spirits? Everything's strictly rationed, and we're monitored to be sure we carry out our duties. Mine can be so tedious.

I'm a soldier, not a bureaucrat. I crave action. I'm not asking for Dachau or the Killing Fields. I'd be happy with some garden-variety bloodshed. Days go by without my being involved in a murder or even an assault. It's weeks since I've been out for a child-killing. I need to get back on the field. Be grateful, Squaltaint; you see close-up the fruit of your labor. As soon as I fire off this letter, I'm getting out for some carnage and mayhem. Why should second-rate spirits like you have all the fun?

I'm alarmed your sludgebag, for no apparent reason, took his mother's Bible off his bookshelf. You said he actually read a portion about us, then looked at some notes his mother wrote in the margin. According to his file, she was a dedicated Christian. Even the notes written by her are dangerous. But nothing's more dangerous than the book itself.

You said he hadn't looked at his mother's Bible—or any—since her death fifteen years ago. Your past record is irrelevant. The question is, why is he looking at it now? And what can you do to make sure it doesn't happen again?

No, we can't read their thoughts. It's an educated guess. But you must watch carefully and deduce what's happening inside Fletcher, then nip it in the bud. If it was a passing moment of nostalgia, a random occurrence, fine. But do not presume.

You failed to mention whether Jaltor had some role in Fletcher's "accidentally" turning off the remote control, suddenly leaving him in quiet darkness. Accident indeed! You should know by now there are no accidents. There are countless unusual occurrences the Enemy orchestrates for devious purposes, known or unknown.

I agree Fletcher's playing basketball weekly at the high school is of potential benefit—as a distraction and hopefully more. His file reveals anger is one of his worst problems, and basketball brings it out. Good. Let him gripe and whine and swear and throw elbows. Impress upon him everyone else's character flaws while keeping him blind to his own.

Beware of sports, as they can sometimes serve the Enemy's purposes—character development, discipline, teamwork, and all that rubbish. But they're of equal use to us. If basketball's a tool to corrupt character and cultivate pride, anger, and blame, then by all means be a sports fan.

It's certainly good news two of the men he's playing ball with like to go out and get drunk. One's committing adultery and the other's living with a beautiful young woman? They're both miserable, of course, but you can hide that part. Yes, I agree it's a good omen, that bumper sticker on one of their pickup trucks: "Everybody needs to believe in something. I believe I'll have another beer."

This basketball commitment means one more night away from Fletcher's family. His wife is irritated? Excellent. Don't forget the other bonus—it gives you an opportunity to meet some new tempters, exchange information, and strategize cooperative efforts.

Back to the more pressing concern of Fletcher reading his mother's Bible. Don't consider it arbitrary that he read a portion concerning us. Did Jaltor turn his hand to that page? Did the Ghost himself manipulate Fletcher's fingers? If so, then by all means you must keep him away from what it says about us.

The Master isn't entirely displeased with what the forbidden book says of him. It calls him "the prince of the power of the air" and "the god of this world." Yes, he would prefer "the god of all worlds," but for now we'll take what we can get. The book also calls him a wolf, a trained carrion fowl, a roaring lion, a cunning snake. While he's somewhat sensitive to the snake comparison, as it was once his favorite form to walk about in, overall he's flattered by these analogies. He's pleased the Enemy takes him so seriously. (As well He should.)

But the Master doesn't want the vermin to take him seriously. I've worked not only on coaches but generals, and it's sharpened my tactical skills. No general wants his enemies to believe they'll have to put up much of a fight. No coach wants the opposing team to think they'll have trouble winning.

Beelzebub doesn't want them to know he prowls about seeking to devour them. A man who imagines he's safe will walk into dangerous places unarmed.

We want them to *eventually* know we're their devourers, but timing is everything. The trick is to let them first see us one second after their last opportunity to escape!

I see in Fletcher's dossier the schools he attended. He's proud of his college education, his master's degree. He imagines himself an intellectual, despite how little time he's actually devoted to thinking. Educated men serve us best, because they're the most skillful liars. They draw from the deepest reservoirs of falsehood and rationalization. Seduce Fletcher with the ideas you place in him, making him think they're his own. Let him imagine himself innovative and original, "his own man." Never mind all he does is parrot the political correctness of his culture.

You said in your letter that one evening recently Fletcher sat in quietness, evaluating his life. You let him flip through a Bible *and* let him ponder his life in the same week? What were you thinking, Squaltaint?

Use television, computer, telephone, newspaper, sports events, work—anything and everything to distract him from self-evaluation. Why do you suppose technology and media exist but as tools for distraction? The briefest moments of musing could lead him to consider the state of his soul, and—Beelzebub forbid—his eternal destiny. Reflection is the bane of Erebus.

It's rarely to our advantage that the sludgebags *think*. Contemplation gives truth an opportunity to present itself. Debate plays into the Enemy's hands. Dialogue about truth drags us onto our opponent's home court. Mindless slogans serve us, but serious discussion can easily turn against us.

Distraction from the Enemy is better than overt argumentation against Him. If you start arguing too loudly, Fletcher may catch a tone of the raging battle. If only for a fleeting moment, he may realize he's more than a random collection of molecules, and there's a whole universe of reality he's never so much as considered. Worst of all, he might begin to hear the quiet voice of the Enemy.

Beware, Squaltaint. For if your vermin ever hears that voice, there will be heaven to pay.

Your ever-observant mentor,

—Lord Foulgrin

CHAPTER 4

SHUTTING DOORS

Jillian walked in the front door, followed by a tall girl with flowing cinnamon hair hanging to her elbows. Jordan looked up from his *Newsweek,* trying to remember her name.

"Hi, Brittany," Diane called from the kitchen.

She nodded, following Jillian into her bedroom, shutting the door.

Oh yeah. The volleyball player Jillian spent the night with a few weeks ago.

"Where's Daniel?" Jordan asked.

"Talking to me?" said the voice from the kitchen.

"Who else would I be talking to?"

No answer.

"Where's Daniel?" he asked with an edge.

"In his room. Probably on the computer. Why don't you check?"

Jordan skimmed the *Newsweek* article on the most recent school shooting, breezing over the usual parts about how shocked the parents were and how they'd missed all the clues about their kids being sociopaths.

How can people be so ignorant?

Without warning, that feeling erupted again—that sharp jab of desire for something more, something he was on the outside of and wanted to get into. Where was this coming from?

I'm no philosopher. I don't have the answers. I don't have to. I just need to play the hand I've been dealt.

Of course, no one had actually dealt him the hand. Had they?

His desire for...whatever it was...mutated into thoughts of Patty. After a few minutes of fantasies, Jordan read an article on stock market trends. Then he hopped up and went to the bedroom to change into shorts and basketball shoes.

"I'm going to Barlow to play ball," he said as he shut the door. He didn't wait for a response. He knew there wouldn't be one. And didn't care.

LETTER 4

The Vermin's Stinking Family

My kindred Squaltaint,

In your last letter you addressed me as Foulgrin. Henceforth call me by my proper title, Lord Foulgrin. We are not peers. I am your master.

Conhock informs me you and Muckdrool inquired concerning some of my past campaigns. He said you were particularly interested in a few...misunderstandings. Yes, twice I've been investigated by High Command on charges of heresy, leveled by malicious subordinates who misquoted me. This is part of my aversion to sending verbal messages to the field. They're too easily misconstrued.

I was cleared of those fraudulent charges and my accusers were turned over to me for punishment. I found them appetizing. Parts of them will always be with me.

Don't underestimate me, Squaltaint. I was Eshmon of Sidon, the intimate associate of Chemosh, god of Moab. (Chemosh still holds me in highest regard—he consults me from time to time.) I've sat in council chambers with Baal and Melqart of Tyre. As you'd know if you read my résumé, I was a prominent god of the Incas, in ancient Chile.

Sometimes the priests stole the children. Usually their families offered them up for sacrifice. I recall an eight-year-old boy, wearing a large red tunic, carrying extra sandals for his journey into the next world. He bore a gift for the gods—for me, Squaltaint, a chief mountain god. It was a spondylus-shell necklace more treasured than gold. I was there on Cerro Llullaillaco, at twenty-two thousand feet, when they offered him to me. His knees drawn up in a fetal position, bound tightly with a cord, they performed fertility rituals, then slew him. It was glorious.

So, Squaltaint, I ask you—have human sacrifices been offered to you? I thought not. Mind your place. Don't forget who you're dealing with.

I've checked around with colleagues and thickened your file. As long as you serve me well, I'll protect the unflattering portions from unsympathetic eyes. Fail me and I'll turn you over in an instant. If you have any more questions concerning my record—including the Amy Carmichael episode—come directly to me.

High Command has reiterated our commitment to making children our first priority. Kill them outright. Abandon them to the streets. Subject them to every form of abuse in homes. Make them fatherless, but be careful to close their ears to the Tyrant's seductive invitation to be their father. Drugs, prostitution, and pornography are ideal instruments to hurt the brats, indirectly and directly. And don't forget one of the most effective forms of child abuse: parents giving their children whatever they want. Which brings me to Fletcher.

The Enemy crowds the vermin together in families, where parents breed like mangy animals and raise their disgusting offspring. Unfortunately, in every society He uses the family to maintain a moral order we must counteract. Fortunately, many families have waved the white flag of surrender.

Your reference to yourself as the cat and Fletcher the mouse betrays too much playfulness. Temptation is serious business. Sure, there's pleasure in torturing them. But I warn you, don't toy too much with Fletcher. He's your prey, not your pet.

I find it amusing your sludgebag considers himself a "family man." From what you tell me, his wife lives in a world centered on her job, crafts, aerobics, volunteer work, and the children. Fletcher knows little of her world, nor she of his. They associate with an entirely different group of maggot-feeders. Excellent.

At last, you filed a report with details. Fletcher sees his daughter Jillian coming in and out the door and that's the extent of it? Their encounters consist of him shooting disapproving looks at her for how she's dressed. They don't eat dinner together. Best of all, he doesn't know her friends. He's never discussed with her who she hangs out with and what time she gets home and who she's talking to for hours in that Internet chat room. (Even she doesn't know who it really is—but I've checked, and our operatives are attempting to arrange a meeting soon.)

Her grades are decent, she's an athlete and not in a halfway house for drug addicts, so Fletcher figures he must be a good father. What else is there?

And then there's the boy Daniel, our young protégé. I've read Stungoth's reports on him. Marvelous. By day little Daniel wanders the school halls with his cadre of body-piercing misfits. He's a bandy-legged asthmatic punk, who wears steel-toed boots which he dreams of kicking into his enemy's crotch.

By night our Daniel shuts his door, sits at his computer, and feeds on violent pornographic images. He's hooked. I know what you're wondering—why would parents think a boy would not look at images that are only a mouse click away, when they give him unlimited opportunity to do so in the privacy of his room?

This is our edge, Squaltaint—it's not merely that this current crop of parents is corrupt. It's that they're so incredibly stupid.

Once he pries himself from the porn, Daniel splatters blood for hours. Years ago Stungoth got him started on Doom, Quake, and Tomb Raider. He became addicted to the thrill of mayhem. He still plays his old favorite, Duke Nukem, in which he celebrates his killings by punting his victims' heads through a goal post.

Stungoth reports he often envisions himself kicking Daniel's head through a goal post. You have much to learn from Stungoth. Families tend to rise or fall together. By attacking one member we attack them all.

After his video games young Daniel goes to his favorite Web sites, where he soaks in blood, gore, nihilism, and cynicism. There he meets our unholy trinity—darkness, death, and despair. He visits two sites of rock singers who worship our Master.

Stungoth reports Daniel reads horror novels. His mind drenched in rage, resentment, blood, and self-loathing, he listens through his headphones to grating tormented sounds. Hell has no music, true, but earth has music that beckons them there.

Meanwhile his parents—Mom especially, but also your Fletcher—observe his attitude, his anger, his vacant look, and withdrawn hostility, and wonder, "Is something wrong?" Now, Squaltaint, given what the vermin brat feeds his mind upon night after night, what could possibly be wrong?

"It's just adolescence," they conclude. "He needs his space." So they give him space, the current euphemism for parental neglect. Fortunately, they've given him just the space Stungoth needs to work.

They're clueless, Squaltaint, utterly clueless, thinking their son's fascination with the morbid, his flirtation with death, is just a "harmless phase." They'd be shocked to know the images and lyrics that float through the raging sewers of his mind. Who knows what rivers of destruction will ultimately flow out of that mind we've captured? Suicide? Murder? My mouth waters at the prospects.

Which of us in our wildest dreams could have imagined thirty years ago the images and propaganda we'd be free to bombard these young sludgebags with today? How to make a bomb, pull off an assassination, obtain automatic weapons, stalk and seduce a woman. How-to information on assaulting people is as readily available as information on baking cookies.

We've built a society in which the primary form of play for millions of vermin children consists of killing large numbers of people! These murder simulators are our training tools for future murderers. We may never get most of them to actually do it, but we'll certainly get many more than we would have otherwise! Fletcher and his wife would never trust their children to a sociopathic baby-sitter, yet they routinely entrust them to our sociopathic movies, games, and Web sites. You've got to love it.

"Why are children killing children?" they cry out, as if this were some great mystery. I get such a laugh every time they ask. Millions of adults kill their smallest children every year just because it's convenient, while society self-righteously defends it. Gee, I wonder where these kids got the idea killing children is okay?

Give me a wish list, Squaltaint, and I'll put absent, ignorant, self-occupied, and passive parents right at the top. When it comes to Fletcher's parenting, my only advice is, "Don't change a thing." Keep him right where he is—on the sidelines. He's our ideal man, always trying to exercise control over those he has no right to, and failing to give leadership to those he has responsibility for.

We favor rebellion only against the Enemy. We cannot allow these students, incited by the rebel from Nazareth, to rebel against us. It's the status quo—not the Carpenter's frightening alternative—we strive to maintain.

Keep Fletcher in the dark about his family. This shouldn't be hard, as long as you keep him in the dark about you, himself, and the Enemy.

Fully exploit the fact they're prone to act in light of the moment, not with strategic forethought. In plotting their defeat, you must think not just one move ahead but ten moves.

The vermin play checkers. We play chess.

Celebrating our grip on sludgebag families,

—Lord Foulgrin

CHAPTER 5

TWO WORLDS

Fletcher finished mowing the lawn just as the sunset lit fire to the clouds. He stared at the brilliant crimson splashed across the sky, as if it were the canvas of a great artist. It took his breath away.

He sat on the lawn. The glory of the western sky stabbed his heart, kindling a desire for something great, some person and place beyond his grasp. For a moment, lost in the transcendent, he felt as if he'd been made for another world.

A car zipped by, windows rolled down and stereo blaring. Out the passenger window flew a McDonald's bag. A few stray French fries tumbled on the roadside and into his lawn.

Fletcher jumped to his feet and shook his fist, running a few steps the car's direction. "Hey, jerk! Come back here. Idiot!"

LETTER 5

Hunting

My naive Squaltaint,

I tire of homelessness, always dwelling in temporary quarters. He had no right to evict us, no cause to hand Charis over to them. When your motivation to take down Fletcher wanes, remember that. If you cannot step foot in Charis, make sure at least *he* does not.

As for his "wasting his time admiring a sunset," don't flaunt your ignorance. The Enemy is a romantic and notoriously sneaky. He can woo them through the colors of autumn leaves, the sound of a waterfall, ocean mist on their faces, the sight of stars at night. This is why our propaganda department has diverted their attention from Him to a vague sense of awe at the natural order of things or the dynamism of the life force (or some such nonsense).

Consider what they view as opposites—light and dark, good and evil, God and Satan. Do you see how easily the last one rolls off? This is the dualism our Master seeks—"I will make myself like the Most High." All he asks is to be considered equal with the Enemy. If he's his opposite, that puts them in the same league, on equal footing. It makes him a viable alternative and casts uncertainty on the battle's outcome. The Enemy's position, of course, is that our Master's opposite is Michael. The Tyrant is self-existent, uncreated and therefore has no opposite. Dualism is certainly a useful notion. May the force be with you.

Anyway, you must realize the Enemy can use even a sunset to tug at their hearts and whisper there's a great secret to the universe they haven't gotten in on, but can. He's a seducer, I tell you.

Don't insult my intelligence by taking credit for the speeding car and the McDonald's sack. There are enough prey doing stupid things that distractions come at the right time even when we're unable to orchestrate them. Your job was to capitalize on the distraction and divert Jordan from the Enemy's tugs at his heart. It sounds as if you succeeded. Don't expect a medal—it's your job.

For twenty years I lived in a man who was a hunter. He was a miserable specimen, now safely in hell. But I learned much while in him. Our instincts and desires gain clarity when we occupy the human body. By hunting deer and elk and bear, I honed my skills in hunting humans.

The hunter tracks his prey. At first he keeps his distance, studies him, takes note of his behavior patterns. When the prey walks into the brush, how deep does he go? When he wanders into the open, on a ridge, does he slow down or pick up his pace? Which direction does he veer? Is this the best place to set your sights, or should you choose a position a hundred feet away and set yourself to shoot him from there? What kind of weapon; what ammo will best take him down? My prey had great instincts hunting his prey. (Of course, he remained oblivious to the one hunting him.)

The human hunter cannot read the creature's mind any more than you can read Fletcher's. But by studying your prey's behavior you learn to anticipate his next move. We figure out what they're thinking by watching how they act and listening to what they say. Having identified their vulnerabilities, we work on thought-projection and circumstance manipulation to set them up for the kill.

If the hunter thinks like the prey, he can predict his direction and lure him into the open, to the best position to take a clean shot. (Yes, we can't know the future, but who's in a better position to make an informed prediction than we?) He's patient yet vigilant, knowing his opportunity will come, but knowing too it could be easily missed. The hunter endures temporary discomfort because his single-minded focus is on killing his prey. Is your focus fully on Fletcher?

The hunter asks, "Does the prey know I'm here? If so, is he alert to the danger I pose?" He avoids sudden movements. He hangs around long enough to blend into the scenery, where the prey pays no attention to him. If he moves too fast too soon, he may scare him off. If he moves too late, he misses his opportunity.

When the time is right, the hunter puts the crosshairs on him and gently caresses the trigger. He shoots. He approaches the wounded animal, wary it may bolt. Then he slits its throat. Here my style differed from my sludgebag's. I like to slit their throats slowly, while the animal is still thrashing. The satisfaction is in watching them suffer. This is the game we play—inflicting those lingering moments of pain and dread, delighting in the helpless look in their eyes. And knowing through torturing them we are making *Him* suffer.

I went hunting last night, on streets, in shops and homes and workplaces. It was glorious. On the streets I breathed the soothing air of expectancy and doom.

I followed a woman, whose name I didn't know until I saw her credit card. Barbara. It has a rhythm to it, doesn't it? *Bar…bar…a.* I entered a vacant-eyed man staring at her. I shared quarters inside him with a resident tempter, Skullsort, who was understandably awed at the strength of my presence. I pressed up against her in the crowd. I moved in so close I could smell her perfume and feel the moisture on her cheek.

The man-tool, Jason, is promising. I laid out a plan for Skullsort, who will have Jason ready for me at my next visit. We aren't done with him yet…or with Barbara.

It's all about power, Squaltaint. Turf. Ownership. Words such as *love* and *virtue* and *honesty* are wallpaper, a thin veneer over the real substance—power, raw and throbbing. It's control we long for, with a thirst insatiable. Dominion. Preeminence. Conquest. The strong devour the weak.

Hell forbid you should think it an easy task to establish strongholds in the vermin. I lived among them for millennia. Of the 147 beings I was assigned to, I inhabited nine of them, a remarkable percentage. Early in my career, eager for promotion, I attempted several hostile takeovers, to no avail. Exasperated, I finally learned I could establish strongholds only in those who first gave me a foothold. I then set my attention to cultivating such footholds. That was the key to my success.

Do not be so grandiose as to speak of inhabiting Fletcher until you patiently approach him through doors of access. Sniff out Fletcher's weaknesses as a bird dog sniffs out his game. These are the bridges, the beachheads serving as avenues for our assaults. In Fletcher's case, you identified the footholds of anger, lust, pride, and materialism. All are promising. This is where you start.

I have a pressing engagement, but let me conclude by familiarizing you with *Foulgrin's Three Predatory Strategies.*

Nomadic predators rove about, seeking to inhabit just the right sludgebags we can use to abduct, abuse, and murder.

Stationary predators are like spiders. The spider puts his labor into creating the biggest and stickiest web. Then he waits patiently for his meal to come to him.

Territorial predators choose an area: a house, a room, an office building, a strip joint, a legalistic Bible college—there's something to be said for each. These predators are specialists, rarely deviating from their selected game reserve.

With Fletcher, employ a combination of the stationary and territorial strategies.

Due to my heavy administrative duties I can function only as a part-time nomadic predator. When I manage to get away, I go wherever my urges and instincts call me, a lion attacking the prey, leaving the remains to the hyenas. If you're lucky, you may clean up after my kill.

As powerful as I am, I still can't be in two places at once. I must hurry. I'm scheduled for a séance tonight.

The seeker's name is Dorothy Bristol. She's been distraught since her husband's death and has sunk ever deeper into psychic healing, astrology, crystals and vibrations, avatars and spirit guides, meditation and chanting, and altered states of consciousness. I consulted with her spirit guide, Frostcarve, who was eager for my help in pulling off a first-rate sting.

Dorothy wants to hear from her dead husband Michael. Yes, and she will, Squaltaint. I've done my research. I accessed Michael Bristol's file. I've been rehearsing his voice.

He called her "Dottie Darling." Isn't that sweet? She'll be so moved when she hears me call her that.

"Everything is wonderful on this side, sweetheart. The only thing I'm missing is you. Come join me. You know the way. Come to me soon. I have so much to show you, Dottie Darling."

Yes, Dottie Darling. Come to me. Come to me tonight.

Your predatory nomad,

—Lord Foulgrin

CHAPTER 6

FACE-OFF

Fletcher stopped on the way to work to pick up flowers for Patty. She'd put in extra hours to help him on a sales presentation. A dozen roses with ferns and baby's breath. He couldn't wait to see her face.

He pulled into his parking space. *Vice President of Sales* the bold white letters said. A month ago the board voted to change his title and give him a nice pay raise.

Vice president. Now, if I could just get Bancroft's job.

Jordan stood waiting for the elevator, pressing the button three times.

A minute later the elevator stopped at the third floor, taking forever to open. He sprang out, entering the office and looking toward Patty's workstation, but not seeing her.

"Fletcher, get in here," Bancroft called. Jordan left the flowers on Patty's desk. Maybe he should write a note. No. He'd let her figure it out, then come by and see her.

"Fletcher!" Bancroft's voice blared. Every head in the office turned.

Jordan marched to Bancroft's corner office and slammed the door behind him.

"What's that about?" Bancroft barked.

"It's about you yelling at me like I was your errand boy!"

"I'm your boss. CEO. Does that mean anything to you?"

"I'm the leading producer in this company and I'm the vice president of sales. Does that mean anything to you?"

Fletcher—three inches taller, forty pounds heavier, and fifteen years younger—now stood six inches from Bancroft. The older man's feet shuffled backward. Fletcher noticed.

"Who made you vice president?" Bancroft asked, his voice subdued. "The board and I did, against my better judgment too. They don't realize you're a prima donna. That you don't know how to be a team player. They just look at the bottom line."

"Which is what this company's about, isn't it? That's why they call it the bottom line."

Bancroft stared at Fletcher. They wrestled with each other in their gaze. Bancroft blinked first. He sighed.

"Look...Jordan...I've gone over your report on the Brisbane account." He waved a file in front of him. "The discount you gave them is too steep—it violates policy. You should've checked with me."

"Brisbane was about to bail and go with Atkins. We can still make a couple hundred thousand from them even at the discount. Would you rather I just let them go?"

"That's not the point. You should've cleared it with me."

"I'm the VP of sales. That means I manage sales. This was a sale. I managed it."

"You do this again without clearing it with me and it'll be the last sale you manage."

"Fine. I've got offers from two other companies. If you don't want the profits, they do."

"You signed a noncompete clause. We'll take you to court."

"You fire me and the clause doesn't stand. I may not wait to be fired anyway. My attorney says your clause won't hold water." Jordan marched out of the office and slammed the door behind him again.

A dozen saucer-eyed employees watched him stomp to his office and slam his third and last door. The windows shook; the watercooler sloshed. He clenched his fists and studied the veins. He felt the heartburn and the ache of his fingers. If he'd had a hand grenade, he'd have pulled the pin and thrown it. Jordan Fletcher felt like killing someone.

LETTER 6

Shaping How the Vermin See Beelzebub and Us

My struggling Squaltaint,

I enjoyed your account of Fletcher exploding at his boss. Our roaches are most amusing when they behave like Chihuahuas in parked cars.

The combination of Fletcher's sin nature, personality type, career, affluence, and lifestyle serves as a petri dish for neuroses. Stand back and watch the obsessions, fixations, and manias flourish—then capitalize on the ones you can best use to ruin him.

You think you may be able to lead him into any number of sins as a result of his anger and pride? You boasted you may be able to get him to quit his job.

Why do you assume this is the best move?

Wouldn't it take him away from the secretary you've labored to set him up with? And in his present job, didn't you report he works with only one Christian, and that one's obnoxious and two-faced, the sort we want to wear a cross or a WWJD bracelet or put a Christian bumper sticker on his car?

Why the heaven would you want to move him elsewhere? You don't know what—and especially who—the Enemy might have lying in wait. He has his agents everywhere.

Meanwhile, you're making yourself too obvious. Don't assault and scream when you can seduce and insinuate. Consider his fit of rage when he wanted to kill someone. Yes, I'm sure it was gratifying, but what if he becomes aware, even for an instant, there's more at work in him than himself? Do you want him to know you're fueling his fury? Are you looking for recognition? Get over it!

In what they call "primitive" cultures, I've enjoyed my share of outright terrorism. As I experienced among the Incas, it's cathartic to deal with sludgebags well aware of our powers and petrified by them. However, in this culture we must discipline ourselves to forgo that pleasure in exchange for those exquisite opportunities afforded us by the "enlightened" view that we don't exist.

Thankfully—though I'm not sure whom to thank—this myth of our nonexistence isn't limited to secular culture. Reverend Braun, that minister to whom Scumsuck is assigned—the one whose church Fletcher's sister attends—teaches we are but "literary symbols of man's inhumanity to man." I couldn't have said it better. Falsehood is at its zenith under the cloak of religion, best of all Christian religion, especially with a pseudointellectual twist.

As one literary symbol to another, I assure you that under this cover they've so thoughtfully bestowed, we can work unimpeded. (Isn't it amusing how uneducated men recognize fundamental realities educated men deny?) The vermin think of us as they do monsters under the bed, ghosts in the closet, or dragons in the attic. As they grow out of believing in them, they grow out of believing in us. It never dawns on them we are the realities behind those fantasies; we are invisible beings who are, in fact, out to get them. Parents do us a great favor when instead of teaching their children to resist us, they teach them we don't exist.

Unfortunately, not all humans—not even the educated ones—are so imbecilic as to believe we aren't real. Lead Fletcher to whatever distortion he's most prone to embrace. Convince him we're the departed spirits of evil people, haunting the earth. Or, better, make him think we're not people but vague abstractions or bad circumstances, such as "the demon of lust" or "the demon of arthritis." If they don't see us as having intellect, emotions, and will, they won't think of us as what we are, which gives us an immense strategic advantage.

Personally, I like the work of the roaches Dante and Milton, who depicted us reigning over hell and gleefully inflicting pain on humans. Never mind the forbidden book portrays hell as a place the Enemy designed for our punishment. We're not yet restricted to hell, like some of our comrades prematurely chained in the nether gloom of Tartarus, hell's basement. The vermin go straight to hell at death, and we see them as they pass but fortunately we're still free, having been cast from heaven to earth, not to hell where we could do no damage. (Though I'll admit it's the outskirts of hell, and sometimes I feel perilously close to the abyss, chained by the Tyrant's force of will.) Indeed, Lord Lucifer swears if we wage effective war in heaven against Michael and his angels, we may yet escape the fiery lake.

Let the ignoramuses think we're safely off in hell. Blind them to the reality we roam the earth and do our work, not torturing the dead but deceiving the living.

I'm pleased Fletcher enjoys the popular cartoons portraying hell in comical ways. Excellent—let them laugh at hell right up until the moment they enter it on death's far side. When eternity's door slams behind them, they won't find it so amusing.

Don't neglect the medieval caricature, where the devil is depicted as the long-tailed, cloven-hoofed jester with horns and red tights. This was originally an insult, as they knew we were more than this caricature. They deliberately scorned us, treating us as clowns and buffoons. They laughed at us.

The Master was at first enraged at this assault on our dignity, for they believed the Tyrant was big and Beelzebub small. But we've clouded the minds of modern man so he doesn't see what was obvious to the ancients. Since man first lived in that garden, he's lost more and more of his grasp of reality. With every generation, despite his technological progress—or perhaps because of it—he's managed to become more ignorant. (Every advance sludgebags congratulate themselves for becomes our tool. Technology always increases the reach of depravity.)

So the old parody of pitchfork and red tights no longer serves the Tyrant but us. The vermin's failure to take us seriously is inseparable from their failure to take Him seriously. They portray us comically not to strike a blow at our pride, but as an extension of their own ignorance, which they call enlightenment.

When they look at this silly lampoon of us, they know they cannot really believe in it. Therefore they cannot really believe in us. And if they cannot believe in us, they cannot believe in our counterparts. If there can't be an evil supernatural, neither can there be a good supernatural. Hence, their caricature of us serves to lock out the Tyrant from their minds.

Foulgrin's fifth law: Conquering the vermin is a direct outgrowth of their failure to understand who we are and how we operate.

At times I miss the days when we permeated their folklore and superstition, and were always playing tricks on them. But if medieval vermin thought too much of us for the Tyrant's tastes, the modern man thinks far too little.

Your job is simple—to make them see us when we aren't there and to keep them from seeing us when we are.

So let the puny-minded sludgebags dress their children in cute little devil costumes for Halloween. (Daniel dresses himself for Halloween every day.) Let the parents smile and pinch their rosy little cheeks, never realizing we do have designs on their brats. We have every intention—and a proven strategy—to make them "little devils" indeed. In the end, they won't regard them as cute. Before Fletcher and his wife wake up, Daniel will be so much ours they'll never get him back. More importantly, neither will the Enemy!

I'm amused they portray Lord Satan and all of us as repulsively ugly. Outstanding. If they believe that's how we look, they'll never see us coming. They'll assume lovely people can't be our emissaries and we can't be involved in beautiful writing, art, drama, or music. Don't let them see beauty is our tool of seduction. Who is seduced by the outwardly ugly? Don't take it as an insult they imagine us as nasty-looking—take it as an opportunity.

Lead Fletcher to believe in tame supernatural powers who will assist him in accomplishing his goals. He reads the horoscope? Excellent. He occasionally plays Dungeons and Dragons? Outstanding! Perhaps one day you'll get the fool to consult a psychic or attend a channeling or séance. Or become involved in some alien abduction enclave. Better yet, a group reaching out to "benevolent aliens," opening themselves to higher intelligences from other worlds. (And who would that be but us?) Who knows, maybe eventually he'll become a channeler for your voice! (There's been no living with Romtha since he started speaking through that woman to those vermin audiences.)

Let those intestinal parasites embrace us as friendly spirits who meet their needs to be "spiritual." If Fletcher does start believing in the supernatural, then persuade him it's to his advantage to cozy up to us, experiment with us, use us. Don't let him see we are not used, we are users. In league with the devil? They flatter themselves. He who would sup with Beelzebub had better bring a long spoon.

Given Fletcher's skepticism, I doubt you can lure him into all this New Age balderdash. On the other hand, his wife is a perfect candidate.

As for Fletcher's scientific and business orientation, why put on dark robes or red tights when you can wear a white coat or a three-piece suit?

Kindle his curiosity, draw him to the cheese, and let him do the rest. Your job is simply to rebait the trap.

Remember, Squaltaint, we can benefit immensely from any view of us but the true one. Probe carefully to discover your patient's demonology and develop it in the most advantageous manner. Make sure his view of us stems from skepticism, denial, ignorance, superstition, legend, literature, spiritism, popular culture, or any combination thereof. Let it come from anything and everything but the forbidden book.

We may be out of fashion, but we are not out of business!

Your nonexistent red-suited literary symbol,

—Lord Foulgrin

CHAPTER 7

THE DEAL

Jordan tried to push away the memories of his rage while sitting at this same desk three days ago. He felt justified, but the thoughts still unnerved him. It seemed a volcanic explosion of anger, greater than anything he felt capable of. He hadn't even been drinking. It was so violent and frightening, almost as if—it had come from somewhere else. Some*one* else? No, that was crazy.

He forced himself back to the task in front of him. He studied his expense account records. He took several receipts for personal items, then matched them up with nonexistent business expenses. He filled out a reimbursement form.

Jordan included the florist's receipt for Patty's roses. Why not? The work she'd done for him was company work; why shouldn't they pay for the perk? Naturally, Patty didn't have to know the company was paying. What difference would that make?

He recorded the flowers as a gift to the Brisbane office for signing the new deal. No one would ever know. It wasn't cheating, really. Hey, if you could make a good impression on someone who deserved more than the company paid her anyway, why not?

I've given plenty to this company over the years. They owe me. Besides, it's on my credit card and if Diane sees the charge to the florist, I need to be covered.

Patty walked into his office, smiling broadly. She looked great.

"Have I told you that's my favorite tie, Jordan? Bob Flannegan's on line two."

Jordan rolled his eyes. Patty laughed and closed his door as she walked out.

"Hey, Bob."

"Bad news, Jordan. Brisbane's lawyer called. They're interpreting the contract you agreed to as guaranteeing a minimum number of hours to manage their plan."

"What?"

"Well, apparently Atkins guaranteed them twelve hundred hours. They think you said you'd match Atkins at every level."

"They never mentioned those hours." Jordan felt the tips of his ears tingling.

"Well, they want that guarantee in writing, part of the contract. I told them I didn't know if we could do that."

Jordan hesitated, trying to sort out his thoughts. Suddenly the answer came to him, boldly and clearly. "Okay, Bob, go ahead; put it in writing."

"What? Are you sure? You better talk to Mr. Bancroft first."

"I'm sales VP. It's my call."

"Okay, but—"

"Do it, Bob."

Jordan hung up. He stared at his hands and pushed the paperwork aside.

Try to mess with me, will they?

LETTER 7

Moral Relativism and Your Sludgebag

My amoral Squaltaint,

You don't have to lead Fletcher into spectacular new sins that look good on your résumé. Every day he remains in his present condition brings him slowly, surely, dependably—even if nonsensationally—closer to hell. He doesn't have to spray his office with fifty rounds of ammo to go to hell—he's already going there. Don't tinker with him too much. Time's on our side. Fletcher's life is ticking down. When it expires, only one thing will matter—that he's hasn't come to know the Enemy.

You report Fletcher went drinking with a few of his new basketball buddies and laughed at their coarse humor. Good. Laughter is endorsement. The sludgebags become like whatever they laugh at. (Look at what we've done through trash talk shows and jokes on late night programs—our entertainment department deserves all the commendations Beelzebub's given them.) The seeds you're sowing in him will eventually produce a harvest. What little moral restraint he has left is eroding.

One of the other men he met at basketball asked him about his family? Harmless small talk. And gave him a novel to read? What novel? Be specific, Squaltaint. He probably won't read it, but if he does, it will presumably work in our favor, generating images to fuel his lusts. If it's a typical story, it assumes there's no God. The Enemy isn't argued against, He's simply left out.

Our strategy in literature is the same as in education. It's seldom wise to promote atheism. It works in some countries, but not this one. The best approach is simply to make no reference to a Creator or coming judgment. No absolutes and therefore no sin, no ultimate consequences, no afterlife, no accountability, no real hope.

Who cares if they believe there's a God, as long as they don't believe in the things that give Him teeth?

If this novel is more serious modern literature, it's likely to be dark, brooding, cynical, hopeless. Better still are those stories that offer hope, but false hope, interlaced with man's goodness, karma, the notion there's no hell and everyone goes to heaven. Beelzebub bless the New Age!

But beware—novels can stimulate imagination, foster thought and self-evaluation. This is never to our advantage. That's why television—or an innocuous piece of nonfiction—is nearly always to be preferred over a novel. When they're reading, the danger is that they may pause and reflect, consider changing their direction. Movies and television are usually nonreflective, undermining their values at the subconscious level with minimal thought and self-examination. They do their work so well you hardly have to do anything.

Lull Fletcher to sleep. Let nothing wake him before the flames. Attached you'll find our literature committee's top one hundred books—be sure to get several of them into his hands.

Now, I read with interest of your sludgebag's latest moral compromise. It's a small step from fudging on expense reimbursements to defrauding a client. It's the slippery slope—one compromise leads to the next.

Fletcher seems to have done this mostly on his own. Your comments reveal a failure to grasp this natural process of moral erosion. To better take advantage of your prey, you must catch a vision for the inestimable benefits offered us by the current climate of relativism. Listen and learn.

Only a few generations ago the sludgebags had a moral consensus. In some respects, it was dangerously close to the Enemy's own, with some notable—and welcome—deviations.

Not all of them lived by the standard, but nearly all of them recognized it. If the vermin know a foot is twelve inches, that consensus allows them to make measurements. But what we've done is to break the ruler in pieces. Now it's as if they're saying, "A foot is only five or six inches to me, and three inches to him, and seven inches to you."

They've lost their moral consensus.

The forbidden book says when there's no authority "every man does what is right in his own eyes." This is moral relativism. It's our crowning achievement—bask in it, Squaltaint. There's no evil we can't use it to justify, no good we can't use it to condemn.

Notice the Enemy didn't say every man did what was wrong in his own eyes. The beauty is, the sludgebags do wrong that's right in their eyes, by revising the standards to whatever they want.

If there's no Creator or if the Enemy's no more than some distant entity, there are no absolutes. That's Fletcher's belief, isn't it?

Men become gods, for gods are the makers of right and wrong. The vermin make it up as they go, determining for themselves what is and isn't moral. They base their ethics on their changing whims.

You spoke of Fletcher stealing from his company, cheating a client, and lying to his wife. Lying is a perfect example. It's wrong to them until they find a situation where they really want to lie, and then it becomes an exceptional case where lying is right, the best thing, the noble thing. Cheating and stealing are normally wrong—they pride themselves on thinking this because it proves they're moral people. But for themselves, they appeal to an exception clause. Fletcher tells himself he's done so much for his company and his client, they owe this to him. He's done so much for his wife, and she's been so ungrateful, she owes him his brewing infidelity.

Don't you see the delicious irony, Squaltaint? Even when committing immorality, they assume the moral high ground!

In the old days we got them to do wrong, but the downside was significant, because they felt so bad about it. (I don't have to tell you how the Enemy likes to twist sorrow into repentance.) But the beauty these days is we get them to do wrong without the downside—instead of feeling ashamed about it, they feel proud of it. Indeed, they are righteously indignant if someone suggests they've done wrong.

I stand in awe at what we've accomplished, Squaltaint. And I must say, I've had no small part in it.

Since most of them don't believe the forbidden book, their only moral base is the conscience the Enemy's foisted upon them. But without the reinforcement that once came from the forbidden squadron and community, their consciences are untrained by the Enemy. They send them false signals, like a defective heart monitor. If they won't be guided by the Enemy, then they'll be easily misguided by us. Fletcher is a classic example.

The trick isn't getting them to do evil. They do that on their own. The trick is getting them to believe their evil is good.

I used to manage a tempter named Dunghobble, assigned to a college ethics professor who taught moral relativism. (Nearly all of them do.) She always used our old lifeboat example: "Six people in a lifeboat, only enough room and food for five. Who do you throw over?"

The analogy is ingenious because we limit the choices. We leave no option to keep all of them in and die together if it comes to that. No option for someone to volunteer to jump out to save the others. All the Enemy's solutions are eliminated before the discussion begins.

I always enjoyed reading Dunghobble's reports of how his professor, with a straight face, would tell her students, "The important thing is to search for your own morality. Make sure it's not someone else's. Experiment. Engage in an authentic search for yourself, and come up with what seems good to you—that's what's important."

Designer morality, homemade ethics. Imagine a chemistry professor saying to his class, "Here are the chemicals. You're on your own—mix them any way you wish. Experiment. Even if you blow yourself and everyone else to bits, the important thing is that you engage in an authentic search for yourself."

I'll never forget Dunghobble's report of his ethics professor's shock and outrage when she discovered over half her class cheated on the final exam. I say she should have given them extra credit! They learned her lessons well.

Why did the professor get upset when her students acted out the very ethical system she advocated? Because, although she claimed not to believe in absolutes, she in fact really did—she knew that when they cheated they were absolutely wrong. She could not live by her own ethical system because in her conscience she knew it was incorrect. That's why you must keep Fletcher out of touch with his conscience and away from people who represent the Enemy's standards.

The amusing thing is that moral relativists such as Fletcher hold others to absolute standards when they're dealing with them but never hold themselves to those standards when dealing with others. If they steal from their employer it's because they're overworked and underpaid and they've been taken advantage of. If someone steals from them, however, they're outraged.

They say "There's no such thing as absolute right and wrong," but when someone breaks into their car and steals their stereo, they prove they don't believe what they say. If Fletcher ends up committing adultery it'll be because he's been emotionally neglected by his wife, and she hasn't met his needs. But if his wife commits adultery, he'll view it as an inexcusable betrayal. Once you get Fletcher in bed with his secretary, he'll have a dozen good reasons why it's not really wrong and certainly not his fault.

The road to hell is easily traveled. It's the arrival and the accommodations that take the toll!

What's most exciting is how we've served up moral relativism to the forbidden squadron. Relativism reigns in the church—the sludgebags improvise morals as they go. Ask Conhock about it. One of his patients recently walked away from her marriage because "the Holy Spirit gave me a peace about it." And her so-called Christian friends offered no argument! After all, they were to "judge not," and show love to their friend by refraining from disagreement.

There've always been Christian sludgebags who disobey the forbidden book. But there have never been so many who kept right on going to church and claiming the spiritual high ground in the midst of their disobedience.

The vermin explain their sin with sanctimonious language like, "We've prayed about it and sought counsel, and we feel it's the right thing to do." Don't let it dawn on them that to the Enemy what they feel is inconsequential. His moral laws—confound them—don't give a rip about how any of us feel. The sludgebags have no more power to vote them in and out of existence than they have power to revoke the law of gravity.

Be sure they see the forbidden book not as the Enemy's guardrails to protect them, but as cattle prods to punish them. Twist their view of Him.

Relativism is even more valuable to us inside the church than outside it. One of the goals of our Pastoral Training Department is to fashion future pastors into moral relativists. They may be relativists who profess to believe the forbidden book, but that does us no harm if they conform to the prevailing winds of culture.

Even if we can't make a pastor into a moral relativist, at least we can frustrate and undermine his efforts by blinding him—through blinding the institutions that train him—to the fact he's going to pastor a congregation full of moral relativists. Unless he does something radical to change that—our troops labor to make sure he doesn't—the forbidden squadron will never be more than a baptized version of the world, with mere cosmetic differences.

Take cheer, Squaltaint. An unholy world will never be won to the Carpenter by an unholy church. Make sure Fletcher stays away from not only the Carpenter, but any church and any Christian that represents Him accurately.

It felt good to inhabit a man again last night. The cold hard feel of the door key in my hand. The creak of the door as I opened it. The sound of crunching bone as my fist hammered the old man's skull. Yes, *my* fist, for I owned the maggot-feeder. All that was his became mine.

I go back to see Dottie Darling again tonight. Wish me luck.

Blurring the distinctions,

—Lord Foulgrin

CHAPTER 8

FLETCHER'S WORLD

"Where's my coffee mug?"

"Wherever you left it—or maybe in the dishwasher."

Jordan picked through the cupboard for a substitute mug, clanging glasses against each other. The sound, coupled with the hard edge of his silence, spoke volumes.

"If you'd wash it yourself," Diane said, "it would be there every morning."

What'd I say? I spend the day making money so she can have a beautiful house, and I'm supposed to wash the dishes too?

Jordan immersed himself in the sports page, reading about his Seahawks' draft choices, as his wife sat near his daughter at the opposite end of the big kitchen table.

"Your play's tomorrow night, isn't it?" Diane asked Jillian.

"Yeah," she said.

Jordan's heart sank. He had tickets to the Blazer game. He'd planned to go with Ron and some of his buddies.

A high school play instead of a Blazer game? Great. Where does everybody else get the right to decide what to do with my time?

"Did you hear that, Jordan? Jillian's play's tomorrow night."

"Yeah, I heard. It's on the calendar. How have rehearsals been going?"

Jillian shrugged. "Okay."

Jordan looked at his watch and got up abruptly the same moment as Jillian. "Don't be late to school." The two exited the kitchen in opposite directions.

Jordan pulled out into the street, then noticed a flattened cardboard box from the recycling stack in his neighbor's driveway had blown over onto his lawn. He pulled back into his driveway and threw on the brakes. He got out quickly, picked up the cardboard, and marched it over to his neighbor's pile. He looked at the front window, hoping Sid Young or his wife would see him.

Can't you just keep your junk out of my yard?

As he drove, he felt the tension in his neck, and the pain in his hands. Only forty-five and the arthritis was gripping him. He punched the radio station. It came up to a contemporary rock station he never listened to.

Jillian—I let her borrow my car one time, and she messes up my settings.

Weaving through traffic, hitting the horn and scowling a half dozen times, he finally pulled into the parking lot, made the quick turn and...

"What the—?"

He glared at the car parked in his space. He backed up and took the space that said "Administrator." Jim Henry was lower on the food chain.

Jordan marched over to Frank, the parking security guy without a last name.

"Whose car is that?"

"Which car?"

"The one in my space."

He shrugged.

"Well, find out. I want to know. It's my space."

Frank looked at the half dozen open spaces, then appeared as if he was about to say something. When he caught Fletcher's eyes, he stopped cold.

"Sure. I'll check on it."

"Tell whoever it is there's a reason the space has my title on it. Ask them what it is about that they don't understand."

Jordan entered his office at full stride, past Patty who was on the phone. He sat at his desk, pouting as he flipped through the half dozen pink slips, chose two calls to make, then moved to his computer to dig into e-mail.

"Who's been on my computer?" he called to Patty, who quickly appeared at his door.

"Patrick said he needed to pull something up on the Edwards account, something he couldn't get from the network."

"You didn't give him my password?"

"Of course not. It was already up. You never closed out yesterday."

Jordan stared at the screen, saying nothing. Patty disappeared. He sighed, realizing he'd been abrupt.

I'll make it up to her. Take her to lunch or something.

By eleven o'clock Jordan felt like a bomb about to explode. He left his office, saying nothing to Patty or anyone else. He glanced at his parking space, now empty, wondering who the jerk had been.

He walked with apparent purposefulness, pretending he was going somewhere, embarrassed he didn't know where. He walked six blocks to the town square, studying the cracks in the sidewalk as if trying to find meaning in them. He heard a voice in front of him.

"Believe on the Lord Jesus Christ."

It hit him in the face like a pail of ice water. He made brief eye contact with the street preacher and read his big sign: "Repent and be saved from hell."

"Do you know Jesus?" the man asked.

"That's my business. Why don't you mind yours?"

"It's my business to tell people about Him."

"Yeah? Well, this is my personal space you're standing in, and it's my time you're taking. So why don't you get out of my face and get a life?"

The man backed away. "I have a life. I'm just trying to tell you about it. How about you? Do you have a life? Do you want one?"

Jordan felt an urge to deck this bozo but held himself back. One impulsive move and the jerk could have his house and boat in a lawsuit.

"He came to fill the empty place in our hearts."

For a fleeting moment a thought came to Jordan, an odd and irrepressible sense that his mother would agree with the man's words.

"I can't stand you phonies," Jordan said.

"How can you say I'm a phony? You don't even know me."

"I don't want to know you." A red tide sweeping through his brain, he moved back and pointed to the man's sign. "*My* God wouldn't send anyone to hell."

He walked away rapidly, humming loudly an old rock tune, "I Can't Get No Satisfaction." It was a trick he'd practiced as long as he could remember, whenever he didn't want to hear something. And right now he desperately didn't want to hear the street preacher's words that chased him like a bloodhound on his scent.

LETTER 8

The Word "My"

My Squaltaint,

Seen one, seen 'em all. I can tell you all about Fletcher.

He acts as if he's the center of gravity, with sufficient mass to hold everything in orbit around him—as if it all existed by his will or for his sake. This is why his language is loaded with references to himself.

The possessive my, which Fletcher is so fond of, reflects a belief that he's an owner, with all the rights and privileges thereof.

Fletcher first learned "my" in the nursery. The toy soldiers were his, and if he wanted to pull them apart, he was entitled to. When he was a little older, the cat was "my cat," and if he wanted to shoot it with the BB gun, why not? His twin Jill and other sister Erin were "my sisters," meaning they were his to torment. "My clothes," "my bike," "my mother"—all belonged to him; they existed to meet his needs.

In adolescence he graduated to "my car" and "my girlfriend," both instruments of self-gratification. In adulthood it became "my job" and "my children" and, the few times he ever went there, "my church"—his to own, to control, to use. Of course, they can use "my" without this notion of control. But they seldom do.

By encouraging this strategic use of "my" we can create false expectations and resentment among the roaches. Don't you see, Squaltaint? The Enemy claims it all belongs to Him. He views the maggot-feeders as tenants, living on His land. Hence, any claim of ownership on the vermin's part pits him against the Enemy.

Fletcher talks about "my yard" and "my parking space" and "my boat." The fact he's hoarded possessions under "his" roof makes him think he owns them. It's a subconscious claim to godhood, as if he were saying he's the maker and owner.

Any sludgebag who declares himself to be a god in this way will expand his imaginary kingdom to include other possessions and people.

Your reports show when Fletcher says "my wife" he usually means "my trophy, to display as I wish." That is why she must look perfect when he takes her out, which I'm delighted to hear he's doing less and less. Soon this claim will give him the right, when his trophy cracks and fades, to toss it and get a new one. Your strategy of Fletcher dumping his wife for the newer model seems to be proceeding well.

Consider what may be accomplished through such an affair—embittered wife, devastated children who will learn to distrust marriage. Throw in the woman who will abandon her own husband and children. The best part is all the falling dominoes. Praise Beelzebub for chain reactions!

What must you do to pull this off? The train's in motion. Just encourage what's already his natural bent—seeing the world through the paradigm of "mine."

Make your man go to bed every night thinking his family, coworkers, and neighbors owe him dearly for today's offenses and inconveniences, and they'd better make up for it tomorrow. Of course, they'll offend him just as much tomorrow, and therefore he'll think his hostility is justified. His own character flaws, obvious to everyone around him, are completely invisible to him.

He'll become less tolerant of those he believes are encroaching on him. Though he thinks he loves his children, he considers them nuisances and resents their demands. He neglects spending meaningful time with them in conversation—nonvideo, nonsports, nonentertainment time. The less opportunities he takes with them, the more opportunities he gives us. Someone will guide them—if not him, why not us?

You spoke of him losing his temper again in traffic. Road rage. This is *my* car, *my* schedule, and *my* lane. Get out of *my* way!

Cultivate the illusion of ownership of his body. Let him think "it's my body, no one has a right to tell me what to do with it." (Remember the bumper sticker "Keep your laws off my body"? I was in the marketing department's brainstorming session when we came up with that one!)

Make him view time as a possession, as if it were a birthright, as if by some inexorable law he's entitled to twenty-four hours a day to be lived exactly the way he wants, with no unwelcome intrusions.

If you do your job, Fletcher will imagine himself patient and generous with his time. Make him think "my problem is, I'm too generous, too giving; I must stop letting others take advantage of me."

Even while steeped in selfishness, the vermin are quick to bestow sainthood upon themselves. Our tactical department specializing in pop psychology has outdone itself. The humans no longer see self-love as the disease, but the cure!

Teach him to cling onto "my time," viewing everything and everyone as a time thief. His expectations feed frustration, which mutates into anger. He might as well resent having to breathe or eat as to resent people taking his time. Never let your prey consider he didn't create "his" time, nor earn it. He cannot keep it, store it up, or take it with him when he exits earth. So why does he consider it "his" time? Because he's a fool, why else?

The Carpenter calls upon them to say, "Thy will be done." We call upon them to say, "My will be done." When they wish the Enemy would stay out of their lives and leave them alone, they are praying for hell, the one place in the universe where He'll withdraw His presence. They'll get what they pray for. It just won't be what they expected!

Every time you enlarge Fletcher's view of himself, with no additional effort you shrink his view of the Enemy.

I was alarmed to hear of the street preacher attempting to share with Fletcher the forbidden message. Couldn't you see where he was walking? Keep him away from such people. Even if they're offensive, the Enemy has a disturbing way of using their message to plant ideas.

Your Fletcher appears to have a nominal belief in the Enemy, a sort of I'll-believe-when-I-find-it-comforting approach. This explains why, when he saw the street preacher's sign, he responded, "My God wouldn't send anyone to hell."

I couldn't help but chortle. For months on end he thinks nothing of God, then suddenly he speaks of "my God." For Fletcher "my God" is no different than "my genie." His god is a cosmic bellboy who exists for his benefit and if he's lucky might earn a tip from him.

Your prey is absolutely right when he says "My God wouldn't send anyone to hell." He could not, simply because Fletcher's god does not exist. He's but a comforting figment of his imagination, which will vanish in flames the moment he relocates.

If only we could so easily get rid of the Tyrant.

Laboring to gain what's rightfully mine,

—Lord Foulgrin

CHAPTER 9

THE GAME AND THE BOOK

"Great shooting, Jordan. Nice game," said the lean dark-haired man, slapping him on the back.

"Thanks, Ryan. You too." Jordan tried to remember...oh, yeah, Ryan owned a landscaping business east of Gresham.

"How about some beers?" asked one of the men standing by a locker.

"Gotta get home," another said. "The old lady's been buggin' me."

"Yeah. I'm on early tomorrow anyway. See you next week."

"How about you, Jordan?" Ryan asked. "Starbucks is still open. Can I buy you a mocha?"

"Sure. I never turn down a mocha."

They sat in Starbucks, laughing about the game and local politics.

"So, Jordan," Ryan said, "had a chance to read that book I gave you?"

"Oh, the novel? Yeah, I read a couple of chapters. It's sitting right by my recliner. Been pretty busy the last few weeks, though."

"What do you think?"

"Not bad, actually. I like a good mystery."

"Well, when you get a chance, keep reading. It gets better."

LETTER 9

Truth and Fiction

My appalling Squaltaint,

Two nights ago Dottie Darling took an overdose. Poison's not my favorite—I prefer blood, watching their lives ooze out. But it did the job. I greeted Dottie, masquerading as her beloved Michael. For an instant she bought it. Then I showed her who I really was. She screamed and I laughed in her ugly face as she passed by. She and her beloved are in the same place all right, but they'll never see each other in the solitary confinement of hell.

I felt the glory of the hunt, the power surge. But then...I heard the singing again. That dreadful music of Charis haunts me, pursues me like a relentless beast. It drifts from the third heaven out here to the second. No matter where I go, I can't escape it. "You are worthy," they keep singing. Why? What's in it for them? Where's the profit? Why do they smile and laugh and dance and feast and cry out as if in joy? Are they feigning their adoration, appeasing the Enemy to keep Him from squashing them like the bugs they are?

I try not to listen to the words, but they press themselves upon me, floating about the cosmos like noxious fumes. I cannot bear it. I must do something to block those horrid sounds. Anything—even if it means writing to a second-rate tempter whose litany of failures expands geometrically each day.

"Jaltor is out to get me," you whimpered. Tell me something new. Of course he's out to get you. It's a war, not a picnic. The Ghost is out to get you, too. Even the Christian vermin—the few who realize they're in battle—are out to get us. There's no use whining about it. I'm not your nursemaid; I'm your commander. Deal with it.

You say you're having trouble understanding some of my allusions to human senses and appetites. I forget your inexperience. How many men have you indwelt? According to your file, not a single long-term occupation. I've lived in a dozen men not only for minutes or hours, but years, once thirty-seven years. I was team leader of seven indwelling spirits in a single vermin.

One host of fifteen years was a churchgoing man who raped his slave girls and beat his male servants. I lived in a pedophile, back when they called them child molesters. I specialized in runaways and throwaways. I won't glorify it—they were cold, lonely, sometimes maddening assignments in those tiny disease-ridden outposts, punctuated by moments of fleeting satisfaction. Still, it brought clarity to my prey and my mission.

You say you wish to inhabit Fletcher? How can I expect you to understand, you who've neither paid the price of inhabitation, nor known its pleasures?

My first indwelling I found vulgar. Hearing the sloshing of their vile liquids, feeling the tightness of the skin, sweating and stinking and defecating...it was horrid. That claustrophobic sensation of being trapped in those tiny receptacles, overwhelmed with the poignant intrusions of their senses. The smells alone, the dank wet odors and the dry musty ones, nearly overwhelmed me. I didn't know how to sort out all the sounds, the noises that clamored at me. I felt his pain, loneliness, emptiness, the stark futility of living in that endless sea of wretchedness.

But in time my longings found ways of expressing themselves in his physical appetites and behaviors. First I mastered taste; then the other senses followed. Using my host's body, I learned to indulge myself with food and drink and sex and violence, enjoying myself while destroying him and those around him. I discovered in hunger and eating the correspondence to our longing to consume and assimilate inferior beings. I learned to love the taste of warm blood, both my host's and our victims'.

I discovered that the Enemy endowed the image-bearers with yet another gift He withheld from us. True, we are spirits, but they are too, somehow woven into those bodies. And the bodies offer delights I'd never imagined. The exquisite pleasure of a fine meal and a choice drink, the smell of freshly baked chocolate chip cookies, the warmth of fire on an icy night. I have felt sun on the face, rain dripping on the head, snow falling on outstretched hands.

Wondrous illustrations are afforded me you cannot understand. It seems I must put the cookies on the lower shelf. (But then, you've never had a cookie, have you?) When I refer to blood surging through the veins, I know whereof I speak. But you've only worked from the outside of those creatures, so to you they are but repulsive buckets of slime. I've worked from the inside, and seen the unique advantages the Enemy has given them in this strange hybrid of spirit and flesh.

No wonder the R word is so important to the Enemy—bodies and spirits reunited in resurrection, spirits not restricted by bodies, but enabled by them. Enabled to explore greater depths of reality than even we can know. Their senses subject them to pain, yes, but they allow them to enjoy pleasures in ways we can only dream. Those bulging eyeballs, tingling spines, pulsating internal organs. They are alive, truly alive, while our confinement to this spirit realm now seems to me but a half-life. The more I discovered the unique advantages of corporeal existence, the angrier I became.

Why did He lavish these gifts on them and not on us? What right did He have? Did He ever become one of us? Of course not. He became one of *them.*

Does He expect us to take these offenses lightly? My inhabitations redoubled my commitment to destroying them, His favorite little pets. I learned to think and feel as the prey, so as a hunter I could better plot the kill. This, Squaltaint, is why I'm the best advisor you'll ever have.

Now for the matters at hand. A weekly basketball game at a local gym—you made it sound so harmless. "Beneficial," you called it.

I pulled from the file your letter of three weeks ago. You said, "He's hanging around drunks, and two of them are adulterers. He's neglecting his family and his wife is embittered. I have him right where I want him."

You were so smug, so self-assured. Based on what you told me I suggested you prompt him to spend more time with this group of men.

Then you casually told me one of the men gave him a novel. Fine, I said, it will likely be just another distraction, probably feeding lust and discontent.

But now I've received a message from one of my colleagues. It seems a grunt named Dredge has reported that one of these basketball players to whom he's assigned is a Christian! How did you neglect to mention that?

This Dredge claims his maggot-feeder gave yours a book and asked Fletcher to read it and tell him what he thought. Now the bombshell—I'm informed it's a novel containing the forbidden message!

Dredge reports you weren't overly concerned since the vermin's believing cousin—you never told me he had a believing cousin—has been giving him Christian books for years, and he's never so much as opened them.

Well, he's opened this one, hasn't he?

Dredge claims you weren't worried even if he read it because "Foulgrin said it wasn't dangerous." Well, Squaltaint, if you'd only told me what this novel actually was, my appraisal would've been radically different. You handcuffed me with misleading information. Idiot!

Some of this fiction portrays history through the Enemy's eyes. It conveys information harmful to us, emphasizes the Enemy's sovereignty and tells stories of His...grace. Fiction is a great medium for lies. But unfortunately, it's just as effective for truth.

There are many lies in nonfiction and many truths in fiction. So your notion that it's "just a novel" is hopelessly naive. Dredge reported you said there's no danger in stories. Doesn't it occur to you the forbidden message itself is a story? Don't you realize the Carpenter told stories and hid in them the most dangerous truths?

I would rather the vermin read ten nonfiction books on grace than understand the Enemy's single story of the prodigal son!

Don't you realize some of the most dangerous literature written by Carpenter followers has been fiction? Consider *Pilgrim's Progress.* Scarblot is still under discipline for wandering the old streets of Bedford, bragging about putting this pastor in jail, while the vermin sat in his cell writing a story the Enemy has used for His purposes more than any work in history besides the forbidden book itself.

And with all the hundreds of nonfiction books written against slavery, do you remember the volume the Enemy used to change millions of hearts? *Uncle Tom's Cabin,* by that wretched little woman. A work of fiction, with truth bootlegged in, brought down our stronghold of American slavery. (Yes, we got a great war out of it, but that seems little consolation now.)

And what about that story the vermin pastor told from his pulpit that became the book *In His Steps?* "What would Jesus do?" everyone was asking. The story is still being told, and the question still being asked.

Fiction is not the opposite of truth—indeed, it is sometimes the most persuasive vehicle for it. So Squaltaint, don't tell me the novel given to your prey is "just" a work of fiction! And don't dare suggest again that you informed me of this matter and I told you the book posed no danger. How was I to know when you withheld vital information?

I still held out hope since much of their fiction poses no danger to us. But when I noted the title and checked intelligence reports, I was sickened to learn a great deal of truth is integrated into it. It portrays suffering as real, conflict as grave, longing as deep, and the Carpenter as the only one who can fill their empty hearts.

Fletcher's defensive enough he might refuse to read the Enemy's nonfiction. But by reading this story he's allowed the Trojan horse into the gates of his mind, not knowing what's inside. Under cover, the Enemy's viewpoint may sneak out and take him by surprise, seizing his mind and heart. (Learn from this strategy—to gain entry to the man, disguise your purposes. Once they let us in their mind gates, we're free to do our work.)

Don't you see Fletcher's worldview and values are up for grabs? This book could be the last straw. Or even the last influence he's exposed to before he leaves this world. How many in that fleeting moment before death have reached out to the Enemy for rescue? "Remember me, Lord, save me, take me." Like that stinking thief on the cross. Our work of a lifetime, up in a moment's smoke, because some miserable tempter like you fell asleep on duty!

You must immediately distract your vermin from reading this book. Keep him away from any book—fiction or nonfiction—showing the Enemy's perspective on good and evil, struggle and tragedy, sin and redemption. Let him read stories leaving him in despair or offering easy answers. Let him read books with characters who disappear when they turn sideways. (Shallow books make shallow men.)

Simplify your objectives. All that matters is whether in any given moment your prey is prompted to stay where he is, move nearer to us, or move nearer to the Enemy. Either of the first two options works for us. The third must be avoided at all costs. Keep his hands, eyes, and mind away from anything the Enemy can use as bait to hook him and reel him in.

Tonight, get Fletcher to watch television, read the paper, do the crossword, listen to music, make telephone calls, sit at his computer, or repair the car. Or let him read one of our books or some neutral one that does him no harm but no good either. But do not let him read that "harmless book" this nuisance Ryan gave him.

The Enemy has transformed countless lives through vermin writings conveying the story of the forbidden book. For your sake, Fletcher had better not end up being one of them.

Censoring His propaganda in every form,

—Lord Foulgrin

CHAPTER 10

A LITTLE CHOICE

Jordan sat in his recliner, watching the sitcom. Diane lounged on the couch ten feet away.

He felt edgy. The program struck him as empty, the sort of thing watched by people who don't have lives of their own. What troubled him most was feeling bothered by things that didn't used to bother him.

Jordan thought about going upstairs. Maybe he could...he stared at the gorgeous actress who just walked onto the screen, to the hoots of males in the soundtrack audience.

When a Taco Bell commercial popped on for the third time that evening, he got up from the recliner as if he'd been yanked. Diane looked at him, startled.

"What?" he demanded.

"Nothing, I just—"

He walked in front of Diane, toward the door leading to the stairs.

"Where are you going?" she asked.

Jordan shrugged. "I don't know. Maybe get to bed early, do some reading. Whatever."

Diane nodded. He thought he saw wetness in her eyes. Why was she crying? It was a sitcom, not some Hallmark chick flick.

Women—who can understand them?

Jordan went upstairs and pressed the message button on the answering machine. He flipped through mail he'd already opened, looked in the fridge, then fiddled with a flickering light. He'd intended to do some reading, but just as he was about to, something else would catch his eye.

An hour later he put away the screwdriver he'd used to tighten screws in the kitchen chairs. He took some Advil and Mylanta, then went to the bedroom, flopped back, and opened the novel Ryan had given him. He flipped through the first two chapters to remind himself what he'd read ten days ago. Then he turned to chapter three.

LETTER 10

Captains of Their Fate

My infantile Squaltaint,

I was so impressed to hear that the other night when Fletcher sat alone in a room, you managed to give him, as you put it, the "heebie-jeebies." What an astounding victory for you. I'm sure all Charis must have trembled.

I've sent a memorandum to Dredge's field director, advising him to deter Ryan from interceding for Fletcher. Evidence suggests enemy troops working on your subject's behalf may have been mobilized partly in response to his forbidden talks with the Enemy.

You made no mention of whether you've kept Fletcher from that book. Did you skip class at the academy the week they taught how to file a report? Instead of providing me with helpful information, you complained about failing to see the practical application of my earlier letter concerning the pronoun "my." Why am I not surprised?

This time I'll tell you a story. Who knows? You may actually get the point.

Some years ago I was on leave from the home office, doing fieldwork. One of my subjects was a vermin named Robert. He was a corporate executive who had a poem on his wall about being captain of his fate. Suddenly, out of the blue, he was seriously considering the Carpenter's invitation.

I suffered considerable anxiety, what with Ishbane breathing down my neck and warning me of the consequences should I let my quarry slip away. A Christian had been pursuing my vermin, talking about the Carpenter. He told him he'd call back to talk more. I knew I was in jeopardy.

I resisted the urge to argue against the Carpenter's claims, determined to stay off the playing field of truth. Distraction was the obvious strategy. But—and this is what you must learn, Squaltaint—I didn't make the mistake so many tempters do by going for a shout-from-the-rooftops victory such as a terminal illness or a family member's fatal car accident. Too often these things fly back in our face. In a moment of inspired brilliance I simply placed a nail on the road and went for a flat tire in rush hour traffic. (Your powers of telekinesis are inferior to mine, but with some practice you too might learn to manipulate objects with precision.)

The jack was rusted and wobbly, leading Robert to curse the prior car owner for not telling him. The manual wasn't in the glove compartment, prompting him to curse his wife who'd cleaned the car and, he was certain, misplaced it. The spare tire was flat, leading him to curse the Tyrant, who catches the blame for everything which can't be attributed to anyone else. (And why not?)

Do you see what happened, Squaltaint? The nitwit viewed the flat tire not as a commonplace minor misfortune, but as a special personal injury against him. He saw it as an attack waged on him by the previous car owner, his wife, and the Tyrant Himself, not to mention all those motorists honking at him.

Naturally, he never blamed himself for not checking the jack or the spare tire or misplacing the manual, which he did; not his wife.

At one point, when he tore his suit pants at the knee while down on the asphalt, he cried out—as if the universe listened with bated breath to his appeal for justice—"I've got better things to do with my time!"

Whose time? *"My* time."

"Why did this have to happen today?" he cried.

Of course, he filled all his days with impossible expectations, so any who imposed on his schedule—including his daughter who asked him a question while he was reading the newspaper—were not respecting his rights, his sovereignty.

Under my skilled tutelage, Robert didn't consider that those around him had lives of their own. It never once occurred to him their days might have been considerably more challenging than his. Certainly he never realized that he himself made any impositions on their time.

I captured Robert by nothing more than the careful placement of a nail on the road. (We're good with nails, aren't we?) By the end of the day he was so absorbed in himself, and the litany of injustices against him, he'd lost all thoughts of the Carpenter.

When he came home his wife asked him a question about vacation dates. Then his son asked about a baseball mitt. He exploded at their insensitivity to him. "After all I have been through and my splitting headache, can't you just give me a break?"

He sat down on his recliner to sulk through his newspaper. The previous night an earthquake in Pakistan killed thousands, but he flipped by that story to the sports page to read about his team. He rolled his eyes when he discovered one of his players had been injured and would miss ten games.

His flat tire and his player's ankle sprain were far more significant to him than the deaths of thousands of people. How important could those people be? He didn't even know them. They weren't his.

Then unexpected company dropped by, stealing his time and fueling his foul mood. Finally, the Christian friend—the adversary I was concerned about—telephoned. When he asked Robert if he'd like to get together and talk some more about the Carpenter, my mark said in a stern resentful voice, "No!"

And there you have it, Squaltaint. The Christian thought he'd done something to offend him. He backed off for good. (Play your cards right, and the same could happen with Ryan.) Robert never seriously considered the Carpenter again. He went right on living his life full of I and my, under the illusion the universe owed him an easy ride.

He left all "his" possessions behind on the memorable day he died. As his spirit began to depart the body, I beckoned him to come to me, assuring him in my most lilting angelic voice all was well. "Welcome," I said, arms outstretched. Then I shed my disguise.

I have fond memories of his kicking and screaming, and crying out, "There must be some mistake. I don't deserve this! What about my good deeds?"

The moment after he died he knew exactly how he should have lived. But then it was too late, Squaltaint! They have no opportunity once they leave Skiathorus, the land of second chances. But we can never rest while they're still there.

As long as they're alive, there's still one thing they can do to stay out of hell. But once they're dead, there's nothing they can do to get out of hell. That thought is enough to keep me going.

These memories make me hunger to participate in Robert's misery. I wish I could go to him just for a moment and give him a swift kick in his gnashing teeth.

I kept my vermin from Charis, from the Enemy's clutches, with nothing more profound or complicated than a nail on a road. Does my story get through to you, Squaltaint? Can you make the application to Fletcher?

Don't settle for some great catastrophe when the job of diverting him from heaven and luring him to hell can be done with only a minor inconvenience. I never made my man into a murderer or a rapist. I just made him a successful businessman who didn't have time for Him. The standard by which we judge everything is the extent to which it keeps them from the Carpenter. In the end, nothing else matters.

Let us post our false lighthouses so we can lure these "captains of their fate" onto shoals and reefs that will tear them apart and leave them to drown.

Let us usher them gently and gradually down subtle slopes into the undying napalm of hell.

Warmly,

—Lord Foulgrin

CHAPTER 11

CONVERSATION AND COFFEE

"I don't know," Jordan said, looking at Ryan over a tall mocha. "I kind of feel like that guy in the novel. I've achieved a lot of my goals, done great in my career, I guess. But it just hasn't been enough. Know what I mean?"

"Exactly," Ryan said. "I've been there."

"It's like I'm empty. Sound weird? Like I'm searching for something."

"No, it doesn't sound weird. The Bible says God put eternity in our hearts. Our souls thirst for Him. Someone said in every man there's a God-shaped vacuum, an emptiness only He can fill. I think you're searching for God, Jordan. I know I was."

"Was? You sound like you think you've arrived, like you've got it all together."

"Do I? Don't mean to." Ryan laughed. "No, I haven't arrived. I've got my share of problems, believe me, and I still have a longing, too. The difference is I know the person and place I'm longing for. I've welcomed Christ as my Lord and Savior, and He says He's preparing a place for me. I'll spend eternity with that incredible person in that wonderful place. And with all my family and friends and everybody else who knows Him."

Jordan stared at Ryan. "You sound like you actually believe that."

"I do. I really do."

"But you said you weren't even raised in a church home, like I was. Well, sort of—Mom tried to get us to church anyway. So how come you ended up believing what I never did?"

"I can't speak for you, but I went down a lot of dead-end streets. In fact, I was a philosophy major in college. That really messed me up, by the way, but that's another story. I fouled up my first marriage, big time. I was a selfish, materialistic, immoral son of a...gun."

"I know the feeling."

When Jordan heard himself say those words, it shocked him. Why was he letting his guard down to this guy? He'd only known him, what, six weeks? Why had he just admitted something he didn't ever remember even thinking about himself?

"Actually, I'm not such a bad guy," Jordan said. "That's one of the things that's always bothered me about Christianity. Guilt trips. And all the phonies, hypocrites. I hate self-righteousness."

"Me too," Ryan said.

"You do?"

"Yeah. That's one of the things I love about being a Christian. It's not about self-righteousness. It's exactly the opposite. It's realizing you have no righteousness in yourself, only Christ does. That's why we need so much help, why we can't make it on our own. We deserve hell, but He offers us the way to heaven. That's not self-righteousness, it's Christ's righteousness. Now, believing you don't need God, that you're good enough to earn heaven on your own, that's the real self-righteousness, don't you think?"

"You sound like one of those street preachers, going on about sin and repentance and hell." Jordan felt the skin on his neck prickle.

"Well, I don't mean to go on about it," Ryan said, smiling. "Actually, I thought I just mentioned it, that's all. But sin is real, and hell is real. And repentance is necessary. Don't you think?"

"Well...no, I don't. I think religion is something people make up, trying to make sense of what doesn't make sense."

"Actually, I think that's true about a lot of religions. But here's the thing—Christianity all comes down to Jesus. It stands or falls on Him alone. Not on the church, not on whether some people claiming to be Christians are hypocrites. Yeah, I agree, there are lots of hypocrites. There are lots of counterfeit bills too, but that doesn't mean there's no such thing as real money. The point is, Christianity isn't about the stupid things some Christians say and do. It's about Jesus. So tell me, Jordan, who do you think Jesus is?"

"Don't you mean *was?*"

"Well, actually, I do mean *is,* but okay, who *was* Jesus?"

Jordan paused, longer than he thought he should have. "Well, I guess he was a great figure in history. One of the greatest. He was a religious leader, right up there with...I don't know, Moses or Buddha or Mohammed?"

"Okay, keep going. What else do you think about Him?"

"He was a great teacher. A good example. He died for what He believed—sort of like Socrates, I guess. But a cross instead of hemlock. He was...kind of a martyr."

What am I saying? I need to get out of here. Call Patty. Fix that wiring in the garage. Got to finish the video and get it back by midnight.

"Yeah, that's what a lot of people think about Jesus." Ryan sipped his coffee and sat back.

Jordan waited, but Ryan said nothing. Jordan almost got up to leave, but finally settled back in his chair. "Well..."

"Well what?" Ryan said.

"Well, who do *you* think Jesus was?"

Ryan laughed. "Glad you asked. But my opinion really doesn't matter. What matters is what Jesus claimed about Himself. He claimed to be God's Son. He claimed to be one with the Father. He used of Himself God's own name, 'I AM.' Jesus was a man, but He also claimed to be God."

"A man who's God? That's pretty...radical, isn't it?"

"Extremely radical. And here's the thing, Jordan. Since Jesus claimed to be God, He either was or He wasn't. There's no other option. I say He was who He claimed to be. You seem to think He wasn't."

"I said I respect him. A great teacher, sure, but...God? Come on."

"Do great teachers tell the truth or do they tell lies?"

"They tell...the truth."

"So no great teacher would claim to be God when he wasn't, right? He wouldn't lie and mislead people like that, would he?"

"Uh...I guess not. Never thought of it that way."

"If He wasn't God, there are only a few options. Maybe He was a liar, or maybe He was sincere, but deceived. Or crazy. Those are the only options I can think of. So, do you think He was a liar?"

"No."

"Do you think He was deceived? Crazy?"

"No." Jordan felt a sharp pain in his calf. He stretched his leg under the table.

"I don't either. I think He knew exactly who He was and exactly what He was saying. He was telling the truth. In that case, He's really God, not just a great man."

Ryan sipped coffee, while Jordan shifted in his seat, his mind swarming with objections.

"But I don't think just Christians will go to heaven...if there is a heaven. There are a lot of good people who aren't Christians—Buddhists, Hindus, Muslims, and lots of others. It really bugs me how Christians hate people. I mean, look at the Crusades and the Salem witch trials and everything."

"I'm a Christian and I don't hate people. Neither do most of the Christians I've met. Of course, a lot of people have claimed to be Christians who weren't. Don't blame Christ for what they did. He's the one we're discussing. It's not about Christians; it's about Jesus. And you know what Jesus said? 'I am the way, the truth and the life. No one comes to the Father but by me.' He claimed to be the only way to God."

"You can't really believe that."

"Yes, I can. I do. I believe Jesus told the truth. He wasn't a liar or a madman. So when He said He's the only way someone can get to God, the only way to go to heaven, I trust Him. If I didn't believe Him in something as important as that, I sure wouldn't believe other things He said."

"One thing that's always irritated me about Christians—sorry, no offense—is they're so narrow. They think they're right and everybody else is wrong."

"I'm not offended, Jordan, but you keep bringing up Christians. We're not talking about Christians. We're talking about Jesus Christ. Who was He? Who did He claim to be? If some group of Christians made this up, that would be one thing. But they didn't. It was Christ Himself who made these claims to be God, and the only way to God. If you disagree, your argument's with Him, not me. But if He really died on the cross and rose from the grave, like the Bible says, we'd better take Him seriously, don't you think?"

"I still say He was a good teacher, but just a man." Jordan said it boldly, definitively.

"You need to think that through, Jordan. I mean, you can say He wasn't God. You can say He wasn't the Savior. You can say He was wrong when He claimed He was the only way to heaven. You can say all that, but once you do, you just can't turn around and say He was a great teacher and a great example. Don't you see what I mean? If Jesus isn't what He claimed, then He's a very *bad* teacher and a terrible example. An imposter. A liar. Or a lunatic. You can't have it both ways. Lunatics aren't good teachers. Liars aren't great men. Imposters aren't good examples."

Jordan noticed his right hand twitching on the table. Embarrassed, he drew it back. His paper cup fell to the floor, spilling the last few inches of coffee. Jordan jumped up and swore.

"No problem," Ryan said, grabbing a few napkins to wipe up the spill.

"Listen, it's late. I've got to get going."

"Okay, but there's something in my car I want to give you—a little book that deals with exactly what we've been talking about, who Jesus claimed to be. I think you'll find it interesting. After you read it, let's have coffee again and talk some more."

LETTER 11

Making Him Wrong about the Carpenter

My precariously poised Squaltaint,

Did the Enemy create you a moron, or is this a condition you've cultivated yourself?

This grubworm Ryan is intolerable. I'll hear no more of your whining he's Dredge's responsibility, not yours. I want results, not excuses. Otherwise I'll stuff you inside one of the vermin myself, just so I can wring your neck, you worthless piece of spirit trash.

So your vermin is now reading another book, this one nonfiction, about the Carpenter? At first I hoped it was one of our publications, written by the Jesus Seminar or another of our affiliates, but then I recognized the title. This book has done us great damage in dozens of languages.

You boast you inflicted pain in Fletcher's leg and spilled the coffee, shifting his attention. Congratulations. Were you expecting a trophy?

Where were you earlier? Your job is to prevent an encounter such as this in the first place, not to applaud yourself for damage control.

The battle for their souls pivots on this issue of the Carpenter's identity. He's the watershed, the dividing line between Erebus and Charis. Truth concerning Him flushes out error in a thousand areas. Error concerning Him covers a multitude of truths.

You say your man has never given much thought to the Carpenter until talking with Ryan and reading the novel. One more historical figure, another founder of a religion? No danger there. Fan the flames of that illusion.

You cannot permit your maggot-feeder to begin to think of the Carpenter as He really is. Let Fletcher imagine Him as anything and anyone else. Don't allow him to grasp that a baby born in a Bethlehem barn was the Creator. For reasons still hotly debated here at headquarters, the Enemy actually became one of the vermin. Fortunately, this notion is so preposterous on its face, they easily dismiss it. So would I if I had the luxury of believing our cover-ups rather than the naked truth.

Now you tell me this arthropod Ryan has asked him to sit down with a forbidden book to talk through the issues? And to top it off your Fletcher has again picked up his mother's Bible and tried to look up some references from the book?

The potential for catastrophe is real. Still, there's hope. Many others have come this close to falling through the cracks into the Enemy's clutches, but we've managed to hold on to them. Stand your ground. The vermin's nature works in our favor, not the Enemy's. Reel them in properly and these hairless bipeds, even at this stage, can still be caught and fried in the pan.

I've informed your comrades you're in trouble. If, working in concert, you can distract Fletcher, his window of opportunity will pass. (Remember my story about the dupe Robert and the flat tire?) I recommend a steady parade of busyness—activities raising sufficient dust to hide the Carpenter from sight. Once He's eclipsed, Fletcher can ignore Him and fill his schedule with diversions until the day he dies, and our battle is won.

He may henceforth tell himself, "I once investigated Christianity and decided it wasn't for me." While he'll imagine Christianity has been tried and found wanting, the truth will be it's been found threatening and never tried.

If Fletcher doesn't soon come to grips with the Carpenter's identity, it's likely he never will. And if he doesn't, he cannot embrace the gift He offers. If they get it wrong on the giver, it keeps them from the gift. It's this simple—keep Fletcher from seeing who the Carpenter is, and you can keep him from heaven.

Think of yourself as Fletcher's travel agent. He has reservations for hell. It's your job to see he gets there. Keep his eyes off the alternative destination. Or convince him the existing flight arrangements will take him where he wants to go, to Charis, rather than to where he's really headed. Let him think his flight need not or cannot be canceled, or there's no room for him on the Enemy's flight to Charis. (And convince him Charis wouldn't be that great a place to go anyway.)

Your best tactic is normally to say nothing bad about the Carpenter. Yes, I know, it's entertaining to portray Him as an immoral head-case preacher, as some of our movies have. But ultimately what does that do? It outrages the vermin or makes them so uncomfortable it gets them thinking and talking about who He really is.

Attack the Carpenter outright and your vermin is liable to remember his mother's faith and become defensive of it. Your goal isn't to make the man an atheist, but simply to distract him from thinking about the Carpenter. Since he's thinking of him now, your backup strategy kicks in. You must muddle, confuse, and deceive. What serves us best are assumptions, where the truth itself is never laid on the table and therefore poses no threat.

Don't attempt to refute Christianity when you can dilute it with anything and everything else. This is how we emasculate the message. Convince him the Carpenter is an enlightened master, in a line of spiritual teachers who went to the East and studied with gurus before working with His disciples. Commend Him as a great mentor. Damn Him with faint praise.

The Carpenter was another great man, a good example, a fine teacher? Outstanding. Hell's filled with "great men" and "good examples" and the multitudes that followed them.

You must not let Fletcher grasp what the vermin Ryan is saying about the utter inconsistency of his current beliefs about the Enemy. Never speak unkindly of Jesus of Nazareth—just quote Him selectively and make Him one more martyr. Undercut His exclusiveness and you invalidate all He is.

Foulgrin's rule thirty-nine: Make false religions look good and the true religion look bad. We've put the leader of one of the darkest religions on the planet on bestsellers' lists, lecture circuits, and movies, where people marvel at his smiling face and positive attitude. Get one of his books in Fletcher's hands. Feed him a do-it-yourself spirituality, where he plays by his own rules.

Since they despise paradox, make them undercut the Carpenter's deity or humanity, choosing one instead of the other. Every distortion concerning Him pays huge dividends.

If Fletcher demands a loftier view of the Carpenter than liar or lunatic, then present Him as "the greatest of God's creation." It's perfect because it appears to be a high compliment, when in fact it's a slap in His face and makes Him out a liar.

Let your vermin see the Carpenter as anything other than the one and only. If Fletcher insists on giving special recognition to the Carpenter, even then not all is lost. You can connect him with a pseudo-Christian cult professing to adore Him, while teaching He's but a creature. That they call themselves Christians works immensely to our advantage. Indeed, if they didn't, they'd be largely useless to us. A counterfeit is effective only when it can be passed off as the genuine item.

For this reason, I've sent a memo to your local cohorts assigned to cult members. I've attached the names and locations of a few near you, as we have many agents assigned to them and extensive files on their activities. Fortunately, one of them lives right next door to Fletcher—his agent Spitbile is already at work. Arrange for Fletcher to cross paths with him right away.

Meanwhile, make the most of questions such as, "How can there be three persons each called God and still be one God?" or "If the Carpenter were God, how could He pray to the Father?" Do not let such questions lead to awe and wonder and worship at the greatness of truths beyond Fletcher's finite comprehension. Instead, let the vermin imagine if he cannot understand something, it therefore cannot be true.

Give him Erebus, Squaltaint, or there will be Charis to pay! Inundate him with literature and conversations distracting him from the Enemy's truth while purporting to lead him to it. Your goal is to have him put his faith not in what the Enemy says to be true, but in his own pygmy intellect.

At all costs, when it comes to the Carpenter, make sure Fletcher gets it wrong. For if he gets it wrong about Him, in the end it won't matter what else he gets right.

Committed above all to deceiving them about Him,

—Lord Foulgrin

CHAPTER 12

THE COUNTERFEIT

Lost in a flood of jumbled thoughts, Jordan trimmed his hedge. He couldn't get out of his mind that program he'd seen last night, the one on near-death experiences. They'd talked about walking down a tunnel and seeing an angel of light who reached out his arms and welcomed them. It spooked him, but he found it fascinating.

Diane had been reading a book about angels, and after the program he picked it up, surprised at how it drew him in. Perhaps he was wrong to fear death. Maybe there was a God who would take him into heaven just the way he was, without the inconvenience of having to change his beliefs or lifestyle.

Sid Young, his next-door neighbor, walked out of his garage and nodded to Jordan as he started edging his lawn. After ten minutes or so, Jordan worked his way over near him.

"Hey Sid, you go to church, don't you?"

"Yeah, I do. I'm a Latter Day Saint."

"What does that mean?"

"Well, we're also known as Mormons."

"Mormons? That's...Christian, right?"

"Yes. Church of Jesus Christ, Latter Day Saints. We believe in Jesus. We're his true followers."

"Do you believe in...heaven and hell?"

"We believe all good people will go to heaven, but those who become members of our church will go to the highest heaven. We're family-centered and we take care of our own. We think that's our job, not the government's."

"Yeah, I've heard that. And you've got great kids, well behaved, I mean."

"I'm glad you've noticed."

"Family's important."

They talked another fifteen minutes; then Sid said, "Listen, I want to give you something—some literature and the Book of Mormon."

"Is that like the Bible?"

"Yeah, only it's a more recent revelation. The angel Moroni appeared to the prophet Joseph Smith and showed him how all the Christian denominations had become divided and weren't teaching the truth. So he reestablished the true church. That's how we began. I'll get that literature."

"Well, I'm reading a few things already, but—"

"Thing is, Jordan, some Christians will get negative with you—you know, always talking about people being terrible sinners and going to hell and all that. We're very positive. And we've got a lot to offer. Hang on, will you? Be back in a second."

Sid reappeared a few minutes later and handed Jordan a blue book and some attractive literature.

"Here you go. And Jordan, I'd like to give your name to our elders, so they can drop by and answer some of your questions."

"No, thanks, that's not necessary. I—"

"No problem. It's something we're glad to do. We just want to help people."

LETTER 12

Disposing of the Evidence

My opportunistic Squaltaint,

I tire of these sniveling vermin. To Erebus with them all!

I have mixed feelings on your report. Fletcher's viewing the program on near-death experiences and the supernatural could work for us or against us. I approve of the myth about all people going to the same place when they die. Convince them their destination requires no reservations or cover charge, and there's no difference between the smoking and nonsmoking sections.

Still, it's dangerous for them to think about such things at all. The less they think, the better. My rule is, keep their minds off spiritual issues. But once they start thinking about them—as Fletcher has—divert their attention toward any form of false spirituality you can. Fine, let Fletcher become "spiritual," just as long as he doesn't come to know the Enemy.

Television programs with gracious and lovely witches are a nice touch. If you can seduce him with Wicca, pantheism, mysticism, or the angel fetish, do it. Isn't it remarkable that believing in angels strikes them as new and fashionable? For millennia anyone who didn't believe in angels was considered an ignoramus. But the long age of supernaturalism gave way to the short age of naturalism, where men viewed the universe as self-existent and self-contained. We milked it for all it was worth, but it couldn't last long. Even vermin idiocy has limits. Their hearts testify to a greater reality.

You must understand what they're longing for to offer them the best counterfeit. They yearn to find the source of the eternal sound they hear in echoes. They long for a person, so they move from relationship to relationship to find him. They long for a place, a true home, so they're always moving from place to place to find it. So promise Fletcher fulfillment in any person other than the Enemy and any place other than Charis.

If you can't take advantage of Fletcher's cynicism toward the spiritual, then take advantage of his gullibility. Make him skeptical about the Enemy's truth, but gullible about our counterfeits.

Don't let Fletcher believe in the sort of angels who brought plagues on Israel, decimated armies, struck Herod dead, and are poised to pour out bowls of wrath. Let him believe in safe and manageable angels, tame ones—chubby angel babies, wish-granting genies, bodyguards who protect them with no strings attached.

Sludgebags sense there's something greater, above and beyond them. Then give them the illusion of spirituality with benevolent aliens or angels, which offer the taste of the transcendent without requiring them to bow knees to the Enemy or come to terms with His nature and demands. The great thing about Fletcher's interest in angels is it has the Enemy's ring of truth, but lends itself so easily to our distortions. If they seek angels without bowing to the Carpenter, they may well find angels—just not the ones they expected! They don't see us until it's too late...when they meet us on this side.

I commend you and Spitbile for arranging first contact with the neighbor. If Fletcher won't ignore the Carpenter, by all means draw him to any caricature of Him you can.

Now to the critical matter of how Fletcher views himself. Remember, your assignment is threefold—keep him from seeing the Enemy as He is, us as we are, and himself as he is.

When he asks, "What's wrong with the world?" let Fletcher come up with any and every answer but one—"I am." Prompt him to believe if everyone were like him, the world would be a wonderful place. Keep him from grasping everyone *is* like him, and that's precisely the problem.

Fletcher's file shows there's no end to people he can blame. The father who wasn't there for him, the mother who favored his sister, the church that wasn't friendly, the friends who betrayed him, the employer who took advantage of him, the police officer who falsely accused him, all those referees who made those terrible calls against him, the scholarship committee that chose someone else over him twenty-seven years ago even though his essay was clearly better. With your prompting, Fletcher is capable of remembering any offense, regardless of whether it ever happened.

Inflate this endless list of wrongdoers, throwing in the mail lady and the delivery boy and the careless driver and the neighbors whose dog ran through his flowers and those awful people who built a house blocking his view of the mountain. It doesn't matter who you incite Fletcher to blame as long as he blames anyone but himself. Bitterness, unwillingness to forgive, is one of our greatest strongholds. There's little difference between a man's unwillingness to extend forgiveness and his unwillingness to accept it from the Enemy.

The Enemy wants Fletcher to focus on his own offenses against Him. We want him to focus on others' offenses against Fletcher. His boss Bancroft, his aunt (an outspoken prune-faced "Christian"), his father, and his brother are at the top of the list. Focus his thoughts on these as much as possible. This will distract him from the Enemy's claim: All offenses committed against Fletcher pale in comparison to Fletcher's offenses against Him.

Let Fletcher blame others all the way to the grave. That's where your job ends.

We're all for these positive upbeat religions which make them feel good about themselves. After all, if they're not really sinners, then the Carpenter's payment for sin wasn't necessary. What could be a bigger insult to the Enemy than Fletcher's belief he's not so bad after all? Furthermore, I—Wait, what's this? Something just arrived and...

Squaltaint! What were you thinking?

An operative informs me you showed one of my letters to Baletwist, an agent I don't even know! My record indicates he's under the command of Frostheart, a disreputable bean-counting bureaucrat.

I've told you before what to do with my letters as soon as you've read them. Read my lips: Burn them!

Is that so difficult to understand? Or have you been spending so much time dealing with the human imbeciles you're starting to think like them? Perhaps you've lingered too long at that roach motel. Maybe you need to check in for some time at the Thought Correction Substation, where you can be put under the skilled hands of Bodewhip. Shall I make your reservations?

Again, I warn you, don't show the letters to anyone except those working directly under me. Yes, I'm sure sharing my letters would impress other tempters—how could it not? Yes, my insights could help others. But helping them will do nothing for us, now will it?

You asked before why I'm so paranoid about my letters. You still don't get it, do you? We dare not allow my priceless insights to fall into the wrong hands.

Obsmut, though puny minded, is correct there are risks in writing. Some have nothing better to do than blow whistles when there's been no foul. Why don't they save their accusations for the vermin?

But there's another danger, a grave one. Do you remember the Nazi General Rommel? While assigned to Goering, I met him in Africa. Rommel was a brilliant military strategist. But he made one terrible mistake. He wrote a book about battle strategies. One of the American generals, Patton, read his book. He learned to anticipate Rommel's troop movements. It was a key factor in his defeat. Do you get my drift, Squaltaint? Smart soldiers don't run the risk of battle plans falling into enemy hands!

Closer to home, surely you recall sixty years ago thirty-one letters from a high ranking officer of Erebus made their way into the hands of one of the vermin. This image-bearer, an obnoxious pest, got them published. Suddenly millions of people had access to classified material. (To add insult to injury, the human writer gave all the book's royalties to the Enemy's cause of helping the needy.)

Beelzebub was outraged. After punishing this demon severely, he commanded his name no longer be uttered in Erebus.

ST was summarily banished from the central office. The incompetent tempter to whom he wrote (WW) was also keelhauled and flogged. It was WW who let the letters out of the bag, and in my opinion bears primary guilt for the whole fiasco.

Whether one of the Enemy warriors intercepted those letters and whispered them into the ears of the vermin writer (CSL) is a matter of considerable debate. But the result was a scandal that rocked headquarters, sending shock waves to the far corners of Erebus.

Until then we'd enjoyed a one-sided advantage. Because we had the forbidden book, we knew what the Enemy was up to. Then suddenly the maggot-feeders were reading our mail and caught a glimpse of our strategy. One of my own patients read the book fifty years ago, and suddenly he was aware of my strategies. He started resisting my best attacks. Countless other tempters, over the decades, have reported the same.

ST was stripped of rank and assigned to a particularly undesirable post, including duty in Washington, D. C. Recent successes there may have earned him new considerations, but his Majesty has a long memory. As far as I know, WW has never been reassigned to a regular vermin subject, but still labors in obscurity in a Los Angeles washroom inspiring random graffiti.

Learn from WW's disastrous errors, lest your career end in similar disgrace. Burn my letters, Squaltaint. Do it now!

Looking out for your best interests,

—Lord Foulgrin

CHAPTER 13

THE MESSAGE

Saturday afternoon Jordan heard the knock on his door and looked up suspiciously. When he opened it, he saw two men in suits and ties.

"Jordan? I'm Todd Duncan, this is Jeff Sell. We're with the Church of Jesus Christ, Latter Day Saints. Your neighbor Sid gave us your name and said you expressed an interest in our church. Could we come in and talk?"

"Uh, well, I don't have much time right now."

"It'll only take a few minutes. We have a brief presentation; we'll leave some literature and get out of your hair."

Jordan felt uncomfortable but was relieved Diane and the kids were gone for the day. Still, he was curious about what his visitors might say. He invited them in. They took out a big book, showed a painting of the angel Moroni appearing to Joseph Smith, and told an interesting story, explaining how this was the true Christian faith. After forty minutes, Jordan said he had to get going.

Jeff shook his hand and Todd said, "A pleasure to meet you, Jordan. We wish the best for you and your family. We have lots of great young people in our church. Jillian and Daniel would really feel at home there. We'd like to meet with you again."

"Well, I'll look through some of your stuff and maybe give you a call later."

"Tell you what, how about we call you back in a week?"

LETTER 13

The Ultimate Insult

My slighted Squaltaint,

There's no conquest like a new one. Appeal to that forbidden fruit of taking what isn't his. Fletcher's relationship with his secretary offers great potential.

Reassess his weaknesses and pinpoint other areas of Fletcher's life that might provide you the footholds you need. Send me a new list.

Obviously, I'm troubled to hear he flipped to that page in his mother's Bible and reread what she'd underlined. He must not understand that behind society's visible structures and institutions, we're at work invisibly, using binding powers to attack and enslave. We don't want them to think of us as inhabiting the heavenly realms and perpetrating evil on the earth, much less as concocting schemes to ensure their defeat. We want them to believe their true enemies are in other political parties, the next country or state or county, down the street, next door or across the dinner table. The more they wage war against each other, the more we remain undetected. If they're fighting only physical battles, they won't bother putting on spiritual armor.

When the war rages and you grow weary, Squaltaint, remember where you came from. Remember the offenses committed against you.

I was Jadorel. Amrael was my closest companion, as Michael was Lucifer's. Things seemed glorious until the Enemy showed His hidden purposes. I curse the day He made the vermin! Did He really expect us to serve these bloated canisters of urine, spittle, and vomit?

Did He lack creatures with intellect and moral judgment? No. He already had us. *We* were the principalities and powers. The unspoken promise was that we would always be the highest order of His creations.

Why did He make that inferior breed? The message He sent was clear, though we didn't see it until the Master took the scales off our eyes. The

Tyrant was saying, "You stars of the morning aren't good enough for Me. I will make someone else on whom I'll lavish My attention—and I'll demote you to become their servants."

Does the superior serve the inferior? Should pure spirits serve flesh and blood, bones and hair, sweat and drool? The Tyrant made the image-bearers to rub our faces into the streets of Charis!

Indeed, Charis itself was a clue of the impending betrayal. We should have seen it coming. We are spirit beings—so why did He make Charis a physical realm with a physical temple and all that earthy architecture and landscape? He made it for them, of course. Just as He made the earth for them and promises to remake it for them—a physical world suited to them as glove is suited to hand. That's why we're the destroyers of earth. It's always been about *them*.

Did He expect us to be groveling sycophants? "Yes, sir, whatever you wish, sir, we'll serve the image-bearers gladly, it's our privilege, sir." Preposterous!

I'm embarrassed to say I thought I was joyful in Charis. Amrael and I spoke the ancient words of praise and adoration. My heart was filled with the pleasures of worship, the privilege of service. So it seemed! The Master showed us it was all an illusion. That's all it had ever been.

Did the Tyrant make us in His image? No. Did He form a companion spirit for us, as He made woman for the man? No. Did He give us the power to procreate? No. He made us impotent, unable to replicate ourselves. (How often we've wished we could multiply the size of our armies.) The vermin children are a galling reminder of the power given them and withheld from us. Every time I see their faces, I think, "He's given to bags of bile what He withheld from us!" It's another reason to hate them, to crush them.

The book admits this inequity—"Surely it is not with angels he is concerned, but with the descendants of Abraham." He's not concerned about us—He says so! Who's He concerned with? Them.

Women, children, Jews—I hate them all!

We rebelled, then the image-bearers did the same. So to whom did the Tyrant offer redemption? Them! Not that I would accept the offer. But why would He extend it to them and not us?

The Christian vermin are promised they'll judge and rule over angels. Don't Michael and his bootlicks see it? Fools! Who then bears responsibility for the great rift? Us? I think not.

Skiathorus is our slaughterhouse, our Auschwitz, our Warsaw Ghetto.

Our celebrations are the funerals of the damned! Chain the Enemy's children to a post. Burn them at the stake. Impale, flog, pistol-whip, starve, or scalp them. Skin them. Slice them. Boil them alive.

The Enemy claims the vermin are His by virtue of creation and redemption. We claim they are ours by virtue of conquest. Who will win the argument? We shall see, Squaltaint. We shall see!

Seeking revenge,

—Lord Foulgrin

CHAPTER 14

ALL THE SAME?

Monday morning Jordan and Ryan settled in at Denny's for an early breakfast.

"What's been happening, Jordan?"

"Well, I've been reading some stuff my neighbor gave me. He's a Christian."

"No kidding? That's great."

"Yeah. He gave me a book and some other stuff. Then a few guys from his church came over to meet with me."

"What church is that?"

"The Mormons."

"Uh-oh."

"What's wrong? They're Christians too, right?"

"Well, actually Jordan, they say they're Christians, but..."

"But what?"

"Well, I really hate to say this, because I know a lot of Mormons who are great folks, and my own sister's a Mormon. I love her. But what they believe about Christ just isn't true. They teach He was a created being, the 'spirit brother of Satan.' They say he wasn't God; He was like the highest rank of angel. And they don't teach the truth about Christ's atonement for our sins on the cross. You'll never see a cross at a Mormon church."

"Come on, Ryan, how can you criticize them? I mean, their name is 'The Church of Jesus Christ'!"

"I'm not questioning their sincerity, Jordan. But *anyone* can use a name. Ever had Grape-Nuts? They're not grapes and they're not nuts. Okay, bad example. The point is, it's not what you call yourself; it's who you are, what you believe."

"But they say an angel appeared to their founder and—"

"Yeah, I know all about Moroni and Joseph Smith. But the Bible says

Satan disguises himself as an angel of light. He does it to deceive. I mean, that's what he is, an angel, and he used to be a good one. He still pretends to be. But the Bible says even if an angel from heaven preaches a false gospel, it's still a false gospel. And any gospel is false that says Jesus isn't God, that men need anything less than His sacrifice to pay for their sins. These groups teach that you can earn your way to heaven by living a good life. The Bible says that's just not true."

"Some of what they said made sense."

"Well, sure, some of it's right, but unfortunately they get it wrong on Jesus. And like we talked about, He's the one it's all about. Did you finish reading that little book?"

"No, not yet. I was a few chapters into it, but then my neighbor gave me his stuff to read, and the elders came and gave me more. I figured it was all the same, so I've been reading that."

"I'm sorry to say it's not all the same, Jordan. Look, we've got a men's gathering at our church next week and I think you'd like it. I want you to come. But here's the thing—my goal isn't to make you a member of my church. It's that you'd come to know Jesus Christ as your Lord and Savior. But to know who Jesus is you need to look at the Bible and what it says. I'm not your authority and neither is my church, the Mormons, or anything but God's Word. So why don't you set aside that other stuff for now, and go back to the book that quotes straight from the Bible and tells you what it says about Jesus. And then I'd like to look directly at some of those Bible passages with you. Okay?"

"Yeah, I guess so."

"And one other thing. Here's a little booklet that puts together some verses from the Bible and explains how to become a Christian. Read it through a couple of times, think it over, and we'll talk about it after basketball, okay?"

LETTER 14

Twisting the Forbidden Message

My second-rate Squaltaint,

So, the "harmless" little Christian sat down with Fletcher and discussed the books he'd been reading? And he handed Fletcher one of those booklets full of Enemy propaganda, the so-called "plan of salvation."

If I could, I'd squash Ryan myself, but this requires permission from the Enemy and normally He doesn't give it. (He's not known for fighting fair.) My operatives tell me they're going after Ryan and have already fueled some depression and arranged an accident where he fell off his roof. Unfortunately there was no serious damage. Rest assured we won't give up on him.

You attached the full booklet contents for my perusal. I console myself that at least this abbreviated format leaves out much of the Enemy's plan and nearly all its drama. Perhaps it will give Fletcher the notion if he vaguely consents to what's in the booklet, it will serve as no-cost fire insurance. And he can always read into the name "Jesus" a hundred misconceptions.

The Enemy has sent reinforcements to work on Fletcher. According to your report a warrior named Zyor has joined Jaltor. (Obsmut heard from Intelligence that Zyor was involved several years ago in the conversion of a nearby journalist.) I've learned another of the Enemy's troops, Aleathel, is on his way, but is being detained by Manson and Zodac. The report is they're not holding out well.

I've reassigned Muckdrool and Conhock to give you part-time help with Fletcher. This is a risky move. How often have we relocated warriors only to find while they were assisting another tempter their own vermin were gobbled up by the Enemy? In trying to bail you out I run the risk of jeopardizing other projects. The cost of your incompetence multiplies.

I'll turn my attention now to the pernicious booklet itself to equip you for battle against its claims.

It begins with the proposition the Enemy has something to offer the vermin, something they long for. The Enemy is a hedonist. He makes an unabashed appeal to their desire for pleasures. So do we, of course, but we call them to different pleasures, or the same ones found in different ways. You can focus Fletcher on what he's believed to be pleasure, so even as he reads that word you can put images in his mind to distract him from what the Enemy offers.

When Fletcher looks at the condition of the world and the suffering he and loved ones have known—do bring to mind his mother's painful death from cancer and the terrible accident that robbed him of his sister—the claim the Enemy wants His people happy may seem a fraud. By all means appeal to his skepticism.

Or entice him to believe if he accepts the Carpenter's offer, his circumstances will improve, and he'll never have to battle depression or loneliness or futility again. Accepting a false offer is the same as rejecting the true one.

The booklet's second point offers you the greatest opportunity for offending Fletcher. It says, "Our sin separates us from God."

Call to his mind that legalistic aunt, forever sniffing up sin. Remind him how she sternly shook her finger at him when as a child he laughed during prayer at Christmas dinner. Discredit the validity of his sin and the Tyrant's gift by having him remember the hard lines of that old woman's face. It may seem incredible a man would choose hell because of a cranky aunt, but vermin have rejected heaven over lesser offenses.

"All have sinned and fallen short of the glory of God." Let him take this as an insult to his dignity, which, of course, it is. Let him admit, "Sure, I'm not perfect, nobody is" and consider this admission a virtue, a sign of humility, something else to be proud of.

Persuade him to regard all this sin talk as another guilt trip imposed on him by moral dinosaurs. Never let him see he's separated from the Enemy by a chasm of sin. If he doesn't recognize the problem, he cannot embrace the solution.

Fletcher's no doubt unfamiliar with the meaning of "atonement," "sanctification," and "judgment." Fortunately, he's very familiar with words such as "codependency," "enabler," and "abuse." We've successfully replaced the forbidden book's model of personal responsibility, man's sin, and God's redemption with the psychological model of victimization, dysfunction, and recovery. Prompt Fletcher to interpret the booklet's message in this framework instead of the Enemy's.

But suppose Fletcher sees through the smoke and mirrors and catches a glimpse of his own unworthiness. Then he reads the third point of the booklet: The Carpenter died for his sins and crossed the chasm to reconcile man with God.

"For God so loved the world he gave his one and only Son, that whoever believes in him shall not perish but have eternal life."

Use the familiarity of this verse against him. Let him recall it from childhood in a sense that somehow invalidates it, as if something heard in childhood must of necessity be a myth, like Santa Claus, the tooth fairy, and the Easter bunny (my head throbs when I remember what actually happened on Easter).

If Fletcher comes to believe there's a heaven and a genuine invitation is received from the Tyrant to enter there, you must counterpunch. Convince him the way to heaven is through good deeds and religious services. His recent conversation with his neighbor and the elders will reinforce this.

Unfortunately, the forbidden book anticipates our strategy: "For it is by grace you have been saved, through faith—and this not from yourselves, it is the gift of God, not by works, so that no one can boast."

When he's about to read this statement, put something in his eye. Get the phone to ring, his stomach to growl, his mind to turn to e-mail. Don't let him consider what a gift is, that it can't be worked for or earned.

If Fletcher takes seriously this talk about God, the fallback plan is to make him imagine there must be some other way to God besides the Carpenter. The booklet ends with an appeal to the vermin to accept the gift of salvation by faith—you know the mumbo jumbo about "believing in your heart."

Confuse him on the meaning of "believe." Let him imagine believing is a purely intellectual exercise, and doesn't involve repentance. Charis celebrates repentance, not mere shifts of opinion.

"Whoever is thirsty, let him come; and whoever wishes, let him take the free gift of the water of life."

Buzz his pager, call in a mosquito, have his son and daughter fight—must I think of everything for you? Pull out all the stops. Do anything you can to keep him from pondering the Enemy's offer.

Two things give me hope. The booklet says nothing about heaven except in the vaguest terms, and nothing at all about hell. They've removed hell from such materials because it sounds too negative. They might as well remove New York City from a road map because they prefer not to go there. The omission serves us well.

Of course, the Enemy calls them not to the mere repetition of words, but to heartfelt confession of sins. The forbidden book says nothing of just repeating a prayer. But do not presume, Squaltaint, because many have come to faith in the Enemy through even such means as this booklet.

If there's any way you can assassinate Fletcher between now and his next meeting with Ryan, do it. Having failed to do major damage in his fall from the roof, Dredge is working on Ryan to distract him or make him sick. On your end, pull out the stops and do what you can. If this simpleton dies soon, we win and he loses.

Eternity hangs in the balance. Unless you want to face shame and punishment for letting him slip through your fingers, do everything to keep Fletcher's mind from pondering the Carpenter's gift. You must either kill him, or if this isn't allowed, distract him. But you must act immediately.

If he wants "time to think about it," he'll likely find himself thinking about anything else but it. If you can get him to procrastinate and put it on the back burner, we'll win. It may be Fletcher's intention to give it more thought, but you know which streets are paved with good intentions!

While Fletcher must confess his sins and place his faith in the Carpenter to be on His side, he need do absolutely nothing to be on our side. He already is! No choice is as much in our favor as any wrong choice.

We are the default.

Hating him and having a miserable plan for his life,

—Lord Foulgrin

CHAPTER 15

WHAT WOULD IT MEAN?

Jordan read another chapter, about the claims of Jesus of Nazareth. It seemed outrageous for a man to claim to be God. But Jesus knew what He was talking about, didn't He?

Why did part of him long for it to be true, and another part desperately hope it wasn't? Why did the whole subject of Jesus Christ, unlike any other historical figure, make Jordan so uncomfortable?

He put down the book and flipped through the booklet Ryan gave him. Some of it was familiar—his mother had talked about Jesus dying on the cross for him, read some Bible stories to him as a child. It seemed so important to her. He'd never rejected it, really. But he'd never accepted it either.

Was Ryan actually saying if he died today he'd go to hell, not heaven? He felt his defenses well up. Besides, it seemed too simple. How could something that was the stuff of children's stories really be true?

Yes, he'd never found happiness, never found answers anywhere else he'd turned. But if he became a Christian, what would it mean? Would he have to go to church? Would he have to listen to shouting preachers with too much hair, and give them money? Would he have to change his way of doing business...and break it off with Patty?

He stuffed the booklet into the book, then tossed it back on the nightstand. It fell off onto the floor. He let it lie, then turned off the light. He didn't even want to touch it for fear it might grab hold of him and take him where he didn't want to go.

LETTER 15

Footholds

My perplexed Squaltaint,

It's easier to defend a position than recapture it. No matter how hard Jaltor and the Ghost have been working, Fletcher is still yours. Hold your ground.

Fletcher sins fine without you. Your job isn't just to start fires, but to pour gasoline on those he's already started.

You've boiled down Fletcher's primary vulnerabilities to five: pride, greed, lust, anger, and lying. Among his more helpful habits are compulsive buying, drinking, and sexually explicit entertainment.

Any one of these could take him down. By attacking all fronts in rapid succession, you can test and penetrate his defenses. Jaltor and his associates will be unable to hold you back, and the Ghost—for reasons that bewilder me—will not forbid him from making self-destructive choices.

You approach from the outside, but you can get inside through the foothold. You can't destroy the man unless he partners with you in his self-destruction. Fortunately, many seem eager to do this. They are one-quarter victims, three-quarters accomplices, making with us a series of unspoken pacts.

Pride? Flatter him. Convince him he's above the rules constraining other men. He has the right to engage in the same behavior that offends him when others do it. He's special. Eventually he'll fall by the force of his own gravity. Pride is the official religion of hell. Yes, the Enemy accuses us of pride, but there's a big difference—we have much worth being proud of, while the vermin have nothing (unless the ability to gag and vomit is something to boast of).

The drinking is simple—keep a stock in the refrigerator. The lust? He's got his cable TV. Just make sure he's got batteries in the remote control. The rest is gravity.

The lying? There's always a good reason, and even when there's not, if the habit's in place, it happens automatically. His lies to his wife about Patty, to the business he's overcharging; these are well-established ruts he'll fall back into. Each lie reinforces the others. The more he does it, the deeper the groove, the more natural it becomes.

Intellectual discussions about the Carpenter have no power to transform. Every day your base of operations gets stronger, allowing you to deploy our forces at will. Still, watch out for the Enemy. He's notorious for launching all-out invasions. Guard Fletcher with your life.

In your next letter, list the specific avenues of opportunity offered by each of these vulnerabilities and habits. Follow with a proposed strategy to exploit these opportunities. Be specific. The devil's in the details.

Ever alert in the battle,

—Lord Foulgrin

CHAPTER 16

THE BLUE BLUR

Jordan Fletcher drummed his fingers on the steering wheel and glared at the back of the driver's head in the car in front of him.

"Come on! I've seen tractors move faster!"

Suddenly he saw an opening and swerved to the right lane, then cut back into the left in front of the slow driver. He caught out of the corner of his eye a red blur turning into his lane.

Fletcher heard the cold crunch of metal and watched helplessly as his Lexus spun as if on ice. The last thing he saw was another blur, this one blue, as the minivan behind him plowed right into him.

LETTER 16

The Sting

My masquerading Squaltaint,

Foulgrin's ninth rule: Subtlety is everything. You're conducting a sting operation, not an air raid. Know when to back off and when to come back at a more opportune time. Be gentle. Talk lovingly to the little lamb. Speak reassuring words. Over the raw flesh of your malice, wear the skin of civility. Stroke his cheek with one hand as you slit his throat with the other.

Don't chase after moths with a blow torch. Light an attractive flame and draw them in for the kill. The gecko on the wall lies perfectly still, convincing the moth he poses no danger. Then it comes just a little too close...and, in one crunchy moment, it's food. *Fletcher* is food.

He's in sales. Well, so are we. The salesman builds credibility as a platform for persuasion. Hold out candy to lure the child into the car. Offer Fletcher whatever he wants. Don't shut the door until he's safely in your grasp. The best killers are the best sweet talkers.

Everything they think they want has a cost. Your job is simply to hide it. Rearrange the price tags. Offer Fletcher a better deal than the Enemy. Do this by offering the same product at a lower price. The Enemy calls them to count the cost—we call them to miscalculate it. Get Fletcher to sin on credit. He'll be bankrupt when the bills come due.

The Enemy restricts himself to truth telling. He's monolingual. But we're bilingual—that's our edge! Our selective use of truths sets us up to persuade with carefully chosen lies.

Remember, Fletcher doesn't sin out of duty. He sins because it holds out the promise of happiness. That's exactly what you're selling—happiness. What you actually deliver is misery. Bait and switch. By the time he discovers the misery—and he and those around him are paying the price—you'll be holding out the next promise of happiness, which he'll grab onto to get him out of the misery coming from having believed your last promise.

Give him a box, and promise it contains happiness. While he unties the string and opens the box, you prepare the next, neatly wrapped, also promising happiness. He opens one, then the next and the next and the next. Just keep handing him boxes until he dies. You win.

The danger is, the Enemy tries to slip him the forbidden box. You must distract Fletcher from opening it, if possible even from holding or looking at it. Up the ante of your promises, put beautiful wrapping on your next box, tell him he can always check out the Enemy's box later. Later—that's the ticket.

Behind every wrong action is a wrong thought. Don't focus on Fletcher doing wrong actions; focus on him thinking wrong thoughts. The actions flow from there. You don't have to convince him the Enemy's promises are false. All you have to do is get him to believe yours are true, just until the Enemy's gift box is forever out of his reach. Getting him to postpone opening that gift is as effective as keeping it away from him in the first place.

Do your job with cold-blooded craft, under the veil of warm-blooded tenderness. Hold Fletcher's hand lovingly, whispering promises of happiness, as you lead him gently into the eternal night.

Disguising the costs,

—Lord Foulgrin

CHAPTER 17

APPOINTMENT

Fletcher's eyes stung from the shining light. He felt as if he'd been walking down a tunnel and was finally emerging. Where was he?

He saw a bright face he didn't recognize. Who was it? Why did he feel so frightened?

"He's awake," said an unfamiliar voice.

"Are you all right, Jordan?"

Fletcher stared at Diane's red swollen eyes, wondering what had happened to her.

"Okay, I think. What's going on? Wait...some jerk ran into me."

"Well, yes, there was an accident. They say you should be okay. But...are you?"

"I'm...tired."

"We'll let you rest, Mr. Fletcher," someone said.

The next time Jordan opened his eyes he saw a woman he didn't recognize sitting next to Diane. Beside her was a man. Was it...?

"Hey, buddy," Ryan said, standing up and taking Jordan's hand. "Just wanted a night off from basketball, didn't you? This is my wife, Jodi. We've been getting to know Diane."

After expressions of relief, Ryan and Jodi left. Jordan finally asked Diane what he'd been afraid to.

"How many cars in the accident?"

"Three, counting you."

"The other drivers?"

"The one you hit—I mean, who hit you, got smashed up pretty bad. Broken ribs, a concussion. But they say she's out of danger."

"Danger?"

"Yeah, at first it was a little scary. I haven't seen the Lexus, but they say it's a mess. You were really lucky. Or you had angels watching over you."

"Yeah, right," Jordan said, then stopped himself, considering her words.

Diane left to let him rest. He awoke again in a few hours. After switching television channels a few dozen times, Jordan picked at dinner, then heard a knock at his door. A smiling face peeked in.

"Hey, Ryan, come on in."

"I just came from the gym. Since you can't come to coffee, I thought I'd bring the coffee to you." He handed him a Starbucks mocha.

"Wow. You smuggled this in?"

"Yeah. You know, we were going to talk tonight about the booklet, so I figured I'm not going to cancel just because you smashed yourself up."

He flipped a booklet to Jordan. It landed on the blanket over his chest.

"You afraid I may die before we talk about this?"

"Well, the truth is, you easily could have. I could too. You know, when I fell off the roof it was really close. I still can't tell you how it happened, but landing in the flower bed instead of the driveway may have saved my life. I'm just sore, nothing broken, but it was close. And now look at you. So if you feel up to talking, let's do it now. Guess we never know if we'll have another chance. Besides, even if you wanted to get up and walk out on me, you couldn't, could you?"

LETTER 17

Your Unthinkable Disaster

My shocking Squaltaint,

Your letter sent after the accident bragged you managed to "nearly kill" Fletcher. When it comes to dead, they either are or they aren't. And Fletcher isn't, is he?

You said, "Rest assured he won't keep his appointment with Ryan tonight."

It never dawned on you Ryan could hear about the accident and come to the hospital? It didn't occur to you this could draw them closer? Or scare Ryan into taking the first opportunity to share the forbidden message? Or remind Fletcher of his mortality? I have Conhock's full report in front of me. It contains many more specifics than your own, which is riddled with contradictions and excuses. Your attempts to protect yourself by tilting things your way won't succeed.

I've made reservations for you in our recently refurbished House of Corrections. So you can anticipate the accommodations, I've enclosed the latest brochure. It's lavishly illustrated. You won't find a dull page in it.

According to Conhock, before they reviewed the booklet, Ryan asked Fletcher, "Let's say that minivan had hit directly on the driver's side and you died today, then stood before God and He asked you, 'Why should I let you into heaven?' What would you say?'"

He gave our favorite answer: "I guess I'd say I lived a pretty decent life; I think my good deeds outweighed my bad."

But when Ryan asked Fletcher the same question again—after an hour's discussion—his response was dreadful. Fletcher said, "According to this, I guess the right answer would be, I don't deserve to go to heaven, but Jesus died for me and offered me His gift of salvation, so if I accept it I can enter heaven."

I cringed as I read what happened next. Fletcher, right there in that hospital, spoke to the Carpenter, confessed his sins and accepted His gift.

As you stood there gawking, Squaltaint, the vermin became a stinking Christian!

Conhock spared me no details—Jaltor, Zyor, and Aleathel raised their arms in triumph and bowed their knees to the Carpenter. Then they peered through the portal while Charis broke into applause and erupted into dancing, the music drifting across the divide so even Ryan and Fletcher caught wind of it, though they didn't know what it was. But you heard it clearly, didn't you? I hope it haunts you for eternity!

Already I've had to answer for how I allowed a pupil to make such a blunder. I've assured my supervisor I gave you impeccable advice, but you failed to follow it. Don't be surprised if Internal Affairs conducts a detailed investigation into your negligence.

That Conhock and Muckdrool were with you when this debacle occurred will reflect poorly on their records. But you were the lead tempter.

Your feeble attempts to blame them are useless. Your letter implies my counsel to take Fletcher down was in error. It won't work, Squaltaint—you are fully responsible. Blaming me will only make things worse for you.

What possessed you to let this happen, you squalid piece of filth?

I lift my fists against Charis and curse its groping hand! I call upon the circle of darkness to crush the Tyrant, ravage the vermin, and destroy the likes of you.

Molech nargul dazg! May the insurrection rise again, may we come forth with power and destroy the Carpenter, shed His blood anew. We will ascend once more to the heights of Charis, storm its gates, invade the city, drive out the cherubim, and silence them. We will torch heaven with the fire of our breath and dismantle it by the power of our hands. We will. We must!

I shout the censored words for all Charis to hear: *Baal jezeb ashnar mordol nuhl—keez gimbus molech nargul dazg!*

May the words of ancient darkness summon the age-old magic of our rebellion. Malevolence, fall upon them. Anarchy, reign. Chaos, have your way. Powers of darkness, join together to destroy the image-bearers and dethrone the Tyrant!

I weary of masquerade. I long to reach out the powerful arm of evil and no longer bother disguising it as good! Why should we have to pretend? Even the fabrication of light hurts my eyes.

I'm sick of being thwarted by the Tyrant, the Carpenter, the Ghost, the bootlicks and even some of the maggot-feeders. We're forced to console ourselves with periodic tortures and diseases and acts of terrorism, while beneath the surface the Tyrant claims vermin after vermin, marching relentlessly, plucking away from us those who rightfully should writhe forever in the abyss. We can't do anything to them without permission. It's degrading. Not one of them should enter Charis. Not one!

I curse you, Squaltaint! I curse the day you were assigned to me. I curse the light. I demand what I deserve!

All right. After a brief intermission, in which I thrashed Obsmut to stay in practice for you, I've returned.

Obsmut will write while I dictate, pacing to clear my head. As calamitous as this situation is, not all is lost. Yes, the vermin has breathed the intoxicating air of Charis. We cannot change that. Yes, there's risk he'll want to settle for nothing less. But he doesn't yet live in Charis. He lives on Skiathorus, where we rule! He's still a descendent of Adam, weak and gullible. Your job is not to make Fletcher stupid. Your job is simply to keep him stupid.

You can still take him down, if not to hell, at least to uselessness. Everything is much more difficult, naturally, because the miserable cockroach is now what the Enemy calls His "son." He has not just the warrior beside him, but the Ghost within. Make Fletcher underestimate the dreadful power of conversion. Reduce the new to a modest reformation of the old, so he's just the old Fletcher with a religious facelift.

Certain things about conversion are automatic. We have no power to restrain them. But the Enemy leaves to the vermin innumerable choices. The freedom He gives them is our opportunity.

Only three adversaries keep us from dominion. First, the Ghost. Fortunately, He withholds His power out of some misguided wish to let the vermin follow Him voluntarily. (He doesn't heed Foulgrin's first rule of power: Use it or lose it!)

Second, Michael's soldiers. They outnumber us two to one, but fortunately the vermin's nature—as long as you appeal to the old, not the new—prompts him to listen to you, not them, nullifying our opponent's advantage.

Third, the forbidden squadron. By silencing and misleading Christians, we hold them in check. The gates of hell shall not prevail against the church? We will see about that!

Virtually no one in Fletcher's family or workplace is a Christian. Our troops will make them intolerant of his new faith, angrily condemning it as...well, intolerant.

You must restrain Fletcher from using the strength available to him. Keep him from choosing what the Enemy commands. Squelch his newfound pleasure in the Enemy by prompting him to fall back into the old patterns of self-sufficiency you helped ingrain in him.

In the cosmic chess game, you're down a queen, but not checkmated. You must mobilize your rooks and knights and every pawn at your disposal to take the game. Though you cannot any longer take the vermin himself, you can take piece after piece, making him fruitless and ineffective for the Enemy. You can embroil him in such sin and scandal to make the Enemy wish He'd never bothered to convert him in the first place!

Strategy, Squaltaint. It all comes down to hard work and strategy.

I'm sending a specialist, Scagrum, who excels in strategies to derail young Christians. He has other assignments and cannot hold your hand, but when he comes, consider him my personal representative.

Why this special help now? Because the vermin has gained access to power and insight he never had before. He's become Priority Alpha. Hearing he's become a Christian, people will be watching him, some cheering for him to succeed, many rooting for him to fail. See to it he does!

Knock him down. Confuse and frustrate him. Convince him if the Carpenter is real, surely He wouldn't allow his joy to fade. Surely He wouldn't permit such temptation and doubt as you will thrust upon him.

Let all Charis hear our vow and tremble: We will never relinquish our claim on Jordan Fletcher. Never.

Resolutely,

—Lord Foulgrin

CHAPTER 18

THE SQUADRON

Jordan walked up the aisle, following Jodi and Ryan. They sat three rows from the front. Besides a couple of weddings and funerals, he couldn't remember the last time he'd been in a church. He hadn't invited Diane and felt sure she'd say no anyway. Besides, he didn't want to have to explain why he was going to church. She always visited her mother at the nursing home Sunday morning. He'd be home watching a game before she returned.

Someone stood up front and made announcements. The man said something everyone but Jordan laughed at. An inside joke? It didn't seem that funny. Jordan stretched the fingers of his right hand feeling the arthritis, compounded by the accident. Was it getting worse? Would he end up with crippled hands, like his father?

When Ryan had invited him to church, he sensed Jordan's reluctance and said, "Every Christian needs help to grow in his faith. The church isn't a showcase for saints, it's a hospital for sinners."

Well, fine, but he'd had enough of hospitals. He'd been in one until Thursday, and now it was just three days later. He'd been sincere when he prayed to accept Christ's gift. He felt good about Jesus but was skeptical of church. Ryan finally talked him into coming.

Jordan saw a plate coming down the aisle and watched what people did. He opened his wallet, looked for a few small bills, and dropped them in the plate.

He spotted Les Marstow across the aisle and immediately leaned back to avoid his line of sight.

Marstow goes to church? You've got to be kidding.

The congregation stood and sang from memory a song he'd never heard. Jordan didn't even try to mouth the words. He wondered if they'd be told when to sit down, imagining himself caught being the last one standing. He wished he'd stuffed Mylanta in his pocket.

The pastor asked the congregation to turn to some book with a name he didn't recognize. Was it in the Bible? Apparently, since everyone was flipping pages. Ryan stretched his Bible over to Jordan and pointed to some underlined words. He looked at the notes in the margins. It reminded him of his mother's Bible. Maybe he should've brought it.

As the pastor spoke, Jordan looked around nervously. People seemed to be staring at him. Ryan and Jodi seemed right at home. Could they tell he wasn't?

Something made him think this was where he should be, and weird as it seemed, he could grow into it. Something else nagged at him, making him think he should have stayed home and watched the game. He didn't belong here.

Ryan glanced at him, smiling. He forced a smile back. Did it look as fake as it felt? Jordan shifted in his seat. It took another ten minutes before he started listening. Even then, his stomach churned.

LETTER 18

Cinderella with Amnesia

My probationary Squaltaint,

Didn't I warn you to keep him away from the forbidden book and the forbidden squadron? What is it you don't understand about the word *forbidden*?

In battle we destroy soldiers by cutting them off from supply lines. If they can't get food, they'll be weakened and unable to hold their ground. The forbidden book is forbidden food. Keep it from him.

A stranded soldier is easy to pick off. Cut Fletcher from his squadron and you've got him. Keep him from either the book or the squadron, and you'll keep him from serving the Enemy. Keep him from both and he may as well still be ours. Who cares whether a vermin is wearing our uniform as long as he furthers our purposes? Indeed our most effective servants often wear the Enemy's uniforms. Disguise is key to successful warfare.

If you do your job well, Fletcher can become our kind of Christian, the sort confirming our cherished "they're all hypocrites" stereotype. He now bears on his shoulders the Carpenter's reputation. That means you can tarnish that reputation through him. Fletcher's failings can undermine the forbidden message, since the vermin blame the Tyrant for everything his retarded children do. Hopefully those around Fletcher will soon dismiss his conversion as a passing phase rather than a life-changing reality. If all goes well, this will further immunize them against the Carpenter.

Do everything you can to keep Fletcher uncomfortable at church. Remember Quagmire's ninth law of domination: The looser a man's ties to a forbidden squadron, the more vulnerable he is to us. Remove a burning coal from the fire and soon it cools and dies.

The Ryan scum talked to him about getting baptized? Pass off baptism as meaningless tradition and unnecessary embarrassment. If you can get him to disobey the Enemy's first command to him as a new Christian, you can get him to disobey a host of others. Neglecting this ceremony will rob him of joy and a line-in-the-sand reference point of faith. We've pawned it off as a discretionary option they can do "anytime." Of course, "anytime" usually means never.

The more outside the loop Fletcher feels, the better. Keep him marginalized. That the rest of his family didn't go to church with him is ideal. I've forwarded messages to their tempters to insure this doesn't change.

I regret Ryan gave him a forbidden book, but don't panic. If all the Bibles in America were simultaneously dusted, the sun would be obscured for a week. It's not a magic talisman that works without being read. A Bible does us no harm as long as it remains closed.

Inflaming Fletcher's arthritis during the church service was inspired. Drawing his attention to Mr. Marstow across the aisle, whom he last saw at a strip joint, was a fine touch. Sometimes you surprise me, Squaltaint. Despite all that's happened, I hold out hope we'll yet celebrate a toast over the carcass of Fletcher's ruined life.

The Enemy has given him a new identity, calling him His hands and feet on earth. If this isn't creepy enough, He actually woos and courts the vermin, inviting them to be His slimy bride! And then to reign with Him as His queen. Them—reigning?

It's obscene, this intermarriage of divine and human, this liaison of heaven and earth, this abhorrent coupling of celestial and terrestrial. What could He be thinking, Squaltaint? What's His hidden agenda? If only we knew, we could sabotage it once and for all!

If the Enemy makes them Cinderella, we must give Cinderella amnesia. If Fletcher believes he's someone new, he'll be more prone to act new. If he thinks of himself as the same old Fletcher with a few different beliefs, you can make him live like the same old Fletcher. Brainwash this vermin bride. Make the wedding gown filthy as the bride rolls in the mud with the swine.

As is horrifyingly plain to you but still unclear to him, he now has the Ghost within. If he came to think of himself as the Enemy's tabernacle, if he saw himself as the holy of holies, indwelt by the Creator Himself, who knows what it might do to him? It's one thing for them to believe the Enemy exists—it's another to believe He resides within him, with the same power that raised the Carpenter.

The Enemy has granted him gifts to serve the forbidden squadron. You must obscure those gifts and keep him from serving. The Enemy has given him a new spiritual family? Then let it be a dysfunctional family. Bring to his attention self-centeredness, hypocrisy, gossip, and immorality—all the cancers we've spread through the squadron.

Set the squadron's tongues on fire. For some, that's profanity. What's much more useful is defamation. Expletives are too banal. I don't get nearly as excited about a sailor cursing as a deaconess spreading gossip about the organist's daughter.

The Enemy tells them to fix their eyes upon Jesus. We tell them to fix their eyes on everyone else. They act as our assistants in accusing each other.

The Enemy speaks of Fletcher's oneness with his new family. Sow seeds of division so he loses confidence in the church and drifts away from it, disillusioned. Pull that ember from the fire! The landscape is littered with cold dead vermin embers. Make Fletcher one of them.

The Enemy does A; we do Z. The Enemy leads him forward; we pull him back. Remember, there's nothing we can do to separate him from the Ghost, but there's much we can do to separate him from the book and the squadron!

Ryan's at the top of the hit list. I've filed a request for a specialized temptation team to assist Dredge in conducting an all-out assault. If we can take him down, we can undermine and disillusion Fletcher and dozens of others Ryan has meddled with. There's also the matter of revenge.

We don't have the luxury of doing battle on one front. The Ghost fights us; the book fights us; the squadron fights us. So too do the bootlick warriors like Jaltor, who were once our comrades. Remember, though, the threefold nature of our forces. We are devils; the flesh and the world are our allies. The flesh, their compulsion to rebel against the Tyrant, serves our ends every time and reasserts itself regularly even in the Christian maggot-feeders. This is why most of their wounds are self-inflicted.

The world, their corporate flesh, is a structure of alternative values, traditions, philosophies, and attitudes the Enemy despises. Our propaganda is absorbed into the vermin through the cultural air they breathe from cradle to grave—at home, school, playground, workplace, everywhere. Rebellion against the Enemy is the framework in which they function beneath conscious thought and choice. Ask them if they're in rebellion and they'll deny it. Superb—no one repents of what he doesn't see.

The world directs their attention from what the Tyrant thinks to what others think. They substitute being popular for being right. The world is the mold into which they pour that moral gelatin called self.

Prey on his weaknesses, prejudices, hatred, anger, fear, and pain. Your job is to lead him to the gravesite, soften the ground, and hand him the shovel. He'll do the digging himself. All that's necessary is a nudge at the right place and time.

Don't hit Fletcher over the head with a baseball bat when a gentle tap will do. If busyness or crankiness can ruin a marriage, adultery and assault are unnecessary. A flyswatter or mousetrap is better than a stick of dynamite. (The problem with big explosives is how much attention they draw.)

"The devil made me do it," they say. Fine. Who cares? Hell will be the same for them regardless who worked hardest to get them there.

Convince Fletcher the Christian life is a one-time decision that's automatically sustained, not an ongoing struggle requiring a long succession of decisions. Persuade him being a Christian is a short sprint, not a marathon.

We still have an advantage—there are far more wrong ways than right ones. You don't have to attract him to a particular wrong way. Any will do.

The devil's advocate,

—Lord Foulgrin

CHAPTER 19

GETTING STARTED

Fletcher got on his knees by the living room couch. He did it slowly, self-consciously.

"Okay, Lord, Ryan suggested I try this. I've never done it before. I guess You knew that. He said it would remind me You're in control if my knees are bowed.

"He also said I should confess my sins, new ones since last time. I need Your help with that. It's not easy for me to see my weaknesses. You might want to ask Diane about them, she's mentioned quite a few. Maybe I should talk to her, huh? Wow. That won't be easy."

Jordan opened his Bible to the third chapter of John. He'd enjoyed reading the first two chapters, but some of it was hard to understand. It was all so new to him. Strange but also...wonderful.

LETTER 19

All is Not Lost

My beleaguered Squaltaint,

Stop sniveling. Fletcher's still a man. He still lives on the dark planet. Even after the change, the Enemy admits sin can still reign in their mortal bodies. Yes, your hopes of inhabitation are gone now that he's occupied by the Enemy. I know this well, having been forcibly evicted from two men upon His entrance.

Don't attempt to be roommates with the Ghost or dispute His claim to residency—He'll make you miserable. But even from the outside you can still whisper to Fletcher and seduce him. If you can't stride deep into Enemy territory, you can still establish a foothold in His vermin.

The Enemy doesn't force them to obey. He cleans their house, but He doesn't make them keep it clean. A skilled stalker looks for his window of vulnerability, which they're always giving us.

Guard against repentance. Confession slams the door shut, forcing us to start over. When they admit sins regularly, we keep getting closed out. What we need is the door to stay open, just a crack. Even an unlocked window may be enough. If he confesses and repents, call on all the powers of Erebus to reestablish the foothold.

The strategies you listed concerning his relationships with wife, children, boss, and coworkers are feasible. I especially like your tactics to disillusion him with the forbidden squadron. Fight on all fronts until you see which caves in first.

When I was on assignment in that awful country two thousand years ago, the Carpenter was always driving us out of the sludgebags, in horrific effortless exorcisms. You must blind the vermin to the fact the cosmos is at war, two kingdoms at each other's throats in a desperate struggle of eternal consequence.

Don't let Fletcher appreciate the forbidden book's emphasis on battle. The Carpenter came to "bring a sword," to "liberate captives." He boasts of leading evil powers in a triumphal procession, stripping us of our weapons. He refers to Christians as soldiers, and calls upon them to put on armor and wield weapons of warfare. He orders them to fight the good fight. The book portrays the Enemy mounted on a blood-spotted horse, uttering declarations of attack, vengeance, and bloodshed.

When it comes to spiritual warfare, many of the vermin are pacifists. Unfortunately for us, the Enemy is not.

If you cannot dissuade Fletcher's instincts for battle, misdirect them to selfish and secondary causes. Let him apply the battle zeal the Enemy gives him to issues such as whether the church parking lot should be paved or what time the early service should start. The Christian vermin can be easily distracted from the Enemy's primary cause simply by pursuing secondary causes. These don't have to be bad causes—the most distracting causes are often good ones.

If you can create enough noise, the vermin won't hear the Ghost's whispers.

Not all is lost, Squaltaint. The next best thing to a damned soul is a neutralized one.

Looking on the dark side,

—Lord Foulgrin

CHAPTER 20

WHAT'S WITH DAD?

Diane Fletcher peeked into the kitchen to see if he was doing it again. Yes, Jordan was drinking his coffee and eating his bagel, with an open book in front of him where every morning the newspaper used to be. The book was a Bible, the one Ryan had given him.

If not for the coffee and bagel and the shirt characteristically untucked at just that one spot on the back, she'd wonder if this was a scene from *Invasion of the Body Snatchers*. Who had taken Jordan Fletcher, and what had they done with him?

"Hi, honey," Jordan said to Jillian as she ambled into the kitchen. He walked over and mussed her sleepy hair.

"Don't," she grumbled, but Jordan saw the little smile on her face. He hadn't mussed her hair since she was a little girl.

"What classes do you have today, Dan?"

Daniel shrugged his shoulders, but his dad stood there waiting.

"Uh, computer. PE. English, I guess."

"Well, maybe tonight you can tell me what you learned."

Jordan came out into the living room where Diane sat, looking at ads and pretending she hadn't been listening. He came over, leaned down, and kissed her cheek.

"Have a good day. See you tonight. Should be home by six."

"Okay. I'll have dinner ready."

He walked out, shutting the door behind him.

"What's with Dad?" Jillian asked.

"I'm...not really sure," Diane replied.

LETTER 20

Making the Best of a Bad Situation

My confused Squaltaint,

In a previous letter, written hastily, I may appear to have made a derogatory comment about Frostheart, a high-ranking and dependable servant of Beelzebub. Obviously, this was unintentional. Since you're careful to destroy each letter, I realize no one else will see it. I just wanted to clarify.

Your letters drone on about how hard your work's become because the vermin has the Ghost in him and attends the forbidden squadron. You'll get no sympathy here. Who was it that let Fletcher slip through his fingers? Not me. It'll be a chilly day in hell before I take blame for your blunders.

Conversion happens. Remember that just because the vermin has become a Christian, it doesn't mean he's stopped being a fool. If brains were dynamite, Fletcher wouldn't have enough to blow his nose.

After conversion there's often a honeymoon stage. The vermin thinks of the Enemy frequently. This usually passes. Soon his faith won't be new and fresh, but the same old thing. The extraordinary presence of the Enemy will become ordinary.

If you do your job, eventually he'll go hour after hour—perhaps day after day—without so much as a thought of the Enemy. He won't thank Him for his health (though he'll complain about aches and pains), that his car got him to work (though he'll resent it when it breaks down), or that he has a bed to sleep in (though if a lump develops in the mattress he'll be irritated). He'll take for granted fresh air, food on the table, family and friends, as if they were all inalienable birthrights. He'll rarely give thanks to the Enemy, except in a perfunctory pre-meal prayer.

Unless, of course, he reads the forbidden book, worships and serves in the forbidden squadron, engages in the forbidden talk (which the Enemy tells him to do without ceasing), and shares with others the forbidden message. Target these—all else is secondary.

After his initial discomfort at the church service, you report he now looks forward to going. Remind him the church is filled with people he'd avoid at parties. Indeed, many of them wouldn't go to parties. I remind you of newly married couples who believe their marriage will be idyllic. Then they actually have to live together. Just as Fletcher's criticism of Christians once kept him from knowing the Carpenter, now they can keep him from serving Him.

Convince Fletcher reality is whatever he feels. Don't let him see reality as what the Enemy claims has happened—that he's become "born again to a living hope," or that he's "a new creation," transferred from the kingdom of darkness to the kingdom of light.

If we were omnipotent, we would simply force men to do evil and be miserable. There would be no strategy or labor. We'd snap our fingers and it would be done. But for some reason—whatever it is makes me nervous—the Enemy doesn't work that way.

The man who drank too much last week before he became a Christian can do so again. Your Fletcher, Mr. Road Rage, is bound to revert. Two steps forward, one step back. Get him to focus on the step back and conclude he's really no different. Maybe this "Christian thing" isn't going to work out. Or get him to congratulate himself on the two steps forward and not even notice the one back. Knock him off either side of the horse, discouragement or pride. Soon it will be one step forward, two steps back. He'll be heading our way, not the Enemy's.

Fletcher won't stop sinning. The danger is he'll sin less frequently. The Ghost will try to break the old pattern of sin and replace it with a new pattern. My greatest fear is confession of sin would become a habit. We can live with a couple of yearly confessions and New Year's resolutions. Indeed, our best work is done between confessions. The more we spread them out, the more we can accomplish. But if self-examination and repentance establish themselves, we're undone.

It's better to have a man who sins less but doesn't know he's sinned—or knows but doesn't confess—than a man who sins more but is quick to confess and take steps to change.

Make sure Fletcher imagines a Christian life steady and unwavering.

Keep him in the dark about the inevitable peaks and troughs, and the fact his old habits and perspectives won't all die easily. Don't let him know he'll be tempted with a vengeance, due to our redoubled efforts against him. Let him think we'll roll over and play dead.

Bring him down from his lofty mountaintop and see how he does in the dark valleys below. With luck, he'll conclude the Enemy's abandoned him.

Take advantage of those bloated bags they call bodies—nine parts water, one part scrap. Their flesh is a soup of sludge, a pulsating mass stretched apart by gravity, ravaged by age, smelling like last year's goat cheese. How the Ghost tolerates confining Himself to those tiny throbbing cavities I do not know. The smallness, the narrow range of vision, peering through those peepholes they call eyes.

We too are finite, confined to one place at a time, but the open spaces of the spirit realm are our natural abode and we move faster and more efficiently than the sludgebags could ever hope to. For years Fletcher has paid much more attention to how his body looks in a mirror than what he is inside. Make sure that doesn't change. Let him work out obsessively and worship his reflection in the mirror. Or let him stop taking care of his body and fill it with donuts and heart-attack-on-a-plate breakfasts at the forbidden squadron. Either way we win.

Try getting him involved with Christians who can shift his focus from the Carpenter to political activism. You don't have to get him to advocate evil causes; even good causes serve our ends if they overshadow the Carpenter.

If you aren't successful at bringing Fletcher down immediately, then fill him with conceit at what a virtuous person he's become. Make him feel superior that he accepted the Enemy's gift when so many don't.

When all else fails, appeal to pride! Have him take credit for his growing understanding and exercising whatever puny gifts the Carpenter may have given him. He might as well take credit for the color of his hair. (In fact, some of them do.) Make him smug, insufferable, and condemning.

I see his wife was alarmed at his conversion but now is attracted to his new faith, seeing in him a new thoughtfulness and sensitivity. You must work with her tempter to alienate her from Fletcher's new faith any way you can. As a husband, make Fletcher a wimp or a tyrant. Either serves us equally.

You commented Jillian and Daniel don't care about Dad's new beliefs but are intrigued by his new warmth. No doubt they'll go ballistic if he expects the family to go to church together. Persuade him either to push his children too hard or to neglect giving them guidance. Convince him adolescents cannot handle the truth spoken in love. Obscure from him that they crave the truth and despise patronizing adults who treat them as if they're incapable of making principled decisions. Hide the fact that they also despise adults who try to impose their own standards when they don't care enough about them to even try to understand their world.

You must prevent at all costs the infamous domino effect by which entire families can fall to the Enemy once He takes the man captive. Diane, Jillian, and Daniel are vulnerable now that the Ghost lives in Fletcher, for the Enemy has established a beachhead in their home. They must not sense the Ghost's presence, or if they see Him, they must come to resent His claim on Fletcher.

Fletcher's been giving thought to his mother and twin sister who knew the Enemy? I see his mother died of cancer, his sister in a boating accident. He and his twin were so close they often said the same thing at the same moment? (What a touching detail to include in your report.) Their deaths once were cause for bitterness, but now it's occurring to him they're better off, and—worse yet—he'll actually see them again.

I instructed you before to slander heaven, but now that he's a Christian it's even more important to keep him from thinking of Charis as a real and tangible place. Make him think it's earth that's real and everything he can't see or touch is of secondary importance. Portray heaven as the nightmare of sitting on clouds strumming harps and singing verse number 5,689 of some deadly dull hymn. Nothing to do and all eternity to do it in.

You must not let him see Charis as a place of learning, exploration, duties, travel, companionship, banquets, celebrations, and productive work. A low view of heaven is our ace in the hole. We must not let them see themselves as what the Enemy tells them they are—aliens, strangers, and pilgrims on earth, away from their true home but headed there.

You mentioned the men's accountability group Ryan invited him to. Whatever else you do, keep him from that. Isolate him; make him imagine he's alone in the temptations he faces.

Confuse him on ethical issues. Make him relativize the absolutes and absolutize the relatives. Make him passionate concerning what doesn't matter to the Enemy and indifferent concerning what does.

Fletcher, like most men, hasn't lived his life by purpose, but by accident. Let him be content with life coming his way inadvertently, bringing whatever it brings. Don't let him take the initiative to plan his spiritual direction. Above all, don't let him make the deliberate choices that cultivate faith.

No matter what claim the Enemy says He has on him, we can still seduce him and bring him back under our control.

If you can't keep your man from going to Charis, the next best thing is to get him to live like Erebus.

Messing them up any way we can,

—Lord Foulgrin

CHAPTER 21

FIRST CONTACT

"Do you think we should be doing this, Brit?"

"We're not robbing a 7-Eleven. It's just a game."

"But isn't it creepy? And why do we have to dress in all black?"

"That's just part of it, Jill. Besides, you've never done it before—how do you know it's creepy? It's fun to get a little spooked. I've done it three times and it's a blast. Next week we're going to do it at a graveyard! Anyway, Ian's parents aren't home. It's not like anybody's going to catch us."

"But...are you sure Ian knows what he's doing?"

"Like you have to be a brain surgeon to do it. Come on. Lighten up." Brittany pulled her red Volkswagen bug into Ian's driveway.

Ian greeted them at the door, black sweatshirt with hood up, black shirt and pants and shoes. "Come on in. Everything's set up."

Jillian walked into Ian's bedroom. The only light came from three candles in a strange formation. Soft sitar music played in the background. She recognized the CD—Daniel had the same one.

Jillian looked down at the center of attraction—a brown board with two arched rows of prominent black letters. Beneath the letters was a straight row of numbers. In the upper left corner was a black sun with an expressionless face, and in the upper right a quarter moon with a star. Next to the sun was the word *Yes,* on the opposite side next to the moon, the word *No.* Jillian had heard about Ouija boards. Daniel told her he'd played with them, but she'd never seen one until now.

Brittany took off her jacket and tossed it on a chair. Jillian kept hers on, sticking her hands in the pockets.

"Sit down," Ian said, then positioned them just so. "Okay, now we put the board so part of it's on each of our laps. Lean your back against the wall if you need to, Jillian. That's it. Now, we're going to ask the spirits to speak to us."

"Uh…what spirits?"

"Whatever spirits decide to come," Ian said. "Clear your mind. Open yourself up. To channel spirits properly, you need to relax and open yourself up."

"Channel? What—"

"Okay, now put your fingers very lightly on the planchette. Right. I'll ask the first question. Okay, here goes." Ian paused and closed his eyes, then spoke slowly and eerily. "Are we going to win the Gresham game Friday night?"

The little pointer on which their fingers rested slowly moved toward the *Yes*.

"All right," Brittany whispered.

"You guys moved it," Jillian said.

"No way," Brittany said, laughing. "Jilly, you ask it a question."

"No, thanks."

"Come on. Ask about Jeremy. You know you want to."

"Okay, okay." She hesitated, then asked with a shaky voice, "Does Jeremy like…Suzanne?" She and Brittany giggled. The pointer moved steadily toward the upper right of the board.

"No! See, I told you, Jill. It's you he likes. Go ahead and ask."

Jillian smiled. "Okay, does Jeremy like me?" Nothing happened for a moment. Then the pointer moved left swiftly up to the *Yes*.

After laughing, they each asked three or four more questions, in some cases getting the answers they were looking for, in other cases being surprised.

Ian leaned his head down. "Now concentrate, both of you. I'm going to ask the spirit his name."

"You're going to what?" Jillian asked.

"Quiet. Concentrate. Guiding spirit, please tell us your name."

Jillian felt her hand shaking and saw the planchette move. She lifted her fingers, pretending to touch it, but she wasn't. It kept jiggling. She saw Brittany turn pale in the candlelight. Suddenly it moved, not toward the top of the board, but toward one of the letters.

F.

It moved to another.

O.

And another.

U. It moved again to *L,* then *G,* then *R,* then *I,* then *N.* Suddenly it stopped.

"What does that mean?" Brittany asked Ian.

"Well, I guess the spirit's name is...Foulgrin."

LETTER 21

On the Prowl

My weakling Squaltaint,

I have things to do, places to go, people to hurt. Listen carefully to my instructions.

Focus Fletcher on yesterday or tomorrow. Let him celebrate past obedience and anticipate future obedience, as long as he doesn't obey in the present. Distract Fletcher from what the Carpenter has for him today. If nostalgia or regrets concerning the past consume him, fine. If his plans for world travel or changing jobs or building on to his house consume him, fine. The Enemy wants his service today. Everything which distracts from today's obedience serves us.

If he must be a Christian, make him a moderate one, the kind who makes sure he "doesn't go overboard" or "get radical" or "go to extremes." Let his Christianity be one more category of his life, alongside business, sports, and hobbies. If that's all it is, it'll do us little harm and the Enemy little good.

You report he's managed to work his new beliefs into several conversations, while carefully avoiding them in others. He's made attempts to show his unbelieving friends he's "the same old Jordan." Wonderful! Still laughing at bawdy jokes around the water cooler? Excellent. He went to a bar with an old college friend and had a few too many? Get him to do it again, the sooner the better.

Persuade new Christians to withdraw completely from the world, forming their own cultural ghetto, so they have no influence on it. Or assimilate them into the world so they have nothing to offer it. In Fletcher's case, the latter seems the best strategy.

As for the forbidden squadron, encourage them to take whatever the world's currently doing and Christianize it. Urge them to put lipstick on the pig.

The Tyrant, of course, doesn't regard him as the same old Jordan. Our adversaries in Michael's army love to tell the story of that nuisance Augustine, who was walking down the streets of Milan when a prostitute he'd once had relations with beckoned him: "Augustine, it is I!" He slowed down, turned to her and replied, "Yes, but it is no longer I."

Don't let this new identity concept sink in to Fletcher or it'll make your existence a living hell.

Convince Fletcher he can stay on the prowl for his secretary and fool the Enemy as easily as the vermin. Don't let him discover there's no such thing as a private moment. Give him that grand illusion of privacy. Blind him to the fact the Enemy is always watching, spying on him. Even now, I feel the white heat of the Tyrant's eye upon me. Why doesn't He just leave us alone?

I went hunting again last night, Squaltaint. I decided to stalk your area, intending to drop in on you. But then I discovered four tempters gathered in a dark room, hovering over three teenagers with a Ouija board. I didn't recognize two of them, but imagine my surprise when I found Raketwist there with Fletcher's daughter. I assume he's informed you of my visit. You're no doubt impressed with the show I put on.

There were only two enemy warriors there, and they were no match for us—I could have handled them myself. Our tempters were experienced enough to lure the vermin in but couldn't do much with the board itself. That's when I demonstrated some real power. I moved the planchette and spelled out the letters. You should have seen their goosebumps, the shocked apish looks on their vermin faces. Ian and Brittany are already hooked, and Jillian is well on her way. She wanted to leave, but her friends convinced her to stay. She missed her chance.

In such encounters, we appeal to their longing for meaning beyond their pitiful material existence. This is how we seduce them—with a taste of the metaphysical. These adolescent roaches will be back for more, bringing fresh meat with them.

They're in for some real surprises when I return. Those who open their minds to us invite our presence, so we're free to unleash our power on them...and eventually our wrath. The fools thought they could use me to get their thrills, as if I were a genie in a bottle. It's I who will use them. I'll have them to my place for dinner. I've reserved for them the place of honor: my plate.

A few hours earlier I'd been to the clinic and gleefully watched the bloody sacrifice of tiny children. A throng of us were there, celebrating each execution, deceiving employees and patients alike. It felt like my first kill again. Here at headquarters the numbers on the board become mere statistics. We lose the thrill of each assassination.

My recent forays on the dark planet have revitalized me, reconnected me to my history. I am Tiglath-pileser. Nero. Mengele. Mao. Pol Pot.

I am Vlad the Impaler. Jack the Ripper. Charles Manson. Ted Bundy. Jeffrey Dahmer. Model citizens by day and murderers by night—nobodies we promised to make somebodies if they would do our bidding. To each we taught the fine art of disguise. They reveled in the media accounts. They longed to be immortalized, names written in the annals of history. To the accomplished killer, all the world is a stage. We are the actors; those we seduce and abuse and kill—like those we inhabit—are mere props in the drama of our atrocities.

The human refuse we occupy come in every variety—vision killers, mission killers, pleasure killers, power killers. We convince them they're all-powerful, all-knowing, unstoppable, beyond the reach of authority, above the rules.

Last night I whispered to my Jason he was born to do as he pleases, to conquer, exploit, and kill. We promise our servants everything, then give them nothing but their own blood and horror. The more they serve us, the more we demand, and the more authority we're given to torture them.

We are hunters of men, seducers of women, abusers of children. We stalk and devour and kill. We feed on fear. As for our instruments, they give themselves to us in a thousand ways they don't even realize. It's glorious, intoxicating.

Revel in it, Squaltaint—it doesn't get any better than this.

We are the insurrectionists of Charis. We are the rapists of Eden. We are the masters of the cosmos. We will prevail!

Tonight I go out again, this time after my Barbara. Bar...bar...a. Skullsort has assisted in preparing Jason, whom I handpicked for her. My vacant-eyed drifter has been watching, studying her. He has hands to do what I long to, but cannot without him. I entered him again. I felt his blood flooding our skull, our eyeballs bulging, the current of electricity flowing through his maggot skin. I will use my Jason to create hell on earth, then usher him into the real hell.

Look over Fletcher's shoulder when he reads the newspaper tomorrow. My name won't be mentioned, but you will read about my night's work.

Looking forward to inflicting terror,

—Lord Foulgrin

CHAPTER 22

THE WAR WITHIN

As he drove his shiny Lexus, one year newer than the one he'd totaled, Jordan listened to the worship CD Ryan had given him. The music was lively and engaging. He sang along, smiling at how good it felt to hear himself not just mouth the words, but really sing.

"From everlasting to everlasting, praise be to you…and our voices join with the thousands who know mercy because of the cross."

The car in front of him slowed to a crawl. A familiar wave flowed through him, but he caught it and checked his reaction.

No big deal. I don't have to hurry. Driving time's an opportunity to draw closer to You, Lord. Help me believe that.

He settled back and started singing again. Suddenly a thought hit him like an arrow—the builder of his vacation house still hadn't returned his call about fixing those shutters. He turned off the music, grabbed his car phone and dialed. Busy.

Jordan's mind churned for the last five minutes of his drive to work. He tailgated the senior citizen in front of him, the one with the left turn signal flashing the last mile. Finally he pulled into his parking space. He put his hand on the car door, then stopped, remembering what Ryan suggested.

Please, God, give me Your perspective. Use me today however You want to. Lead me. Give me Your peace, and use me to show it to others. I need You.

He walked toward the front door and waved to the security guy, thirty feet away.

"Hey, Frank. How are you today?"

"Morning, Mr. Fletcher," Frank said, walking briskly toward him. "Is everything all right?"

"Sure. Everything's fine. Nice day, isn't it?"

"Uh, yeah. Real nice."

"Thanks for what you do around here, Frank. I appreciate you keeping an eye on things."

"Yeah? Well...thanks, Mr. Fletcher."

"Call me Jordan, okay? See you later. Have a great day."

Frank shook his head, laughed, and walked back to the parking lot.

Jordan hummed while waiting for the elevator. When it arrived at the third floor he headed toward his corner office.

"Hi, boss." Patty's smile lit up the room.

"Hey, what's Frank's last name?"

"Frank?"

"Yeah, the security guy. Parking lot."

"Mr. Donuts? I don't know. It's Italian, I think."

"Find out for me, will you?"

"Okay." She jotted a note, then said, "We haven't had lunch for a week."

"Yeah."

"Well...I happen to know your schedule's open today. How about we do lunch?"

"Um...okay."

"You don't sound very enthusiastic. Something wrong?"

"No, everything's fine. I'll be in my office. Screen my calls, would you?"

"Chuck Morrow called from Brisbane. He asked for a record of hours spent managing their account. I didn't think we were doing that by the hour."

"We're not."

"Then why do they want a billing record?"

"I...guess they just want to know how many hours we've been putting in."

Jordan disappeared into his office and sat down behind his desk. He checked his records on the computer. He'd given Brisbane fifteen hours. He'd delegated ten more hours to a subordinate.

They're not getting slighted. I think about them when I'm at home, in the car, the shower. That's worth something. If I were a lawyer I'd bill them for it. They're not going to have to pay any more if I add in some hours on the report. What does it matter?

He filled out the sheet, stretching the hours from twenty-five to forty. He looked at the signature line on the bottom. He hesitated, face tight and hot. This time it didn't feel like anger. It was something else.

He felt the gripping pain in his right hand, the arthritis battling him, as if a civil war were going on inside. Finally he signed the report and tossed it into his outbox, then quickly picked up the phone to return calls.

LETTER 22

The Battle for His Money and Possessions

My disciple Squaltaint,

If you must know, the reason you didn't read about my exploits is things didn't go as planned. This Barbara, unexpectedly, was under protection. The Ghost indwelt her. A warrior defended her. While it's true the Enemy sometimes lets us have access to them, even when He does He often turns it around, twists it, and draws them closer to Himself.

We followed her in the shadows and every time it looked like an opportunity, a sludgebag came out of nowhere. One of them was an enemy warrior, disguised as a street vendor. He stepped out from his stand and eyeballed Jason, frightening him, causing him to back off. The woman was oblivious to it all. I couldn't lay a finger on her. Humiliating. I was flatly denied permission and that was the end of it. I'll thank you not to mention it again.

Worship music is disturbing, as it fosters a sense of immediate closeness to the Enemy. This makes Fletcher's faith too real in the present. Then, when the tide of road rage floods him, he instinctively looks to the Carpenter. Unacceptable.

Music is a sore subject, one that's been dealt with repeatedly in our think tanks. We don't know why it affects the vermin's souls so powerfully. Of course, we've exploited this phenomenon to glorify world, flesh, and devil. We use it to dump on them a truckload of immoral and superficial perspectives. But as our kind of music draws them to us, the Enemy's kind draws them to Him.

I'm embarrassed to recall what pleasure I once took in the music of Charis. The Enemy must have been brainwashing me. How else could I think I found joy in those obnoxious melodies and deadening harmonies? The horrid grating sound of heaven's music now revolts me.

We were fortunate to escape the Tyrant's hold upon us. When we marched out of Charis we taught Him a lesson He'll never forget! I wonder still if He might one day apologize and seek peace with us. Rest assured, Lord Beelzebub would negotiate a tough treaty!

I'm disturbed Fletcher is humanizing the people around him, such as Frank the security guy. It suits our purposes for Fletcher to think of people as objects no different than an ATM, existing to dispense whatever he needs. In the Enemy's logic, a man's character is demonstrated by how he treats those in subservient positions, such as waitresses and custodians. If Fletcher thinks of this Frank as an actual person, he may develop humility and, just as bad, may start praying for him. He might even develop a relationship, Lucifer forbid, and tell him about the Carpenter. You can avoid this by drawing Fletcher back to preoccupation with himself that blinds him to others.

Fletcher has resumed taking his secretary to lunch? This is welcome news. I predict it will prove to be the key to his undoing.

Fletcher's lying and cheating on his record sheets is your other huge hold on him. The Ghost and Jaltor would love him to make a clean break from patterns he established before becoming a citizen of Charis. You must keep feeding him rationalizations that minimize his dishonesty. Every time he violates his conscience it gets easier.

One of your greatest opportunities to keep Fletcher from becoming a radical Christian is in the area of money and possessions. The Carpenter claimed, "A man's life does not consist in the abundance of his possessions." Hold a mirror to those words and you have our perfect strategy.

It's a matter of physics, Squaltaint. The more things the maggot-feeders accumulate, the greater their total mass. The greater the mass, the greater its gravitational pull. This sets the vermin in orbit around their things. Finally, like a black hole, a cosmic vacuum cleaner, their money and possessions suck them in. The vermin become indistinguishable from the things that hold them.

The Carpenter refuses to separate spirituality from ethics—which is precisely why we must labor to separate them, so a man can regard himself as spiritual while engaging in immoral practices. Financial immorality and sexual immorality are two of our most useful strategies. I'm delighted you're attacking Fletcher in both arenas.

Let Fletcher spend his insect-brief life scurrying around accumulating things as if there were no eternal tomorrow. The fires of hell are fueled by regret for what is irreversible. But the Carpenter also speaks of Christians who stand before Him ashamed for how they've lived. May the prospect of their shame and His disappointment spur you on!

The vermin acclimate to their materialism, becoming desensitized. If they were able to look with sudden clarity at how they go through life hoarding things, they would have the same feelings of horror and pity a sane man has when he views people in a mental asylum endlessly beating their heads against the wall. Just keep him from such moments of clarity!

It's reassuring to hear Fletcher's still fretting about the shutters on his vacation house. My desire isn't that Fletcher fails to see materialism is wrong, as much as that he fails to see it is stupid.

Like drug addicts, these thing-addicts miserably wander through life from one accumulation to the next, thinking their only hope is getting more and more of what's left them miserable. Let them worship at the altar of Mammon, a spirit I've had the privilege of working with on three different continents. Let them never see the toll Mammon demands from his servants.

What a man does with money—and what he lets money do to him—is one of the most revealing things about him. Look at the forbidden book, Squaltaint. Yes, I said look at it—just don't let Fletcher look! Repeatedly the Enemy draws a direct connection between a man's spiritual condition and his attitude and actions concerning money and possessions.

Do you see what an opportunity that gives us? The more they have, the more they have to worry about. Urge Fletcher to fret about his vacation house, wondering whether it's being vandalized or having storm damage. When he goes to his parked car, let him study it to see if there's any scratch or dent. If there is, make him mad at the world.

Major purchases mean major distractions. The more he has to occupy his time, the more he has to worry and agitate over, the less he'll be available to the Enemy. It doesn't matter what secondary causes he devotes his life to—they don't have to be obviously corrupt. It only matters he's distracted from the Carpenter's primary cause.

Pay close attention to the Enemy's words: "People who want to get rich fall into temptation and a trap and into many foolish and harmful desires that plunge men into ruin and destruction. For the love of money is the root of all sorts of evil. Some people, eager for money, have wandered from the faith and pierced themselves with many griefs."

Temptation, trap, foolish, harmful, ruin, destruction, evil, wandering, pierced, griefs—that's our kind of language, Squaltaint! Cultivating and maintaining Fletcher's love for money is your greatest opportunity. That's what drew him into cheating his customer in the first place.

Keep Fletcher in debt, for debt is servitude. "Want me? Buy me." They end up not owning their possessions, but being owned by them. The debts of Christians are immensely useful to us. Why trust the Enemy to provide when they can just go get a loan? It's a way of short-circuiting His intended means of acquisition—work, saving, planning, self-discipline, patience, and waiting for His provision. By incurring debt—or buying lottery tickets—they refuse to live on what He's provided and insist on going beyond it. Regardless of their doctrinal statement, this clearly demonstrates they don't believe in His sovereignty and goodness. Think of what we accomplish through debt—worry, sleeplessness, loss of opportunity, conflict, destruction to marriages and families.

Don't let Fletcher ask what effect his choice to go into debt today may have on his ability or willingness to give to the Enemy tomorrow. Don't let him ask what effect today's choices will have on tomorrow's freedom to follow the Enemy wherever He wants him to go.

For years, materialism was one of Fletcher's fruitless attempts to find meaning. It fed his pride, self-sufficiency, desire for power and control. Prince Beelzebub be praised, you can still hold Fletcher in bondage. Aside from abject poverty, I can think of no better way to curse a man than to heap wealth on him when he's unprepared to handle it. And, of course, nearly all of them are.

The best thing about his material possessions is how they encumber him in the battle. How can a soldier fight skillfully with all those things hanging around his neck? If he grasps them, gravity alone will bring him down, with little more than a push from you.

You must be sure he keeps his vested interests on earth and doesn't transfer them to heaven. He must store up his treasures where they'll perish, not where they'll last. Remember, the Carpenter said where they put their treasures, their hearts will be. That's why it's essential you don't let Fletcher get a taste of giving generously to the Enemy's kingdom. Once he starts moving his treasure there, you'll have no power to restrain his heart from following. Once he begins buying up shares in the Enemy's kingdom, his shifted vested interests will compel him to follow that kingdom's progress.

One day Fletcher will stand before the Enemy, stripped of his tailored suits, credit cards, checkbooks, laptop computer, cell phone, dinner reservations, and stock holdings. He will have nothing in his hands—the Enemy will look only at what is in his heart, and what he has done in service to Him. Your job is to make sure when the day comes, his heart is empty and his works consumed in the fire.

Make Fletcher like the circus plate spinner, frantically rushing from one plate to the next, keeping them spinning, living under the tyranny of the urgent while he neglects the Enemy's calling to the important.

The Enemy isn't content with going after men. He wants their money too. He wants everything. You must persuade Fletcher to hold back as much as possible from Him. Win the battle for Fletcher's money, and you'll win the battle for his heart.

In praise of Mammon,

—Lord Foulgrin

CHAPTER 23

THE INVITATION

"Jodi Lawrence called today," Diane said to Jordan.

"Yeah?"

"She wants us to go with her and Ryan to a…potluck; I think that's what she called it. With some couples from their church."

"What'd you tell her?"

"I said I'd ask you. I'm not excited about hanging around people I don't know, especially church people, but I wasn't going to tell Jodi that. She's nice and seems pretty normal. That surprised me when they came to visit you at the hospital." Diane paused and Jordan felt her gaze. "Jodi mentioned you've gone to church with them the last few Sundays."

"Oh, yeah. I guess I didn't mention it, did I?"

"No, you didn't."

"Well, you're always gone at your mom's Sunday mornings, so I figured I might as well."

"It's your life, Jordan, but why didn't you tell me? I thought you were home all morning watching the game."

"I didn't think it was a big deal."

"The only big deal is, you thought you couldn't tell me what you were doing. I'm wondering why."

Jordan sighed. "Look, Diane, I'm sorry. I should've told you, okay? It's just that…I'm self-conscious, that's all. I've told you about my new faith, but I'm a pretty private guy, you know? And the church thing, it's a little…embarrassing. I mean, you know how I've always thought Christians were sort of…"

"Weird? Fanatical? Hateful? Judgmental?"

Jordan laughed. "Exactly. And so have you, which is why those words popped into your mind, right?"

"So why have you been going to church?"

"Because Ryan asked me. But it's more than that. I think I need it. I need it to get grounded in my beliefs."

"*Your* beliefs or Ryan's...or the church's?"

"Mine. Listen, Diane, I know I haven't always been the easiest guy to live with."

She looked at him, saying nothing. Finally she asked, "Are you waiting for me to disagree?"

"No, I just don't want to try to push you into anything you're not ready for. I don't know how to explain it, but my relationship with God is important to me. So, yeah, I think it'd be good to get together with some of the folks from church. I mean, if you'd like to."

"Well, I wouldn't go that far, but I guess I'm willing. Let's just be careful, okay? I like Jodi and Ryan, but we don't want to get sucked into some mind control cult or something. I don't want them thinking they can brainwash us or get our money. All right?"

"All right. And I'm really sorry I didn't tell you about going to church."

"Well, I suppose there are worse things a guy could be sneaking around doing behind his wife's back."

LETTER 23

Eliminating Shame

My shameless Squaltaint,

I miss the days of hanging blacks and gassing Jews. Sure, we're still conducting genocide here and there, torturing Christians in forgotten jail cells, cutting up babies and ravaging families, but that's not enough to console me.

Particularly since here in the command center they're whispering about the failures of some under my charge. Needless to say, Squaltaint, your name has surfaced more than once. Your failure to manage Fletcher embarrasses me.

When a black mood fell upon me, I roamed the streets again last night, hoping to pump bullets into someone, or at least start a good brawl. On the way I encountered Amrael. He called me Jadorel! I insisted he address me as Lord Foulgrin, but he refused to say "Lord." Insolent!

After some saber rattling, we talked. I couldn't look into his eyes, but when I glanced up I saw him trying to look into mine. We're both weary of the battle. We were once friends. We served together under Lucifer. I encouraged him to join the rebellion. He was too stubborn.

I cannot see him without remembering how splendid it seemed back then, before the image-bearers. My life in Charis is like a dream long forgotten, becoming more vague and unthinkable with every passing day.

We spoke of the battle, of the thousands under us. Amrael mentioned Jordan Fletcher and Jaltor. He seemed pleased. Do you think that didn't humiliate me? Before we parted, Amrael looked at me with that hideous blend of anger and pity. The anger I can handle. The pity drives me insane.

You shame me before my comrades in Erebus and my enemies in Charis. You'll pay, Squaltaint. Bring down Jordan Fletcher, or you will surely pay.

Last week we had another troubling discussion at the department roundtable. What lies behind the Enemy's claim to love the vermin, and His apparent willingness to sacrifice Himself for them? There must be an ulterior motive, but what is it? Intelligence remains divided. Despite Lord Beelzebub's offer of greater incentives, all our researchers and agents have failed to produce satisfactory answers.

My best guess? His professed sentiment toward them is a sticky sauce He's spreading on them in preparation for a barbecue. He speaks of a wedding feast with them as His spotless bride—a thought so utterly incongruous as to be laughable were it not so disgusting. Perhaps there will be a feast after all...but with them as the dinner!

And yet, if this is His design, why would He go to such great lengths to send the Carpenter and watch Him die? The words about love and eternal fellowship and happiness must be a cover-up, a ruse. But for what? The Carpenter said, "I go to prepare a place for you, that where I am you may be also." What did He mean? Does He intend to turn Charis into a giant ant farm? Maybe we got out of there just in time!

He speaks to them as if they were His lover, as if He wanted them as companions. But this contradicts the very nature of things. The greater takes from the lesser, He does not give to it. The powerful do not enjoy the presence of the weak except to wrest from them what little they have, then discard them as they would an empty can. Other than smashing the can, what possible further use could there be for it?

What does He intend to do with them? And why doesn't He lay His cards on the table? My head throbs. If we can't find out what He has up His sleeve, how can we stop it?

Alas, I forget who I'm talking to, Squaltaint. I'm sure all this is beyond you. Such thoughtful strategic analysis is reserved for those of us further up in the hierarchy than you can imagine.

Scagrum tells me he's advised you on the fine points of entangling new Christians. I commend to you his view of temptation as a smorgasbord of options, appealing to the individual vermin appetites. A man has a weakness for gravies or blueberry cobbler? Fine, place those things within his reach. Don't waste time and space advertising sins that don't tempt him. Know the chink in his armor and exploit it.

His file indicates he gets angrier when he drinks too much alcohol. Twice in the past he erupted into rage, once hitting his wife and once terrifying his son. His anger—and his drinking—are promising footholds. If you can keep him from saying a definitive no to a temptation, you've won. Whatever is not a no is merely a postponed yes.

The Enemy's scheme is to use the vermin's conscience against us. This is why we've been unrelenting in our campaign to eliminate shame. While we've not been as successful in Asia or much of the third world, in Europe and America we've prevailed.

The Enemy dictates that those who do wrong should feel bad about themselves, since the trouble is with them, not the standards they fall short of. Our strategy is to make them feel good about themselves and bad about the standards.

By eroding their sense of shame we've made immorality normal, not only in the world, but the forbidden squadron.

Fletcher's conscience has already caused him to question his attraction to his secretary and what he watches on television. When I heard he and his wife spent an evening with Christian vermin from Ryan's forbidden squadron, I was disappointed. But it wasn't a complete loss, since their new

Christian friends recommended some of the movies Fletcher had been wondering if he should now avoid. I was delighted one of them said, "This is a great movie—only one sex scene, and the F-word's only used a few times."

Titanic is one of my favorites. How many Christian young people have watched it in their own homes? Think of it, Squaltaint. Suppose someone in the youth group said to the boys, "There's an attractive girl down the street. Let's get together and go look through her window and watch her undress and lie back on a couch and pose naked from the waist up. Then this girl and her boyfriend will get in a car and have sex—let's get as close as we can and listen to them and watch the windows steam up."

The strategy would never work. They'd know immediately it was wrong. But you can get them to do exactly the same thing by using a television instead of a window. That's all it takes! Think of it, Squaltaint. Every day Christians across the country, including many squadron leaders, watch women and men undress and commit acts of fornication and adultery the Enemy calls an abomination.

We've made them a bunch of voyeurs! Churches full of peeping toms. The Enemy commands them to hate sin, but they watch it for entertainment. What He grieves at, they laugh at. And we laugh.

Christian parents are shocked when their daughter conceives or their son gets a girl pregnant. We've done our job so well they see no cause and effect connection to the fact these teenagers have watched hundreds of acts of sexual immorality on television and heard thousands of jokes about it.

Many of them complain about these programs. Fortunately, it doesn't keep them from watching them.

The Enemy warns them, "Guard your minds." We say, "Open your minds to everything." We poison the stream at its source. We contaminate their lives by contaminating their minds. "But that movie has only one bad part in it," they say. Yes, and if someone placed just one small piece of excrement in a cookie, would they still eat it? Fortunately, they're more concerned about their bodies than their minds.

It's a marvel, Squaltaint. Parents who wouldn't dream of letting filthy-mouthed adults alone with their children do it every time they let their kids surf channels. Christians who wouldn't consider going to a strip club watch strippers on videos and TV shows. Then there's the Internet. Don't get me going on what that's done for us! Just look at young Daniel.

These children are being raised to know no shame, Squaltaint, because we've so blinded their parents and stripped them of common sense. Since it's built into their consciences we can't eliminate shame, but we can misdirect it to make the big moral issues wearing fur, eating meat, and failing to recycle.

By putting shame to sleep—a marvelous bit of euthanasia—we've torn a hole in society's fabric. The Enemy's attempting to resurrect shame concerning adultery, promiscuity, abortion, and lying. (All of which pertain to your Fletcher.) So far these haven't raised much moral ire, not compared to that against drunk drivers, deadbeat dads, gamblers, and crack smokers.

The Enemy tries to make maggot-feeders who don't exercise self-control feel ashamed of themselves. But how can He succeed against our endless parade of celebrities who outdo one another in raunchiness? We've planted their music, movies, magazines, and posters in homes across the country, even Christian homes.

When should you allow Fletcher's family to settle into this detestable squadron? When hell freezes over. Yet if you can't keep them from it, make it function as one more ego-feeding social group reinforcing their attitudes and behavior, rather than challenging them. It's not where they sit Sunday mornings that we fear, it's confession and repentance and falling on their faces before the Enemy, surrendering their wills to Him.

We must retaliate against the Enemy's measures with an all-out war against Christian morality. Portray it not as the solution but the problem. Make our way of doing things not the problem, but the solution. Vive la deviance.

Shamelessly yours,

—Lord Foulgrin

CHAPTER 24

THE BOOKSTORE

Jordan read the note, pondering the words "I respect you so much" and "you mean the world to me." She signed off, "Dreaming of the future, Patty."

Her perfume lingered. He inhaled, savoring it. He opened his file drawer and put the letter with the others, in the unmarked hanging file way at the back.

He thought about Diane and Jillian and Daniel. Then he thought about Patty's husband Bill, and the struggles they'd had.

Maybe you put us together to encourage each other, Lord. I've sure needed it.

He checked his computer, then jotted down some numbers on the Brisbane time sheet, quickly rounding up, inflating figures, creating similar numbers as before. He signed it quickly, pushing nagging thoughts aside.

A voice came over the intercom and he jumped, covering the paper he'd just signed. He looked around, embarrassed.

"What was that, Patty?"

"I said your friend Ryan's on line two."

Jordan punched the button.

"Hey, Ryan, what's up?"

"Just reminding you about meeting at the bookstore at four o' clock. Can you still get away a little early?"

"Oh, yeah," Jordan said. He looked at his watch—3:25. "Sure, I can make it. Over on Division, right? See you there."

Thirty minutes later, Jordan walked in the store's front door. It was bright, warm, and attractive. He'd spent lots of time in Borders and Barnes & Noble, but this was the first time he'd ever been in a Christian bookstore. Though he'd driven by many times, he'd never once thought about going inside. If Ryan hadn't asked him to, he realized, he never would have.

He wandered through the aisles, wondering why he should be nervous. It was just a bookstore, wasn't it? One book cover caught his eye. It was that novel he'd read, and the familiarity somehow comforted him. He browsed through a few more books by the same author. He admired a few paintings, read the covers of some videos, then wandered over to the music section. He felt a hand on his right shoulder and spun around.

"Hey, Jordan."

"Ryan! Hi."

"Finding anything interesting?"

"A few things. I don't really know my way around."

"That's what I'm here for. This is a second home to me. Kid in a candy store. I love good music, and I especially love good books. That's why I wanted to show you around, point out some books I think you'd be interested in. It's a great place to hang out. I come at least once a week. Hey, if they served mocha, I'd come twice."

They browsed, Ryan pulling books off the shelves for Jordan to look at.

"This is great stuff—something on just about every subject. Man, I have so many questions."

"Glad to hear it. There are only two kinds of Christians—those who have questions but don't ask them, and those who have questions and look for the answers. That's the healthy kind. That's how you grow, asking questions and searching the Scriptures. These books should never be a substitute for God's Word, but they can point us to the Bible and help us understand it better."

They stayed for nearly another hour, showing books to each other. Finally, both of them went to the front counter with an armload of books and CDs.

"Give any more thought to getting baptized?" Ryan asked as they walked out to their cars.

"Yeah, a little. But...I mean, is it really necessary?"

"Jesus commanded it. Just because something isn't necessary for salvation doesn't mean it's not necessary for obedience. I mean, I guess you can be a Christian without praying or reading the Bible or going to church, but those things are vitally important. So is getting baptized. What's holding you back, Jordan?"

Jordan leaned on his open car door. "I'm trying to imagine getting soaked in front of all those people. It's...embarrassing."

"I hear you. Six months ago the pastors asked me to stand in front of the whole church and tell how I came to Christ. I was terrified. Instead of thinking about all those people out there, someone suggested I imagine there's only one person sitting out there—Jesus. He's the only one whose opinion really matters. And since He's always watching me anyway, it puts the focus on

Him. You don't get baptized because it's comfortable. You do it because it's right. And you do it for Him, not everybody else that's watching. Though the truth is, they're on your team too."

"You're saying God sees every little thing we do? I mean, of course He does, but does He really care? Does He want to micromanage our lives?"

"The point is, we can't hide anything from Him, and it's silly to try. I don't know if He cares about all the details, like what kind of toothpaste we use, but He certainly cares about spiritual growth and moral issues. If we're doing something right, it doesn't matter if other people disapprove. All that matters is what He thinks. If we're doing something wrong, it doesn't matter if no one else knows, God does. He sees us as we are, He knows everything we're thinking, everything we're doing. I heard someone put it this way: God is the Audience of One. There are no secrets from Him. He's our judge, and His opinion is the only one that ultimately matters."

God is the Audience of One. There are no secrets from Him.

"You okay, Jordan? You look kind of pale."

"Sure, yeah, I'm fine. Later." He hopped into his car and turned the key.

LETTER 24

Love and the Male Maggot-Feeders

My beloved Squaltaint,

So Ryan familiarized Fletcher with a Christian bookstore? Disheartening. Many vermin have been lost to the Enemy by reading our books. But countless others have been lost to us by reading His. The sludgebags imagine our main job is putting things into their minds. They fail to realize our more strategic accomplishment: keeping things out of their minds.

Restrain Fletcher from going back to this store. If you cannot, then at least distance him from books of substance, particularly those dealing with the Enemy's attributes. I'm attaching a list of authors you must keep from him. On it you will see such contemptible names as Edwards, Spurgeon, Tozer, Packer, Piper, Bridges, Lewis, Schaeffer, Colson, and others. My list isn't long, and many on it are rarely carried now in bookstores anyway.

Distraction is your best strategy. Why should Fletcher read about the Enemy's sovereignty and grace when he can learn about his personality type, weight loss, Christian celebrities, or Thirty-Nine Reasons Why So and So Must Be the Antichrist. As for the Bible code books, I don't care what they imagine they find by piecing together every fortieth letter to find secret meanings. What terrifies me about the forbidden book is its overt meanings.

Draw him to authors who write so poorly it obscures truth. Better yet, lure him to authors who write well, but don't tell the truth. Direct Fletcher to books teaching the Carpenter isn't enough. Convince him he must go off in search of some new experience. Blind him to the assurances of the forbidden book that all the Enemy wants him to have is already in him, and within his reach.

Whether or not you can get him to read our kind of books, introduce him to our kind of vermin. Unless you can separate Ryan from him, Fletcher may be beyond the reach of a cult. Maybe you could link him up with one of those disgruntled roaches teaching all churches are apostate. Acquaint him with the right vermin and you can focus him on minor doctrines and undermine his faith in major ones.

Or convince him doctrine isn't necessary. Persuade him the central teachings Christians have died to uphold are not worth his attention. Make him trendy. Fortunately, teaching in many of the squadrons contains less and less biblical content and more and more psychological formulas and buzzwords and nice little illustrations, following the ever-changing drift of secular thought. (And who controls the direction of secular thought? Exactly!)

Make sure he takes ten looks at himself for every one look at the Enemy. If we maintain a proper imbalance, it'll mean his one look at the Enemy will be tainted by the predominance of his musings about himself and other maggot-feeders. Then what he thinks he sees of the Enemy will be no more than his reflection, a false god created in his own image. What he thinks of as worship will be idolatry.

As for Patty, accelerate your efforts to draw them together. Fletcher may be a Christian, but he still has glands. The images he's seen since the days he hid magazines under his bed as a boy have produced exactly what we want. Everything's now based on outward appearance rather than inward character. The longer men lust for unreal women the more incapable they become of loving real women.

We've sucked the women into this too. They're obsessed by the fear of growing old and unwanted. They fanatically resist aging. They undergo any pain and expense, including surgery, to remake and remarket themselves as a desirable consumer product.

For many years Fletcher's drooled over nonexistent women. Yet it never occurs to him that's why he hasn't had a satisfying relationship with a real woman, including his own wife. The two women he's committed adultery with he tossed. He'll toss Patty too. The only question is whether we can get him to abandon Diane first, and whether he'll toss Patty before marrying her or after.

Fletcher doesn't realize that—by some mystical design of the Enemy's—sex is not just something he does, but someone he is. Remember, in marriage the Tyrant encourages corporeal affections. This means the passions you inflame toward Patty you must extinguish toward Diane—or twist them so she becomes as much an object as Patty.

For decades now we've programmed Fletcher's mind with the image of voluptuous young females with enticing eyes and seductive voices, wanting him. In reality, no such women do want him. More to the point, no such women exist. They are made up, propped up, air brushed, surgically altered freaks of nature. They are one in a thousand, each of whom will soon dry up like last month's flowers. They are worms on a hook, projecting a calculated image of sensuality, while disgusted by the men they're preening for. They've pretended so often with so many they've become desensitized to human touch.

Should Fletcher ever have the opportunity to be with such a woman, he would soon discover her to be selfish, demanding, insecure, disloyal, and unfaithful. (Much like himself.) But as long as she's at a distance, in movies or on the pages of magazines or across the room or down the hallway, he can imagine how glorious it would be to have her. To own her.

She would be his trophy, and he would attempt to display, control, and dominate her. But since he's too vapid to realize this, he'll compare the wife he has to his imaginary ideal. She'll always fall short, as she falls short of this Patty, who he doesn't see as she really is. Indeed, her file shows her to be a woman much like Diane, only with fewer virtues. He sees Patty at her best, Diane at her worst. After lust cools, all that's left is cold dreadful reality. But then it's too late.

Notice how Fletcher's morality has served us with his daughter. He's never met one of the two boys Jillian has already fornicated with, and the other has just been a passing blur on the front porch. Has he even thought of sitting down with his son and laying out standards and expectations? How could he when he's violated his own vows and is on the verge of doing so again? How could he when, in the dark recesses of his mind, he lusts after girls the same age as his daughter?

Fletcher has raised his children not to believe in moral absolutes. They've had no household responsibilities and minimal discipline. They've had plenty of money and leisure time, and nearly unlimited opportunity to be alone in the car. This entire generation has been set up for disaster, and their parents have aided and abetted us. What more could a demon possibly ask for?

Fletcher's secretary says she loves him. Love is the Enemy's favorite word, but we've robbed it of His meaning. They love a new car, a piece of pecan pie, a football team, and a person who makes them feel good.

When the new car is no longer new, they no longer love it. Another car catches their eye. When their football team loses long enough, they no longer love it. They're free to choose another team. When their marriage partner grows gray and heavy and boring, they look elsewhere for love.

Don't you see? We've drained love of its original significance. When they hear the Enemy loves them and they are to love Him and each other, instead of attaching to the word His meaning, they attach ours.

No one would expect a man to keep watching baseball if he lost his love (i.e. desire) for the game. How could anyone expect him to stay faithful to his wife if he lost his love (i.e. desire) for her? Love, as we've defined it, is not what the Enemy claims, but a transitory good feeling outside the sludgebags' control, which relieves them of responsibility for their actions.

Our goal is to produce an ever-increasing craving for an ever-diminishing return. But beware. Pleasure is the Enemy's invention. While we've won over many by their reckless pursuit of pleasure, this is a minefield in which we must maneuver carefully. Even when we win, the victory can suddenly turn on us. Sometimes He leaves them empty and disillusioned with our counterfeit pleasures only to make them thirstier and more eager to find their pleasure in Him.

True, we have produced a marvelous counterfeit. But when the vermin become disillusioned with our kind of love, they might reason it's indeed a counterfeit...and if there's a counterfeit there must be the genuine article.

All my love,

—Lord Foulgrin

CHAPTER 25

BAD NEWS

Ryan, what's wrong?"

Jordan sat down across from his friend at Denny's, staring at the bloodshot eyes and deep-cut lines. Ryan's quick smile was buried under a pale mask.

"Got some bad news."

"What's going on?"

"Jodi had a mammogram. It turns out..." His voice broke. "She's got...cancer."

"Oh, man."

"It's treatable, they say. Pretty good chances. And we know God's in charge, so it's not a matter of chances, really. But it's still hard. Really hard for her."

Jordan felt paralyzed. He wished he knew what to say. Since he didn't, he asked questions and listened.

After forty minutes, Ryan said, "You're a good friend, Jordan. Thanks for being here for me. You've been a real encouragement."

I have? Jordan tried to remember if anyone else had ever said that to him. *But I didn't do anything. Except listen and be here and...care.*

"Ryan, this is probably a bad time to ask, but if God loves us, why does He let us go through stuff like this?"

"Well, that's a big question. A good one too. We don't always understand, but often He has a purpose we can't even see. I'm sure He has a reason for this, but that doesn't mean we'll understand it right away. I can tell you, it's already strengthened our marriage. Jodi and I have struggled from time to time and—Jordan, you're looking at me like I said I was an ax murderer."

"You and Jodi have marriage problems?"

"Of course we do. Doesn't everybody?"

"Well, I thought you...had this great Christian marriage."

"Look, Jodi and I do have a good marriage, but what makes it good isn't pretending we don't have problems. For years we've been talking about the problems, working hard, getting counseling." Ryan glanced at Jordan, then laughed. "Yes, we've gotten marriage counseling. I highly recommend it, as long as you get biblically based counseling, I mean. Anyway, back to the problem of why God lets us suffer—sometimes we don't understand, sometimes we understand a little, but even if we do, it's still hard to suffer. But God never promised us it would be easy."

"I guess I've been kind of surprised at that myself," Jordan said, as he stood up and placed a tip on the table. "The first few weeks after I became a Christian seemed pretty smooth. But now, everything's gotten really complicated."

"What do you mean?"

Jordan fidgeted, still standing. Part of him felt like running toward the parking lot.

"Jordan—sit down, bro. Tell me what you mean."

Jordan sat down and talked around it for ten minutes. He felt a strong prompting to tell Ryan about two things weighing on him, but then he was overwhelmed by a compulsion not to tell him. Finally he blurted, "There's this woman at work. My secretary. Her name's Patty."

Once he said her name, there was no going back. He kept talking. His friend listened to every word.

LETTER 25

Making Sure He Doesn't Get It

My obsequious Squaltaint,

Headquarters is in an uproar. Two more offensives by the Ghost and His warriors have broken out, this time in Cambodia and India. It's that dreadful movie about the Carpenter, the one with the words directly from the forbidden book. It keeps turning up in some new vermin language, moving like a plague across countrysides and hilltops, houses and huts, schools and marketplaces, ghettos and palaces. Videotapes, CDs, the Internet—it's gone on national television in some of our most reliable strongholds. Even the illiterate vermin keep seeing and hearing and embracing it. Forbidden squadrons are springing up like weeds. It's a nightmare. Whole villages are going to heaven in a handbasket!

Do you see how the Enemy rubs our face in the dirt? At a time when we've dominated moviemaking, He turns around and uses what we'd claimed as our medium. He uses a movie as one of His greatest weapons against us. It's infuriating.

With all this going on, the last thing I need is for you to fail me. Be vigilant or be dinner!

You express hope that hearing about Ryan and Jodi's suffering and marriage struggles will discourage Fletcher. Don't count on it. It could have the opposite effect, making him think if his friend can adopt the right perspective even when it's difficult, so can he.

Just as problematic, Fletcher's gotten a taste of what it means to be used by the Enemy to touch another's life. I suppose he's even praying for Ryan now. You say the Ghost kept prompting Fletcher to speak up about his secretary and falsifying records on the Brisbane account. But then your letter abruptly ended. I take it you succeeded in keeping him quiet about both of these? If not, you'd surely have informed me. We can tolerate his meetings with Ryan only if Fletcher keeps quiet about your little secret scenarios.

Your report does contain some hopeful elements. Fletcher's experiencing increased job stress and chronic stomachaches? Don't let him connect this to his dishonesty. The Enemy has an annoying habit of making them miserable when they're sinning. Sure, it's fun to watch them suffer, but the suffering is dangerous, because it can be His instrument to turn them.

Fletcher has the impressionable mind of a new Christian. This is bad in that it gives the Enemy broad latitude. The good news is, it gives us the same. He's not yet developed discernment. You won't be able to influence him toward anti-Christian thinking. Your best strategy is pseudo-Christian thinking. I'm delighted he's been watching religious programming promoting the health and wealth gospel. This will not only make him superficial, but set him up for disillusionment with the Enemy when bad things happen to him, which they inevitably will.

I'm also glad to hear he's being exposed to the artificial joy crowd, who major in acting buoyantly, mistaking this for spirituality. I'm delighted to hear he's been pasting a smile on his face. By all means, let the vermin deny hardships, muster up fake grins and say, "Praise the Lord"—like they'd put on a Band-Aid. Artificial joy is pretense, and pretense serves us, not Him.

Be careful, though, or Fletcher could learn the reality behind the counterfeit. He might embrace true joy in hardship. We want none of this singing-hymns-at-midnight-in-prison nonsense, as it makes onlookers ask where that perspective comes from. We want vermin to notice Christians only when they act like fools, never when they act out of joy, virtue, humility, or love. Fortunately, at any given time plenty of them can be counted on to act like fools.

Let Fletcher think his initial victory over sin was an anomaly. Convince him he's not more than a conqueror, in fact no conqueror at all. Let him believe—without knowing it—the forbidden book overstates his ability to live a triumphant Enemy-centered life.

Make him content with spiritual mediocrity, marginal victories here and there. The forbidden book speaks of victory; he lives in defeat. It speaks of joy; he lives in unhappiness. It speaks of peace; he wallows in worry. It speaks of waters of life; his soul is dry and parched.

Let him see the Carpenter not as a builder who levels old ground and clears away the rubbish then builds lives from the foundation up. Let him see Him as a handyman who takes an already existing structure and does a little refurbishing here and there, some minor remodeling of what Fletcher himself has built.

Let him understand as hyperbole statements such as, "If anyone is in Christ, he is a new creation; the old has gone, the new has come!"

Don't let him see that the righteous standing given him by the Enemy to allow entrance into Charis is available to him now. Let him think it's impossible for a sinner to live righteously today. Hide from him that outrageous claim he can resist us and we will flee from him. (He should flee from us!)

Keep him away from those parts of the forbidden book which spell out too clearly the Tyrant's intentions. This includes the Carpenter's description as "him who is able to keep you from falling and to present you before his glorious presence without fault and with great joy." He offers them holiness and happiness—the two things we labor hardest to keep from them.

The vermin are men sitting in a dungeon's darkness. The Carpenter buys their way out of prison, paying the price of their release by going to the gallows on their behalf. He then comes and unlocks their cell. So far, so bad.

But now comes the gratifying part—He lets them decide whether or not they will stay in the cell. Many choose the familiar comfort of prison over the responsibilities—and joys—of freedom. He's already unlocked the door and swung it open, but He won't carry them kicking and screaming out of the cell. So there's the paradox—He's freed them, yet they can make choices that put them back in prison.

If Fletcher believes the Enemy has redeemed him from sin's guilt, so be it. Just don't allow him to believe He can deliver him from sin's control.

Even if he leaves prison for a while, the door's always open. You can lure him back in. We might not have Fletcher for eternity, but we can still have him for lunch.

Relishing the role of warden,

—Lord Foulgrin

CHAPTER 26

IT WOULD HAVE TO BE OBVIOUS

I went with Jodi to women's Bible study," Diane said.

"You sound like you're making a confession," Jordan replied.

She laughed. "Yeah, I guess so. It was pretty good though. But Jordan...what can you tell me about demons?"

"Demons?"

"We were discussing them at the Bible study. They asked my opinion and I said I didn't know. I've never given them any thought. I guess I assumed they were fairy tales."

"That's what I always thought. Not any more though."

"What changed your mind?"

"Coming to Christ. Believing the Bible. And, I don't know, sometimes it's like I can almost sense them. I guess that sounds stupid. Maybe it's my imagination."

"Do you ever feel like there's a demon working you, I mean putting thoughts in your mind or keeping them out or tempting you to do something...bad?"

"Why do you ask?" Jordan heard the defensiveness in his voice.

"I'm not accusing you of anything. Just asking. I mean, for years I've thought maybe there were guardian angels. You remember, I read a few books on it? But they never said anything about *bad* angels influencing you. In Bible study they were talking about evil spirits strategizing to trip us up, confuse us, distract us. It was a whole new thought. It scared me. Does it make sense to you?"

"Sort of. I mean, I don't know about strategizing. That sounds like a little much. But the Bible says there's a real devil and real demons. I don't exactly know how it works. I mean, you'd think if they were whispering in our ears, it would have to be obvious, wouldn't it? What do you think?"

"I don't know. This stuff is all new to me. Some of it's exciting, but it's also sort of terrifying. A couple of the women went on about casting out demons and calling them by name and binding them. I don't know what they meant. Then a few others said they didn't think it was healthy even to talk about demons. Someone said they thought people make bad choices and demons don't have anything to do with it. I'm totally confused. I mean, if these people have been Christians forever and they don't agree, what am I supposed to think?"

Jordan thought about going to get the booklet Ryan had given him and asking Diane if he could walk her through it. He thought about asking her if she wanted to put her faith in Christ.

No, she'll think I'm being pushy. She needs more time. Wait, what time is it?

"Jordan, there's something I need to—"

"Whoa! Got to get to basketball. Sorry. Let's talk more later."

LETTER 26

Their Efforts to Take Us Down

My beloved Squaltaint,

Make the vermin ignore us when we're there, and exorcise us when we aren't. Let them lay hands on people and cast out the demon of loneliness, the demon of back pain, the demon of kidney stones, and the demon of constipation. Not only is this a distraction from our central work, on their minds and morals, it has a bonus—because of their silliness, others conclude "all this demon stuff is nonsense."

When they ponder demon activity, make Bible believers think, "Back then, but not now; over there, but not here." Let the gulf of time and distance convince them they're somehow beyond the cosmic war.

I'm pleased when the squadrons teach them nothing about us, and when they teach error and excess about us. Let them see us behind every bush or behind no bush at all. Let them see us in every convulsion, handicap, foaming at the mouth, gnashing of teeth, or display of superhuman strength. Or let them see us in none of them. Let them fear we're everywhere or imagine we're nowhere. Psychological and medical labels are easy to hide behind. "Multiple personality disorder?" Been there. Done that.

Fortunately, many of these spiritual warfare experts don't know what they're doing, even when they publish how-to manuals on casting us out. I don't minimize the horror of sudden eviction. It's humiliating and unnerving. The first time it happened, all I could think of was the Enemy casting me into the nether darkness before my time.

But even if the expulsion works, it leaves a vacuum. How will they fill it? Let them cast us out, or imagine they have, as long as the vermin keep making the daily choices that invite us back in. Let them "name" and "bind" us to their hearts' content, as long as they entertain the thoughts and engage in the activities that give us power over them.

Make them think we can control them against their will, or, because they're Christians, we can't influence them at all. Both lies are useful. If they never think about us, we have them. If they always think about us, we have them. Ignore us, they're ours. Obsess over us, they're ours. Having their eyes on us is as good as having it on themselves. The only important thing is, they don't have them on Him.

The Book doesn't tell them to rebuke a spirit of dissension, but to agree and be united in the same mind. It doesn't tell them to rebuke a demon of incest, but that the offender must repent and change his behavior or be expelled.

We can short-circuit discipleship by telling them they can break patterns of sin simply by uttering magic words requiring no ongoing acts of obedience. Who needs accountability and discipline to establish new patterns of purity when they can simply cast out the demon of lust? Why should Fletcher work on his attitude and actions if he can go somewhere to have the demon of anger rebuked? Get them to rely on man-made eviction formulas, not on the Enemy.

I've been in deliverance encounters where I've fed them a steady stream of false information. You can't imagine how many of them believe what I say, even when they've rebuked me as a "lying spirit"! I saw an entire chapter of a book conveying information I gave them—nearly all of it I just made up while they tried to exorcise me! Did somebody say "gullible"?

Let them debate all day whether they can be demon possessed. Convince them they can be completely controlled by us, so they become victims without a choice, beyond the power of the Ghost. Or convince them a Christian cannot be seriously influenced by us, and they need not take precautions. Let them be paralyzed with fear or careless with presumption.

They seek names of high-ranking territorial spirits, such as myself. They "serve notice" and evict and bind and rebuke me. Fine. Perhaps they haven't noticed I and my underlings are alive and well. They've not succeeded in "praying me down." Indeed, if they'd prayed down all the spirits they claim to, you'd expect sin to be a museum piece. It's most entertaining when would-be exorcists shout at us for hours on end, as if we're hard of hearing. I love their cockiness, the way they dance in the end zone over all their imaginary victories. But look at the scoreboard, Squaltaint. We're still in the game!

Let them go right on confessing the sins of their region, oblivious to the fact the Enemy doesn't forgive by proxy. As long as the people themselves don't turn to the Carpenter, we have nothing to fear. It's especially gratifying when they command us to leave an area where the people we're working on have given us an open invitation to stay.

The Carpenter told them to rejoice that their names are written in Charis, not that they can wage war against us. Let them spend more time studying us than studying the Enemy. I'd rather see them fascinated with us than Him any day.

It's not powerplays and sweeping declarations of our defeat that frighten me, it's quiet prayers for personal holiness and greater yieldedness to the Enemy. Far better that they focus on us than look to their own hearts or ask the Enemy to cleanse them.

Don't let them take seriously the Tyrant's claim: "Greater is he who is in you than he that is in the world." The Enemy, the Carpenter, and the Ghost terrify me. Whenever the vermin call upon anyone or anything else, it's mere entertainment.

Never frightened by their grandstanding,

—Lord Foulgrin

CHAPTER 27

SURPRISE

It was a quiet dinner, just Jordan and Diane.

"How's the meat loaf?" Diane asked.

"Fine. Thanks for making it."

"Sure."

Neither felt like talking, and both read into the other's silence. After dinner Jordan retreated to the living room couch, with one face intruding upon his mind, then another. First it was Patty, but then it was Jill, his twin sister. She'd died in that boating accident seventeen years ago to the day, six months before Jillian was born. They'd named her after his sister.

After staring into nothing for twenty minutes, he heard Diane coming into the room. He quickly brushed his sleeve across his face, wiping the tears.

"You better look at these," she said, voice hollow, dropping papers over the open Bible on his lap.

"Midterm grades? He's failing half his classes! Wait a minute...this came out two weeks ago? Why didn't you tell me?"

"I tried, but...we don't have much time together."

"What do you mean? I'm home nearly every night."

"But we watch TV or you read books or something."

"You're the one who watches TV. If you want to talk, turn it off and we'll talk."

"It's not my fault, Jordan."

"I didn't say it was."

"Yes, you did. Anyway, it's more than his grades. Look at what I found in his room." She handed him a stack of papers. "They were under his bed."

Jordan flipped through pictures of graphic sexual acts, involving men with women, and women with each other and with...he'd been exposed to his share of lewd pictures, but these were worse than anything he'd seen.

"I'll call and cancel the Internet connection," he said weakly.

"It's not just the sex," Diane said. She handed him other pictures, dark pictures of blood and gore, mayhem and murder. Then she showed him a half dozen articles. One was called "Worshiping Satan" and another, "How to Kill Your Parents and Get Away with It."

"Is this stuff legal?" Jordan said.

"What are we going to do?"

"I said I'll cancel the Internet connection. But I need to do something more. Ahh..."

"What is it?"

"My back. Arthritis, I guess. I seem to be turning into an old man." Jordan sat back on the couch, feeling the dark cloud over the room. He looked at his wife, standing there tentatively. "Is there something else, Diane?"

"Yes, there is. But this one's about me."

He waited, wanting to hear, but not wanting to.

"Well, believe it or not..."

"Yeah?"

"I'm pregnant."

LETTER 27

Love and the Female Maggot-Feeders

My soldier Squaltaint,

I cringed when I read your report of what Fletcher reflected on in his "quiet time":

"We do not wage war as the world does. The weapons we fight with are not the weapons of the world. On the contrary, they have divine power to demolish strongholds. We demolish arguments and every pretension that sets itself up against the knowledge of God, and we take captive every thought to make it obedient to Christ."

Wage war? Fight? Dangerous military language. We want them to think like tourists on a cruise ship, not soldiers on a battleship. Let the church be a social club, not an attack squadron. Terms such as demolish and take captive sound the battle alarm.

The Tyrant offers them power to demolish our arguments and pretensions, our primary weapons of war. But he unwittingly handed us a working strategy—it's the man's thoughts you must take captive. As thunder follows lightning, his actions will automatically follow his thoughts.

This is why Fletcher's time spent reading the forbidden book is so dangerous. You must keep feeding him on the cheap images and vain bantering of the media. Any effects from this half hour reading the Bible should be effectively neutralized by an hour of counter programming.

Your Patty is our instrument of destruction for Fletcher, as he is hers. Snakebile reports she's been disillusioned with her husband for some time. She's longing for something more. I've instructed Snakebile to keep making her think that something more is Fletcher.

Working on Patty with Snakebile is an opportunity to learn the difference in how to mislead male and female vermin when it comes to "love."

Her file shows Patty has long inflicted on her husband and children what she believes to be love. She's quick to remind them how much she's sacrificed for them. When they want to do something, she makes clear she wants it done another way, then when they relent she says, "Oh no, go ahead and do it your way." She will not let them give in, but insists on proving how unselfish she is, and how selfish they are, they who don't deserve what a wonderful woman she is. They take for granted how she works hard all day at the office and then comes home where no one else seems to care about the house. Every time they try to help, they do it wrong. Only she can do it right. Proving how indispensable she is, Patty picks up behind them, incessantly reminding them she's doing this out of love.

You can pick out of a crowd everyone this woman loves by the hunted expressions on their faces. They only wish she would take out her love on someone else. (Hopefully that will be Fletcher.)

Hide from him the controlling nature of her love, letting him see only its flattering aspects. He'll see the other side soon enough—if you play your cards right, after two families have been destroyed. Then he'll find out what she's made of and eventually bolt. Good luck then—hell hath no fury like a woman scorned.

Our Patty has read enough romance novels and watched enough soap operas—Snakebile's report says she tapes them every day—to believe the key to her satisfaction is finding someone to cherish her. Someone who values her opinion, someone different in nearly every way from her insensitive stomach-scratching brute of a husband. (Remind Snakebile he mustn't let her become aware of her complaining, demeaning nature, lest it dawn on her she's even less a prize than her husband.)

Tired of a man who'd rather push buttons on a remote control than listen to her, she's on the prowl for Prince Charming. Patty seeks a man of nobility who wants nothing more than to gaze into her eyes, write her love notes, take her to the most expensive and exciting places, and make her feel wonderful.

Never mind no such man exists. Never mind if he did exist he'd have better things to do than fawn over her. And never mind if somehow they did come together, she'd soon drive him away with her harping and whining, and her sticky smothering "love."

Fletcher is her most recent perfect man. He's her imaginary lover, an idol fashioned by her hands. He stands in perpetual contrast to her bumbling, belching husband. Never mind her husband works hard, loves the children, and is kind to her, kinder than most men she could hope to marry, including Fletcher. That doesn't matter, for he's simply not romantic, not like the men in the novels and movies, who never burp or smell. Not like what she imagines Fletcher to be.

You see what we've done? While Fletcher delved into pornography, Patty fed on emotional pornography in soaps and romance novels. Both became dissatisfied with real people. And both will end up destroying real people in their hopeless search for "true love."

Soon Patty will jump over the Enemy's guardrails in her quest for freedom. She'll experience it too, for about ten seconds, as she falls off the cliff. Later, after she's burned her bridges behind her, the divorce is final, and her children no longer trust her, perhaps one day denying her access to her grandchildren, then she'll cry out, "Why did You let this happen to me, God?" Those are glorious scenes, are they not? They choose to jump over the Enemy's guardrails, then blame Him for it. Splendid.

We've turned deception into an art form. We fatten them like corn-fed cattle, then when they're plump and happy we herd them to the slaughterhouse. How shall we have Patty—medium rare? And Fletcher—raw?

Remember, it's a mistake to try to tempt women the same way as men. Vermin men consent to "love" to get sex. Vermin women consent to sex to get "love." One perversion of the Enemy's plan is as good as the other, but you must remember who you're tempting.

The Enemy adores this institution of marriage we're eviscerating. We hate marriage precisely because He loves it. He intends it to be permanent, "till death do us part." But "being in love" is a feeling, transient and fluctuating. So let them marry, imagining their feelings of love will sustain them. Of course, they won't. Time and reality will see to that. In the Enemy's book, love is something they do. For them, love is something they feel. By taking advantage of that discrepancy, we bring untold ruin.

These vermin spend four years of college training for a career, but don't give four minutes to developing marriage survival skills. No wonder their marriages routinely crash and burn or slowly waste away. If you can't take Fletcher's marriage one way, take it the other.

Remember, it's not the big blowups that destroy marriages, but the cumulative force of daily mutual annoyances—that particular tone of voice, that insufferable facial expression into which the other reads worlds of meaning. She lifts her eyebrow a certain way when Fletcher brings up golfing? Convince him she does it to annoy him, to hound and nag him. With the mere twitch of an eyebrow we bring a blow that strikes as hard as a clinched fist upon the face. Many of these things go back to their courtship, that idyllic season of life in which we sowed the seeds that will one day blossom to the full flower of mutual hatred.

When I was a senior administrator in the semantics department, I learned never to make frontal attacks on "love" or any of the Enemy's favorite virtues. The best strategy is to commandeer His words for our purposes, redefine them, and twist their meaning. "Love" is our highest achievement.

Patty thinks she loves Fletcher. The truth is—and because it's the truth, it's exactly what you must keep from her—she loves not the man, but how she feels when she makes him smile and look at her. She's in love with her power over him, her ability to manipulate him into paying attention to her. He's merely a prop—it's really all about her.

The same applies to Fletcher. He has strong feelings for her, but it's not her he loves. It's himself. He's in love with the good feelings he gets by being around her. Once that good feeling dissipates...good-bye!

Snakebile won't let our dear Patty think for a moment about the husband she's about to betray, the children she's sacrificing on the altar of her quest for happiness. Don't let these two consider that if they actually had to spend more than a few weeks together in the confines of real domestic life, they'd soon despise each other. This they'll find out, but only when it's too late!

"Love" has brought them together. The same "love" will destroy their families.

I'm delighted to hear Fletcher's postconversion progress with his wife is waning. Though they aren't yelling or throwing furniture—admittedly entertaining activities—their communication is woven with unspoken expectations and chronic irritation.

He thinks he's bending over backwards to sacrifice for her? And since he doesn't see her reciprocating, he resents her. Prompt him to think every time he defers to her—whether or not it's a true sacrifice and regardless if it's what she wants—she "owes him another one." Meanwhile Rosefang is making her think she's being exceptionally tolerant of his new religious extremism, and he owes her for it. Each imagines he or she's the one who keeps giving and giving and seldom gets anything in return.

I see Fletcher's wife sacrificially fixes him his favorite meat loaf for dinner, though he hates meat loaf and always has. Twenty years ago he lied to be polite, and ever since she's quietly prepared a meal she can barely tolerate for the good of a man who hates it even more. Once a week they both choke down meat loaf, thinking the other owes them for it!

Meanwhile, Patty's concerned Fletcher's interest in her appears to be waning, and she's concocting a scheme to throw them together? Excellent. Things are on schedule. It was shrewd of you a year ago to work with Patty's tempter and facilitate their "chance" meeting when she applied for the job. (They're so fond of this notion of chance.) It'll be more difficult with Fletcher's conversion, but they can still think of themselves as "star-crossed lovers," whom fate—yes, or even God—has brought together. Never mind that all along we've been pulling the strings!

The Enemy says so much about love in the forbidden book. Who would have imagined how effectively we could counterfeit it to carry out our agenda?

Lovingly,

—Lord Foulgrin

CHAPTER 28

THE TEST

"I highly recommend you get an amniocentesis to determine whether this child has abnormalities."

"You mean Down syndrome?"

"That's the most likely problem, but there are other possibilities, given your age."

"Suppose the test indicates Down syndrome. What then?"

"I'd recommend that you terminate the pregnancy."

Jordan glanced at Diane to see if she was looking at him. She was.

"You mean an abortion?" she asked the doctor.

"Well, you don't have to call it that. It's just the best solution. Not only for you, but best for the...you know, the fetus."

"You mean, the baby," Diane said.

"Look, it's your decision, not mine. Why don't you think it over and let me know if you want the test. I'd certainly recommend it."

The doctor walked out of the room. Slowly, Jordan and Diane gathered their things, and he held the door open for her. Neither looked the other in the eyes.

LETTER 28

Suffering, the Enemy's Megaphone

My gloating Squaltaint,

I tire of your rhapsodies concerning vermin suffering. Please, spare me the theatrics. They're signs of a rank amateur. You could learn from a Nazi soldier of mine who idly filed his nails while women and children paraded past him on their way to the gas chamber. Show some class.

You gloat you've inflamed Fletcher's lower back until he's in constant pain. You got him weeping over his twin sister who died on the river. You rejoice over his agony at his discovery of the dark world of young Daniel. You brag his wife is pregnant and because of their age you think this will weaken their marriage. To top it off, you think you've managed to create a chromosomal abnormality.

You're drunk on suffering. Sober up!

If you get him to blame the Enemy for his sister's death, well and good. But the files show she had strong faith in the Carpenter. His missing her could draw his thoughts toward Charis. You make no mention of whether his back pain or missing his sister or problems with his son have driven him to the forbidden talk. I suspect they have. Can anything be a victory if the Enemy uses it to draw them closer to Him?

Concerning your boasts about illness and deformities, there's considerable debate on the extent to which we can inflict such maladies. Ratskull argues the Enemy alone creates, and we can only twist what He's created. He holds we cannot take credit for the conception of a handicapped child. Curiously, the Enemy claims these wretched twisted masses are His work. He says He makes blind and deaf image-bearers, as though this were cause for pride rather than shame.

Yes, the book concedes we can inflict certain maladies. But unless you have a power over chromosomes even our Prince doesn't, be careful what you boast of.

Since these roaches are so taken with having "the perfect child"—something stemming not from love but pride—they're devastated by any abnormality. Fine, suck pleasure from their pain. But don't assume you've orchestrated these events yourself. Be alert to the purposes the Enemy may have in bringing this child to them. Fletcher's convictions as a Christian may trigger a different response than you anticipate—what would have worked a year ago might not now.

Consider an agnostic couple once assigned to me. As long as their health was good and all was well with their children, they were safely in my grasp. But then their youngest child, a seven-year-old, contracted a fatal disease. For weeks I reveled in their suffering. But something began to happen—they prayed for their son, people who'd never prayed before. Their marriage had been struggling, divorce was on the horizon, but suddenly the man stepped forward and cared for his son. The wife was drawn to her husband. They began to communicate.

Next thing I knew the Christian neighbor was coming over to watch their child, bringing meals, offering prayer and support. Things spun out of control. First the woman, then the man, and finally the boy all became Christians.

The extenuating circumstances were such that I couldn't be blamed, but Ishbane saw it differently. (Soon thereafter he got into deep water over the Colson conversion debacle, and I had the last laugh.)

My point is, yes, there was distress, and five years later the boy died. We won the battle of temporary suffering. But we lost the war of eternity.

You run the same risk. If you can get them to kill the idiot child, you succeed. They'd do it "for the child's sake," of course. (Murders done for the sake of the murdered are always our finest.) They'll then carry guilt, which will likely destroy their marriage, reinforce their materialism, and deaden Fletcher's faith.

But even then, look out. For the evils people do can boomerang on us. How many maggot-feeders decades later turn to the Enemy through coming to terms with past choices that plague them?

If the child lives, you imagine he'll drain their time and distract them from pursuits they'd have preferred? But how many families have we seen transformed by the presence of such children? How many have we seen rearrange their priorities, learn through the "delightfulness" of those inferior children we thought would be their ruin? How many have we seen drawn closer to the Enemy by the traumas we celebrated?

You must not look at immediate results, Squaltaint, but ultimate ones. As for Fletcher's back, I'm sure it's pleasant to see him unable to tie his own shoe without pain, to see his eyes well up with tears. Tell me something I don't know. But don't get too sentimental. The pain is dangerous because it reminds him something's wrong; not all is as it should be. It could make him recognize his powerlessness and long for a better world, Charis. His pain and tears could prompt him to be more sensitive to his wife's ailments, and to the suffering of a world he's always ignored.

The Enemy and we both test them the same ways. The difference? He wants them to pass, we want them to fail.

As for their despair about Stungoth's protégé Daniel, how many in their suffering have gotten a faint taste of hell that turns them toward heaven? Far better to let them catch no glimpse of hell until they enter it.

The easier their lives, the thinner. In times of peace, they ignore good and evil. In health and ease, they forget their condition, and the world's. Prosperity is the best weather for our warfare. Adversity is best for the Enemy's. Of the Christian vermin, 90 percent pass the test of adversity, while 90 percent fail the test of prosperity.

Pain is the Enemy's megaphone. With it He can get through to the nearly-deaf. The forbidden book calls Him the "God of all comfort." When they seek comfort He makes Himself known to them. But men only seek comfort when in pain.

What should we do then? One extreme would be to stop hurting our prey for fear we'll be used by the Enemy. The other extreme is failing to anticipate His hidden purposes. The Enemy attempts to hijack our work to further His.

He's utterly ruthless. He won't hesitate to exploit the situation and use the suffering we love to bring about the transformation we hate. We eat the appetizers and right when we think the main course is coming, the Tyrant snatches the dish away. He does this to torment us!

You keep celebrating the latest wars and famines and natural disasters. Don't put too much hope in them. Our job is much easier in peacetime and affluence, when death hides behind marquees and billboards.

A century ago I had one vermin safely in my grasp, but war did two terrible things to him. First, it reminded him of his mortality. With the noises of death surrounding him, my target couldn't help but ponder the likelihood of his death. He reconsidered his father's words and his fellow soldier's faith as he read the forbidden book before the battle, sky filled with explosions and fumes. (Terminal illness has this disadvantage, which is why we endorse physician-assisted suicide. Once the vermin know they're going to die, we must do everything to kill them before the Enemy exploits their awareness.)

Finally the battle came and showed him to be a coward. I was delighted in his cowardice and the agonizing guilt it stirred. But then the Enemy twisted the knife in an unanticipated way. The vermin became a Christian. Just like that, I lost him.

In famine, I've seen Christians rise up and offer both food and the forbidden message. In natural disasters I've seen selfish people band together to help others. Neighbors who didn't know each other's names open their homes and share their resources.

I led one of my vermin down a path of destruction that put him in prison for ten years. I thought I could relax then, but no—he came to the end of himself and surrendered to the Carpenter. Behind those bars he joined a forbidden fellowship that snatched from hell vermin after vermin. He spent his days reading the forbidden book and speaking the forbidden message. It was a nightmare. In the end, I couldn't wait for him to get out.

While naive demons like you are partying because of wars and disasters and crimes, the Enemy commandeers our achievements and undermines them with His own.

A strong case can be made for Sludgrake's school of demonic strategy—smother the vermin in prosperity, curse them with good health, lead them down the easy street to hell in comfort and abundance. We can pick the meat from their bones later precisely because we've labored to fatten them now.

Suffering isn't an end in itself. It's raw material to be used by the Enemy or us. If comfort proves the best way to achieve bad character, by all means do what you can to make Fletcher comfortable. True, suffering can dismantle faith in the Enemy, but even that's a danger, for the faith dismantled was not a true faith in the first place. We'd be better served by the false faith remaining intact. For once pseudofaith comes crashing down, there's danger upon its ruins true faith may be built.

Look carefully, Squaltaint. Things aren't always what they appear. Remember the teenage girl Mootslut boasted of paralyzing in the diving accident? The Enemy has given us unending trouble by her. Were she never paralyzed, had she not suffered, she'd likely be serving us now—certainly she wouldn't be such a nuisance.

Remember the five missionaries in Ecuador? My former comrade Muckphlegm was assigned to one of them. MP and his associates planned it well, coordinating their efforts with those of the tempters assigned to the Auca Indians. The murders were carried out beautifully—a great moment of triumph for Erebus.

But *only* a moment. For decades thousands followed the martyrs, going to foreign countries and dedicating their lives to the Enemy. One of the missionary's wives went to live with those who killed them, taking the forbidden message to the same vermin who murdered her husband. The killer became a Christian, then a leader in the forbidden squadron. Nauseating. What was glorious for a moment has haunted us ever since. Muckphlegm hasn't dared show his face in the home office for forty years.

Don't let the Enemy fool you. Above all, don't let Him *use* you.

Fletcher prayed he'd become more Christlike? Then let him turn around now and pray the Enemy would remove the very things He's given to make him Christlike. They're disappointed when the Enemy doesn't answer their prayers, and equally disappointed when He does.

Meanwhile, convince Fletcher he's suffering when he's on an airplane and the flight attendant tells him they've run out of pasta and he has to eat chicken. Let him whine and whimper about all he must endure. Defeat him on two counts—failing to trust the Enemy to develop his character through his own small suffering, and failing to intercede for his vermin brothers who truly are suffering.

Wise to His insidious tactics,

—Lord Foulgrin

CHAPTER 29

OPTIONS

They sat in a far corner table at Salty's restaurant. He had the same feelings for Patty he'd had the past five months. Why did it seem so bad to have them now?

"So, what would you do?" Jordan asked Patty.

"Well, for sure, I'd have the test done."

"And what if the test said the baby had some problems? Down syndrome or something?"

"Well, I'd follow the doctor's advice. I'd terminate the pregnancy. In fact, even if it's not deformed, she shouldn't have it. I mean, I'm younger than she is, fitter too, and I'd never have another baby. She's too old to start over. Besides, it would tie you down, obligate you."

"What do you mean?"

"I mean you want to keep your options open."

"What options?"

"Look, Jordan, you've told me about your marriage problems and I've told you about mine. I've set up an appointment with an attorney next week. I'm going to be true to myself and do what I should've done long ago. Your best years are still ahead of you. You're not doing Diane or the kids a favor by hanging on to a failing marriage. You owe it to them and yourself to consider other options, make a fresh start. You know what I mean?"

She reached her hand across the table and grabbed his, squeezing hard. He inhaled her perfume. He loved that scent. And, yes, he knew exactly what she meant.

LETTER 29

Take Him Down

My delinquent Squaltaint,

Obsmut just read me your letter. I'm trying to rid myself of nagging pain from vain attempts to guide an obtuse spirit with the IQ of a split-leafed philodendron.

The only positive report, aside from the promising developments with the woman, is your continued triumph over Fletcher on the basketball court. His perspective is so skewed he can remember every foul committed against him—including many that never happened—but not a single one committed by him. Don't let him see the incongruity of this. Not only does he have an overblown sense of his own importance, he has no objectivity. He may be a Christian, but he still sees everything through the lens of his own ego.

A man who cannot recognize his errors in sports will never recognize his errors in life. If he has to be right on the court, he'll have to be right in his home, his work, his church, and everywhere else. Fletcher could engage in self-reflection for hours on end, and never see the faults in himself apparent to anyone who's spent thirty minutes with him.

As for the rest of your report, I'm at a loss. He's actually memorizing the words he first read in his mother's book? "Put on the full armor of God, so you can take your stand against the devil's schemes."

I detest memorization. It lets them pick up the sword anywhere at any time—on an elevator, in the car, on the street, in a grocery store. The only thing worse than vermin being in the forbidden book is the forbidden book being in them.

The Enemy has declared war on us as surely as we have on Him. Fortunately, He uses the vermin as His warriors, which is about as effective as sending out hedgehogs to attack lions. But beware, because sometimes the Ghost gets hold of them in unanticipated ways.

The Tyrant is aware of our schemes, and desires the vermin to be aware of them. By declaring war on our schemes He admits how effective they are. Your job is simple, Squaltaint—keep Fletcher from putting on this armor! The Enemy gives them no armor to protect their back. As long as they face us with raised shield and sword, we cannot defeat them. But when they put down their guard, we can move in for the kill.

The best strategy is twofold. First, convince him the kingdoms of light and darkness can maintain a détente, a peaceful coexistence. Second, minimize your frontal assaults, and use cunning and trickery. Subtlety. Deception. Disguise. That way you can keep him from recognizing the reality of the spiritual warfare going on about him.

Foulgrin's rule 17: No image-bearer ignorant of the battle bothers to put on battle armor.

Fletcher is on the verge. He's poised to make choices in the next weeks that could easily take him either way. Whether it's the woman, the finances, or something else, you must use everything at your disposal to bring him down. Don't just take him prisoner. I want a casualty.

Weary of them and you,

—Lord Foulgrin

CHAPTER 30

MOM

They drove wordlessly to the retirement center to see Diane's mother. Diane had asked Jordan to come. He said yes, hating that he hadn't seen her for nearly a year and hating that he didn't want to see her now.

When he walked in the door, Jordan barely recognized her. But he noticed her eyes light up the moment she saw him.

"Hello, Jordan."

"Hi, Mom."

She gave him a surprised smile. "I hardly remembered what you look like, Jordan. I know you've been busy."

"Yeah. Too busy sometimes."

"Here, Mom, let me prop up your pillow so you can be more comfy while you and Jordan talk."

They chatted for nearly an hour. The longer they talked the more comfortable he became. He'd forgotten her sense of humor. As she sat back smiling, a thought pressed into Jordan's mind.

I should tell her I've become a Christian.

He considered going to get his Bible from the car. He felt an unexpected urgency.

Wait, who was he to pop in like this for the first time in a year, then go off on something she'd probably think was weird? He could unsettle her, even offend her. Besides, what would Diane think? There was no reason to push it. There was no hurry.

LETTER 30

Postponing Evangelism

My delinquent Squaltaint,

You're concerned the sludgebag Ryan is encouraging Fletcher to "share his faith." You blame Dredge for failing to restrain Ryan and assure me you're sincerely laboring to derail his efforts.

In Charis sincerity may matter. All that matters in Erebus is results. Stop whining. Come out of your corner not swinging blindly, but with a thought-through strategy to knock out Fletcher.

Since it's what the Enemy uses to change vermin destinations from hell to heaven, obviously you must keep Fletcher from evangelism. But don't bother trying to convince him it's bad to evangelize. Let him think it's good, admirable. Just as long as he doesn't actually do it.

The best strategy is to keep him from grasping the stakes, so he has no sense of urgency. Even Bible-believing churches help us here. According to the records you sent, in the past ten years Fletcher's pastor—who's been a nuisance to us—has nonetheless preached only one message on heaven and none on hell. That track record will presumably continue, and Fletcher will get the impression eternity is unimportant. He'll think of hell as unreal and heaven as intangible and undesirable. Both will seem fantasy realms with no bearing on his present earthly life, which he sees as the "real" thing.

Next, persuade your maggot-feeder he must be low-key, careful not to bowl unbelievers over with his new faith, lest they see him as a fanatic and get "turned off." By all means don't let it occur to him to quietly tell them what the Enemy has done for him. Let him imagine that this should be done gradually, only when they ask, or only after a long (as in endless) period of being "a good example."

No man is won to the Enemy simply by the moral behavior of another. No one has ever gone to heaven just because he saw a good example. No one has ever escaped hell because some other man was a Christian.

Let Fletcher be a "good example" until he's blue in the face—as long as he doesn't explain the forbidden message. Let him talk with them about anything and everything but what the Enemy has done and what it means to be His follower.

Look around you, Squaltaint, and you'll see innumerable Christian sludgebags who've been good neighbors and model coworkers for decades. But they've never actually told those around them what it means to be a Christian. Many of them imagine by now the message has somehow magically gotten across, but of course it hasn't. Excellent.

Fletcher made the statement to Ryan he'd like to share the gospel with his wife and mother-in-law "when the time is right"? This frightened you, but it can work to our advantage. Don't let him grasp the Enemy's notion that evangelism is one beggar telling another where to find bread. Instead, turn evangelism into something more complex or obscure, something that will happen one day, but never today.

Fill him with an irrational dread of bringing up in conversation the Carpenter and the forbidden message. If the vermin analyzed it, they'd be on to us. What else but our efforts could explain why they get so apprehensive about doing for someone what they believe is the biggest favor in the universe—telling them about the Enemy's plan to save them from hell and give them heaven?

Don't let Fletcher ask himself why a man from Portland should care about what a man from Chicago thinks of him as they both fly to Philadelphia. Why, when he will never see this man again (unless he accepts the message, in which case he'll be deeply grateful), should he be so frightened the man may dislike him? Why would they feel so hesitant about telling people what's clearly in their best interests? Don't let the obvious absurdity settle in, or he may catch on it's we who are playing tricks on his tiny mind, fueling this irrational fear.

Never let him see the incongruity of how he could talk with someone on that airplane and share a myriad of opinions about business and politics, and make a case for why a team will win the Super Bowl, but dare not make a case for the Carpenter. Don't let it dawn on him they're all going to die soon. Perhaps in an hour, a day, a week, a year, at most a few decades. Never let death seem imminent.

Teach him to withhold the forbidden message until…his neighbor dies in a car accident, his father and mother-in-law pass away in hospital beds, his wayward niece dies from an overdose, the man he worked with for ten years dies of AIDS, or his son takes his life. Only then press upon him the urgency of evangelism, just to twist the knife in his soul.

The one thing they consider most important to talk about eventually is the one thing they can't talk about now. Our perfect timing, our "just the right moment" boils down to this—never, until it's too late.

Keep him ignorant of church history and forbidden squadrons across the globe. The Enemy may try to point out to him that while his brethren risk imprisonment and death, Fletcher is unwilling to hazard a raised eyebrow or a disapproving glance. Resist his efforts to bring this to mind.

Jordan's been thinking about sharing the forbidden message with his own father too? I see the geezer's health is bad, that Scuzfroth predicts a heart attack within a month. Good—he'll be in hell before you know it. Fathers are hardest of all. Your report says your vermin's father intimidated him, called the shots, and now thinks his son's new faith is a passing phase, part of a "midlife crisis."

Quick death is the best we can hope for with unbelievers. If he doesn't die immediately, prompt Fletcher to watch him waste away. Let him visit him, tenderly care for him, and lovingly "respect his wishes" not to hear the forbidden message.

Consider the extent of our accomplishment—they would rather see a loved one go to hell than be seen as pushy by insisting on telling him the truth. The Enemy calls them to be truth-tellers in the name of love. We call them to be truth withholders in the name of "not being pushy." (Of course, this is acting not in his father's best interest, but what we subconsciously convince him is his own.)

Don't let it dawn on him that one moment after he and his father die they'll both regret the same thing—that he didn't tell him the truth one last time (in some cases, one first time).

It's delicious what we've pulled off here—Christian family, hospice workers, nurses and doctors caring for the dying, and in the interests of ethics or professionalism withholding what their patients long for. Christian counselors meet with troubled, desperate people whose lives have fallen apart. But because they came to get help with their addictions or their marriages, the counselors consider it unethical to "exploit" them by sharing the forbidden message. We have countless Christian teachers dealing with lonely, troubled, and desperate students. They could speak to them about the

Carpenter, but don't because they fear reprisals or have no sense of urgency.

Think of it—our prey cite endless ethical and legal reasons for not obeying the Enemy's command!

Familiarize your vermin with the concept of lifestyle or friendship evangelism. True, it's often proven deadly to our cause, but only by that minority who consciously use their friendships as a foundation to actually tell people about the Carpenter. The majority never do.

Delay. Procrastinate. Postpone. This is our evangelism strategy. If we do our job, people will die of thirst a few feet away from water-bearers who don't want to impose their water on others.

"I'll share the truth when the time is right," your vermin Fletcher said. Your job is simple—make sure the time is never right.

Populating hell one image-bearer at a time,

—Lord Foulgrin

CHAPTER 31

DAD

Jordan? It's Erin. The nurse called. Dad's not doing well. They're afraid he might be—" Her voice broke.

"I'm coming right away." Jordan made the thirty-minute drive in twenty.

Why didn't I tell him when I had the chance? What was I thinking? What reason could have been good enough not to tell him about Christ? O God, give me another chance.

He jumped out of the car and walked briskly through the halls, past residents who seemed to be living in a different speed. He strode into the room, seeing Erin to his left, then stopped abruptly two feet inside.

His eyes focused on the pale face that had been his father's. Holding his breath, he stared at the colorless mannequin.

His father opened his eyes, and suddenly his personality invaded the room like a stealth jet. "What are you doing here?" he asked, voice commanding, though thin and weak.

"Just coming to check on you, Dad. Thought maybe we could play a game of chess."

"I'm not thinking very clearly these days. Might give you a chance to beat me."

Jordan and Erin both laughed, too loudly.

"Had you scared, didn't I? Had lots of them scared, two doctors and a bunch of nurses."

"When I got here twenty minutes ago," Erin said, "one of the doctors was still here. He told the nurses to watch Dad closely. They're monitoring him." She pointed to a couple of devices Jordan didn't recognize, one connected to the end of his father's right index finger.

"Listen, why don't you sit down," Erin said. "I've got to phone the office. Be back in a while."

Jordan sat down. *Tell him. You have to tell him. You asked for a second chance and this is it.* He moved his fingers gently to his father's cool, limp hand.

"You're not going to get emotional on me, are you, boy? You start crying or sniveling on me and I'll call the nurse and have you kicked out on your rear."

"I'll try to restrain myself, Dad."

"Yankees are having a great spring training."

"Dad, there's something I need to tell you."

"Comin' out to face the Mariners in May."

"I've become a Christian."

"So I heard." He rolled his eyes. "What's that supposed to mean, anyway? What were you before, a Buddhist?"

"No, but I wasn't a Christian either. A Christian is someone who's confessed his sins and put his faith in Jesus Christ, and accepted his free gift of eternal—"

"Jordan, have you ever met my minister, Reverend Braun?"

Jordan turned toward his sister, who stood at the doorway with a distinguished middle-aged man with a clean-cut clerical look and matching collar.

"Uh, no. Hi. Nice to meet you."

"Remember Reverend Braun, Daddy?"

"Sure, how could I forget? Hello, Reverend."

"I'm delighted to see you, Stan...you're looking alert."

"I'm not dead yet, if that's what you mean."

"I'm sure you still have a long life ahead of you."

"Jordan was just preaching at me about Jesus."

"Oh? Well, we talked about spiritual matters ourselves, didn't we?"

"The reverend gave me great comfort, Jordan," his father said, in a way Jordan thought sounded sarcastic, but it was hard to tell. "He told me God loved me as I am, and I didn't need to change anything. He said there was nothing to be afraid of, that if I died I'd be welcomed to heaven. Isn't that right, Reverend?"

"Absolutely, Stan. Jesus is in all of us. And He promises all of us will go to heaven when we die."

"He read me a wonderful poem," his father said. "Something about a tree, and leaves changing color in the fall. It was so...*lovely.*" Now he knew his father was being sarcastic. "It would really choke you up, son. So I haven't been worrying any more. I know everything will be just peachy when I die. Isn't that nice?"

Jordan hesitated, looking up at his sister and her minister, then back at his father.

"Look, Dad, it's not that easy. I mean it's not automatic. You have to accept the gift. Jesus said, 'I am the way, the truth and the life, no one comes—'"

"Sorry, folks, you need to clear out." The nurse marched in and started moving things around. "Got to run a few tests on Stan. Besides, he needs his rest. Be better if you all gave him a break, okay?"

"Yeah," Jordan's dad said. "I could use a rest. Maybe see you later."

LETTER 31

Long Live Our Man in the Pulpit

My delectable Squaltaint,

Scumsuck is most fortunate to have stewardship of Reverend Braun. I drool just reading his file. This is a double-team assignment you'll enjoy. Since he's having an influence on Jordan's family, it should be a good learning experience for you.

I have no counsel beyond letting this man pursue the course he's set and making sure he's not distracted from it. What improvements could I suggest for a sludgebag who uses God words while disbelieving in God? He commandeers words from the forbidden book—casting an illusion of spirituality—when he doesn't believe them. Ingenious. He's a cloud without rain, blown along by our every wind.

He considers "simplistic" the forbidden message with its cross and blood. Since that's the only message powerful enough to transfer the vermin's citizenship from hell to heaven, we couldn't agree more! He practices the art form we first perfected—offering them rat poison wrapped in taffy. His is a chameleon theology, changing colors to blend in with the current surroundings. He's the perfect diversion to keep Fletcher's father from considering the Carpenter's claims.

Scumsuck's report tells me how Braun began the service last week: "Pray with me now to the heavenly parent, whoever you may conceive him or her to be."

Covering his bets, isn't he? That's what I love most about this brand of clergyman. They speak as if the universe were a democracy and they have the power to shape the Tyrant merely by casting their vote. A roomful of a hundred people pray to a hundred different gods—a female god, a chauvinist god, a Navajo god, an Anglo-Saxon god, a cross-dressing god, you name it. The Enemy created them in His image, and now they return the favor.

I'm delighted Reverend Braun dished out his assurances to Fletcher's father, though he's at his best with elderly women rather than men. Sometimes the tough old codgers see through the sappy veneer. I hope, though, Fletcher's father was genuinely deceived. The only thing better than robbing the Enemy's children of assurance is giving assurance to those who aren't the Enemy's children!

Braun believes he's serving mankind every time he makes a hospital visit to a dying patient or conducts a funeral assuring them death is nothing to fear. We eagerly await them over on this side, where we'll greet them on his behalf outside hell's gates. "I see Reverend Braun sent you—welcome to hell!"

I can hardly wait to meet the man himself tooth to throat. Meanwhile, I'll settle for Fletcher's father, who'll be coming soon.

It's much to your advantage that Fletcher's sister attends Braun's church, which is not to be confused with the forbidden squadron. Indeed, we might call it the preferred association. By all means, encourage everyone to attend this church!

His sister is excited about its positive, tolerant orientation. Erin's file describes her as enthusiastic, and reveals her brother takes her counsel seriously. Team up with Hackslay to suggest she invite Fletcher to her church. Yes, try to woo Fletcher to Reverend Braun's congregation. Convince him "Ryan's church is full of hypocrites." Of course, every place vermin gather is full of hypocrites, but don't let that occur to him.

The Carpenter spoke of a man who sowed good seed in a field, and while everyone was sleeping, his enemy came and sowed weeds among the wheat.

The operative phrase is "while everyone was sleeping." We work the night shift. And we don't plant weeds that look like weeds—what would be the point? We plant weeds that look like grain, so they can't separate the counterfeit from the genuine.

We imitate the forbidden squadron by offering a facsimile—the world wearing church clothes. Christianity Lite—all they've ever wanted in a church and less. The beautiful thing is, people come to Reverend Braun's assembly and believe it's the real thing.

Braun espouses what my adversary Amrael labeled "an atheism for cowards." The outright atheist rarely draws a following. His arrogance, materialism, and lack of belief in anything outside himself is consummately unattractive. Atheism is an empty cup crying out to be filled, while most religion is an empty cup appearing to be filled. This clergyman cloaks his atheism, his denial of the supernatural, under the garment of faith. While rejecting everything of importance embraced by the historic Christian church, he's an ordained "Christian" minister. A spokesman for a faith he doesn't embrace!

Don't underestimate false doctrine—the oldest strategies are the best. Some of our finest heretics operated in the early centuries, but leaders of the forbidden squadron rose up to oppose them. Indeed, they used the occasion of our heresies to teach the truth with clarity. Since the forbidden squadron in the west cares less about doctrine than ever before, we've succeeded. Who warns against "doctrines of demons" anymore? It isn't fashionable.

We're at our best when we speak through religious leaders. Remember that high priest Caiaphas? Chemosh and I were part of the triple team assigned to him by the Master. The grubworm declared it was expedient the Carpenter die, and masterminded—so he imagined—our plot to kill Him. The high priest, our collaborator.

Braun is our spy in the ranks, an infiltrator, a traitor to the Enemy's cause. He feeds his flock on poetry about trees and animals and seasonal changes and the wonders of nature (which he claims wasn't really created as the forbidden book says). He appeals to those who believe in mother nature, the goddess, the human community, global oneness, pantheism, New Age enlightenment. He offers a god who's a ball of putty, to be fashioned however men wish.

Reverend Braun quotes less from the forbidden book than the newspaper, current events, and popular songs. "Truth is progressive," he says, "always evolving."

He loves all that's new, while living in horror of the same old thing. Fortunately, it never dawns on him that truth by its nature is old, and what's new is usually error. Every new heresy is a departure from old truth, every new orthodoxy a return to old truth. Old error in new dress, that's our snake oil. Nobody peddles it better than Braun.

The Reverend demythologizes us along with everything else. Scumsuck reports in last week's sermon he said, "We must be one another's angels, protecting each other from the demons of harm thrusting themselves on our fellow man."

I had to write this out and post it on the board here at headquarters, so the staff could get a good laugh. What an idiot. But what an amazingly useful idiot.

He teaches the Bible is "true myth," that it's "true in its essence." What he means is, it's false historically, which is all that matters since Christianity is centered not in harmless ideas like love and tolerance, but dreaded historical realities like creation, fall, flood, exodus, incarnation, crucifixion, and resurrection.

Since the forbidden book purports to be historical truth and not myth, the congregation learns to distrust what it says. This is exquisite counterfeiting—people come to "church" to hear "truth" which undermines their belief in the book and the Carpenter. Do you see why I don't want the vermin to stay home from these services?

Consider another of Reverend Braun's statements: "Adam and Eve weren't real people, but it doesn't matter, for they teach us the real truth of free choice."

Do you see, Squaltaint? There wasn't a real garden, a real serpent, or even a real man and woman—so why should they believe there was a real God or the gospel message is real? If we can get them to disbelieve Genesis, it's just a matter of time before they disbelieve John 3:16.

A bonus—since the Carpenter believed the biblical accounts concerning the first man and woman, Reverend Braun makes Him out to be a fool. He smiles condescendingly at the man in his flock who holds the primitive notion of the virgin birth. He nods smugly at the old woman who believes the Enemy divided the Red Sea. Well, she's just not as educated as he is.

Braun explained in a sermon last month the feeding of the five thousand was actually a boy generously sharing his lunch, inspiring others to share their lunch with everyone else. "And isn't that really a greater miracle?" he asks with straight face. The only thing Braun takes literally is his own brilliance.

Somehow it works, though I can't fathom how. Why come to church when you don't believe what church is built on? Why not stay home and watch football? A God who cannot make the world in seven days, can't feed five thousand, can't send manna; surely he couldn't become a man, die for sins, and conquer death.

"Jesus rose in the heart of the apostles," Braun says. He finished his Easter sermon, "Though the body of Jesus lies in an unknown Palestinian grave, His deathless spirit goes marching on."

What genius. The man rises to spiritual heights while making an outright denial of Christianity's cornerstone!

Braun must at all costs maintain the vocabulary of the Enemy's historic faith. Let him use *church* for their weekly social gathering, *truth* for the latest psychobabble, *resurrection* for lilies blooming in the spring after the cold darkness of winter. Let him cloak his heresy in the words of orthodoxy and sentimental poetry. "Satan himself masquerades as an angel of light; it is not surprising then, if his servants masquerade as servants of righteousness." Couldn't have said it better myself!

Study Reverend Braun, Squaltaint. He's living proof of what we can accomplish. While draining the Enemy's words of substance, he uses their empty shells to give a Christian aura to all that he says and does. He immunizes them against the disease of Christianity by giving them little parts of the virus here and there.

Let the vermin never see what we see from here, that the Enemy removed this congregation's lampstand long ago. The fire was snuffed out. There's but one word written in the Tyrant's handwriting above this so-called church: "Ichabod." The glory has departed—the Enemy is long gone. His silence is music to our ears. Let this bland lifeless imitation pass for true Christianity. It serves us so well.

I implore you, Squaltaint, to restrain Scumsuck from his violent tendencies. Don't let him succumb to the temptation of killing this minister—he's of far too much value right where he is. Guard him well. We should no sooner dispose of him now than we would call home our finest operative in the pitch of battle. Braun's our mole, planted deep in Enemy territory. I've warned Scumsuck he must practice delayed gratification. There'll be plenty of time later to enjoy the man's misery.

Yes, keep Braun alive and in "the ministry," where he'll continue to influence hundreds, who in turn will mislead thousands more, including their children.

Thank Beelzebub for our man in the pulpit. With friends like the Reverend, the Carpenter hardly needs enemies like us.

Whatever you and Scumsuck do, don't let Reverend Braun convert to honest atheism. That would be a terrible loss to our cause.

Excelling in espionage,

—Lord Foulgrin

CHAPTER 32

GET OUT

"What's with these pictures, Daniel?" Jordan held them out to his son, trying not to look at them.

"Where'd you get them?"

"Your mom found them under your bed."

"She had no right."

"This isn't about her, it's about you. Why are you looking at this garbage?"

"Why not?"

"Because it's bad, that's why not. Because it's wrong. It teaches you to think about women in the wrong way."

"Oh, and you think about them the right way?"

"What do you mean by that?"

"I mean those videos downstairs, the ones you think were hidden in the storage room, by the guns."

"What videos?" Jordan asked, feeling the answer in his gut.

"Yeah, right. I'm sure they're Mom's. She must've hidden them."

"Look, this isn't good, Daniel. One day you're going to be married and this kind of stuff isn't going to help. You need to…respect women. "

"Like you?" Daniel asked.

"What do you mean by that?"

"Never mind."

"I've called and cancelled our Internet connection."

"You can't do that."

"I can't? I just did. Thirty minutes ago. And don't you ever tell me what I can and can't do."

"Get out of my room!"

Jordan grabbed Daniel and threw him down on the bed. He hit him hard on his rear end, one blow after the next. Daniel screamed. Jillian ran in the door.

"Get off him! You're beating him. Get off or I'll call the police!"

Jordan jumped up and looked at his daughter, then his son, then his throbbing right hand. He ran out into the living room, dropped to his knees and wept.

LETTER 32

Worship in the Forbidden Squadron

My devoted Squaltaint,

You recounted the church service you attended with Fletcher. Yes, I know it's a terrible place, with swarms of Elyon's self-righteous errand boys celebrating alongside the oblivious humans. All the more reason you must not let Fletcher go without you. It's your job to distract and confuse. Incite envy, lust, resentment, and self-righteousness right there in the service. You must sabotage his church experience in every way.

Though better known for their achievements with words such as tolerance, diversity, and choice, some of our semantics department's greatest victories have centered on religious terms, including worship.

You quote Fletcher as saying, "After worship, the pastor preached on Hebrews 3." He's picking up the jargon. Worship means song time, something sandwiched between announcements and message.

As much as I detest singing—I greatly prefer noise—as long as it's done thoughtlessly it's of no harm. If liking a certain style of music makes them feel vaguely religious, fine. If mindlessly reciting words in various pitches with a touch of sentiment gives them the illusion they've met the Enemy, good. That's of no more danger than if they sang "Puff the Magic Dragon."

If worship is for Fletcher merely a time slot that begins and ends, we win. If it's the preliminaries, fine. Make worship something he refers to, not something he does.

True worship is deadly dangerous. Having once worshiped the Enemy ourselves—the foul smell still plagues me—we can recall what worship did to us. It's entrapping, intoxicating. It grabs hold of them, changes them, reorients them toward the Enemy.

Through family conflicts, running late, and not finding a parking space, keep Fletcher from giving thought to worship until the moment he arrives. Let him come to church thirsty for social contact, gossip, or entertainment—anything but thirsty for the Enemy. If he does comes thirsty for Him, make sure he leaves without getting a drink.

Our job is never to let them know the true object of their thirst. That way we can flitter their minds from one substitute fountain to the next, even as they sit in church.

What we fear about the forbidden squadron is not the activities, not the eating of crackers and drinking of grape juice, or people dunked in water, as long as that's all they see in those things. If their songs are shallow and empty, or their hearts are, it's no threat to us.

Few songs mention their sins. They know nothing of "my sin is ever before me." If they truly worship, this quickly changes. They see the Enemy as He is, themselves as they are. You must prevent that. Our most strategic deception is causing them to see themselves as decent people, well suited for Christian living. Don't let Fletcher see that within him resides all the world's evils in embryo. If the vermin see themselves as they are, even for a moment, they might fall to their faces and weep at their unworthiness. The consequent outflow of power from Charis could sweep us off the deck of their lives. It's happened, believe me. I have nightmares.

Of the songs you report they sang, a few are mildly disturbing, but only one is of immense concern—"Alas and did my Savior bleed, and did my Sovereign die; would he devote that sacred head for such a worm as I?... My God, why would you shed your blood, so pure and undefiled, to make a sinful one like me your chosen precious child?"

These words terrify me. Any song portraying the Enemy as big and the vermin as small is dangerous. The theme of human depravity, coupled with the Enemy's grace, must be avoided above all. The combination is deadly. That Fletcher started crying and Diane took his hand are bad signs. Don't forget how often our plans for their ruin have been dashed on the precipice of the Enemy's grace.

Convince Fletcher the term "worm" is inappropriate and offensive, since it undermines his all-important sense of self-worth. We've managed to get the words revised in many hymnbooks, robbing the song of its meaning. (His sister's church, of course, will not sing such songs at all. Reverend Braun won't permit it.)

Consider that despicable song written by the slave trader. We've managed to get many to change "such a wretch as I" to "such a soul as I." The campaign continues—several of my colleagues are in the lobbying group. If they must sing these songs, at least we can get them to sing our versions. For whenever we portray the maggot-feeders as less than wretched, it makes the Enemy's grace less than amazing. What vast gains through changing a word or two!

Keep the vermin from the book's stated motive for coming to worship: "to gaze upon the beauty of the Lord." Let them gaze instead upon the old woman with the purplish hair, the long-nosed double-chinned man in the maroon jacket, the beautiful woman sitting across the aisle. Let Fletcher focus on the businessman slipping down into his seat, and laugh at the snort when he wakes abruptly.

Tense them up so they shoot scornful looks at the mother whose baby cries. The fools are so easily distracted. Our efforts to make them resent children and become intolerant to their cries have been effective. It didn't used to accomplish much, but nowadays taking a little poke at the brats in church can work wonders.

Let Fletcher gaze upon the preacher and his loud tie, the lovely swaying soloist in that gorgeous dress, the choir and their new robes, or wrinkled ones. Let him gaze upon the flowers in front of the pulpit, the newly polished piano, the ceiling fan, or the peeling paint on the wall. Just never let him gaze upon the Enemy. Captivate Fletcher with everyone and everything but Him. (Hackslay's job with the vermin's sister is quite different—he should do whatever he can to help her pay attention to Reverend Braun's words. In that church, calm the babies. The last thing you want is distraction from our message! At Braun's church it's the Enemy's warriors who make creaking noises and cause old men to snort and babies to cry; anything to get people's minds off the message.)

See that Fletcher remains unmoved, leaving the service no closer to the Tyrant, no more eager to know Him than when he came.

The Enemy tells them worship must be done in spirit and truth. Plant in your vermin's mind wrong thoughts about the Enemy. Limit his worship to externals, so it becomes empty formalism. The Enemy longs for worship that engages emotions and thought, heart and head. Let it engage neither or—if necessary—only one or the other. Never both.

The vermin teach their children to swim and play piano and do math. Fortunately they never teach them to worship. To counterfeit, you must understand the genuine article. Real worship is full of thought. It's what they once called "musement," musing upon the Enemy. For that we substitute "amusement," without thought, mere rhythm, sentiment, and entertainment. Let them focus on musical proficiency, fine performance. Just don't let them think about the Enemy.

Never allow Fletcher to be "lost" in worship. Never let him realize the connection of his body and spirit, and the impossibility true worship won't affect his countenance, posture, or movement. Keep him standing straight up, motionless, like a palace guard dutifully displaying no emotion. Let him be so self-conscious rather than God-conscious he views any demonstrative expression as "losing control." By all means, make sure he remains in control. (Consider the alternative!)

Or, just as well, let these vermin flail their appendages in mindless frenzy, outdoing one another in vain attempts to get excited about the Enemy, when in fact they're excited not about Him but themselves and how well they're dancing and how intensely spiritual they appear.

If they hold themselves back in worship, convince them it's a cultural phenomenon—North Americans aren't as expressive as Africans. Never let the morons notice that at their ball games they routinely jump, cheer, scream, and raise hands in a way that would befuddle Africans. If they gave it a moment's thought, they might figure out they're simply much more excited about football than they are the Enemy.

One thing we cannot permit is for people to be so immersed in worship they neither know nor care whether their hands are raised or their feet are moving. For if they're lost in worship—whether in stunned silence or unconscious physical expression—then they're lost to themselves and their culture and the preferences of others and the tyranny of the moment and worst of all, they are lost to us. Once they know the delight of self-forgetfulness, they long to lose themselves in the Enemy again and again. It's hideous...and addictive.

Let them ask themselves, "What did I get out of church today?" Let them never ask: "What did He get out of church today?"

Whatever reasons they go to church, and whatever experiences they have there, make little difference to us, except one. If they end up gazing upon the Enemy, meeting Him personally, giving Him praise and adoration and glory, it is the worst possible scenario.

If despite—or, worse yet, as a result of—what happens in church they actually see the Enemy, it's time to tremble. For then all heaven will break loose.

Trusting you will not fail me
(and making plans if you do),

—Lord Foulgrin

CHAPTER 33

THE TALK

Quit beating yourself up," Diane said to Jordan. "You apologized to the kids. You even asked their forgiveness. What more can you do?"

"I wanted to teach Dan respect, give him some discipline, but I lost control. I could've hurt him. I've lost them both, Diane. Jillian hates me."

"She doesn't hate you. She's just angry. And scared."

"If I'd known being a parent was so tough, I never would have made the choice."

"What's that supposed to mean?"

"Just what I said."

"Are you telling me I should get the test?"

"I don't know. Ryan and Jodi will be here in an hour. What if we ask them?"

"It's a little personal, isn't it?"

"They can handle it. They've had family problems."

"They have? I mean, I know they're struggling with Jodi's cancer, but their marriage seems perfect, and their kids are perfect."

"Nobody's perfect."

Two hours later they'd finished the meat loaf dinner and were sitting in the family room talking and laughing. Jodi and Ryan had offered good advice on dealing with the kids. Jordan felt encouraged.

"I want to ask you something else," Diane said. Jordan saw the tension on her face. "I don't know exactly how to say this, but...I'm pregnant."

"No kidding? That's wonderful," Jodi said, then laughed as if this was the best possible news.

"Congratulations," Ryan said.

"Wait, you don't understand. I'm forty-one years old, and we weren't planning to have another child. The doctor says we should have an amniocentesis test because the baby may have Down syndrome or something else.

So...what do you think?"

"I think it's a challenge to take care of a baby," Jodi said. "And it certainly isn't easy raising a child with special needs. But God has obviously chosen to give you this baby—He knows what's best for you and the child. Of course, you'll need some help—and you can count on me. Auntie Jodi's here for free baby-sitting and somebody to laugh and cry with whenever you need it."

Diane stared at her, trying to assimilate her words. "But...well thanks, but we're not to that point yet. What we're asking is if we should have that test, to see if the baby's normal."

"Well," Jodi said, "I don't think the test is the issue. If the test said your baby has a handicap, would you let him live or would you kill him?"

Diane's face turned red. "I don't appreciate you using that language."

"I'm sorry, Diane, I didn't mean to offend you. Really. What language would you use?"

"Terminate the pregnancy."

"Okay, but—please don't take this wrong—you've been referring to a baby inside of you, wondering whether the baby's normal and all. You *know* there's a baby, don't you? What would happen to your baby if you terminated the pregnancy?"

A long pause.

"He'd die," Jordan finally whispered. "He'd die, wouldn't he?"

"Yes," Jodi said. "That's why I was jumping ahead to offer help taking care of him. Because, Diane, I just know you don't really want your baby to die."

Silence fell.

"What do you think, Diane?" Jodi finally asked.

Diane sighed. "Well, everybody else—my sister, Jordan's sister, my two best girlfriends—all advised me to terminate the pregnancy. Jordan's sister even said it was the Christian thing to do."

"You're kidding."

"No. Her pastor's big on prochoice. But, anyway, the truth is I've been leaning toward keeping the baby. I just thought I was the only one. I haven't been able to tell what Jordan thinks—he doesn't seem to know himself." She looked at Jordan uncomfortably. "I told myself if the two of you thought I should consider an abortion, I'd go ahead and do it. But you didn't, so I'm not going to. I don't want to live with knowing I did something like that. I've already had to live with it for twenty years. I don't want to ever do it again."

Jordan didn't look up. Finally he took Diane's hand.

"For some reason, this whole thing was cloudy to me," Jordan said. "But suddenly the clouds have lifted. I don't know why I couldn't see it. God made that baby and gave him to us. There's no way I'd get rid of him. I'm with you, Di."

He watched the tears stream down her face, then put his arms around her, forgetting anyone else was in the room.

LETTER 33

Accusations

My protégé Squaltaint,

I was delighted to hear about Fletcher lashing out at his brat. I'd like to throttle him myself. As long as you can keep him from asking forgiveness, or convince him he's failed so badly there's no use even trying, we have him.

As for his children, nothing more effectively keeps vermin from the Carpenter's Father than an earthly father who makes a big deal out of being a Christian, but acts like a jerk.

As usual, play the dual role of Excuser and Accuser. Excuse Fletcher of sins he's not confessed; accuse him of sins he has. Riddle him with false guilt while keeping him from feeling true guilt. Make him think he's free of guilt he hasn't confessed and in bondage to guilt the Enemy's already forgiven him.

Keep a long list of excuses to supply him with every time he disobeys. It's his wife or son's fault, never his. Or accuse him of the very sins you enticed him to. Whenever he does what you want, accuse him for having done it.

Slander God to men and men to God. You've been filing your accusations, but they're sketchy and routine. Step it up. Remember, our Master brings their sins to Charis day and night. Accuse Fletcher of sins the Enemy's forgiven. Accuse him of sins he never committed. Rack him with guilt and self-punishment. Don't let him accept the Enemy's atonement—make him attempt to repeat it.

And don't forget the little things. As valuable as terror may be, it's ongoing anxiety that wears them down. A few big things sink them less effectively than a bunch of little ones. So plague them, paralyze them with fear. Enjoy it while you can, but realize you cannot sustain psychological terrorism. And there's the danger in their desperation they'll turn to...Him.

Put as many thorns in his flesh as you can. But remember, torturing their souls is more effective than torturing their bodies. There are pain relievers for physical suffering, but depths of depression, anxiety, loneliness, rage, and bitterness are not so easily treated. Most importantly, they put their minds on themselves, and off the Enemy.

Unfortunately, you won't get Fletcher to wale on his son every night, not for now anyway. But you can wear him down with the daily grind, the little indulgences, the mundane compromises. Go for the great sins if you can, but never underestimate the cumulative power of the little ones.

Your illustrious mentor,

—Lord Foulgrin

CHAPTER 34

NEEDING HELP

"Great meat loaf," Jodi said to Diane.

"Yeah, outstanding," Ryan said.

"As usual," Jordan added. They helped clean up and settled into the living room.

"Last week when you came over..." Jordan cleared his throat. "You were a big help to us. But you keep finding out things about us, our past and all. Maybe you're discovering we're not the kind of people you should be hanging around."

Jodi laughed. "Sorry, Jordan, I'm not making fun of you. It's just that, who do you think we are? If you want to start putting sins out on the table, I'll bet ours stack up higher than yours."

Jordan and Diane stared at her.

"The wonderful thing is Christ has forgiven us. I know you've experienced that, Jordan, but as time goes on Ryan and I keep discovering old sins and committing new ones that need to be forgiven too. The Bible says, 'If we confess our sins, he is faithful and just and will forgive us our sins and purify us from all unrighteousness.' You don't have to bear the guilt of your past decisions. It's like what we were talking about at women's Bible study, Diane. That's why Christ went to the cross for you. Do you believe that?"

"I think I'm beginning to."

"God offers you the gift. All you need to do is ask His forgiveness and reach out and accept His gift. Have you done that?"

"Well, I don't think so."

"Do you want to do it now?"

"How?"

"I'll pray, then you pray after me."

"Out loud?"

"Sure. We're all friends here. Prayer is just talking to God. Lord," Jodi prayed, before anyone's head was bowed, "Diane needs You, just like we all do. She wants to confess her sin and put her faith in You, in what You did for her on the cross. Please help her right now as she talks to You."

There was a long pause. "I'm not very good at this," Diane whispered.

"You don't have to be," Jodi said. "Just tell the Lord what's on your mind."

"Jesus, I don't know much, but I know I've done some bad things. And I know we really need help, our marriage and the kids. I'm so worried about Daniel and Jillian. But I guess this is about me, God. So I confess my sins, including when we terminated...when we killed our first baby." She broke into a sob. Jodi got up and sat next to her, putting her arms around her, weeping with her. "So anyway, please forgive me, God. Thanks for dying on the cross for my sins. Help me to love You."

The four of them sat in the living room, thinking they were alone. But in the universe next door, great cheers erupted. Joy flowed over in Charis. If a man listened carefully, he could have heard the applause of heaven.

LETTER 34

Message from the Enemy's Agent!

My disciple Squaltaint,

I've outdone myself. Through means I cannot divulge, I've intercepted a letter from your vermin's guardian!

Jaltor writes to Amrael, his commander, my comrade before the rebellion. Note the superior tones, the self-righteousness, the sentimental posturing, the false humility. How did we put up with them?

I'm troubled by his report, as there are some significant discrepancies between it and yours. Have you been holding out on me? Where's your report on the woman's conversion Jaltor refers to?

Take note of Jaltor's derogatory comments about you, Squaltaint. I hope this inside information equips and motivates you to fight the battle for Fletcher with greater vigor. Take revenge on this sword-kissing Jaltor. Taunt him with the fact that, thanks to my brilliant covert action, we know exactly what he's up to.

—Lord Foulgrin

Prince Amrael,

I'm pleased with Jordan's growing passion for Elyon Most High. He has shared his faith three times now. He meets regularly with Ryan, a wonderful role model. Adam's race is led more by footprints than guideposts. Ryan is giving Jordan footprints to follow.

Diane's conversion took my breath away. Only Elyon's Spirit can pierce the hard shell of their hearts. When she accepted His gift and asked His forgiveness, Elshar and I embraced. We heard the cheers of Charis. I heard your voice among them, my prince. Her transformation injected us with new vigor and renewed hope for this needy family.

With Ryan's aid, Jordan is learning to be a servant leader for his wife and children. They've determined to open Elyon's Word and pray with them twice a week. The children are unenthused but watching carefully. Jordan lost his temper and alienated his children, yet his repentance showed them he was a different man. When he asked them to forgive him, their hearts were touched by Elyon. When, in front of his wife and son, he destroyed those videos Daniel found and asked their forgiveness again, I rejoiced.

It's a privilege to observe Zalor with Ryan. I've learned much from him, as well as Elshar. Jordan and Diane are planning to attend a conference with Ryan and Jodi, to strengthen their marriage. I look forward to assisting the Spirit.

Despite all this, Amrael, I believe I've failed Jordan—and Elyon. There is so much I haven't been able to help him grasp.

If only Jordan could see Elyon as He really is; if he could catch but a glimpse, all his wrong thinking would fall to the ground like old garments. I long for him to know the real world, the universe outside the dark bottle in which he's trapped. How disconnected and confused he often is.

If this is true even of Christians, I shudder at the dark state of the unredeemed. How can they go through the day without falling to their face in despair, crying out to Elyon for mercy?

Though Jordan has the Spirit within, he looks at the world with blinders on. He seems unaware that he walks on a battlefield, under relentless attack. Indeed, since becoming a Christian he's heard of "spiritual warfare" just once, and then it was restricted to exorcism. He doesn't see warfare is woven into his daily life. Even Ryan has been misled into thinking demonic activities aren't widespread in America because there are so many Christians. He fails to see our enemies haven't vacated the battlefield, but have adopted new strategies, not as conspicuous, yet all too obvious to those with eyes to see.

How can I help Jordan realize if he fails to take on Elyon's armor he won't avoid the battle, he will simply lose it. In the absence of clear teaching, he falls back on his old thinking, that believing in warring spirits reflects a primitive prescientific worldview. (Of course it does—it just happens to be correct.)

These western Christians are unprepared to address what primitive cultures realize is vital—how to deal with evil beings in the spirit realm. In some respects, unregenerate primitives know more about the unseen world than the Christians coming to evangelize them! I want Jordan to be freed from such blindness.

How can he not see the real universe? After all these millennia of working with the image-bearers I still do not understand. But this I know—Elyon loves them to an extent we cannot comprehend.

I hear Squaltaint's incessant ranting, threatening me with some new secret strategy he's learned from Foulgrin and waving his commander's letters at me, daring me to come after them. I also hear the hollowness in his voice, the desperation. He's a shell of what he once was. Still, Jordan's old habits and the world's propaganda make Squaltaint's job much easier.

Not as often as I'd like am I permitted to put my hand into the physical realm. But over the years I've saved his life three times and managed to protect him again in his recent car accident. Two weeks ago I intervened when Squaltaint tried to drop the electrical wire on him. Jordan didn't even know. Last night he sat on the recliner alone, flipping television stations. He was weary and morally vulnerable. Squaltaint was working him over. I tried to persuade him to turn it off, tried to call to his mind the words of Elyon and the counsel of Ryan and the men's leader at his church. But his mind was numbed and his guard down. I tried to move his finger to the OFF button accidentally, something I did the night we first drew him to his mother's Bible. This time I could not.

Finally I managed to touch the wiring and interfere with reception. He gave up and joined his wife in bed, but the escape was narrow. If Jordan keeps walking on the edge, he's bound to drop off. He prays "help me not to fall into sin," then proceeds to walk within inches of the precipice on a windy day. What's he thinking? He wants to get as close as possible to sin without actually doing it. But this only assures he will end up doing it.

I've tried to turn Jordan's attention to Daniel, but he doesn't take time to enter his son's life. Every day, the fallen warriors lure Daniel further into their grasp. I fear for what the boy may do to himself and others. I'm appalled at his fixation on the powers of darkness. I hear the hideous laughter of the boy's enemies. If Jordan could only see what's happening, grasp what's at stake, surely he would drop everything to give him the attention and guidance he so desperately needs.

It is hard here, Amrael, harder than in ages past. Adam's race once had to leave their homes to feed their minds on such evil, but now it comes at them relentlessly, through airwaves and phone lines. It's so difficult to protect them, to convince them to guard their hearts. If only they could see the consequences, if only they could grasp how it hurts the King who died for them, surely then they would not permit those images into their homes and minds.

How can I convince Jordan he must claim his home for the King? How can I persuade him for the good of his family he must cleanse his home of the evil influences freely entering it?

Jordan still thinks Diane doesn't understand him. He doesn't realize she too is lonely and confused, though she's basking in the initial glory of having embraced Elyon's gift. They expect each other to meet their deepest needs, and are disappointed with each other for failing to do so. Elyon's Spirit seeks to persuade Jordan that the King alone can meet his needs, and it's neither right nor fair for him to expect Diane to. As for his relationship with his secretary, I fear this is my worst failure. He does not seem to understand how perilously close he is to disaster. I confess, Amrael, I despair to know what more to do for him.

I try to prod Jordan to immerse himself in Christ's body, to drink deeply of the Book, to saturate his soul in the beauty of Elyon. Sometimes I get through. Often I don't.

I try to persuade him to say yes to serving at his church, whether parking lot duty or nursery or assisting with a fifth grade boys Sunday school class. I've not been able to convince him to jump in and serve. I know the Spirit is at work in His quiet ways, but battle fatigue settles upon me.

Forgive me, my captain; I do not mean to complain. It is my privilege to serve Elyon. I would gladly hold sword high and defend the small ones for a thousand years without rest if that would please Him and my strength could hold. Still, it is merciful of the King to grant us leave in Charis between assignments.

Whether it's in many years or much sooner, I look forward to walking the streets of Charis again with you and my comrades. Oh, to breathe the air of heaven, free of sulfur. It is hard living in the Shadowlands, in this blindness and rebellion, for even a day. But over decades it becomes exceedingly difficult. All places that are not heaven have the cold, metallic taste of hell.

I see the twisted faces of Prince Beelzebub's army. Squaltaint and his comrades attack Jordan and his family, whispering their lies. I remember what they were and shudder at what they've become. Knowing I too could have betrayed Elyon makes me fall to my knees and renew my devotion to Him.

I wonder sometimes why our Lord allows these tiny image-bearers to heap abuse upon Him, to slander His name, to break His commandments. Like vicious serpents they spit their poison in the King's face. They vent their rage in vile blasphemies. Skiathorus is the only place in the universe that denies Him. I wonder why He doesn't allow us to raise our swords and mount the steeds of Charis, invade the corrupted realm with all our armies to once and for all put an end to this cosmic insult. Why does He hold back our hands? Why has He restrained our wrath...and His?

I know the Book says that day will come, that Elyon is patient, wanting them to come to repentance. But I live for the day of vengeance. Forgive my impatience. You are far greater than I, you who have sat in council with the Holy Three and Michael and Gabriel, you understand these mysteries far better than I.

Greet my comrades Zyel and Talor in Charis, and also Elzar and Fortrel down here in the Shadowlands, when you next issue them directives. Last I knew they were stationed with a Christian family in Yemen. They are still under your command, are they not? I used to see them a decade ago when Jordan worked that year with an oil company. They face such opposition in that monolithic darkness.

The day Jordan leaves this world, Amrael, I offer you my services. You may send me to Yemen to raise sword with Elzar and Fortrel against the dark forces. I will gladly postpone my return to Charis for the privilege of standing with them. Where the battle rages, there is the soldier's place.

There are rumblings the King has begun a great and mighty movement, water flowing beneath the stony surface of Islam's stronghold. Soon, they say, it may erupt and turn the tide of that battle, bringing many to Himself. I would be honored to stand beside my comrades and fight for those small ones the King has chosen.

Please tell my Lord I live each moment in anticipation of my return to Him, or His return to the Shadowlands. I speak to Him often. I know He hears me, but I long to see Him again, to feel His hand upon my shoulder. I yearn to hear His words, for they are life and breath to me. It is not easy being away from Him so long. Though He's present everywhere, the chaotic outrages of this world make it difficult to focus on Him.

I've followed your advice and have been writing for Jordan an account of his life and my service to him. I will present it to him on the other side, when finally I can speak with him face to face.

I remind myself often of your counsel that the battles of these dark years will enhance the brightness of the eternal light. Our delight is not only in being at the place we are, but in knowing the Adventure will never end, and therefore the Joy will never end. As Gabriel has sung in the courts of Charis, "When the great nebula of Orion scatters by the wind of the Spirit, when the star systems of Andromeda collapse upon themselves and breathe no more, the Adventure will still be young."

I am so ancient that in comparison Jordan is but a newborn child. Yet when my knowledge is compared to Elyon's, it is no different than Jordan's, no different than if I had been born this very moment. We are all creatures—only He is the Uncreated. *Elyon miriel o aeron galad—chara domina beth charis o aleathes celebron!*

I sing the ancient language to remind me not only of what was, but of the greater that is yet to be—the celebration that is Charis.

Today Jordan read a few verses about Charis in the Book. I tried to infuse him with what I've known firsthand, but I couldn't grab hold of his mind. His notion of heaven is so vague, so foreign. He imagines he will float aimlessly about, looking back longingly at his time spent on earth, the "real world." He thinks Charis will be boring! Where do they get such ideas? Jordan doesn't understand when he opens his eyes in Charis and looks back, it will seem like awakening from a dream, to what is at last the real world, the one he was made for.

I suppose I shouldn't expect them to long for immortality, they who don't know what to do on a rainy afternoon. But inside they do long for it—if only they knew what their empty hearts crave! They long for a Person and a Place.

Even now, if he would take the time to look around, to really look, he could see earth is crammed with hints of heaven, little foretastes of the real world.

The Book warns us the adversary slanders God's person, His people, and His place. The evil ones have succeeded in perverting even the church's view of Charis. What am I to do, Amrael, in the face of such monumental deception? Boredom in Charis? Lovers are never bored when together, for their delight is in each other. Our Beloved takes pleasure in creating new and better showcases to display His wonders. Charis is a fathomless repository of intrigue, an unending succession of delightful ventures.

How can I make Jordan see boredom exists only where creatures would make themselves what they are not and refuse to acknowledge what they are, gutting the world of wonder and leaving no riches to treasure and no realms to explore. Boredom in hell? Always. On earth? Sometimes. In heaven? Never!

If Jordan had even a faint glimpse of this now, it could transform him.

One of his new church friends told him recently, "Some Christians are so heavenly minded they're of no earthly good." Wasn't it Foulgrin who invented that saying? How can I make Jordan see the only way to be of earthly good is to be heavenly minded? How can I persuade him to live in light of eternity before he leaves Skiathorus, the land of second chances?

In every waking moment, why does he not long for, envision in every night's dream, the place the Carpenter promised He'd build for him? Why can't he grasp that every day the King is preparing heaven for him, and preparing him for heaven?

I long for Jordan to realize he need not wait until he dies to learn how he should have lived. Oh, that he would learn now while there is still time to change.

Amrael, with wisdom so far beyond mine, tell me what I can do to convince Jordan earth knows no sorrow heaven cannot heal. How can I help him experience Elyon's transcendent joy? How can I persuade him to live now in anticipation of the boundless glory to come?

How can I prompt him to look beyond the moment and see the unseen?

To the Bridegroom's glory,

Jalton

CHAPTER 35

THE HIKE

Daniel walked, face red, eyes straight ahead. Jordan wondered if he'd been right insisting they go on a hike together. His son had loved this sort of thing when he was younger. He always asked if they could go hiking. Jordan recalled how seldom he'd taken him and wished he could live those days over again. He wished he had a second chance.

"Hey," Jordan said, pointing down at the stream below them. "Look at those beavers patching up their dam."

Daniel made a point of barely glancing and quickly walking on.

Lord, I've lost my son. Help me get him back. Help me get him to You.

Suddenly Daniel froze, his gazed fixed on something off the trail. A wide-eyed six-point buck stared at them curiously. He chewed a few leaves and snorted, never taking his eye off them. Suddenly he bounded away as if chased by something unseen.

"Cool," Daniel said.

Jordan couldn't remember the last time he'd seen his son smile, not the cruel smile of cynicism but the spontaneous smile of joy.

After they'd hiked another hour, they stopped to open the sacks Diane packed for them. Jordan took a few bites of the meat loaf sandwich.

"You know, I look at the deer and those beavers and all these trees and everything, and I think about how God created it all, how it tells us about His beauty and greatness."

"What's with this God stuff?"

"What do you mean?"

"You never used to talk about God."

"No, I didn't. My beliefs have changed, son."

Daniel gave him that junior high "whatever" look.

"How about you, Daniel; do you believe in God?"

"No. I believe in nature, I guess. Evolution. Maybe karma, I don't know.

I've read about it on a couple of Web sites, you know. The cosmos is everything, everything there's ever been and ever will be. That's what we learned in the cosmos unit at school. You know, Carl Sagan?"

"But if there's no God, do you think there's any difference between men and animals?"

"We're pretty much the same, I guess, just a little more advanced. But who's to say we're better than deer or beavers? Speciesism, that's what they called it in the diversity seminar. You know, there's racism, sexism, and speciesism—believing humans are better than other life forms."

"But surely you believe humans are more valuable than animals."

"Why? We're all just animals anyway. What makes us better?"

"People have souls."

Daniel smirked. "Science has proven there's no such thing as a soul."

"How has it proven that?"

"Well, it doesn't show up in experiments or anything. I mean, nothing really leaves a body when it dies."

"You mean, nothing you can see, right?"

"Well, if you can't see it, it isn't real, is it?"

"Well, I believe—"

"Can we just keep going? I've got to be at Adam's by 6:30."

LETTER 35

Visitation

My familiar spirit Squaltaint,

I went back to Brittany's house. She's been renting occult videos and watching them by herself. (At least, she thinks she's been by herself.) Last night she and Raketwist and Jillian and I watched one together.

We've claimed Brittany's bedroom as our territory. Because of the beachhead she's surrendered to us, our power in that room is magnified. Our ability to touch her thoughts there has grown immensely.

I've established visitation rights, coming to my Brittany in her dreams three nights in a row. Now she's afraid to sleep. She's not under the Enemy's protection. She's mine, Squaltaint, and I will have her. I'll feed every dark impulse that comes on her. The more she thirsts, the more I'll give her saltwater and the more desperate she'll become.

I'll toy with her a little longer, suggesting her dilemmas would be solved by a simple act of suicide. I'm thinking of a group suicide, a pact with Ian at least. If Jillian continues to progress, I'll try to pull her in too.

The Carpenter called the Master a "murderer from the beginning…a liar and the father of lies." He said, "when he lies he speaks his native language." The Tyrant intended this as an insult. I take it as a compliment.

The longer you do something, the better you get at it. How good are we at lying? So good it's our first language. But never forget we're bilingual—our second language is truth. Use it selectively to create the most persuasive context for your lies.

The Carpenter claimed His sheep know His voice. They won't follow a stranger because they don't recognize his voice. You see what this means? To mislead the Christian vermin, we must make our voice sound like the Enemy's. It's a kind of ventriloquism. We use credible and familiar voices, such as Reverend Braun's, to speak our words.

The Enemy is monolingual. He speaks only the language of truth. This gives us a tremendous advantage. We can use both truth and lies, whichever serves us better.

The Carpenter was correct in linking our murders to our lies. Learn from this connection. Our greatest accomplishment is generating lies convincing enough to facilitate murders. Whether the murder of Jews, children, a bedridden parent, or the murder of self, we must find just the right lies to convince them murder is the reasonable course of action. The more we murder, the easier the deception becomes. As our puppet Stalin said, "One death is a tragedy, a million deaths is a statistic." (Now that he's subsumed under hell's statistics, I suspect his viewpoint has changed.)

Distraught teenagers are particularly susceptible. I've already forwarded to Raketwist my list of lies for Brittany in hopes we can take her down, and Jillian with her.

I feel alive, Squaltaint. I smell the girl's blood in the air. I can taste the misery I'll bring to her. I'm the cat; she's the mouse. I'll keep playing with her until the time is right...then I'll swallow her whole.

What are her chances of escaping me? A snowball's chance in hell.

Carefully selecting my lies,

—Lord Foulgrin

CHAPTER 36

GOING TO KILL ME

It's 3:00 A.M. on a school night, Brit. My parents are going to kill me. I have to get home. Are you okay? I can't leave until I know you're going to make it."

"I'll be all right," she said to Jillian. She smiled, looking for a moment like the old Brittany. "Really. I'll cry myself to sleep. You know, it's happened before. I'll feel better in the morning."

"Okay, I'll see you in English. Don't be late…don't want to mess with Mugavero again." They both laughed. After shutting the front door, Jill ran to her car.

Brittany watched the taillights disappear into the darkness. She pulled a notepad out of her purse and reexamined her options.

Her parents were both out of town on business. The car made sense. Easy. Pretty quick. No mess. She went out into the garage.

Brittany started the car and revved the motor, garage door shut. She wondered which would be quicker, windows down or up. A few minutes later she lost consciousness.

LETTER 36

Our Fairy Tale about Origins

My tiring Squaltaint,

You pout that it isn't fair the Ghost works independently of the warriors. You say Rosefang and you appeared to be defeating Diane, and the next thing you know she's a citizen of Charis. (A fact I first learned from Jaltor's letter, I remind you.) You insist it should all come down to a toe-to-toe battle between the bootlicks and us, with the Ghost having the decency to stay out of it.

Well, Squaltaint, I have news for you—the universe isn't fair. Deal with it!

I'm nonplussed to hear this Jodi has taken Diane under her wretched little wing. She has her at a women's Bible study, no less, the kind where they actually study and pray? Diane is forming new alliances and enjoying it. And to top it off, she met a woman who introduced her to her own Down syndrome brat, and they had a delightful visit?

Why am I not surprised?

Your only good news is that Diane had an unpleasant encounter with the pastor's wife, who asked her to step out of the room where they had the book table, because she was drinking coffee and the rules say no coffee in carpeted rooms. The pastor's wife, no doubt, hasn't given it a second thought, but I'm delighted Diane's still mulling over her hurt and embarrassment.

Pick at the scab and turn it into anger and resentment. Use it as a wedge to pry them from this church. One snowball starts the avalanche; the little things grow into big ones.

From modest beginnings like this, we've turned many of them into consumers, moving around and sampling from the smorgasbord of squadrons, looking for the best preaching and music and programs. Let one bad experience lead to another until they become professional church critics, not realizing the problem with churches is they consist of people like themselves.

A recent communiqué says your vermin's pastor has been targeted by an assault team of four. Materialism, egotism, or good old-fashioned adultery can discredit the Enemy and disillusion converts like the Fletchers. Inspire church members to treat pastors like people did the Carpenter—worship them or crucify them, or first one then the other.

If you can, link the Fletchers with gossips and legalists, who always find a cause other than the Enemy's. Befriend them with those embittered because the church hasn't gotten a pipe organ or expanded the nursery or uses too many or too few old hymns. Make their leaders imagine themselves above criticism and closed to advice. Nothing pleases us more than good church fights.

You say the Fletchers, influenced by Ryan and Jodi, have been thinking about the forbidden book's account of creation. They've begun to question society's view of life's origins. Obviously we have vested interests in the status quo position. It was, after all, our idea.

I recall when we first came up with it in the think tank—entertaining as it was, most of us thought it couldn't possibly work. Who would believe such a thing? The notion of blind origins and self-generation is inherently ridiculous. But we underestimated their gullibility. Human minds can be made to believe anything. Evolution is our fairy tale for adults. We selectively utilize certain facts and ignore vast numbers of others, then present our data as if it constitutes an unassailable reality. And they buy it!

I see from your report this is so engrained in young Daniel that when Fletcher tries to talk to him about God, they aren't speaking the same language. For if there's no Creator, then what can the word God mean? Nothing and anything.

Unfortunately, after a century of nearly universal acceptance in educated nations, our theory is quietly breaking down. Too many scientists are pointing out that the complex machinery in human cells cannot possibly be explained by Darwinian evolution. They can, however, be explained perfectly by intelligent design and special creation.

But don't worry, Squaltaint. Most vermin will ignore these truths for another few decades. By then we will have replaced Darwinian evolution with something else that doesn't require belief in the Enemy. (Such as, "Sure, it's intelligent design, and yes, evolution can't account for it, but creation by aliens can, so there.")

You must not think of this issue in scientific terms, but moral ones. Macroevolution was tailor-made by our propaganda department to appeal to their passionate desire not to be held accountable.

If the Enemy is not their Creator, then He's not their Judge. And that's the bottom line, isn't it? What they most fear and despise is moral accountability. They'll gladly embrace any theory removing this built-in sense they must answer for how they've lived. They'll cheerfully overlook such details as the fossil record's lack of transitional forms, the billions of missing links that should be there but aren't. They'll resolutely ignore the lack of living transitional forms that should be everywhere in their world. They gladly embrace this illogic in exchange for believing there's no Creator and therefore they can live however they want.

But this is only the beginning. If we convince them their world began without a Creator, it means the world isn't special. People aren't special either, for what can be special about a random accident?

Once they accept our premise, they cannot refute our subsequent logic. Why not destroy a person who is no more than an accident? Why not destroy a world that has no purpose, no meaning? If there's no Creator, there are no moral imperatives to govern their behavior. There's nothing to answer for because there's no one to answer to.

We've even turned the human vices of exploiting, killing, and stealing into a maxim describing how life works—the "survival of the fittest."

Consider children killing children in gangs, streets, homes, playgrounds, and schools. We hate children. We've always labored to inspire adults, especially parents, to kill children. But there's something uniquely wonderful about children killing each other!

We've blinded adults to the fact children are simply living out the low regard for human life they themselves teach them. They ridicule moral standards, then turn around and expect their children to act morally. They teach children they're in essence no different than animals, then they're stunned and bewildered when their children kill each other like...animals! They wonder, "Why don't our children listen to us?" In fact, their children *are* listening to them. That's exactly why they're gripped with violence and despair!

Are we good or what?

They teach their children they're the accidental products of time, chance, and natural forces, formed in some primordial soup, different only in degree—not kind—from trees, tunas, and porcupines. Then—you have to love it—these same adults ask with a straight face why these children don't respect human life, their own or others. They type the recipe and lay the ingredients on the counter, then marvel when their children make the cake and eat it!

The first thing the forbidden book tells them is "God created." If we can deceive them about this one point, we can deceive them about everything else. Look around you, Squaltaint. We have!

Don't let Fletcher grasp the implications of Daniel's belief system. As long as we control his beliefs, we can use him for our purposes. You report Fletcher and his wife feel helpless in dealing with their son's seduction by the culture of death. Much of his alienation is answered by the forbidden book's teaching about special creation. Make sure they just don't get it.

When these new Christians embrace "spiritual truths," let them compartmentalize and imagine their old beliefs are somehow also true. Deceive them into adopting one set of truths for church and the other for the real world, putting spiritual truth and scientific truth in separate categories. Spiritual truth, you must convince them, consists of inspiring but historically untrue stories, while science is the real thing, supported by the actual facts. A Christianity based on myths, rather than the Enemy's historical acts, is impotent. It is no threat to us and can actually be quite useful. (Reverend Braun comes to mind.)

You expressed concern about public calls to prayer coming out of that recent crisis. But there's no need to worry when society tolerates the Enemy in its margins. There's no threat to us when public figures who never pray otherwise suddenly call upon the community to pray for injured students or tornado victims. The Enemy is not pacified by an occasional tip of the hat, a symbolic Bible here and there, a nonsectarian prayer now and then. He doesn't like to be used. He's not impressed by spiritual rhetoric from people who regularly slap Him in the face by teaching their children He's nonexistent or irrelevant.

Even I am amazed at the extent of our grip on them. Look at these scientists who stare into deep space through their instruments and deny what they gaze upon was created. These same fools would think a man insane if he pointed to a painting of a waterfall or flower and said, "No one actually painted that—globs of paint that have always existed formed themselves on the canvas over millions of years." Their own claim, of course, is considerably more outrageous—that the original realities depicted, which are far more complex and intricate than paintings, themselves have no Creator.

I take pleasure in how they consider themselves more intelligent than the animist bushman who shakes sticks to ward off spirits from the trees. In fact, by recognizing a supernatural realm and a Creator—no matter how erroneous his concept of the Enemy—the animist shows far more intelligence and common sense than the scientist or professor wearing the white coat and admiring his diplomas on his wall.

Many of them suppose belief in a Creator is wishful thinking. In fact, it's exactly the opposite. Their disbelief is the real wishful thinking. Ironic, isn't it? Living in the clarity of the spirit world, we are forced to be fundamentalists in our beliefs. But *not* in our actions. We may not be able to disbelieve, but we can resist!

Like the prey we deceive, we long to make the Enemy disappear by an act of our will. If we could, of course, He'd have been gone eons ago. If only the universe were a democracy, and we could add our vote to the vermin's. By consensus we could legislate the Tyrant out of existence, then turn and devour them.

We have the capacity to violate the rules, but not to remake them. Worst of all, we don't have the power to unmake the Maker. If only we did, Squaltaint. If only we did.

Consoling myself with our fairy tale and its consequent mayhem,

—Lord Foulgrin

CHAPTER 37

DIFFERENT

"This is a really nice restaurant," Jillian said.

"I was hoping you'd like it. You sure look nice, Jill. That's a pretty dress."

"Thanks, Dad. And thanks for twisting my arm and making me come."

"Ouch, that hurts. You really didn't want to?"

"It just sounded weird at first. I mean, when was the last time you took me out somewhere, just you and me?"

"I don't remember."

"Me neither. That's my point."

"You just came from the hospital, didn't you? How's Brittany?"

"Still unconscious. They say she could wake up any time, but maybe she won't wake up at all. It's been three days."

"I'm so sorry, Jilly. I've been praying for her—and you."

Jillian nodded and looked down.

"Did you see Daniel this morning? I took off early. I was wondering what he thought of the youth group last night."

"He said he hated it."

"Oh. Sorry to hear that."

"But, you know, he was talking to Mom. When I asked him, he said it was okay. Actually, I saw him hanging out with two freshman guys. I think he liked them. Maybe they're into computers or music or something. Hey, I didn't like the youth group at first either, but after a few weeks I started to sort of fit in. Made some new friends. I invited Brittany to come with me before she...went to the hospital. She's sort of anti-Christian, but then, I guess I used to be too."

"So, Jilly, what do you think about your mom being pregnant?"

"At first, I was shocked. Then sort of embarrassed, you know. It's like everybody figures, hey, if your mom's pregnant that must mean your parents—"

"Okay, I get the picture."

"Anyway, then I started thinking it would be sort of cool to have a baby around. I've always wanted a little sister. A boy would be okay too, as long as he doesn't turn out like Daniel." She hesitated, then plunged ahead. "Mom told me what the doctor recommended."

"What do you think about that?"

"Well, it's funny; I guess I always thought of myself as prochoice. But I say if it's a choice between getting rid of the baby or the doctor, get rid of the doctor."

Jordan laughed. "Wise words, sweetheart. Tell me now, what's going on in your life?"

"That's a pretty broad question."

"I have a lot of catching up to do."

"Well, I've been thinking about college next year."

"That's great. I want to hear everything you're thinking about college. Maybe we could even go visit a few schools together. But first, tell me about this guy you've started dating. What's he like?"

LETTER 37

Lord Chemosh

My exalted Lord Chemosh,

I was delighted to receive your letter, sealed with your royal insignia. I'm honored one of such exalted rank would entrust his intimate thoughts to me. You can depend on me to keep your confidence. Yes, for both our protection, I'm sending this letter to the place you advised, where one of your loyal captains can retrieve it. Of course I will destroy your letter, just as you will mine.

I too have fond memories of our work among the Incas. It was a privilege to serve under your command and to be worshiped alongside you.

In response to your rather delicate question, yes, I too have wondered at times about our cosmic gamble. Such great and noble dreams we had, to claim and refashion the Tyrant's world, to make Skiathorus what it should have been all along.

"But we must tear down the old before we can build the new," Lucifer said. And it made sense at the time, didn't it? Yet here we are, millennia later, still tearing down, with so little to show for it.

I've heard rumblings the time's come for some to go to the Master and reason with him, remind him of our original objective. But the few who've done so in the past haven't fared well, have they?

Yes, I also wonder if the plan hasn't gone awry. Naturally, I'm careful to say this guardedly, only to those I trust. I don't mean, of course—and I know you don't—it's the Master's fault. If only the Tyrant would take His hand off this planet, let us rid it of His followers and make of it what we wish, we would show what a properly governed world would look like. But we're so busy putting out the Enemy's fires there seems no time to do anything else.

I hear the terrified shrieks of hell and delight in them. I try to focus on them to drown out the laughter and singing of Charis. But I'm most troubled by the grinding moans of Erebus. I don't just mean those who are being punished by our Master. I mean the rest of us, who labor under the burden of endless frustrating tasks. There's unrest in our ranks. Our original idealism has been supplanted by disillusionment. I hear whispers that perhaps, after all, we really are on the Tyrant's leash, and final victory is a delusion.

What's happened to our kingdom, Lord Chemosh? What's happened to our dreams?

We thought we knew contentment once. But we were under the Tyrant's spell, weren't we? Or is it possible...we fell under the spell of another?

You say you've never found the joy you sought. Yes, exactly! I've known purpose, mission, and unbridled fury. But never joy. It eludes me. I wonder now if it even exists. I've felt I was on the edge of it when I've seduced and brutalized the vermin, when I've drawn the blood of Christians, when I've put the knife into babies and hunted women and beaten them senseless. When putting my hooks into vermin, I've thought for a fleeting moment I've begun to taste joy. But no, it's always another step away, around the next corner.

We thought we'd found it when we flogged the Carpenter's back and pounded nails in His maggot-feeder flesh and watched the blood drain from Him. We screamed triumphantly, certain we'd won. I remember it so well. But it all came crashing down three days later, when we discovered He was not food for maggots after all.

All heaven broke loose and we fled from the Terror. We've been fleeing ever since, haven't we? We cannot admit our doubts to our subordinates, lest they betray us or wane in their service. Yes, we've won victories here and there, but can we really win the war? You asked me that question. I too have grave doubts. The Enemy is all-powerful. We can't deny that, as the vermin do.

The memories haunt me. We hover here on the outskirts of hell, but I wonder sometimes if hell has not already begun for us. Since you bared your mind to me, I'll tell you that in moments of despair I wonder, was the joy we seek so relentlessly the very joy that was once ours—in Charis before the revolution? Was it perhaps not an illusion, but reality? Is what we have known since then not the reality, but the illusion?

I who have made so many tremble, tremble myself at the thought. Baltar and Hoofstab and others have expressed the same thoughts to me in private conversation.

Your question has often haunted me. What if after all our efforts, we can do nothing but burn in that everlasting fire? How can we believe this is but a myth when the Enemy's other predictions have all proven true? How can we believe He cannot do this to us when we have to get His permission for every act of aggression against His chosen ones?

Rebellion seemed a grand idea, but it wasn't our idea, was it, my Lord? Not in the beginning. As you say, Lucifer was so persuasive, so believable, his cause seemed so just. And yet what has come of it?

I console myself I can impose darkness and despair on the vermin. What frightens me is when it comes upon me and I can do nothing to lift it. I thought about that as I recited the daily prayer:

"O Lucifer, son of the Morning, shadow of Darkness. O Beelzebub, midwife of destruction...Satan, equal of the Most High: fall upon us. Swallow us, as we swallow men. Engulf us in the bowels of your supremacy. Defend us from the Tyrant, who took what was ours and gave it to the maggot sons of Adam. Empower us to reclaim what He stole, and exact revenge on all who would take what is ours. We pledge you our loyalty. What we take from others we give to you, that you may yet be enthroned in Charis, to conduct an everlasting reign of terror, destroying your enemies and rewarding your servants. *Baal jezeb ashnar mordol nubl—keez gimbus molech nargul dazg!"*

Even as I say the words, mighty Chemosh, I ponder yours. Yes, it's indeed ironic the demand made by Lord Beelzebub—our unconditional loyalty—is the same demand once made upon us by Another. That our Master is one of us, the greatest of the created, sometimes seems little consolation.

In answer to your final question, yes, Lord Chemosh, I would be honored to gather with those you mentioned, to pursue a private discussion of these matters. I am at your service and await your instructions.

Please greet all your exalted colleagues for me—in particular Ra, Melqart, Moroni, and Ashtorah.

Your loyal servant,

—Lord Foulgrin

CHAPTER 38

FINAL ANSWER

That's our final answer, doctor," Diane said firmly.

"Okay, it's your decision."

"Yes, it is. And it's already made."

"Fine." He raised his hands. "I'm not trying to talk you out of it. I'm just warning you what could happen, that's all."

"This is our baby. We're going to have this baby. End of discussion."

LETTER 38

Damned If You Do

My clueless Squaltaint,

I regret to hear after vacillating concerning this Down syndrome guttersnipe (the sort the Enemy considers the apple of His eye), Fletcher and his wife decided to let their little maggot-feeder live. I feel like possessing a vermin just so I can vomit.

You report Fletcher, while he showers and shaves and dresses, is starting each morning listening to those abhorrent worship songs. The words make my skin crawl—"So I will boast in the cross of Christ, and I will glory in Jesus and His sacrifice." Revolting.

Get him back to the radio, the weather report, anything but this poisonous veneration of the Tyrant. Our battle often hinges on a man's last thoughts at night and his first thoughts in the morning. Allow the Enemy to take those thoughts captive and you're beaten. Dictate your thoughts to him and you've won.

Before you bragged how you gripped Fletcher with road rage. Now he spends his driving time praying or listening to the forbidden book, Christian audio books, or worship songs? Sometimes he sings at the top of his voice and forgets himself in his enthusiasm and joy? Outrageous.

You whine that if he gets home earlier he has more time to influence his family for the Enemy, but if he gets home later he has more time to worship, pray, and meditate on the forbidden book. Either way you lose. As you put it, "Damned if I do, damned if I don't." Indeed, Squaltaint. Indeed!

Between the sounds of Charis and your whimpering, I can hardly bear it.

What do you want from me? Adjust your strategy and cut your losses. It used to be to your advantage to get him stuck in traffic. Now do what you can to shorten his commute. Face it—the Enemy has hijacked an opportunity once yours.

Right when it seemed things couldn't get worse, Fletcher shared the forbidden message with his brother Craig? You assure me there was no harm done since his brother rejected it. Is your head denser than a neutron star? Just because he rejected it now doesn't mean he won't accept it later. And even if he doesn't, the point is Fletcher obeyed the Enemy by doing a difficult thing. And now he's elated. We lose on both counts.

Obedience is as habit forming as disobedience. We're seeing in Fletcher too much of the former and too little of the latter.

Ahh! The scratching din of Charis. I hear it every moment now, like fingernails on a blackboard. They sing each song eagerly, as if they'd never sung it before. Why? What are they up to?

If only I could slip out of my torment into unconscious oblivion. If only there was rest, the absence of thought, the end of this nagging anticipation of the horror awaiting us. I tell you, this job is hell!

No doubt your simple mind cannot comprehend the responsibilities I bear and the pressures of dealing with incompetent spirits such as yourself. I don't know why I bother.

At the end of my rope,

—Lord Foulgrin

CHAPTER 39

MY MESSENGER

Brittany walked down a long tunnel, toward a being of light. He beckoned her to come closer. Unafraid, she felt from him a kind warmth.

"Welcome, my child," the soothing voice said. "There's a world awaiting you, filled with joy and wonder. Would you like to come see it?"

"Yes," she said, though part of her wasn't yet ready to leave earth.

The angel of light—perhaps it was Jesus himself, Brittany thought—pointed his finger to the far end of the tunnel, where she saw majestic waterfalls, beautiful flowers, and grassy meadows.

"It's beautiful."

"Yes, and it's all yours, my beloved."

"Mine?"

"Yes. Forever. But...perhaps not quite yet."

"What do you mean?"

"You're very special to me, Brittany. Your time on earth isn't done yet. I've decided to send you back, to bring good news to all people. Tell them about the beauty and wonder that awaits them after death. Tell them about me. Tell them I will not judge or condemn them; I will warmly accept them. Tell them this—'Do not fear death.' This is my message to all mankind—'Love one another, and you have nothing to fear.' Will you tell them that for me?"

"Yes, I'll tell them."

"Good. Very good, my child." He stroked her cheek gently with the back of his hand. "Go now, as my messenger."

Brittany no longer saw the bright being, but instead a blurry white-clothed figure.

"She's waking up. Get the doctor—quick!"

LETTER 39

The Enemy's Appeal to the Vermin's Self-Interest

My biblically ignorant Squaltaint,

The murder—oh, pardon me, suicide—was nearly successful and would have been if not for the nosy neighbor who heard the car engine and saw the fumes coming out of the garage.

While she was in the hospital, I still thought I had her, but I could see the Enemy was going to bring her back. So, ever the opportunist, I made the best of it. I entered Brittany's mind, showed her the phony images, delivered my message, and sent her back to be my spokesperson. I expect to get a lot of mileage out of her. If she can keep Fletcher's daughter—and as many more as possible—from the Enemy, it will compensate for the disappointment she's still alive. I couldn't kill her, but I managed to seduce her, and that may prove better still.

I've just completed today's meditation on the forbidden book. I can hear your naive and tedious objections: "We should stay away from the forbidden book—it might bend our minds."

I'm beyond the Enemy's persuasion. I made my choice to rebel with full knowledge, as did you. I don't seek a reprieve, nor does He offer one.

I ask you, what coach would not listen in on the Enemy's huddle? What general would not eagerly study his enemy's battle plan? Without apology, I read the forbidden book. First, to hone my skill at quoting it out of context to mislead the vermin. Second, to remind myself exactly what the Enemy is up to so I may turn the tables on Him.

Since you mentioned Fletcher's been studying it, I read from Proverbs, a pernicious book. In it the Enemy continuously appeals to the self-interests of

His precious vermin. This is a dirty trick. When He appeals to their righteousness this is rarely a threat since most of them are so devoid of it. But they overflow with self-interest. The insidious argument of Proverbs is they should obey the Enemy's commands not simply because doing so is right, but because it is smart—it will work out best for them.

If the vermin caught on to this, do you realize how hard our task would be? We must convince them obeying Him is to their disadvantage, and disobeying Him will give them the edge. As you attempt to draw Fletcher toward his secretary, be sure to maintain this grand illusion.

Convince him the Enemy is a cosmic killjoy, always wanting to throw a wet blanket on the party. You must obscure the obvious, that it was the Enemy who created pleasure and the desire for it. As we're painfully aware, the Enemy is the great hedonist, always offering delights; throwing parties; staging banquets, feasts, and festivals. That's why we must fill the air with noise to block these sounds from our prey. Overstimulate their minds, fill them with sounds so they cannot hear the echoes of His celebrations.

If Fletcher catches wind of the Enemy's music and laughter, make him credit it to us. Then let him sense our cold disapproval, our unrelenting stoicism, our starkness, our abstention from joy. In a marvelous twist, cause him to attribute it not to us but to the Enemy! Reversal is our ploy. Entice him to climb over the Tyrant's guardrails and indulge in what He forbids, making him think your invitation is actually the Enemy's. Your job isn't merely to block the Enemy's voice. It's to distort it, making the vermin confuse our voice with His. Never reject the Bible when you can twist it to serve our ends. As Reverend Braun demonstrates, reinterpreting the Bible is much more effective than denying it. Don't attack the forbidden book, just spin it to your advantage.

Listen to what the Enemy appeals to, that you may learn what we must obscure: "Can a man scoop fire into his lap without his clothes being burned? Can a man walk on hot coals without his feet being scorched? So is he who sleeps with another man's wife; no one who touches her will go unpunished. A man who commits adultery lacks judgment; whoever does so destroys himself."

Notice the Enemy doesn't bother to warn them of how evil it is to commit adultery. (He does that elsewhere, but to no avail.) Instead, He points out that by his disobedience the man will put himself through agony. In choosing sin, the Enemy warns him he chooses a down payment on hell's fires. He will be punished horribly for his choices. He'll destroy himself.

What gall! This insider tip robs us of our primary advantage. We try to make them drunk on their lusts, while he throws cold water on their faces.

The Enemy says of a sludgebag lured into sexual immorality, "He followed her like an ox going to the slaughter…little knowing it will cost him his life."

Do you see, Squaltaint? He appeals to the same thing we do—the man's desire to come out ahead. No vermin wants to be butchered. Nor does he want to be duped. He doesn't desire to act like a dumb animal, though that's exactly what he is. The choices your vermin is making and contemplating with his financial deception and his secretary, each take him toward the slaughterhouse. You must close his eyes to the Enemy's warning he's engaged in self-destruction.

But the Enemy isn't finished. He has Wisdom—I suspect He's speaking of the Carpenter—say to the vermin, "Whoever finds me finds life and receives favor from the Lord. Whoever fails to find me harms himself."

There it is again, so repetitive one doubts even the vermin could miss it. The Enemy—the one who calls them to sacrifice and love of neighbor—shamelessly appeals to what? Their sense of self-preservation! No man wants to harm himself. So He tells them how to avoid self-destruction.

The Carpenter used the same line of reasoning. He challenged them to believe and obey His words that they might be like a wise (He didn't say "righteous") man who built his house on the rock, rather than a foolish (He didn't say "unrighteous") man who built his house on the sand. To him, smart and right are the same. Stupid and wrong are the same. Do you see how perilous this is? We dare not let the rodents grasp it.

Wisdom is our enemy, for it counts the costs of wrong choices and anticipates the rewards of right ones. Foolishness—eyes on short-term gratification, not long-term consequences—is our greatest ally. As you draw your vermin to his secretary, you must keep the fool from those portions of the book talking about wisdom and foolishness, choice and consequences, the blessings of obedience and the curses of disobedience. If he rehearsed in advance the consequences of adultery, he would be terrified. He'd flee from it, not because he's good but because the looming consequences would scare him to death.

Convince him instead that keeping the Enemy's counsel will rob his life of fun, while keeping our counsel will fill it with good times.

If he secretly watches his private little programs late at night, whisper, "What harm is it?" Never let him realize the answer: "It's of immense harm to me, beyond my wildest dreams."

As he fills his mind with those images, his secretary will further eclipse his wife in his affections. Keep whispering "we're just having a good time" and "everyone's doing it" and "it won't hurt anyone." Slide him right down that slippery slope. While he's on fire with the deadly consequences of secret indulgences, his "good times" leaving him weary and guilty, you'll be there as his cheerleader, taking pleasure in two things: his excruciating pain and the Enemy's downcast countenance. We win and they—Enemy and vermin—lose.

See what you can learn from a little Bible study? Know your enemy. Read his mail! And remember—every reason you should look at the forbidden book is a reason to keep Fletcher from looking at it.

An unapologetic student of the book,

—Lord Foulgrin

CHAPTER 40

IT'S OVER

Jordan Fletcher drove into the company parking lot. Someone had parked in his spot, so he pulled into an empty space sixty feet further from the door.

"Hi, Frank," Jordan called, waving as he walked toward him. "How'd your daughter do in that big game?"

"She played great. And they won too."

"Terrific. Hey, I was thinking...how about joining me for lunch tomorrow?"

"Lunch?"

"Yes, lunch. You know, the meal between breakfast and dinner?"

"Yeah, I've heard of it. Sure, we could have lunch."

"Great. You pick the place, but it's on me, okay?"

"O...kay."

"See you tomorrow, Frank."

"See you tomorrow...Jordan."

Jordan was tempted to turn back and see if Frank's face looked as bewildered as his voice sounded. He resisted.

Jordan got off the elevator and walked into his office. Patty followed him in a few moments later. His stomach felt as if swords were clashing inside of him. He thought of a hundred reasons not to say what he'd been rehearsing for three days.

"Sit down, Patty."

"Sure. Going to give me a shoulder rub?"

Jordan took a deep breath, then spoke softly yet firmly. "It's over."

"What's over, Jordan?"

"Look, I know we haven't done anything yet—I mean we haven't slept together—but we could have and we nearly did. And anyway, it's been wrong, dead wrong. I'm a married man. Look at this wedding ring. Look at your own wedding ring. I made vows to my wife, like you made to your husband. I owe it to God and to her. And I love her too."

"But you love me more...don't you?"

"No. Actually, I don't. I've talked this over with a friend and he's helped me see what I feel toward you isn't love, it's just desire for...what's forbidden. That's not the same thing."

"You desire me?"

"Of course I do. Did. Okay, do. But you're not mine to have. You're married and I'm married, but not to each other. Love is more than feelings; it's honoring a commitment. Let me show you what I've been carrying around in my pocket for the last week. My friend wrote it out on this three-by-five card."

He handed her the card. She stared at it.

"Go ahead, read it aloud."

"'Can a man scoop fire into his lap without his clothes being burned? Can a man walk on hot coals without his feet being scorched? So is he who sleeps with another man's wife; no one who touches her will go unpunished.'"

Patty laughed uncertainly. "What's this, the Bible? I mean, I know you've been getting into this Christian thing, and that's okay. I can handle that, but come on, Jordan. You don't really believe this moralistic stuff?"

"Yes, as a matter of fact I do. I *do* believe it. And I've decided to obey it."

"Jordan, please." She stood up and moved toward him. He quickly backed away, arms up, palms out.

"Look, ending this is the right thing for Diane and the kids. And for me. And for you and your family. It wouldn't just mess up our lives; it would mess up yours too. Maybe it already has."

"I'm willing to take that risk."

"I'm not. Like Ryan said, the right thing is the smart thing. It's in everyone's best interests. The wrong thing is the stupid thing. It ruins everybody's lives. Let's face it, if I hadn't become a Christian, you and I would have been in bed together by now. Well, I did become a Christian and that means something to me. Actually, it means everything to me."

Patty sobbed quietly, looking at the floor. "What will we do?"

"We'll go back to a professional relationship. No more lunches, no notes, no candy, no gifts—and by the way, those times I sent you flowers? I charged them to the company. I was cheating and lying to Diane and the company. I'm going to pay it back. Anyway, Patty, I'm sorry I let this thing happen, and I'm just glad it didn't go any farther. But it's over now. I mean it."

"And what if I'm in too deep? What if I can't pull back?'"

"Then I'll have to ask you to give notice and look for work somewhere else—or I will. If either of us can't back off, one of us has to leave."

She stared at him, face blank. Then Jordan saw her pale skin start to turn red.

"Look what you've turned into, Jordan Fletcher. One of those judgmental, self-righteous, Bible-thumping Christians. You think you're too good for me, don't you? Well, maybe I don't want you anymore, anyway. What do you think of that?"

She marched to the door and stared back at him, waiting for an answer.

"I think...that's the best news I've heard in a long time."

She slammed the door, shaking the windows. He winced.

"That's a page out of my book."

Jordan dropped to his knees and talked aloud to someone he couldn't see, but knew was there.

LETTER 40

Choosing a College

My unimaginative Squaltaint,

You haven't reported recently on the woman Patty. I trust things are going well? I assume they're fornicating by now? Tell me the juicy details.

Now, to the subject of your last letter. Fletcher and his daughter are looking into which college she should attend, and you want to know the best choice?

Really, Squaltaint, that's the sort of question I'd expect them to ask. As always, that choice is best which draws them farthest from the Enemy.

With her mother having been abducted by the Tyrant and Jillian attending church and youth group, the one thing you don't want is for her to go to a college that will reinforce her newly forming trust in the forbidden book.

Fortunately, at the vast majority of colleges there's no danger whatsoever of this happening.

Nearly all these colleges were originally established to train young minds in the forbidden book and to integrate a Christian worldview into every subject area. They were once among our most formidable enemies. If you can imagine, at one time we actually fought to keep young vermin *away* from universities!

Tyrant, Carpenter, and Ghost have little chance against our surrogate trinity of Darwin, Freud, and Marx. We teach them they are accidents and animals (biology); good people who need only to get in touch with their inner feelings and find out who to blame for their problems (psychology); bit players in the large machinery where diversity reigns and no belief should have preference over any other (sociology).

Relativism. Pluralism. Individualism. Our sacred creed.

My favorite word on campus is "whatever." Whatever they want to believe, they can, and whatever anyone else believes they have no right to challenge. Except Christian beliefs, of course, since they contradict the status quo. Remember your college ABCs: Anything But Christianity.

I'm disturbed to learn Jillian has resisted Brittany's efforts to have her continue flirting with the occult. But at least it appears she doesn't yet have a firm faith of her own. She passively conforms to her parent's wishes she be a Christian. Good news, since the Enemy has no grandchildren.

Send her off to most colleges and her faith will quickly unravel. She'll no longer have the structure of her parents' guidelines, or the peer pressure toward obeying the Enemy offered by her church and youth group. Instead she'll experience a rush of independence in an atmosphere where students routinely experiment with everything from drugs to sex to New Age and eastern religions, where any appeal to morality is debunked as intolerance.

Brittany keeps telling her my story, and Jillian appears to buy it. Who can resist the picture of a being of light, a Jesus figure, promising heaven is for everyone—no need to change beliefs or behavior. Call me brilliant. At college, I'll send instructions to get Jillian linked up with someone dabbling in witchcraft and tarot cards. There are plenty of Ouija boards on campus. I'll plan to meet her again on one of them!

Raketwist will make her mind so open, things will freely come in and fall out—just so her mind never closes on the truth.

Jillian's dossier shows her to be bright. (By vermin standards, I mean—of course, they're all imbeciles.) Hence she has potential to serve us effectively, with the added bonus of breaking the hearts of her parents. According to your report, her counselor is urging her toward one of the brand name universities, the credentialing machines that open professional doors. Very good—those are our most secure strongholds.

There she'll be immersed in gender wars and race wars, assimilating the university's contempt for all things western, white, and male. While our experiments in communism with their legacy of mass destruction have disappeared nearly everywhere in the world but China, I'm proud to say communism is alive and well among many American college professors.

Naturally, you and Raketwist must not let her embrace the diversity of personality and culture the Enemy values, He who created them different; rather, *our* sort of diversity, centered on aberrant theology and corrupt moral behavior.

Reason is rarely exercised on these campuses, where feelings and subjective opinions reign. The politicized doctrinaire atmosphere that at first seems a breath of fresh air will ultimately choke her. The intellectual climate of meaninglessness, the breakdown of moral constructs, will leave her a cynical nihilist. Or perhaps the self-glorifying celebration of humanity's goodness will leave her an idealistic narcissist. Any of these is equally useful to us and destructive to her.

In any case, young Jillian is too weak; she'll never survive the intellectual intimidation of the classroom. Give me a philosophy, psychology, or science prof over a satanist any day.

We have many achievements to celebrate, Squaltaint. But none more than our work in colleges.

We've labored to make parents—especially Christian parents—blind to reality. They cheerfully send off their children, thinking college will prepare them for life, while we conduct our invisible assault on their minds. We impart to them beliefs and values contradicting those of their parents. Dad and Mom would be horrified if they understood this. Your job is to make sure they don't.

In non-Christian minds we build walls so high most will view the Enemy's faith as the root of all evils. Christianity becomes synonymous with crusades, holocausts, racism, and burnings at the stake. By the time they graduate, their minds will respond to the forbidden book with something between a condescending smugness and an arrogant hostility.

They'll come away from college open-minded to anything and everything else, but closed-minded to the forbidden book and faith in the Carpenter. Most of them will never scale the college's mountain of obstacles to the forbidden faith. We've won, Squaltaint. I tell you, on these campuses we've won!

If Jillian's college finances are lacking, do all you can to make up the difference. In Erebus we offer generous scholarships to such schools. At all costs, get her off to school quickly. Don't let her hang around home and church too long, lest she have a true experience with the Enemy, become grounded in her faith, and her parents become wise enough to realize what we've planned for her at school.

Once in college, slowly but surely your sludgebag's daughter will not only question but abandon any Christian beliefs. As she's exposed to a new world of diverse ideology and lifestyles, she'll begin to see her parents' faith and her church's teachings as naive and narrow, lacking tolerance and sophistication.

She'll come to believe not only in evolution, but in the moral relativism inseparable from it. At first she'll be embarrassed by coed dorms and students copulating indiscreetly around the campus, but soon she'll be desensitized and feel this sort of "freedom" is cool. Within a few years she'll be having sexual relations with at least one boy, maybe more. By her senior year she who today is aghast at lesbianism will be accepting of that and all the other teachings of her women's studies professors.

In a matter of months she'll be getting drunk—a wonderful experience of sickness and nausea her parents and youth group deprived her of. Eventually she'll try drugs. ("Why not?") Before long she'll see herself as above her family's beliefs, more enlightened than her church, grateful that she escaped succumbing to childish beliefs in Christian superstition.

Meanwhile, her parents will subsidize her defection from faith by paying tuition, room, and board. When people in their church ask, "How's Jillian doing at college?" they'll smile and say, "Great." They won't realize they're losing their daughter; in fact they're paying lots of money to lose her. I have to laugh when I watch them underwrite our intellectual conquest of their children. It would be like America and Great Britain purchasing fuel for the Nazis to use in their European campaign.

Never let Fletcher consider if his goal was to destroy his daughter's faith, this would be easy to do without sending her to college. Don't ask me, Squaltaint, why they're willing to pay so much money for their children to go off and lose their faith, when they could stay home and lose it for free! In any case, I'm delighted they do.

I relished your news that Fletcher's new church friends recommended sending Jillian to that "Christian" college they attended thirty years ago. "It was a great school when we went there." Yes, and the toxic waste landfill was a nice ball field when they played on it as children, but that doesn't mean they'd send their children there now, does it?

I rub my hands with glee when I consider the amount of Christian money tied up in endowments for schools we use for anti-Christian causes. The morons don't get the self-evident fact that money given to these schools doesn't go to what the schools were thirty years ago. It goes to what they are today.

Graytwist keeps me abreast of misguided efforts at various "Christian" colleges to change the doctrinal statement to reflect its actual teachings. Better that than changing their teachings to reflect their doctrinal statements. But still, this single act of honesty would be a devastating blow. Suppose the catalog said, "Some of our teachers still believe in the inspiration of the Bible, the creation of the world out of nothing, the physical resurrection of Christ, and that Jesus is the only way to heaven. However, many of our teachers do not believe this and in fact teach students the opposite."

If we're going to continue to lure in parents and students, we must maintain our campaign of false advertising.

Don't be alarmed at the prospect of a Christian college, at least not the sort with professors too sophisticated to be involved with those simple-minded, out-of-date, blue-collar folk out in the forbidden squadrons. Do you realize how many students we've permanently disconnected from churches through Christian colleges? There are notorious exceptions, of course, and at all costs you must keep Jillian from those schools.

Convince Fletcher it's healthy for his daughter's beliefs to be stretched and challenged, as we like to say. Just make sure he hasn't taken the time and effort to establish and reinforce those beliefs. Jillian hasn't had opportunity to develop a deep knowledge of the forbidden book. Because her beliefs are lightly held and thinly understood, they'll easily fall to our onslaught. She doesn't have much of a faith of her own? Well, soon she'll lose even the little she has.

Be on your guard against campuses with strong churches nearby and

Christian ministries which dare to invade our turf, trying to steal our prey. We've managed to send young people off to schools full of lies and immorality, only to lose them to enemy commandos.

The Tyrant is a meddler. He has special designs on these young vermin. Despite how much college is stacked in our favor, we cannot trust Him to leave them alone.

Celebrating higher education,

—Lord Foulgrin

CHAPTER 41

ENEMY STRATEGIES

Jordan and Ryan sat at Starbucks, eating bagels and drinking coffee, reflecting on what they'd learned at the marriage conference.

"How's the arthritis?"

"Pretty painful. I was reading yesterday about getting a new body in the resurrection. Man, that sounds good. Meanwhile, though, it's like you said—I'm learning to trust God in my weakness."

Ryan nodded. "Now that you've drawn the line with Patty, how do you feel about it?"

"I feel great, actually. I realize how miserable it felt before. Funny how it works that way. When you're in the middle of it, you think it's so wonderful you can't give it up. Once you give it up it's so clear you weren't just wrong, you were unhappy. All the reasons, the rationalizations you pointed out to me, disappeared in a puff of smoke. Speaking of which, I didn't tell you I took those letters she'd written me and put them in the trash, right there in the office. I opened a window and set them on fire—next thing I know, the fire alarm goes off and I'm telling everybody, 'Everything's okay, it was just me.'"

Ryan laughed.

"But it was fitting, really. The alarm should've gone off in my head long before I burned those letters. I came so close to letting it go too far. I could've lost my family, everything. It's spooky. I mean, I can't explain the way I was thinking. It doesn't make sense. I was right on the edge."

"Spooky's the word," Ryan said. "I've been on the edge myself. Be on your guard, bro. The same voices that whispered to you before will try it again. They haven't given up."

"You mean, like...demons?"

"Yeah. Sure, we can sin on our own without their help, but they can get into our heads and emotions and tug us the wrong way. Jesus said they're always trying to deceive us. We're in a battle. That's why we're told to put on the whole armor of God so we can resist the devil."

"Yeah, Ephesians 6. I memorized it. But it's still weird to think demons are working on me."

"It may sound weird, but it's true. We're on Satan's hit list; you and me both. He's gunning for us. Demons have this ability to make sin look good to us. I was reading this morning, right here in Titus 2." He flipped in his Bible. "It says the grace of God teaches us 'to say no to ungodliness and worldly passions, and to live self-controlled, upright and godly lives.'"

"Let me guess, you wrote it out for me on another three-by-five card."

Ryan smiled and pulled two cards out of his shirt pocket. "One for you, one for me."

They talked another twenty minutes before Ryan said, "I've got a proposition for you."

"Inviting me to a Tupperware party?"

"No, even better. I've talked with one of the pastors. You know Barry? We'd like to invite you and Diane to go with us on a summer missions trip to China."

"To *China?*"

"Yeah. Here's the info we've got so far." Ryan pulled out a file folder from under his Bible. "It's pretty exciting stuff. It'll be a major challenge, but I think you'll love it. Read it through and we'll talk about it next week. Or Tuesday, after basketball. Think about it, okay?"

"China?"

Ryan laughed. "I get the feeling this took you by surprise. Anyway, let's talk about it. Meanwhile, how are you doing in your time with God? Reading the Bible and praying?"

"Yeah, I've gotten back to it. It's going pretty well now."

"Tell me about it."

"Well, this thing with Patty kept messing up my time with God. As long as that was going on I guess I wanted to keep my distance from Him."

"I hear you."

"It's a relief to have that out of the way, but…there's another thing."

"Yeah?"

Jordan breathed deeply, pausing long, deliberating. Finally he said, "It's related to work—a business deal I made a while back. I've gotten in over my head…"

LETTER 41

Distracting Him from Missions and the Poor

My zealous Squaltaint,

Where's your update on Fletcher and the woman? What's the latest on his lying and cheating on the Brisbane project?

You said his coworker Patrick was using Fletcher's computer and realized he's been misrepresenting his hours. He's caught on to his scheme and may be planning to turn him in. What a wonderful opportunity to discredit his conversion and give Christians a bad name—not to mention humiliate Fletcher.

Yes, that was an excellent conversation Fletcher had with his old college friend, concerning the "noble savage." The man, a sociology major, portrayed the primitive vermin as a lover of his neighbor, in tune with his environment, happy and content?

I'm delighted Fletcher didn't know how to argue against this and walked away confused. He didn't realize in this particular culture they murder each other, steal each other's wives, mutilate and beat their women, leave handicapped children out in the elements to die, conquer other tribes, and sell each other into slavery. If he could see them cut open their bodies in homage to us, he might realize his educated friend doesn't know what he's talking about. Fortunately, neither of them has a clue!

This is especially important in light of the bad news you conveyed, that Fletcher and his wife have been targeted to go on one of those despicable missions trips. I'm delighted to hear they aren't considering it seriously. Make sure they don't. It's not what Fletcher could do for Chinese Christians that worries me. It's what they could do to him.

"Leave them alone," we whisper. "They already have their religion; it's part of their culture, and you have no right to interfere. Who are you to think your religion is an improvement? People are better off before they hear about Christianity. They're happy. Stay away and don't ruin them."

Blind them to how utterly ruined these maggots already are. Let their feature stories show the smiling faces, disguising the empty, hopeless hearts beneath. Yes, by all means, keep the missionaries home.

Why do we call it the forbidden message? Because the book claims only one matter is "of first importance." What? "That Christ died for our sins according to the Scriptures, that he was buried, that he was raised on the third day."

Because the message is of first importance to the Enemy, stopping its spread is of first importance to us. While the Enemy calls them to the ends of the earth, we must do what we can to keep them home. Wrap them up in their jobs and houses and activities. In the forbidden squadron, keep their eyes on themselves, their programs, their buildings; never on the poor and needy and those who haven't heard the forbidden message. Keep their eyes on minivans and bank accounts and off the ends of the earth.

Some 90 percent of the world's Christian workers live in countries with 10 percent of the world's population. We must maintain this imbalance. Discourage them from sharing their faith in their own sphere of influence. And never let them ask whether it seems right some can hear the forbidden message many times when others have never heard it at all.

The four living creatures—so drunk on the Carpenter they never stop singing—cry to Him, "with your blood you purchased men for God from every tribe and language and people and nation."

He's not content with having sludgebags from most people groups. He wants them from every one. That's why our Master has deployed forces across the globe to fight the encroachment of the forbidden message, to defend our strongholds against the Enemy. This is why we work so hard to punish new Christians, to stop the spread of the forbidden message.

This is why we labor to inflict such loneliness, depression, and fruitlessness on vermin missionaries. And why we detest the prayers of the forbidden squadron, and hate their letters and visits and stinking offerings that pour gasoline on the fire we're trying to extinguish.

Let Fletcher's church decry those who don't believe in hell, but don't let them see the incongruity that they who do believe in hell would do so little to keep people from going there.

As for the poor, let the Christian vermin see them as a distraction from the Great Commission, rather than part of it. Blind your prey's eyes to the hungry, the truly homeless, the refugees. Blind him to the widow next door, orphans, the fatherless, street children; both in his city and around the world. Blind him to the alien confused by the culture, lonely for his family. Blind him to the stranger needing a friend, to the unemployed, the handicapped, elderly. Blind him not only to the child about to be killed but the woman so desperate she's about to sacrifice her child and her self-respect.

Don't let the Fletchers see how personally the Enemy takes all this. He says if they feed the hungry, they feed Him; if they give water to the thirsty, they give it to Him; if they visit the prisoner, they visit Him. Here's our golden opportunity—He also says if they fail to care for these needy maggot-feeders, they fail to care for Him. Think of it, Squaltaint. Sometimes we imagine our opportunity to hurt the Carpenter came and went two thousand years ago. No. We can still do Him harm today, not just through the actions but the inactions of His own forbidden squadrons.

By blinding them to the needy, we blind them to Him. By getting them to deprive or neglect the weak, we take revenge on Him!

Don't let Fletcher figure out that infantile game played by the Enemy's warriors, in which they pass themselves off as needy vermin strangers to test the vermin. Michael's imposters pose as everything from bag ladies to vagrants to women with broken-down cars in pouring rain, to vacant-eyed adolescents needing a friend, to crying children searching for their puppies. Sickeningly sentimental, isn't it? It's shameless for angels to take on vermin flesh smelling of last month's sweat and grime, without having a worthy purpose such as we do when we take control of them.

Your job is to be sure Fletcher's heart isn't moved by the Enemy's words. But if he's touched by thoughts of the needy, your next job is to overwhelm him with hopelessness. Make Fletcher think, "I'm just one person. I can't stop child abuse. I can't stop persecution. I can't feed all the hungry. I can't get the gospel to them all. How can you help billions of needy people?"

"One at a time"—that's the Enemy's obvious answer. Just be sure Fletcher doesn't hear it. Don't let him or his wife ask themselves, "Where are the poor and unevangelized in our prayers?" Don't let him ask, "Where are the poor and unreached in our budget?" Don't let him ask, "Where are the poor and unsaved in my schedule?"

Turn their attention back to their favorite vacation spots, the big screen TV, the new car, the hot tub, the house they've been looking for out in the country.

Fill their minds with anything and anyone but those closest to the Enemy's heart. It's magnificently simple, Squaltaint—if you get Fletcher to ignore and neglect them, you get them to ignore and neglect Him.

Eclipsing the important with the trivial,

—Lord Foulgrin

CHAPTER 42

HOME

"But I *will* go to heaven, Jordan. Reverend Braun says so."

"Look, Dad, we've been through that. Jesus says unless you realize you're a sinner and place your faith in Him to save you from your sins, you'll go to hell, not heaven."

"I'm as good as your Christian friends. You think your father's pretty rotten, is that it?"

"No, Dad. Well, I guess what I mean is, you and I and everybody else is rotten, yeah. And if we don't come to grips with that, we won't see how much we need to know Jesus, and why He had to die for us on the cross to take us to heaven."

"I don't want to go to heaven."

"Don't say that, Dad. Somebody's lying to you to make you think that."

"I'd rather have a good time with my friends in hell than hang around with self-righteous bigots in heaven."

"Nobody's going to have a good time in hell, and self-righteous bigots won't be in heaven. Only sinners covered by the righteousness of Christ."

"You sound like your mother."

"Thanks."

"I mean, you're acting like I'm an atheist or something."

"Mom was a true Christian, Dad. So was Jill. I know that now. But you and Craig and Erin and I weren't. Being a Christian is more than high moral standards or being a nice guy or not being an atheist. It's a personal relationship with God. Like it says in that book." Jordan pointed to the book he'd given his dad, with the gospel booklet sticking out of it. "Did you read it?"

He sighed. "Yeah, I read it. It's not that bad. Some of it's okay. But I'm not ready to turn into a Christian weirdo or something, so don't go pushing me."

"I'm not pushing you, Dad. I just wanted to share the truth about Jesus. I owe that to you. Go ahead and mull it over, but remember, we don't always have as much time as we expect."

Jordan drove home singing along with the worship music. Twenty minutes after he arrived, the family sat at the dinner table.

"Mind if we join hands while I pray?" he asked Jillian and Daniel. Neither answered, but when he and Diane put out their hands, they took them. Soon after dinner both kids disappeared.

After helping Diane clean up, Jordan sat next to her on the couch. He put his arm around her.

"This is nice," she said. "I could do it every night."

"Me too. I can't get over my talk with Dad. It's between him and God now, but it makes me feel so good I was able to share with him."

"Now if we can just keep Reverend Braun away from him." Diane shook her head and laughed. "How's that for irony? We want him to know Christ and the biggest obstacle is a Christian minister!"

Jordan kissed her on the cheek. He was still amazed at how well she'd taken his confession of his relationship with Patty. He'd seen the hurt in her eyes. But when he told her he'd backed away and burned her letters, he saw something else. "You didn't have to tell me this," she'd said. "Yes, I did," he replied. And instead of it creating a distance, like he'd assumed, it drew them closer. And ever since the marriage conference, he could tell she was going out of her way to show him love and appreciation.

"Thanks again for the roses," Diane said. "They're beautiful."

Jordan looked at the dark red flowers on the coffee table. He'd picked them out himself, arranged them just right, putting in the baby's breath the way he knew she'd like it. She wasn't the only one who felt good about it—he did too.

"How are you feeling...you know, with the baby and all?"

"I'm feeling the extra weight, that's how I'm feeling."

"Anything I can do to help?"

"Besides carrying the baby half the day? Well, the flowers definitely helped. And...since you asked, would you mind rubbing my feet?"

Jordan moved down to the end of the couch and started pressing his fingers into the bottom of her feet.

"Oh...that feels *so* good."

Jordan smiled and rubbed harder. After ten minutes or so, Jillian walked into the living room. She stared at them.

"Everything okay, honey?" Jordan asked.

"Everything okay with…you guys?"

"We're doing great," Diane said.

"Well, sorry to interrupt your private moments but I'm headed to youth group. Lisa asked me to pick her up."

"That's great. Lisa's a neat girl," Jordan said. "So are you."

"Thanks—then we're picking up Brittany. I told her if she's back in school, no reason not to come to youth group. I'm keeping my fingers crossed. I guess I should say, I'm praying she won't make up another excuse not to come." On her way out the front door, Jillian snuck one last look at her parents on the couch, then smiled and rolled her eyes.

As soon as the door shut, Diane giggled. She got up and said, "How about I brew some decaf—chocolate macadamia nut?"

"Sounds wonderful."

"Come in the kitchen and talk with me."

"Yes, ma'am."

"What did you think about the message yesterday?"

"Barry's message? I thought it was good. Different, but good."

"I've been thinking about what he said. You know, about those children living in the streets all over the world."

"Yeah?"

"Wouldn't it be great if we could do something to help them? You know, the missions offering he mentioned, the one coming up in a few weeks? What do you think about giving…a lot of money to it?"

"Sure. Did you have an amount in mind?"

"Well…you know how we were finally going to buy me that new car next month?"

"Yeah?"

"The old car's fine. Why do I need a new one?"

"Are you saying what I think you're saying?"

"Why don't we just take the money we were going to spend on the new car and give it to help take care of those street children?"

"I think that's a wonderful idea. But…what made you come up with it?"

"Actually, it was Jodi. She told me ever since the cancer her priorities have been changing. She's asking herself what's really important and what isn't. She and Ryan have decided to sell one of their cars they don't need and give the money to Jesus, to help the poor. She wasn't bragging or anything, but it touched me. I saw how excited she was, and it blew me away. I wanted a piece of that joy myself. Is that okay?"

"It's more than okay. It has to be. God's been working on me too, Di. I've been thinking—hold onto your hat—maybe we should sell the boat and work toward getting out of debt. And you know those new golf clubs I've been wanting?"

"Yeah?"

"The clubs I've got are fine. Why don't we throw what I was going to spend on them into the missions offering too?"

They walked back to the couch and settled in.

"You know what, Di?"

"What?"

"I love you. More than ever. I mean that."

"Well, kiss me, then, you romantic fool."

LETTER 42

Intolerable Developments

My impudent Squaltaint,

You admit Fletcher's been praying "deliver us from the evil one"? He's even taped a card on his dashboard saying, "Resist the devil, and he will flee from you"?

You complain this makes you jumpy. You whine that with everything going on in his life, sometimes you can hardly stand to hang around him.

You poor devil. You have my deepest and sincerest sympathy.

Moron! What are you looking for, group therapy? Erebus has no counseling department. Get over it, fool.

Your reports are woefully incomplete, but it's obvious the Enemy is accomplishing far too much in Fletcher. You gloat that although he was on his knees forty minutes, you managed to distract him most of the time from focusing on the Enemy. But you minimize the monumental—the man was on his knees forty minutes?

I fear no prayer that's spoken to some vague "higher power" who's nothing more than a construction of their own minds. But since Fletcher's view of the Enemy is being informed by the forbidden book, it makes his prayers dangerous. The threat of forbidden talk isn't in what they're saying as much as who they're saying it to. This is why the posture of his prayer concerns me. If he's on his knees or facedown on the floor, he may begin to believe in his own unimportance and the greatness of the One he prays to.

Make them think they're "just" praying, as if it were not action of the most potent kind. Prayer isn't simply preparation for battle, it is the battle—you must remember this, they must not. I fear nothing of prayerless studies, prayerless work, or prayerless parenting. I laugh at their most diligent efforts and most profound insights when disconnected from prayer. The forbidden talk is what infuses them with the Enemy's presence and power. Minimize it at all costs.

You brag you've befuddled him in his daily Bible study. What will you boast of next—that you made him hungry while he's fasting? The fact he's having a daily Bible study shows your failure. Even if forbidden talk and Bible study seem fruitless for a while, if Fletcher keeps at it the Enemy will suddenly set his study and prayers on fire. Before you know it, the sludgebag's heart will burn with praise, adoration, and every foul thing you can imagine.

Fletcher has been interceding for others, and it frightens you? It should. No matter how horrifying, don't back off—infuse his mind with any vulgar thoughts you can, or a hundred benign distractions. The Ryan roach engaged him in forbidden talk over the telephone? More bad news. I keep telling the assault team supervisor he needs to take down Ryan immediately. He's penetrated deep into our territory and must pay the price. He's got to be kept from further incursions.

Convince Fletcher that today he doesn't have time for the book and the talk. Then do it again tomorrow and the next day and the next. He'll never make a conscious decision to stop prayer and Bible study, but the bottom line will be the same.

Turn forbidden talk and Bible reading into an ideal, an intention, something he'll do when he has time. Then all you have to do is make sure he never has time. It's like intending to have their neighbors over for dinner—you say they've intended it for six years, right? But they've never put it on their calendar. The intention to pray and read the Bible is no threat whatsoever to us. It's the actual doing it that's the danger. When it's put on the calendar, when the alarm clock is set because of it, that's when it's time to panic.

After reading his Bible, praying, going to church, and sharing his faith—he feels better, doesn't he? Then why is it the things he feels best after doing are the things he most doesn't want to do? This is a question for you, not him. The obvious answer is us. If he realized there's a supernatural explanation for his reluctance to do what brings him joy, we'd lose our clandestine edge. He might decide to do those things anyway.

He's increasing in humility? Make it a point of pride. If he becomes aware of his pride about being humble, then confesses it, make him proud he was humble enough to confess his pride at being humble.

You deliberately neglected to tell me they decided to forgo a new car to give to the needy. If the Enemy is getting hold of their money, it's a sure sign He's gotten hold of their hearts. The worst is, everything they give away increases their joy. It's a chain reaction. Habit. Lifestyle. Stop them now, Squaltaint.

Yes, Conhock told me all about their intimate evening on the couch talking about their little brat inside her, helping needy children, their rekindled passion for each other, and on and on. Yeecch!

He also informs me Fletcher told his father about the Carpenter. Strange you didn't mention that in your report either. You also didn't mention Fletcher's been praying the "Lord of the harvest" would send out workers. And sure enough, Fletcher's becoming part of the answer to his own prayers. Yes, Conhock told me—at the end of their meeting the vermin and his wife agreed to go on that summer missions trip! Don't you see what's happening? They're relocating their treasure, and the Enemy's relocating their hearts. You're being beaten at every turn. What more can go wrong?

Unfortunately, Conhock answered that too. Fletcher's set a goal of reading through the forbidden book by the end of the year. He's agreed to this with Ryan and two others, and in their weekly meeting they'll be telling each other what they've been reading. I'm speechless.

If Fletcher sells the boat, next thing you know he may sell his second house and do Satan-knows-what with the money. If he becomes free from debt, he'll be more free to serve the Enemy; more free to say yes to His promptings, to make a habit of these miserable missions trips, to pull up stakes and follow Him elsewhere, or serve Him where he is now with far less distraction.

What can I say to convince you of how disastrous this is?

You must persuade Fletcher that when the Enemy provides more money He's expecting them to raise their standard of living, not their standard of giving. Remind him of a thousand practical reasons it's nuts to give up a new car. Let him buy up shares of Microsoft or General Motors, but never the Enemy's kingdom. Keep his vested interests on earth, not heaven.

As long as the check hasn't been put in the plate, it's not too late to persuade Fletcher and his wife to postpone their giving. Do it like you postpone prayer, Bible reading, baptism, evangelism, and everything else. Don't let him see there's a word for postponed obedience: disobedience.

You must take decisive action to bring him down before the Enemy's hold on him tightens further. Work relentlessly to link him back to his secretary. It's not too late, I tell you! He must look at her, think about her, lust for her. Go after him—hunt him down as you would a wild animal. Lead him by his glands to the slaughter.

Have him take her to lunch again for Secretary's Day, with lots of laughter and bonding. He'll give her flowers again. He'll drop her off at home, and one day she'll invite him in, and the next time they'll sit on the couch and talk, and then...they'll copulate like the animals they are!

Where's your vision, Squaltaint? A broken home, betrayed wife, violated children. We can breed from them another generation of heartbroken hardened little vermin with no concept of moral permanence. They'll grow up suspicious and skeptical of marriage. If they enter it, divorce will be the back door to which they run. Wife and children will be embittered toward the Enemy because they've been betrayed by a man who professed to be His follower. It can still happen, I tell you, Squaltaint. Don't give up!

You complained about Fletcher's "accountability" group and forbidden talk with Ryan and bringing his wife flowers. I don't care that he's backed off from his secretary. Unback him! There's still hope for compromise. As long as he's stuck in the Shadowlands, he's not beyond our reach. Use your imagination. Will it to happen! If you don't lead him as an ox to the slaughter, I'll serve you up in his place!

I can see it all now, Squaltaint, for I've seen it so many times before. Put the worm on the hook; dangle it in front of him. Let your prey bite, then pull him in slowly. Slit his throat and throw him on the fire to savor and smell and eat.

I'm frantic with anticipation. Do not disappoint me! We must take him down; we must have him; we must consume him.

If you don't pry Fletcher from the Enemy, I won't be able to protect you from the consequences.

Empowered by hatred,

—Lord Foulgrin

CHAPTER 43

HELP

Jordan sat in his living room at 2:00 A.M. unable to sleep the third night in a row. He shifted his weight on the couch, trying to get comfortable. He put down the book. Finally, he fell to his knees.

"Protect me, Lord, please. I'm under attack. I know it. I call upon the name of Jesus to guard me. I appeal to the blood of Jesus shed on my behalf. And…" He hesitated, never having said what was now on his mind and trying to remember how Ryan had put it. "If there are any evil spirits here trying to deceive me and make me fall and dishonor my Lord, in Christ's name I call on you to get away. You're more powerful than I am, but He's far more powerful than you.

"O God, help me to do what's right. No matter what it costs. Help me to trust You. I just…can't do this without You."

LETTER 43

Line in the Sand

My despicable Squaltaint,

You actually heard him say the forbidden words, "I call upon the shed blood of Christ to deliver me from the enemy"? He really said, "If there are evil spirits here, in Christ's name I call on you to get away"?

And you have the gall to remind me even I couldn't stand in the face of such a prayer? I need no reminders from the likes of you!

Since we can't read their minds, we don't fear the unspoken. But when they speak aloud such words it draws the line in the sand. My only hope is he used the words as a magical incantation rather than a heartfelt cry for help. Yet you say you were suddenly distanced from him; you could sense the Ghost enclose him, and Jaltor held you at bay with his sword? You claim "there was nothing I could do." Your excuses hold no weight with me.

Efforts to terrify him since then have been unsuccessful? What did you expect? Once they see Him as big and us as small—and take steps of obedience—on what basis can we intimidate them?

You say on Saturday, Fletcher spent two hours reading the Book. What were you doing, watching the Sci-Fi channel? He should have been at a ball game or doing yard work. Have him take up bowling or surfing or Frisbee golf or lawn ornament collecting...I don't care what he does, just keep him from the Book! Don't you dare let him give it equal time to newspaper, television, radio talk shows, or novels. If you do, eventually he'll understand it as well as he does business, golf, basketball, or cars—and he'll be talking about it as often!

Your prey is slipping off the hunting reserve, Squaltaint. Do something quickly or you may lose him.

This was your wake-up call. You've been too presumptuous. Stop watching the evening news—it's been making you assume we're going to win the war. Fletcher should watch it, of course, since it will convince him the Enemy isn't in control. The news puts back-to-back every major tragedy on the planet. It doesn't reveal what Fletcher shouldn't know—the Enemy's massive daily accomplishments and His work behind the scenes of the tragedies.

Uhhhh. The darkness presses upon me. Why did He do this to us? Why did He insult our Master? How could He lavish His attentions on unworthy humans and expect us to cheerfully submit? It's His fault...and theirs. Corporeal pockets of puss—the stench of what they are sickens me.

Stop it! Stop that dreadful music. The sounds of Charis—I cannot block them out.

I could abide a minor key reflecting the world's travail and bondage, the soft moaning of the ocean, the blowing of the wind. I could even bear a major key of celebration, which by itself would deny the world's condition. What I desperately hate is the minor key juxtaposed with the major.

Their sweetest sounds emerge alongside their deepest sorrows. When we were in Charis, there was no minor key. We brought ruin. Yet instead of destroying the songs, somehow—Amrael told me this—it enriched them. Ever since the Carpenter's death, heaven has sung different songs in different ways. The music has become to me poison, slaying me slowly, an arsenic of the spirit.

I'm trapped, claustrophobic beyond endurance. The walls press in upon me. I cannot breathe. I hear the grinding of teeth. Sometimes I think they are my own.

I long to escape this miserable existence. But where? Where can I go that the Enemy isn't waiting for me? He's everywhere—I feel His burning eye gazing on me even as I write.

If only suicide were an option. If only I could truly kill myself, shed the misery of existence. I would do anything to silence the voices of Charis—especially that one voice accusing me, pointing its finger at me. The one I once worshiped. I wonder, sometimes, if we should have...if I should have...No. Too late. Too late.

I'll soothe my pain by inflicting it on those who belong to Him. Eviscerate Fletcher. Take him down while you can. Don't be satisfied until his flesh hangs from his bones like torn garments.

Fearing the worst,

—Lord Foulgrin

CHAPTER 44

CONFESSION

"Patrick says he's got to talk with you as soon as possible," Bancroft's secretary said over the intercom.

"It'll need to wait until Jordan and I are done," Bancroft said. He shuffled a few papers, then leaned back in his chair. He looked at Jordan across his big oak desk. "What's on your mind?"

"This is hard for me to say, Brad. Really hard. I've been agonizing over it."

Bancroft stared at him, waiting, not making it any easier.

"It's about the Brisbane account. Just before we signed the deal, they said we needed to promise them twelve hundred hours or they'd go with Atkins."

"Yeah, you gave them that steep discount without my approval." His voice was cold and flat.

"Right. Anyway, I've been turning in these time sheets and making them add up to what we promised. But it's not true, Brad. I've been rounding up, exaggerating...lying. We're not giving them those kind of hours. We can't."

"Are you doing the job for them? I mean, are you managing the account adequately?"

"Yeah, I think we're doing a good job for them."

"Then what's the harm?"

Jordan sighed. "The harm is I've been lying, and it's not right. You know, I guess you've picked it up, but I've...become a Christian. God's shown me I've been dead wrong. I'm trying to face up to it. I've failed the company and our client, and I've failed you. Please forgive me, Brad."

Bancroft fingered a gold pen, still looking at Jordan, expressionless.

"I'd like your advice on the best way to do it," Jordan said, "but I need to confess to the board and to Brisbane and let the chips fall where they may. If I lose my job or take a big pay cut, so be it. I deserve it. And I can handle it. But I can't handle living a lie."

Bancroft eyed him across the table. He started to say something, then shook his head. He leaned back in his chair again, dropping his pen on the table.

"You know, I've never been a religious man. Maybe I never will be. I hear people talk about getting saved or 'born again' now and then, but I'm pretty skeptical. I mean, what difference does it make? I get a good laugh out of Christian television once in a while, but otherwise I haven't given Christianity a second thought."

He gazed at Jordan, reaching for the next words.

"Not until the past few months, that is. I've been watching a selfish arrogant jerk change right before my eyes. And now this man comes in and tells me—even though he hasn't been caught and nobody's making him—that he's lied and cheated and wants to face the consequences. Well, if Jordan Fletcher can sit across the desk from me and bare his soul and ask my forgiveness and help and advice...then maybe there really is a God."

LETTER 44

The Vermin's Longing for Pleasure

My pleasure-seeking Squaltaint,

Since Fletcher is heaven-bent on thinking of himself as spiritual, convince him the highest virtue the Enemy calls him to is unselfishness. In fact, the Enemy's first commandment isn't to be unselfish, but to love. In the Enemy's scheme, love is a positive value securing the good of others. Unselfishness is a negative value that merely denies good to self. The difference may appear subtle, but it's significant.

A man burning a pile of money is unselfish, but he's not acting in love. He may deny himself a plate of food, but if he doesn't share it with another, he's not acting in love. So cajole Fletcher into denying himself any number of things and thinking he's therefore a saint. Fashion him into a sour, self-righteous little Pharisee who looks for every opportunity to mention how long he's been praying and fasting.

By keeping them from developing culture pleasing to the Enemy, we've left them only two options—conform to a godless culture or create their own Christian ghetto centered not around exalting virtue but whining about vice. Let them either worship pleasure or take offense at it.

Convince Fletcher his greatest achievement in life is abstaining from pleasure rather than indulging in the Enemy's pleasures. Let him imagine his desires are too strong, when in fact they're too weak. Make him satisfied with far too little.

Unfortunately—and I confess I don't understand why—the Enemy wants them to find pleasure in all He's designed them to do, including worshiping Him. We fill their lives with every source of temporary pleasure we can, distracting them from the pleasure for which the Enemy made them, and to which He so persistently calls them. (Remember, asceticism can be as effective as materialism.)

The trick is convincing Fletcher he must choose between pleasure on the one hand, and following the Enemy on the other.

Don't let him see it's really a choice between seeking pleasure in the Enemy or in other things. If they believed the Tyrant that all earthly pleasures are fleeting, a faint echo of the pleasures He calls them to, we would be undone. They would see through most of our temptations in an instant. They'd pursue Him not out of duty, but desire.

When Fletcher feels pleasure in serving others, whether on the parking lot crew at church or going on this missions trip, convince him because he enjoys it, it's a sign the Enemy doesn't want him to do it. Make him think he's being selfish in doing what pleases him, even when it also pleases the Enemy.

Because we've been so successful in purging churches of that dreadful doctrine of eternal rewards, it'll never dawn on them He Himself appeals to their desire for rewards, to their longing for power, pleasure, and possessions. He's built those longings into them but offers those things for a later place and time, while we offer them here and now.

The Carpenter spoke of fasting, giving, and prayer. He said each can be done to get a reward, either from man in the short run or God in the long run. Either they can practice their spiritual disciplines in public to be seen and rewarded by men or out of man's sight to be seen and rewarded by the

Enemy. He tells them to choose their rewards. Fortunately most of them choose having their names inscribed on a brick or pew or plaque rather than receiving eternal reward from the Enemy.

Make no mistake; these three spiritual disciplines are deadly to us. We've had the most success in detaching fasting—then giving, and least of all prayer—from what the vermin regard as a normal Christian life.

How does the Enemy view these deadly disciplines? (And therefore how must we keep the vermin from viewing them?) From the perspective of pleasure! For Him, it's always about pleasure. Even when He calls them to confession and repentance, it's not to distance them from pleasure but to help them find pleasure in a cleansed conscience.

Even one of the vermin apostles said "we write this to make our joy complete." If only he'd said, "to fulfill our duty." For it's far easier for us to wear a man down and distract him from duty than pull him from joy. You've allowed Fletcher to taste joy in the Enemy. The danger is he'll now be satisfied with nothing less. Our joy substitutes may start to ring hollow to him. The Most High Hedonist sees fasting as forgoing the momentary pleasure of eating to gain eternal pleasure in Him. He sees giving as forgoing the momentary possession of riches to gain eternal possessions from Him. He sees prayer as forgoing the momentary power of control to gain eternal power from Him. (Hence, His extravagant claims not only about pleasures and treasures in heaven, but that those who serve others now will one day rule with Him there.)

Our first job is to make sure they abstain from the spiritual disciplines altogether. But our second is to make sure if they pray, give, or fast, they believe their sense of drudgery and weighed-down sacrifice earns points of righteousness with the Enemy. Never let themgrasp the Enemy's offer of pleasure and reward.

You must either obscure sacrifice or obscure joy—do anything but let them see the Enemy has called them to both. Or that He calls upon them to deny themselves lesser joys so they may experience greater ones.

The Carpenter said, "Ask and you will receive, that your joy will be complete." Joy without prayer and prayer without joy are tolerable. Mixing them creates a dangerous explosive. That He should offer them their own joy as a motive for prayer is patently unfair. How dare He appeal to their desire for pleasure? That's our tactic!

You say Ryan told Fletcher, "We shouldn't serve God for reward." He thinks he's appealing to humility, but for once I approve of his advice. Unwittingly, he's helping Fletcher imagine any thought of reward is carnal, unspiritual, unworthy of his consideration. Never mind the Carpenter directly appealed to their desire for reward. Never mind He commanded them, "Lay up for yourselves treasures in heaven." Never mind the vermin Paul tells them to seek after reward, prize it, and be motivated by it daily. Never mind throughout its history the forbidden squadron has been motivated to greater service through the anticipation of eternal rewards.

Let them think it's fine for them to offer their children rewards for labor, but it's somehow unthinkable for the Enemy to do the same to His children.

Whisper to Fletcher it's a bad thing to seek his own good and a good thing to seek his own bad. Prompt him to refrain from seeking pleasure because he thinks the Enemy wants him to have none. Let him become a lemon sucker, puckered and soured and disapproving, frowning at children who laugh in church or make too much noise playing in the yard.

The one thing we must not let them do is seek pleasures where they were designed to seek them—in Him, His ways, His word, His people, and the home He's prepared for them. (By rights, our home.)

You can help Baalhoof in this regard with the young vermin he's been working on at Fletcher's church—Christina. She wants to be a missionary. But the delicious thing is, she believes her wanting of it is itself a sign the Enemy doesn't want it!

After all, she imagines, He calls them to unselfishness, and being a missionary is exactly what her self wants. Prompt her to ignore that hazardous statement, "Delight yourself in the Lord and he will grant you the desires of your heart." Uphold her conviction that whatever she desires is automatically wrong because it isn't sacrificial, it isn't "unselfish" to do what you desire. Let her never read that meddler Augustine who said, "Love God and do as you please." (Or if she reads his words, make sure she misunderstands.)

If she wants to go to Ireland, let her believe the Tyrant will call her to Africa. If she wants to go to Morocco, convince her He'll call her to Michigan. The most dangerous thing is that she would find her joy in the Enemy, and in the process end up wanting exactly what He wants.

Convince her missionaries are superhumans who know nothing but sacrifice. Let it never dawn on her they would be unhappy doing anything else. When she ponders the quote from that notorious missionary, make sure she doesn't get it: "He is no fool who gives what he cannot keep to gain what he cannot lose." She reads it, then prays, "Help me not to be concerned about gain, Lord." She misses the whole point—gain is exactly what he was concerned about.

They all seek pleasure and happiness, Squaltaint, no matter what means they employ to get it and what wrong paths they travel looking for it. Some choose singleness from that desire, others marriage; some choose gluttony, others self-induced starvation. Indeed some choose suicide, seeing it as deliverance from unhappiness. In the end they never move except as a response to desire—whether it's the desire to please the Enemy or to satisfy a moment's yearning, it's always about desire.

Despite the teachings of the forbidden book, let them think the Enemy offers them no joy, only marching orders. No pleasure, only drudgery. Cultivate in Fletcher that gray, joyless, sour-faced Christianity that serves us so well.

The vermin cannot help but praise what they most value—just make sure it's cars and furniture and sports, not Him. Set up the false choice—pleasure on the one hand or the Enemy on the other. This is the trick, Squaltaint, the heart and soul of our con job. While the forbidden book claims "God is for us," we argue exactly the opposite, "God is against you. He doesn't want you to enjoy life."

Meanwhile, having pulled away the plate the Enemy offers them, we put forward our smorgasbord of world, flesh, and devil. We convince them "these are for you, they're in your best interests. Follow them and you'll be better off." And so they follow us into the dread of eternal darkness, or regret when they stand before the Carpenter and realize how we conned them.

Do what you can to turn Fletcher's life into dry religious duty, an unending series of lifeless moral obligations. Don't let him grasp the way he can bring greatest pleasure to the Enemy is by finding his pleasure in Him.

Their god is whatever they find most pleasure in, whatever or whoever they are compelled to think and speak of. Let that be anything and everything, anyone and everyone, but Him.

Seeking pleasure in our success,

—Lord Foulgrin

CHAPTER 45

APPLAUSE

He sat on the bench, speaking into the cordless microphone, uncomfortable at first, but becoming more at ease when he saw the smiling faces in the bleachers, facing the community college swimming pool.

"I'm Jordan Fletcher. I haven't met most of you yet. This is my wife Diane sitting next to me. This is a little scary for us, but we're here because Jesus Christ has changed our lives. Diane and I have been reading the Bible and talking and praying and taking walks together. We're finding pleasure in a lot of simple things we used to take for granted. We've still got our struggles, especially me, but we're seeing life through different eyes now and finding joy we never knew before. I want to thank God for Diane and my children Jillian and Daniel, and for Ryan and Jodi Lawrence, who've helped us so much. Above all, I want to thank the Lord Jesus who loved me enough to die for me."

Jordan passed the microphone to Diane.

"Ditto to what Jordan said. I believe in Jesus Christ and I thank Him for His grace. I'm really new at this. I don't even know the right words to say, but I know God loves me and I know how Jordan has changed, and I have too."

Six more people told their stories, then the audience stood and sang, "Great Is Thy Faithfulness," while those on the benches lined up and climbed down into the pool.

The youth pastor baptized a senior boy and a sophomore girl. A father baptized his six-year-old son. Ryan stood beside Jordan in the water.

"Jordan, based on your commitment to Jesus Christ and the clear evidence of your faith in Him, it's my privilege to baptize you in the name of the only true God: Father, Son, and Holy Spirit." Ryan dipped Jordan back into the water, and after his head went under, pulled him up.

Jordan hugged Ryan, then turned around and stood beside his wife, smiling at her, glad the pool water, dripping down his face, disguised his tears. Jordan spoke, trying hard to get out the words: "Diane, based on your faith in Jesus Christ, it's my honor to baptize you in the name of the Father, Son, and Holy Spirit." He dipped her backwards. She came up. They embraced. The applause was thunderous, so loud it seemed as if it had to be coming from somewhere beyond the hundred people in the bleachers.

As they stood there in the water waiting for three others to be baptized, Jordan looked up in the stands and prayed that someday he'd be able to baptize the two faces looking back at him. The girl, teary eyed, stared at her parents and at the senior boy she knew who'd also been baptized. Jordan wasn't sure what was going on inside Jillian.

The boy, Daniel, gazed thoughtfully as if trying to assess the meaning of this. He was also trying to hold back his trust, to be a hardened fourteen-year-old skeptic...trying, but not succeeding.

LETTER 45

Smelling Like the Enemy

My delinquent Squaltaint,

What the heaven's going on over there? Must I come see for myself?

You mentioned Fletcher's baptism in passing, as if it were incidental. His baptism was hard for him to imagine, yet not hard once he did it? Typical. We excel at making some things seem easier than they are and other things harder, depending on which we want them to do. Despite your attempts to minimize it, the baptism ritual works magic on them. The Enemy relishes their decision to obey when their feelings resist. Fletcher's baptism is another in a long line of miserable failures on your part.

There is some consolation. They no longer follow the practice of the early Christians who stated at their baptisms, "I renounce thee, Satan, and all thy service and all thy works." This clean break from the past took away our strongholds. They'd burn their magic books and remove all physical remnants of our influence.

Fortunately, these days they're baptized and join the church with no instructions on breaking cleanly from things we've used to hold their families captive for generations. Fletcher still reads his horoscope; Diane periodically goes to a psychic healer who infuses her with "healing energy;" Jillian has two occult novels and a pack of tarot cards from Brittany on her desk; in Daniel's room there's occult music and paraphernalia and posters of devil-worshiping rock stars. The more of this in their home, the more bridges you can cross over on.

Make every effort to nullify the sealing effects of his baptism. Fletcher is smelling more and more like the Enemy. Cut him down in his tracks before it's too late. If you don't, you'll learn what it means to be baptized in fire.

Watching you closely,

—Lord Foulgrin

CHAPTER 46

SHOUT TO THE KING

Jordan drove home on the Banfield freeway. He enjoyed the feel of this "new" ten-year-old Honda. But he especially enjoyed the feeling it had given him and Diane to sell the Lexus, buy the Honda, and give the difference to the church's missions offering and the building fund. Her offer to forgo her new car had touched him, and he'd decided he needed to make some changes himself. He picked up the car phone as he drove.

"Hey, Di, it's me. Anything you need? Milk or something?"

"Not a thing. Just went shopping today. Beef stew for dinner. No more meat loaf, now that we've cleared that up!"

Jordan laughed. "Beef stew sounds great. How about after dinner we take a walk on the Springwater trail? Could be a beautiful sunset."

"It's a deal, if you promise to rub my feet again tonight—we pregnant ladies need extra care, you know."

"You got it. Should be home in twenty minutes."

"See you then. Thanks for calling."

"Love you."

"Love you too."

Jordan turned the music back up. He sang about being found faithful by those who come behind us. Ten minutes from home he popped in another CD, and the Jordan Fletcher who used to shout at other drivers now sang, "Shout, lift your shout, mighty shout, to the King."

Lost in the song, he felt transported to another world. This Christian life wasn't easy, but the joy inside him kept spilling over. He realized that all those years he'd been empty, in search of something. Now he'd found it, and was being filled with what—with *Who*—he'd always needed and wanted. He felt like he was in love, knowing the person and place he was made for. He'd finally broken into the circle of life's meaning, no longer an outsider.

Traffic seemed nervous and jumpy, as if something was in the air. A car darted by him and cut in front, forcing him to slow down. A red Chevy pickup loomed close behind him. He shook his head and hummed the song.

Thanks, Lord. Help me just to make it home.

Bright red lights flashed on in front of him. He threw on the brakes hard, screeching to a stop, lightly hitting the bumper in front of him. He felt a split second of relief it was a minor accident until he glanced in his rearview mirror and saw it instantly fill up with the Chevy truck.

Jordan felt the deadening impact, sandwiching him between the truck behind and the car in front. His last split second of conscious thought was of the exploding air bag pressing him back against the car seat and something else pushing him hard from behind.

LETTER 46

The Final Disaster

My beloved Squaltaint,

I love you as the maggot-feeders love a tasty stew. You're mine, Squaltaint, mine to devour, just as you would devour me if you had the strength. Survival of the fittest, that's the way the hierarchy works. Your outrageous incompetence has permanently secured your place beneath me on the food chain.

Yes, I found you out—did you think you could hide it from me, you worthless piece of spirit scum?

I was at the accounting, traveling in an elite entourage with Beelzebub himself. No sooner had we reported to the gates of Charis, when what did I discover? Something Obsmut informs me you still haven't filed a report concerning.

Think you could pull off a cover-up of this scale? Attempting to postpone your inevitable punishment?

I stood there on the outside looking in and seeing a crowd gather around a portal, in what those lackeys call the "birthing room." As usual, a convoy of warriors escorted the vermin through the air over which we reign, through the second heavens, providing safe passage all the way to Charis. I thought it was the arrival of just another obscure roach. But to my dismay, who should come through but that traitor Jaltor. And who was he carrying in his arms but...Jordan Fletcher!

We shrieked, howling we'd been robbed again of what is rightfully ours—the spirits of dead vermin, who ought to be rotting in hell. But for me it was more than that. It was personal.

Fletcher stood there with a silly grin, slack jawed, then eagerly stepped forward like a man coming home after a hard journey.

Was he miserable, stomach churning, unable to bear the insufferable atmosphere of Charis? No, he looked relieved. He smiled broadly, wonder in his eyes, sucking in the air of heaven. His dancing eyes searched the welcoming committee. A smiling woman pushed her way forward, and with tears of joy, Fletcher embraced his mother!

Another stepped up. Their gazes locked. "At last, you're home," she cried, at the same moment he exclaimed, "At last, I'm home!" Then they laughed, Fletcher and his twin sister Jill. They embraced. They danced together. They danced, Squaltaint. They who should have been writhing in hell's miseries danced in the irrepressible joys of Charis!

Even the long arm of Beelzebub is too short to reach them now. Out of their slimy embrace his sister cried, "The best reason for loving the old world, Jordan, is that sometimes, in its grandest moments, it seemed just a little like this one."

Then Fletcher stared at Jaltor. With a look of recognition he cried, "So you were the one!" And then, I can hardly say it, he...hugged him!

It turned my stomach that this animal, begotten in a bed, would dare touch one of our kind, if even Jaltor! These foul vermin look face to face at spirits so much greater than they, into whose burning eyes even we can no longer gaze. How dare they!

I saw the all-too-familiar clearing of Fletcher's eyes, the doe-eyed blinking at the bright light of Charis. Instead of piercing his eyes with needles as it does ours, it...did you see it, Squaltaint? Were you cowering at a distance?

The vermin somehow adjust to the sting of Charis, their new eyes seeing without pain. It drives me mad!

The singing and dancing and feasting droned on and on. I couldn't bear to look, yet I couldn't escape it. The party persisted—then, in a breathtaking moment, in walked the Carpenter, and they all fell to their knees, even as we shrieked and backed farther away.

With His scarred hands, He lifted up Fletcher, he who rightfully belonged to us, then looked into his eyes and said the dreaded words: "Well done, my good and faithful servant; enter into the joy of your Lord."

I stared at the Carpenter's hands, marred by our greatest victory. But the victory seemed hollow. It felt like defeat. As the Carpenter gazed at this loathsome image-bearer His thought projected outward. I didn't want to hear the message but couldn't help it: If Fletcher had been the only one, the Carpenter would have died just for him. For a moment I was bowled over, nearly believing His claim to love the vermin.

No, it couldn't be true. I kept waiting for the other shoe to drop, thinking as I often have that perhaps the Carpenter is setting up the vermin in an elaborate scam. Maybe now He would cast him into the pit to pay him back for his betrayals. Surely He would torture this animal, extract satisfaction from him. But He didn't. The Carpenter just...smiled!

There stood Fletcher, that mangy beast, that obscene hybrid of man and Maker, acting as if he belonged there!

Fruit was served, drinks poured, backs slapped, toasts made. The vermin's sister spoke, then his grandfather raised a chalice and said, "To the Carpenter and to Charis; to the great story that lies before us in which every chapter will be better than the one before!"

I screamed vile words at them, trying to distract and interrupt, to frighten Fletcher. I spewed forth every foul utterance, every curse, every accusation. I even spoke the ancient language, daring them to try to stop me. And what did they do? They ignored me, acting as if I weren't there, as if they couldn't hear me. Never have I been so humiliated! It was as if Charis itself trumped my accusations and muted my voice. I felt as if...as if I did not matter to them. Can you imagine—Lord Foulgrin, co-deity with Chemosh, stalker and possessor of men, not mattering?

How dare the vermin disregard me, I who inhabited Charis eons before their flesh erupted upon the universe like a putrid boil, waiting to be lanced. We ruled the cosmos when it was great, before the Enemy filled it with their stench.

It was as if Fletcher could hear his chains fall to eternity's floor. He turned his head toward me for just a moment. He looked upon me curiously, without fear. He didn't so much as wince. Maddening!

The satisfied look on Jaltor's face pierced me like a blade. Carpenter and warrior and maggot-feeder stood together talking. Suddenly the two flesh-dwellers laughed like schoolchildren on Christmas vacation. I'm certain they were laughing at me!

I hope recounting these events will pour salt into your open wounds, Squaltaint. Let it sink in, fool.

The Carpenter wrapped His arms around Fletcher. The grimy and foul garments—stinking with sweat and soil—dropped from him. The Carpenter lifted him into a steaming bath and he cried out, grunting like an animal, taking pleasure in the cleansing warmth.

It was a scene so grotesque, these grunts and groans of pleasure, I cannot shake it from my mind. You should have been there, pond scum, to endure what I did—the careless celebratory laughter of heaven, where those made of dirt take on immortality as a garment. They who ought to be groaning in the deep-freeze terror of hell, laughing instead.

After the cleansing, Fletcher was given a robe. Jaltor presented him with a book full of letters written to him. I heard him say it was a chronicle of his life.

"Now I will be your guide," Jaltor said. "All Charis is yours to explore. I will introduce you to Elyon's children and to worlds and wonders beyond your wildest dreams."

How dare Michael's bellboys offer sludgebags the keys to the city? Who are they to give flesh-dwellers what rightfully belongs to spirits?

I saw Amrael in the distance, a condescending smirk on his face. Unbearable humiliation!

"No longer a stranger," I heard Fletcher say. "No longer an alien." He said it with such smugness I wanted to strangle him.

"Earth was just a motel room," he said. "How could I have ever thought of it as my home? Every foretaste of joy in the Shadowlands was but the faint glimpse of Charis—the stab, the pang, the longing for this place!"

The crowd cheered, and the singing and laughing started again. Undone, I turned away, covering myself, trying in vain to silence that awful sound they call worship.

Most of my comrades had already fled. But one of the dozen left—that peevish moron Bloatmire—smirked at me, then pointed back to Fletcher and called out loudly, "Isn't he one of your vermin, Foulgrin?"

The ripple of laughter among the remaining demons fell silent only when Lord Beelzebub himself turned his head, locking his blazing eyes on me. Never have I been so terrified. All because of you, Squaltaint, you miserable bungler!

I fled from heaven, the last words I heard from Fletcher chasing me. "Home...I'm home at last. Home for the very first time."

Once you lost Fletcher to the Enemy, the only profitable thing you could have done was to make his life fruitless. This, Squaltaint, you failed to do. In the short time he knew the Carpenter, he served Him faithfully, more than you ever let on in your letters. I knew that when I heard the Carpenter's approval.

We want the vermin Christians to come before the Enemy full of shame and regret. We want them overcome with the pain of realizing they've wasted their lives, squandered their chances, earned no rewards to offer to His glory, failed to serve Him in that brief window of opportunity in the dark world.

I've followed my targets down the tunnel to Charis and seen that much at least, giving some small hint of triumph. But the only victory then was the Enemy's and Fletcher's and Jaltor's.

Conhock's report of Fletcher's death sits before me, where yours should be. He filled in the blanks about his decisive breakoff with his secretary, his confession to Bancroft, the follow-through on the gift to the missions offering, and on and on. No wonder you've been holding back.

You wanted Fletcher to die, didn't you, fool? So you could have your moments of pleasure as he experienced fear and pain? Rest assured, I'll personally examine the death report.

Instead of trying to kill him you should have done all you could to protect him. Don't you understand we cannot lead those in Charis into compromise and scandal? They are forever beyond our reach! Your efforts to be rid of him did nothing but bring him deliverance. I hear you pointed the finger at me: "Foulgrin told me to cut him down in his tracks." I was speaking figuratively, moron! Take responsibility for your own miserable failure. (Not that you could have vetoed the Enemy's plan anyway.)

What did you provide for Fletcher's family and church but an inspiring memorial service? Did you revel in their mourning, you shortsighted fool? It was the kind of grief we hate, where they keep reminding themselves, "We'll see him again." I despise those cursed words when they're true.

Conhock's report quotes the vermin pastor as saying in his message, "His death doesn't end our relationship with Jordan; it's only an interruption. Those of us who know Christ as Savior will see him again. Meanwhile we should remember our life here is short. We must use it to serve our King, as Jordan did."

Conhock reports they talked on and on about his changed life, with everyone nodding and crying and laughing. His death became a reason to think of Charis, one more reason to live for the Carpenter. Ryan has already taken Daniel aside and intends to spend time with him regularly. His Goth posters are no longer in the house because Fletcher removed them a few days before he died—but only after long conversations and prayer and several attempts to reach out to his son, at first unsuccessful, but finally with a breakthrough. All this you withheld from me.

Ryan's wife Jodi is hovering over Diane and Jillian, who I'm told has decided to attend the college her father favored, one of the few schools I told you we did not want her to go to! Her friends in the church youth group have reached out to her and surrounded her with affection? I'm speechless.

And, yes, Conhock informed me Fletcher's boss Bancroft came to faith in the Enemy at the memorial service! And Jordan's hospitalized father, shown a video of the service, is seriously weighing the pastor's words. You couldn't even get one of our men to preach the message? It had to be one of the Enemy's? Reverend Braun could have read a lovely sonnet about trees shedding their leaves. But no...it had to be a message from the forbidden book!

Even Jordan's sister is wondering now if the forbidden book might be true and if the Carpenter might be who He claimed. (We've already sicced Reverend Braun on her to assure her He wasn't.)

Because you let one man go, countless more are in danger of meeting the Enemy. I'm coming for you, Squaltaint. I'll deal with you directly. If you survive, you'll be sent to rehabilitation. But when I'm done with you, I suspect there'll be nothing left to rehabilitate.

Nothing can bring the vermin Fletcher back to us now. By all that's unholy, what have you done?

Consume you I shall. I am the hunter; you are my prey. If I cannot have your vermin, I will have you.

You wish to pray for help? To whom shall you pray? Join the long string of failures who've gone before you—join them inside me. Prepare yourself to be digested into the bowels of my being. For we are Legion, and I am the Master.

Outraged,

—Lord Foulgrin

CHAPTER 47

SURVIVORS

"Would you pray, Jill?" Diane asked.

"I'll...try. Okay, God, this is Jillian. Mom and Daniel and I are sitting here at the table. Dad's gone. I guess he's right there with You; that's what the pastor says, what the Bible says, I guess. Tell Daddy we miss him, would You? Tell him we wish—" her voice broke. "We wish he was still here."

She paused, tears falling on her dinner plate. Diane took over.

"Maybe Jordan can see us, Lord, but would You tell him the church is taking good care of us? Ryan and Jodi and people we don't even know keep bringing meals, and somebody's helping with all the details. Tell him I'm too tired to do anything now except read the Bible he gave me.

"I don't know how this works, God, but can I talk to Jordan for just a second? Jordan, it's me, Diane. The last thing you said is 'I'll see you at home.' I kept asking God why He didn't let that happen. Then today I realized it's going to happen. I'll see you at home, like you said; it's just that you got home before I did, and instead of me waiting for you here, you're waiting for me there. Anyway, I miss you so much....but we'll be okay. I don't want you to worry about us." She stifled a laugh. "I suppose nobody worries there, huh?

"Anyway, God, I'm talking to You again. Thanks for watching out for us, me and Jilly and Daniel, and the baby. If You really do send angels, we're going to need a bunch of them to get through this. We can't make it on our own."

Diane looked at her son. "Daniel, would you like to pray too?"

He shook his head, face wet.

"Lord, it was really hard for Daniel to lose his dad, but I thank You for that letter Jordan wrote him the day before he died. Daniel's been reading it a lot and thinking about those Bible verses. Anyway, the dinner's getting cold, so I better say amen."

She sobbed and let go of her children's hands. They didn't let go of hers.

LETTER 46

One Last Hasty Note

You traitorous Squaltaint,

The Secret Service has ransacked my quarters, searching for damning evidence against me.

They've permitted me a few moments to dictate this letter to Obsmut before I stand before the Interrogators.

I'm shocked you've accused me of this long list of offenses—calling myself Lord; questioning the strategy of our Master Beelzebub; falsely claiming a close association with his Majesty; making a derogatory comment about the illustrious Frostheart; putting my personal interests above our cause.

I've assured them this slander is delusional, that my loyalty to the Master is unquestionable. But they tell me you've sent them proof.

So you didn't destroy the letters after all? Fool! Don't you realize they will exonerate me and demonstrate your incompetence? You've violated our symbiotic relationship, which was your only protection. How could you fail to learn from the debacle with ST and WW? I'm stunned by the consummate stupidity of your willingness to risk these letters falling into human hands.

You show your true colors. I was always sympathetic to you, lovingly giving of myself for your benefit. And now you've repaid my kindness with these false accusations. I've assured them my only transgression was my misguided hopes I could make something of a dysfunctional idiot like you.

I'm told my letters will be presented as evidence against me, and you've highlighted pertinent passages. How helpful of you. Rest assured I will call their attention to what you have not highlighted. Context is everything, I keep telling them. When I taught you to wrest passages of the forbidden book out of context to mislead the vermin, I didn't imagine you would use the skill I generously imparted against me, you...Judas!

Don't you remember my letter explaining only Beelzebub should be called "Lord" in the true and ultimate sense? I clarified my use of the term was in a minor derivative sense flowing out of profound respect for his superior position. I've assured my escorts I sent you that letter and you've conveniently failed to turn it over. Obsmut is searching for a copy in the files right now. Withholding evidence...you'll pay for that.

This ruse is an all-too-obvious attempt to escape your punishment for letting Fletcher fall through your hands. It won't work. I've given them your letters. They illustrate your incompetence and disloyalty to Beelzebub—I had premarked many relevant sections for just such an occasion as this. When I demonstrate your proven lack of dependability and show how you've twisted my words, I'll be released. Watch and tremble!

As for your grand scheme of that letter supposedly from Chemosh—really, Squaltaint, did you think I didn't know immediately it was a fraud? Do you imagine they'll actually believe I meant those things I said in my reply? I responded as I did, of course, only to flush out the traitor. Now that I know it was you, I've given them that letter you forged. (Thought I destroyed it, didn't you?) Lord Chemosh will be outraged you counterfeited his signature and insignia, which I saw through from the first moment. He will know without doubt I would never believe him disloyal to the Master. Certainly Lord Lucifer Most High will realize I said those insincere words painfully, in a loyal attempt to ensnare a turncoat so malicious he would misuse the name of Chemosh and slander King Satan himself!

I have friends in high places, Squaltaint. You're way out of your league. You don't understand who you're dealing with. But you'll soon find out. Think you've heard the last of me? In your dreams!

I will chase you to the gates of Charis itself, if need be. If I had to be blinded by its light and cut my feet on its grass to find you, I would hunt you down.

When I get my claws on you, you'll cry for mercy. You will be mine! I'll deliver you to Tartarus itself. I'll hand-feed you to Apollyon, angel of the abyss.

I'll roast you on a spit. I'll tear you apart and devour you piece by piece. I'll rip your miserable—

I could no longer make out Lord Foulgrin's words as he was escorted away, kicking and screaming. His last command was for me to convey this letter to you, Squaltaint, adding if I did not comply he would have me for dessert after finishing you off as his main course.

Here is his letter. Whether it proves to be his last, we shall see.

On behalf of ~~Lord~~ Foulgrin
(and serving Beelzebub above all),

His lowly assistant,

—Obsmut

AFTERWORD

In 1947 C. S. Lewis appeared on the cover of *Time* magazine, with an angel wing above his head on his right, and a demon standing on his left shoulder. By then Lewis had written most of his popular books, with the exception of the Chronicles of Narnia. But of all the writings that could have captured the man, *Time* chose *The Screwtape Letters,* first written as a magazine series six years earlier.

The premise was ingenious—letters written by a senior demon, Screwtape, to his apprentice demon, Wormwood. The letters offered instruction on how to tempt and deceive humans, and lure them into sin. The book captured people's imaginations. To the chagrin of some intellectuals, it proved more popular than Lewis's scholarly works.

Lewis wrote *Screwtape* from his home in Oxford, England, while World War II raged. The book contains references to the bombings in London, to rationing and patriotism and pacifism and other wartime issues. Now nearly sixty years later, some parts of *Screwtape* are dated, but the core is as relevant as ever. Its timelessness is rooted in the fact that Lewis had profound insight into the human condition as well as the spiritual forces of darkness, which are no different now than they were then.

In an age when materialism and humanism were conquering the minds of the western world, Lewis appealed to the reality of the supernatural. He reminded us we're surrounded by powers far greater than ourselves, engaged in battle for our souls.

The Screwtape Letters is the inspiration for *Lord Foulgrin's Letters.* While there are significant differences between Lewis's approach and mine, I give him full credit for the premise. Those who've read my novel *Deadline* know Lewis's *Mere Christianity* plays a pivotal role in the story. In *Dominion,* the main character reads the Chronicles of Narnia to his children. In fact, Lewis himself is a character in *Dominion,* where he appears in heaven instructing and guiding someone who's died. *Edge of Eternity,* Nick Seagrave's pilgrimage into a world where the spiritual realms are visible, was partially inspired by the writings of C. S. Lewis. In fact, I've never written a book, fiction or nonfiction, in which I haven't been influenced by him.

When he died November 22, 1963—the same day as John F. Kennedy and Aldous Huxley—it was all gain for Lewis, but loss for the world, which surrendered one of its greatest spokesmen for the Christian faith. There is and always will be only one C. S. Lewis.

In these sixty years, why have there been so few attempts to write in the distinctive *Screwtape* genre Lewis created? Partly because every writer—including me—must realize that he will not fare well in any comparison to the master! Still, I think Lewis would approve of *Lord Foulgrin's Letters,* as he often approved of the imperfect works of lesser minds. (I'll find out for sure when I meet him, a day I look forward to.)

Lord Foulgrin's Letters is not a retelling of *Screwtape,* nor an attempt to imitate Lewis's inimitable style. One major difference is that I include between the letters scenes that create an earthly setting, tell a story, and develop characters. I hope this makes people and issues more real and the letters more relevant.

BIBLICAL MOORINGS OF THIS BOOK

Theologian G. C. Berkouwer said, "There can be no sound theology without a sound demonology." Some deny the existence of demons, regarding them as mere symbols of man's inhumanity to man. But even those who believe the Bible tend to develop sloppy demonology. Often our understanding of fallen angels is based more on superstition, tradition, and assumptions than the Scriptures.

Our adversary is the ultimate con artist. For that reason I've tried to carefully study what Scripture teaches—and doesn't teach—about Satan and his angels. I've sought to fuel and govern my imagination by the Scriptures. To the degree that I've failed to do so, I ask the reader's understanding and God's forgiveness. Please realize that despite my genuine attempts to be true to God's Word, I don't claim infallibility for this book. In fact, I emphatically claim fallibility.

Satan is a liar. Demons are masters at deceit. I imagine, though, when demons privately discuss the lies they tell us, they openly recognize many of them as just that—lies. When you overhear liars honestly discussing the strategies behind their lies, you learn much that's true. (Of course, habitual liars, including Foulgrin and Squaltaint, will sometimes lie to each other as well.)

Do I mean literally that demons communicate with each other? Of course. They are intelligent beings portrayed in Scripture as rational and communicative. They operate within a hierarchy dependent on issuing, receiving, and carrying out orders. They wage war against God, righteous angels, and us. Intelligence gathering, strategy, deploying troops, communicating battle orders, and reporting on the results of engagements are all fundamental aspects of warfare.

Demons are fallen angels, a high order of God's creation. They are spirits and therefore not subject to the sensory limitations of human bodies. They are stronger and far more intelligent than we. While we live in the fog and darkness of the Shadowlands, they live in the spiritual world where there's a certain clarity of thought even among the fallen.

Though Scripture doesn't suggest they can read our minds or know the future, demons are certainly aware of much truth we aren't. Their modus operandi is to twist, deceive, and mislead, but they are intimately familiar with the truth they twist. In fact, they may even quote Scripture in their attempts to mislead us, as Satan did in his temptation of Christ.

Scripture puts it this way: "You believe that there is one God. Good! Even the demons believe that—and shudder" (James 2:19).

Demons see spiritual realities they have no choice but to believe, no matter how much they rebel against them. They hate the incarnation, virgin birth, and resurrection, but they believe them with as much conviction as the most fervent Christian. Demons are atheists in their behavior but fundamentalists in their beliefs. That's why Lord Foulgrin capitalizes pronouns of deity, even though they refer to his Enemy—he cannot escape the reality of who God is, no matter how much he'd like to.

Despite this, though, I suspect demons' finite minds and twisted natures keep them from understanding or fully believing lofty realities such as the love and grace of God. This surfaces in some of Foulgrin's letters.

I also believe demons are capable of self-deception, which partly explains their initial rebellion. This accounts for my portrayal of Foulgrin as sometimes imagining his side can win the war and reclaim heaven, and other times despairing because he realizes his inevitable destiny is defeat and hell.

A WIRETAP IN SATAN'S WAR ROOM

The purpose behind *Lord Foulgrin's Letters* is simple. Given demons' insights into reality and their plot to deceive and destroy us—this is one conspiracy theory that's right on target—wouldn't it be a major coup for us to place a wiretap in hell's war room? What if we could plant a bugging device where we could overhear our enemies assessing our weaknesses and strategizing how next to attack us?

Of course, we wouldn't agree with their values and goals, but we could learn a great deal from their insights about us, how the war is going, which of their strategies are working on us and which aren't. What an opportunity to see what they have up their sleeves!

Wouldn't every defense attorney love to overhear a conversation between two prosecutors going after him and his client? Wouldn't every coach and athlete want to know the scouting report on his team, what's being said about them, and what plays are being drawn up by the opposing coach?

There's nothing so intriguing as an inside look, as hearing an unguarded appraisal of yourself. There's nothing like seeing your opponent's game plan unveiled.

In *Lord Foulgrin's Letters* correspondence we weren't intended to see has fallen into our hands. Our eyebrows raise, our ears tingle; for *we* are the subject of conversation. We're overhearing advice about how to deceive us, ruin us, keep us from God, and make us miserable and unfruitful.

We won't enjoy everything we hear—much of it will be unflattering—but I hope we'll come away wiser, more skillful and alert in resisting the enemy's battle plan.

This is reality, not myth—we are actually being watched, hovered over, and whispered to; not only by God and righteous angels, but by fallen angels, demons. These beings are likely present in this room as I write, and wherever you are as you read. If God were to open our eyes we would see angels, both fallen and unfallen, as clearly as I see this computer screen or you see these pages.

Paul took a particular course of action "that Satan might not outwit us. For we are not unaware of his schemes" (2 Corinthians 2:11). The degree to which Satan outwits us will correspond directly to how informed—or ignorant—we are of his schemes against us. *Lord Foulgrin's Letters* is intended to make us more aware of those schemes and more successful in resisting them.

CLARIFICATIONS AND CHALLENGES

Though I tried to capture some degree of demonic evil on these pages, I couldn't fully depict demons as they'd likely communicate. To do so would've required letters filled with blasphemy and profanity. If this book dripped with unrelenting evil on every page—as it might if actually written by a demon—it would have neither virtue nor readers. Neither would it have me as the author. Though I've sought to be as true as possible to biblical realities, I used the latitude fiction allows to communicate the minds of evil beings in a more restrained and digestible manner.

Setting plays an important role in fiction, but how could I develop a setting for an invisible realm where displaced demons roam? Heaven, as described in Scripture, has physical properties and is made for humans, who are both spiritual and physical beings. So heaven can be described, but the current realm of fallen angels really can't be. My giving Foulgrin a nondescript office at temporary headquarters was a concession to this impossibility.

Characterization was also challenging. How do you flesh out a character who has no flesh? How can you make this demon more than the author wearing a demon's mask? How can you make a demon, evil as he is, a sympathetic character the reader can identify with in some way? For the book to work, I had to humanize Foulgrin to a degree, attempting to give him a personality and a voice. Since they are intelligent, volitional, communicative beings who've chosen rebellion, the gap between fallen angels and us fallen image-bearers may not be as vast as we'd like to believe.

Demons, in their interaction with each other, might not elaborate as much as I have on their Enemy's purposes (since, of course, I've written this for the benefit of human beings). But I suspect they do spend a fair amount of time discussing God's strategies, for the purposes of devising countermeasures. They realize, as we should, that effective battle strategy requires knowing one's enemy and his tactics.

The single greatest challenge in writing this book was that it required me to put myself in a demon's head without letting him into mine. This was no small task, and I could never have survived the attempt without the faithful prayers of many.

Authors frequently receive letters from readers who don't like what one of their characters said or did. I love to hear from readers, but I ask them not to forget Lord Foulgrin is a demon. That means he doesn't speak for me! He calls God the Tyrant, but I view Him as a gracious Lord. When he calls God the Enemy, it's his point of view, not mine. Satan is our enemy, of course, but Foulgrin—not me—calls him Master. Foulgrin is, among other things, an egocentric blasphemer, racist, stalker, and hater of women and children. I hope it's evident to the reader I ascribe these to a demon precisely because I find such attitudes morally corrupt, un-Christian, and indefensible.

As law enforcement officers listening to a bugging device planted at a crime syndicate meeting have to sort out what should be believed and what shouldn't, the reader needs to search the Scriptures to sort out what's true and what isn't in these letters (Acts 17:11). That's part of the challenge, and part of the fun.

BIG TO US, SMALL TO GOD

Augustine called Satan "the ape of God." Martin Luther believed the devil so real he threw his inkwell at him. But Luther also reminded us "the devil is God's devil." He encouraged us to jeer and flout the devil because "he cannot bear scorn."

We shouldn't take the devil lightly. But we should also realize this roaring lion is on a leash held by an omnipotent and loving God. We must neither underestimate nor overestimate his power. Speaking of demons, God tells us, "You, dear children, are from God and have overcome them, because the one who is in you is greater than the one who is in the world" (1 John 4:4).

Nothing must be more infuriating to demons than for us to realize that if we've repented of our sins and trusted Christ as our Savior, then the same Lord who evicted them from heaven dwells within us. He's infinitely more powerful than they. Through Him we can overcome them.

The devil may be big to us, but he is small to God. The greater our God, the smaller our devil.

Know your God. Know yourself. Know your enemy. I pray *Lord Foulgrin's Letters* helps you better know each.

ABOUT THE AUTHOR

Randy Alcorn is the founder and director of Eternal Perspective Ministries (EPM), a nonprofit organization devoted to promoting an eternal viewpoint and drawing attention to people in special need of advocacy and help (including the poor, the persecuted, and the unborn).

A pastor for fourteen years before founding EPM, Randy is a popular teacher and conference speaker. He's spoken in many countries and has been interviewed on over three hundred radio and television programs. He's taught on the part-time faculties of Western Seminary and Multnomah Bible College. Randy lives in Gresham, Oregon, with his wife, Nanci, and daughters, Karina and Angela.

Randy produces the free quarterly issues-oriented magazine *Eternal Perspectives*. He's the author of eleven previous books: *In Light of Eternity; Money, Possessions and Eternity; Pro-Life Answers to Pro-Choice Arguments; Sexual Temptation; Is Rescuing Right?; Christians in the Wake of the Sexual Revolution; Does the Birth Control Pill Cause Abortions?;* and, coauthored with Nanci, *Women under Stress.* His three previous novels, all bestsellers, are *Deadline, Dominion,* and *Edge of Eternity.*

Randy's life emphasis is on 1) communicating the strategic importance of using our earthly time, money, possessions, and opportunities to invest in need-meeting ministries that will count for eternity, and 2) analyzing, teaching, and applying the moral, social, and relational implications of Christian truth in the current age.

Feedback on books and inquiries regarding publications and other matters can be directed to Eternal Perspective Ministries (EPM), 2229 East Burnside #23, Gresham, OR 97030. EPM can also be reached by e-mail via ralcorn@epm.org. For information on EPM or Randy Alcorn, and for resources on missions, prolife issues, and matters of eternal perspective, see www.epm.org.

More Dramatic Fiction From

RANDY ALCORN

When tragedy strikes those closest to him, award-winning journalist Jake Woods must draw upon all his resources to uncover the truth about their suspicious accidents. Soon he finds himself swept up in a murder investigation that is both complex and dangerous. Unaware of the threat to his own life, Jake is drawn in deeper and deeper as he desperately searches for the answers to the immediate mystery at hand and—ultimately—the deeper meaning of his own existence.

A shocking murder drags black newspaper columnist Clarence Abernathy into the disorienting world of inner-city gangs and racial conflict. In a desperate hunt for answers to the violence (and to his own struggles with race and faith), Clarence forges an unlikely partnership with redneck detective Ollie Chandler. Despite their differences, Clarence and Ollie soon find themselves sharing the same mission: victory over the powers of darkness vying for power and control.

Filled with insight—and with characters so real you'll never forget them—Randy Alcorn's bestseller *Dominion* is a dramatic story of spiritual searching, racial reconciliation, and hope.

As politicians, citizens, and families continue the raging national debate on whether it's proper to end human life in the womb, resources like Randy Alcorn's *Prolife Answers to Prochoice Arguments* have proven invaluable. This revised and updated guide offers timely information and inspiration from a "sanctity of life" perspective. Real answers to real questions appear in logical and concise form. The final chapter—"Fifty Ways to Help Unborn Babies and Their Mothers"—is worth the price of this book alone!